Forbidden Obsession

C.S. Berry

Dear Reader

Dear Reader,

We need to talk. See, what I've written is a lot of smut with some plot. It does have a plot! Part of the plot is the sex so, it works. I promise the other plot is worth it too, but I really like writing smut. My characters will fall in love and have a hell of a time getting to their happy ending... well at least the ending of the series (4 books, 1 romance). Everyone gets their *happy endings*(if you know what I mean) throughout the book. Because if you're going to make cookies, everyone gets one or two or more.

Fair warning, I like group scenes and because there's only so many ways to fit that many bodies together, I apologize if it seems repetitive. Sara is a very lucky girl, who apparently doesn't get UTIs or sore (look it's a fantasy, let the poor girl live a little).

Obsession was originally written as a serial. If you read the serial, you may find some changes where it makes sense to help make the serial into books.

Now a little airing of the dirty laundry, if you have issues with primal, dp, bondage, brat behavior, kidnapping, other women making drama, or discreet public play, this probably isn't the book for you. If that sounds like a good time, strap in because this ride is about to get bumpy.

XOXOXO,
C.S. Berry

Content Warnings

Content Warnings:

If you don't want any spoilers, stop reading now because I'm going to list out some things that might make some readers uncomfortable and I want them fully informed. Some of the content is in subsequent books, but within this series.

- No sword crossing
- Story elements: stalker, kidnapping, other woman drama (no cheating), shooting, fighting
- Affectionate, controlling men
- BDSM play time
- Group Sex
- Office Romance
- Strip club, but not a sex club (sorry for those who love a sex club)
- Consensual play, including:
  - BDSM
  - Lots of group scenes
  - Bondage

- CNC
- Spanking
- Primal
- Brat Submissive
- Public play, but discreet, not done for an audience or anyone outside her guys

Chapter 1

Spinoff

Sara

Clarity. That's what I found when my newest friend barely escaped her stalker. It took a few weeks, but I found it. For years, I've waited for Wyatt Hawkins to give me the time of day, but I'm done waiting for him. No, I'm not going to force his hand like I've tried dozens of times before. Fuck that.

I've got just the man in mind who can help me with the one tiny problem that remains.

But first, brunch. It's ten o'clock on Saturday. An odd time for a first date, but Drew Young isn't your typical guy. And we didn't meet in the typical fashion. Meaning my mother didn't set me up with him.

Nope, I chose Drew Young myself. He made me laugh. But mother would approve. He's socially acceptable, having dated a much wealthier woman than me. He's new money, which isn't a problem with our family because so are we. Kind of.

Newer than most families, at least. My grandfather squirreled away a fortune and my father was a brilliant investor until he passed. My brother Tom, well... he did get a degree in accounting, so we're hopeful.

"Sara."

Turning, I smile at Drew as he strides toward me in front of the restaurant. His sparkling brown eyes capture mine. His light brown hair has some wave, but it's styled nicely. He has on a blue buttoned shirt tucked into his dark jeans. His sleeves are rolled up, showing his muscled forearms.

I've seen him in a tux at events and even nice clothes at the restaurant, but I've never caught sight of his muscular forearms. Didn't think that would do it for me, but damn.

When he reaches me, he pulls me into his arms and envelops me in a rich, spicy scent. "I'm so glad you called."

I have to admit, the draw I feel for him isn't as strong as the one I feel for my brother's best friend, Wyatt, but it's still there. There's this buzz of attraction that makes me want to do naughty things with him.

"How could I not?" I step back and self-consciously try to tuck my hair behind my ear, but it's in a bun. The dinner I met Drew at was an ambush on the two women he was fucking at the time. So he's perfect for what I need. "You definitely kept me entertained."

His eyes twinkle with mischief. "Just a warning. I only fake date women I fuck."

I laugh as he opens the door to the restaurant. "I'm not looking for a fake date anymore."

He takes hold of my elbow and leans in close to my ear. "So only a fuck then?"

"Maybe." I try to be nonchalant while everything in me is wondering, *What the fuck am I doing?* I can be forward when I need to be, but I'm not typically this forward.

His heated smile makes my heart skip and my panties melt. He turns to the host. "Table for two."

The woman is dressed all in black with her blond hair sleeked back in a high ponytail. Her flirty smile is all for Drew. "Right this way, Mr. Young."

Drew leads me through the tables to a two-seater right next to the window. One of the best places to be seen. I almost ask for a dark corner, but the host is already returning to her station.

I won't flat out proposition the man, but I'm definitely open to the possibilities.

He holds out my chair for me. I gather my skirt before sitting and allowing him to push me in. When he sits across from me, he doesn't pick up the menu. Instead, he leans on his elbows and looks at me.

"So, is this a revenge fuck then?" He winks. "Getting back at an ex?"

My cheeks flush with heat. "No, not revenge."

His eyes widen when I once again don't deny the *fuck* part of his statement. I set the menu to the side. Both of us have obviously been here before. I don't need to casually peruse the menu before getting what I always get.

I lean my elbows on the table and fold my hands together to rest my chin on them. "I'm curious about you. You made me laugh, and I have to admit, I felt a little spark even though you were fucking two of the women at the table."

"Currently, fuck buddy free." His brown eyes twinkle with mischief. "Are you applying for the position?"

I blow out a breath. I can do this. "Can I be honest with you?"

"Of course."

"What can I get you today?" Our server stops beside us. She's attractive. Her dark hair is pulled up to show off her face. She checks out Drew, but he doesn't look at her, keeping his gaze steady on me. My pulse kicks up a notch.

Drew nods for me to go first.

"Belgian waffle with strawberries and extra whipped cream." I've never had a guy give me this much attention. Granted, the last guy I went out with was in a secret relationship with my friend and we'd agreed to fake date to appease our matchmaking moms.

"Eggs benedict with a side of your sourdough toast." Drew continues to look at me not the server.

"Coffee?" the server asks.

"Yes, please." We answer at the same time. His attention is a little unnerving, especially for what I want to discuss with him.

"Be right back with that." She walks away, leaving us relatively alone.

"You were about to be honest with me. Something I greatly admire." When he smiles, butterflies flutter in my stomach. How fucking cliché. But they respond more to him than most guys.

Okay, being honest with myself here, they don't take flight for anyone besides my brother's best friends. Yes, all three of them. Not that they feel the same way. Drew fascinates me because, outside of those three, I've never felt like this about a guy.

"Right." I exhale. "For years, I've had a massive crush on my brother's best friend."

"Dante Stone?" Drew relaxes in his chair as he searches my eyes.

My face heats. "Um, no."

Does Dante stir up something desperate and needy inside me on certain occasions? Yes, but I wouldn't call it a crush. But there have been moments. Breathtaking moments.

Drew nods. "Finn?"

Finn Lawson, my brother's other best friend. A certifiable flirt who makes me hot and achy when he's close. But I always figured, that's just Finn. Most women drop their panties for him. And while he'd be perfect for my current mission, I can't do that to Wyatt, even if he doesn't look twice at me. Or look at me ever.

"Also no. Wyatt." I blush and fidget with putting my napkin on my lap. "He doesn't see me that way though and I'm done waiting."

"Sara." He waits until I lift my gaze to his. "I'm open to whatever you want. You want someone to fuck Wyatt out of your system, I'm just the guy to do it. You need someone to go to events with and laugh at all the people, I'm down. If we're being honest?"

The server comes and fills our coffee mugs before walking off again. If I didn't have impeccable table manners, I'd release a frustrated breath. She has crap timing. And most days I hate having impeccable manners.

I take my cup and sip at the hot brew, waiting for him to continue.

"I noticed you that night at the restaurant. I'd noticed you before that too. It may have been a thing for redheads at first." He flashes me a cocky smile.

I touch my red hair pulled up into a loose bun.

"Or the first time I saw your pale green eyes that look like a color out of a fairy tale. So honestly, I'm up for whatever you want because I want to spend time getting to know you. If that's okay with you?"

"Oh." My cheeks heat. I'm surprised I feel the same way. What if this could actually be ... something? I smile. "I'd like that."

I knock on the door, then slap my hand against the solid wood. It's almost noon, and you'd think one of the four guys who live here would be awake. I glance toward the elevator. There's only one door on this floor and it belongs to my brother and his merry band of pricks.

My date with Drew got cut short because of Tom. Grrr, Tom is the biggest cockblock of my life. I blame him for Wyatt's disinterest.

Drew was about to kiss me when I got bombarded by texts that made no fucking sense. My heart rate is elevated. If this is a prank, I'm going to rip Tom a new one.

I pound again and this time a voice comes through the door.

"Hold your fucking horses." It's muffled enough I'm not sure which guy it came from. I don't care as long as someone lets me in, so if my brother isn't being murdered, I can murder him.

The door swings open to a dripping-wet Viking of a man in a scrap of a towel that barely conceals anything. Damn. I bite my lip. His blond hair falls in curls to his shoulders. His chest is wide and cut, his waist narrow. Black ink starts on his pec and winds around his neck.

My mouth goes dry and my panties get wet. My attraction to him annoys the piss out of me because it most definitely isn't mutual.

"What do you want, Sara?" His icy-blue eyes narrow on me. He never shows any emotion except irritation when it comes to me. Which is fine, because I'm done with all these guys. They should be relieved. I finally moved on from the nothing they've offered me for six years.

"Where's Tom?" I brush past the giant of a man into the dim living room, shaking off the sparks my arm rubbing against his hard muscles triggers. "Tom! Tom, get your ass out here. I swear to God I will come into your room, and if I see boobs or dick, I'm telling Mom."

I ignore Dante, who follows me as I move deeper into the apartment. His presence makes my skin tingle with an awareness I wish I didn't feel. I'm still in the sundress I wore on my date. My hair is still up and I can almost feel Dante's breath on my neck. Which would be difficult given how fucking tall he is.

I'm not really short, but no one would call me tall or even average.

Tom's bedroom is toward the back. I don't care if I wake the dead and whatever woman or women might still be here from last night. My brother has a lot of explaining to do.

"Tom!"

A door opens and Finn Lawson steps out. He's not as tall as the Viking but still much taller than me. I'm not prepared for so much lovely man chest this morning. His body is a work of art and he works hard at the gym to keep it that way. His dark hair looks mussed, like someone's been running their fingers through it.

Chances are someone has.

His green eyes focus on me and he gives me this smile that would melt anyone's panties. Mine are, unfortunately, not immune. His flirty smile is full of temptation.

"For fuck's sake, flower. Keep it down or come in here and I'll make you scream real good." He strokes his fingers over his lips. If any other guy spoke or acted this way, I'd roll my eyes, but heat floods me when Finn does stuff like that.

Why couldn't my brother find ugly friends? Like seriously, did he hold auditions and only let the most attractive guys through to the final round? Because that sounds like an excellent way to meet a guy that will make my mother turn blue trying not to say bad things about him.

Unfortunately, Drew is perfect for my mother. Which means she'll love him and won't ever let me dump him. He's from a good family, knows how to dress, and actually likes me. My heart speeds up thinking about how he was just about to kiss me when my phone blew up with Tom's texts.

Ignoring Finn, I walk to my brother's door. Ignoring Finn takes dedication. It's hard to ignore someone so blatantly pretty, but I'm currently on a mission and can't be waylaid even by the pretty fuckboy.

When the door behind Tom's opens, I don't look. No matter how tempted I am. I know it's Wyatt. While I've been trying to get his attention for the last few years, today is not the day. Today, I have to make sure my brother is just fucking with me.

"Tom, I hope you're decent," I warn before throwing open the door. The bedroom is dark and there's no sign of life. In fact, it's a mess. Clothes are strewn all over the place, but that could be the way he lives.

I don't normally storm into my brother's room.

"Why are you here?" the dark, gravelly voice that haunts my dreams says.

Shaking off the shiver of delight working down my spine, I don't stop to fill Wyatt in on the details. I walk into the room and to the bathroom door, checking to make sure no one's there.

"Fuck." The word slips from my lips. Okay, hot guys aside, we have a problem.

My hands tremble as I take out my phone and doublecheck the

text message conversation between me and my brother, or more like between me and five quick texts.

"What's going on, pipsqueak?"

I sigh at Dante's voice and the old nickname. Being a giant, he's always been taller than me, and even more so when I stopped growing and he didn't. Pretty sure that nickname is to keep me at arm's length.

"Tom." I hold out my phone. Dante takes it and looks over the conversation I know by heart.

TOM:

I've got to go

Don't stay at home.

Go to my apartment.

Don't look for me.

They'll protect you.

Followed by a flurry of texts from me asking *what the fuck* in various ways. What the fuck did he get into this time? He's an accountant not a fucking superhero or spy. Why would he have to go anywhere?

"I swear, if this is about a woman, I'm going to kick his ass." I flop down on the edge of his bed and look around his room. This would be an extreme way to ghost someone, but who knows with Tom.

His closet door is open and the suitcase that's usually in there is gone. Half of his hangers are empty. A few are on the floor.

"When did you get this?" Dante leans against the wall, scrolling through my text conversation with Tom. He's probably looking at earlier messages. Not that Tom and I talk much.

The most recent texts were me threatening to tell Mom about his high school hookup that's still going on if he didn't give me an internship.

Dante knows how to see when a text was sent. Is he just trying to get me to talk?

Shaking my head, I stand and go into Tom's bathroom. When I turn on the light, the room looks like someone grabbed things in a hurry. His toothbrush and toothpaste are gone, but his floss is on the floor.

His razor is gone but his shaving cream is tipped over.

Silence falls over me as I think more about Tom's words. *I've got to go.* What the fuck is he into? What is happening? If anyone knows, it's these three.

I storm out of the bedroom and poke Dante in his chest. Ow. And just hurt my finger.

I glare up at him, rubbing my finger. "You live with him. Where is he?"

Dante returns my phone and crosses his arms over his chest, making his muscles bulge out even more. Fuck, he's so fucking hot and that towel isn't really covering much except his cock. My tongue darts out to lick my lips before I lift my gaze back to his face.

"We don't keep tabs on each other." His eyes lock on mine for a second longer than they should. Flames lick at my spine. Fuck, I'm done with this shit.

Focus. Tom. I need to find Tom.

"So what the fuck are his texts about?" I leave Tom's room and the hot Viking to look for more clues. I didn't see his laptop or phone or even his chargers in the bedroom.

"May I see the texts?" Wyatt steps in front of me and holds out his hand. My breath catches as I lift my gaze to his dark brown eyes and sleep-rumpled dark hair. His pajama bottoms cling to his hips. My insides soften. I swear if a woman comes out of his bedroom, I will lose what's left of my mind.

He dates. He sleeps around. He flaunts the fact he's with other women. Every other woman, except me. I'm the one who gets ignored. And I'm done with it.

Drew is my step in the right direction to prove I'm finished with Wyatt.

I hand Wyatt my phone and wander through their living room and kitchen. In the kitchen, there's a note.

Need to lie low for a while. Not sure if they know about my family except Sara, but watch out for Sara and my mom, Roger, and Caitlyn. With me gone, they should be safe.
-Tom

Heat floods my back as Finn reaches over my shoulder and takes the note from my hand. "What do we have here, flower?"

Finn smells like sex and sin. My body perks up at his scent. Ugh. These guys have always made my head spin, but usually Tom is around to pull me back down to earth.

"Tom left you guys a note." I move away from the tempting warmth of his body. "I don't know who *they* are, but I'm still scheduled to start my internship on Monday, whether or not Tom is there."

I'm holding firm to that because I need this internship to graduate. My gaze meets Wyatt's eyes as he places my phone on the counter.

"Of course, pipsqueak." Dante still hasn't found clothes, and I'm pretty sure that towel isn't going to hang on much longer. Fuck. I really don't need to see that.

I've seen the man in gray sweatpants. He's packing some serious heat behind that towel.

"Would you go get dressed?" I gesture to him. "We all know you're hot. Cover that shit up."

Dante's eyes flash with heat for a second before he nods and heads into his bedroom. I go to the bar in the living room and put a glass on the counter. I glance over the liquors before choosing a whiskey, because fuck, I need something strong to deal with these guys.

"Early for a drink," Wyatt grumbles, running a hand through his hair.

"You want one?" I pour myself a little and set the bottle on the bar. "I was on a date when Tom sent me his vague texts and wouldn't answer my calls."

"A date?" Finn asks while starting the coffeemaker.

"Yes, a date." I down the contents of my glass. It burns my throat, but I don't care. I pour a little more and walk away from the bar to slump on their living room sectional.

I rest my head against the back and close my eyes. Tom left in a hurry. He told me to come here. Why? And why do I need protection? From what? Or who?

Chapter 2

Work in Progress

Sara

Dammit, Tom. I was going to get over whatever I have for Wyatt by getting under someone else. I swear, Tom doesn't want me to have a love life.

"Coffee with your whiskey?" Finn asks.

I open my eyes and he's holding a steaming cup of coffee out to me. "Thank you."

I set it on the coffee table and pour the whiskey into it, because why not?

Finn sits close, but not right next to me, with his own cup. Wyatt comes over carrying the creamer. He pours a little in my coffee before sitting down, but he doesn't add any to his.

For as much as the guy ignores me, he knows things like how I take my coffee. That I prefer white wine over red. I'm always a little shocked at what he knows about me and that's what kept me obsessed with him for so long. I always thought it meant something, but it just means that we grew up around each other and he's observant.

I drink my coffee and exhale. "What is Tom into now?"

"He's been working with a new client." Finn stretches and his pants dip a little lower, showing off his Adonis belt, that V that points directly to his cock. He has a totally droolworthy body. Fuck.

I blink and lift my gaze. I just need a good fuck to straighten my head out. Pretty sure that will cure whatever this is. But right now, I need to focus on Tom.

"Okay, new client, what do we know about them?" I glance at Wyatt, but he's on his phone scrolling through something. His jaw clenches, and I can imagine how it would feel if I pressed my lips against that muscle.

"He's been pretty tight-lipped about them." Finn shrugs and takes a sip of his coffee. "He brought in a few new clients and hasn't been real talkative about any of them, actually."

"Is that normal?" I take a sip. The cream really makes it better, but I'll never tell Wyatt that.

"No." Wyatt doesn't even look up.

"Okay." I draw the word out. "So do you guys understand his note? Is he into something shady? Or was he dating someone shady? Is this all an effort to ghost some woman?"

"He hasn't been seeing anyone that I know of." Finn looks to Wyatt. "Do you know if he's fucking someone?"

Wyatt's dark eyes collide with mine and my heart squeezes. He doesn't normally look at me, so to have his attention makes me long for more. My insides flutter.

"No." He looks away and I can breathe again.

Fuck, I need a life.

"Okay, so maybe this has to do with business. Maybe something else. Can one of you try to call Tom? I tried after the texts and it went straight to voicemail." I look from Finn to Wyatt.

"Already tried." Dante steps out in a black t-shirt that clings to his muscles and dark jeans that cling to the rest of him. He's barefoot and he's pulled his blond hair back into a loose bun.

He's never been easy to ignore, no matter if he has on clothes or doesn't.

I push the heat that pulses through me to the back of my mind, just like I've done for the past six years. When I was younger, these guys were like gods in my eyes. They could do no wrong. But when I turned sixteen, my mind strayed to a slightly darker side of the gods.

By then they were twenty and I was still Tom's kid sister. I'd always crushed on Wyatt and out of misguided loyalty tried to be true to only him. But Finn and Dante have always stirred something wicked inside me too.

After my friend admitted to having a sexual relationship with her four bosses, my dreams got a lot darker and starred all three of them. Wyatt, Finn, and Dante sharing me, fighting over me, fucking me.

Resisting the urge to fan myself, I swallow some more of my coffee with whiskey. Fantasies that will never happen and I'm not even going to entertain anymore. I'm going to fuck Drew because he actually wants me. He doesn't ignore me like Wyatt or act like a protective older brother like Dante. He does flirt with me like Finn, but unlike Finn, Drew's willing to take it further.

"Okay, what do we do?" I draw in a breath and look at the guys around me.

"We'll look into it." Wyatt doesn't meet my eyes. "We'll search the files and see if we can find out who he might run from."

"You let us know if anything happens." Dante steps forward, blocking my view of Wyatt. "Your parents are home, right?"

I swallow a sip of coffee and nod. No, they aren't. They left yesterday for an extended European tour. Something my mom planned for years and decided now was the time. They took Caitlyn, my little sister, with them.

Tom knew that, which may be why he said don't go home, but fuck him, I'm not locking myself in with these guys. I'd go insane.

And there's no way I'm telling these overprotective bastards that I'm home alone. Because I made plans too. I'm dating Drew Young and I'm going to seduce him. Though that shouldn't be too difficult to do.

Having an empty townhouse with just our Pomeranian, Peabody, is the perfect opportunity to have some alone time.

I finish my coffee. "If that's all we have, I've made plans. As soon as you hear from Tom, let me know."

"What plans do you have, pipsqueak?"

I walk over and rinse my mug before sliding it into the dishwasher. "Plans that don't include you guys."

I was so proud of myself for walking out of there. As I rode down the elevator, I texted Drew to come over tonight for dinner, to make up for ditching him earlier. I have a coffee date with my ladies this afternoon though.

The last thing I need is more coffee. When I walk into the corner shop, Madison Harris sits at one table and Cooper Graham is at the next. He's turned in his chair, whispering something in her ear that's making her blush.

Serious relationship goals right there.

Her blond hair is pulled into a loose bun like mine. When he draws back, her blue eyes stay locked on his blue eyes. His dark hair is pulled into a low tight bun. They look good together.

She doesn't see me, so I go up and order a bubble tea. When it's done, I walk over and sit across from her. She smiles. Now there are no shadows lurking in her eyes like before.

"How are you?" I ask.

Coop leans in and kisses her. "I'll be back for you later, sweetheart."

Madison waves him off and then turns to me. "So good."

"Did Kayla's flight get in?"

Kayla Wagner is the sister of one of Madison's bosses and part of our group of friends.

"Blake picked her up and they're on their way."

The door opens and Hope Williams walks in. She's shorter than me with brown hair and huge bright blue eyes. She sees us and comes over.

"I ran into Coop outside and he hugged me." She looks over her shoulder like she still can't believe it.

"He's in a good mood." Madison stirs her tea but doesn't elaborate.

"My bitches!" Kayla bursts in the door. I laugh at her larger-than-life personality. She's gorgeous with her dark hair and green eyes. After finding out Madison was dating four guys, she decided *we* should all date, even though she's the only bisexual among us.

"So is it official?" I ask.

She dangles a set of keys. "Officially moved to New York City and unfortunately, alone. Bea and I broke up, but we agreed to stay friends."

There's a hint of sadness in her green eyes. She loved Bea but they couldn't agree on where to live. Kayla's work wanted her to move here. Bea wanted to stay put.

"Let's get something to drink, Hope." Kayla's smile rebounds and she drags Hope up to the counter. They don't take long and soon we're all seated around the table.

After a few minutes of pleasantries and drinks, Madison looks at me. "So...?"

I smile.

"Yeah, how did brunch go?" Hope asks. She keeps looking at the door, like she expects someone to burst in. It's been a few months since she got abducted, but the fear still clings to her. We usually meet at her brother's bar, but we're trying to branch out like her therapist wants her to.

"Did you fuck him?" Kayla drinks her coffee with a smirk. "I mean, I saw the guy at the benefit. Drew is hot. I bet he's good in bed. Come on. Details. I need something to get me there tonight."

"First off, ew, I'm not giving you spank bank material." I hold my hand up in front of Kayla. "Second off, we didn't get that far. We had a lovely brunch, and just when he leaned in to kiss me and I was going to invite him inside, Tom texted me."

"Big brothers are the worst cockblocks." Kayla shakes her head.

Hope nods in sympathy. "Jason keeps interrupting any date I have these days."

"As long as Madison keeps Blake occupied, I should be free and clear to narrow the playing field of potential lovers this city has to offer." Kayla winks. "So when are you seeing Drew again?"

"Tonight." My cheeks flush hot. I really don't know what I'm doing anymore. "Dinner at my house. But Tom sent me these cryptic messages. I'm worried about whatever he's gotten involved with, but I'm also wondering if he just needed a break and took off."

Tom is a hard guy to read most of the time. He's good at his job, but he's got this impulsive streak that he never really reins in. Am I shocked that he left without stopping by to say goodbye? Not really. Am I surprised his cell phone is off? Also no.

But he usually doesn't leave behind orders to not go home and to have them protect me. If anything, Tom is the hugest cockblock of my life when it comes to Wyatt. Even Finn and Dante. There's this whole *no dating my little sister* vibe that Tom puts out.

The others look around the table at each other. Unfortunately, we're relatively new friends. So they know some of the backstory, but not all of it.

"Tom takes off sometimes. So it's not completely worrisome." But my gut keeps nagging me that something is wrong.

Madison reaches across the table and takes my hand. "I'm sure he'll be fine."

I hope so.

Something outside the window catches my attention. A guy in black stands across the street. He's tall and thick. He draws on a cigarette and then flicks it at the cars going by before blowing out the smoke.

It looks like he's looking right at me, but that can't be the case. We're not seated by the window, and the sun is probably glinting off the glass, blocking his view of the inside. A shiver creeps over me.

I shake it off.

Most likely it's just Tom's cryptic messages playing tricks on my mind. The girls and I talk about our dreams of the future. We're trying to position ourselves to work together on something, kind of like Madison's guys did.

They graduated college and formed Morrigan Technology Group.

Between the experience she's receiving as their assistant and the mentorship with Deidre Bryne, a self-made millionaire with her company focused on women, Madison is primed to become a CEO.

Hope will make an excellent VP and Kayla is a marketing wiz. I'm the final piece. My master's in accounting is complete after this internship and a few more classes. I just need more experience, which is why I begged Tom to let me intern with his company, meaning Tom, Dante, Wyatt, and Finn.

"You're still good for your internship?" Kayla asks.

I nod. "Start on Monday."

Which means I have two days to fuck those guys out of my system, so I can focus on learning and figure out what the hell Tom was up to that he had to run from.

Nervous doesn't quite fit how I feel currently. Anxious gets closer. Pretty sure it's not just butterflies zipping around in dizzying circles inside me, but bees, wasps, maybe a few hornets. Honestly, I feel a little ill.

Maybe it was all the caffeine. The whiskey earlier probably didn't help.

The doorbell rings and I jump. Glancing at my video doorbell app, I see it's Drew. I smooth down my skirt and brush my hair over my shoulders. I've never done anything like this before.

I just hope I don't fall on my face.

With a deep breath, I open the door.

"Fuck, you're breathtaking." Drew's dark eyes sweep over me and shivers work down my spine. He's wearing gray slacks and a white buttoned dress shirt with the top buttons undone. It contrasts nicely with his golden skin. He takes my hand and lifts it to his lips. "Sara."

Sparks float up my arm. "Come in."

He steps into me and I back up a step, except he keeps coming until my back is against the wall. My breath catches. He shuts the door and tips my chin up.

"We got interrupted earlier." His gaze drops to my lips.

I swallow hard around my thumping heart, which feels like it's stuck in my throat. "Yes."

His thumb brushes down my neck. "Should we make up for lost time?"

"Yes." It barely leaves my mouth before his full lips brush gently over mine once, twice, three times. My insides turn molten. My hands cling to his arms, feeling the muscles shift beneath them.

"One taste before dinner." He captures my lips, taking me hostage as I follow his lead.

This kiss isn't the typical first kiss. It's carnal and dirty and makes me excited for more.

I've been kissed before, but never quite as consuming as this. He explores the edges of my mouth before demanding entrance, which I happily give. He tastes me and slides his tongue against mine until my pussy throbs with need.

When he lifts his head, his darkened eyes search mine for a heartbeat. He could fuck me right here in the entryway and I wouldn't care. If he fucks like he kisses, I'm in for one hell of a ride.

He brushes his thumb over my bottom lip. "Dinner?"

Chapter 3

Unrealized Loss

Dante

"What the fuck was Tom thinking?" I sit across from Wyatt and Finn in our conference room. It's late and this is not exactly what we hoped to do on a Saturday night. We've looked everywhere for his most recent files, but they're missing. Not on the server and not in the office file room.

"Whatever he got messed up in must be serious." Finn rubs the back of his neck and cracks it. "He thinks he's in danger."

"He thinks *she's* in danger." Wyatt rubs his chin.

None of us have to ask who *she* is. Sara. Fuck, just thinking about her being in trouble makes me itch to be near her. To watch over her. But her family is home and she should be safe.

"Why did he tell her to not go home?" Finn pushes away the laptop. "It doesn't make sense. Did he want her to stay with us? Maybe he meant for her to stay with her boyfriend?"

Wyatt growls low enough that we might not have heard it if the room weren't so fucking quiet. There's one thing in this world that Wyatt wants but won't let himself have. I help where I can to drag her away and protect her from herself.

But she doesn't hide that she wants Wyatt. She refuses to admit she wants Finn and me too. I'm just glad she doesn't have to make a choice between us. Because according to Tom, she's off-limits. We all want her, but none of us can have her.

It doesn't make hearing about her dates any easier.

"It's a date. Not a boyfriend." I know Sara. She barely dates. The one guy she dated a few times this past year turned out to be in a relationship with another woman, along with his three friends. I've never contemplated sharing a woman, not even with my friends.

I've seen some porn with double penetration but never really considered it since I usually stick with one woman at a time and never thought to ask a guy into the bedroom with me.

"All we can do is keep trying to reach him." Finn stands and stretches. "I feel like drinking tonight."

"We should go by and make sure she's okay." Wyatt's voice is gruff, but by *we*, he really means Finn or me. He does everything he can to not be alone with Sara. The guy's willpower is good, but if anyone can make him break, it would be her.

I'm good with holding his line. I'm just lucky that Sara doesn't look at me the way she looks at Wyatt. There's desire there, and lust, but it's something she chooses to ignore.

"I'll go by." Finn smirks. "I'll check out the new guy and see if we need to do a background check on him."

Wyatt makes a noncommittal noise. But I'm all for it.

"We don't know what Tom has gotten into and can't be sure whoever is getting close to her isn't involved." I put that out there. Or maybe I'm just making up excuses.

Not that I need much ammunition to check on her.

Sara

Drew sits catty-corner from me at the table while he tells me stories about his adventures with the two women. I made sure the lights were low. There's a few candles in the room for ambiance.

"Let me see if I have this correct." I set my fork on my plate and put my elbows on the table, resting my chin in my hands. "You were fucking three women at the time. Woman one was using you to placate her parents, but didn't know about the other two. Woman two was using you for revenge sex against woman one, but didn't know about woman three. And woman three got off on you telling her what you did with woman one and two?"

"Yes, she did." He rests back in his chair and his dark eyes hold me motionless. If ever there was a smolder, Drew perfected it. My lips part and an aching need claws at my insides.

"And now? How many women are you currently fucking?" I raise an eyebrow in challenge. I shouldn't care. I'm not looking for something long-term, though he indicated that this may lead to something else. As long as he uses condoms, who am I to care where else he sticks his dick?

I cringe internally at that thought. Yeah, maybe I'm not good with the cheating stuff, but if everyone knows the score, no one gets hurt.

He leans forward and takes my hand. "Hopefully, just one."

He brings my hand to his lips and kisses my knuckles. I laugh.

"Damn, you're smooth." I draw my hand back and try to cool down my libido.

"I aim to please." He gives me that smolder again. A little hint of fear races through me with the desire.

Can I really do this? Casual sex? Am I up for this?

"How about dessert?" Standing, I grab our plates. I don't wait for his answer, just take them into the kitchen and set the plates on the counter. What am I doing? I mean, this is what I want. This is how I free myself of Wyatt.

"Hey, are you okay?" His words are soft, but I don't turn around.

"I'm sorry. I don't want to screw this up." Blowing out a breath, I stare at the countertops.

"We can go slow, princess."

"Princess?" I turn and smirk at him.

He closes the space between us and reaches out to brush my hair behind my ear. "You're gorgeous and proper. You have the most beautiful eyes in all the land. Pretty sure that makes you a princess."

My breath increases at his nearness. He's as tall as Wyatt, as flirty as Finn, and crowds me like Dante, but there's still something missing. Definitely not the sparks because those are running riot through my veins.

Maybe *missing* is the wrong term. He doesn't lack anything. I want him. He wants me. Maybe I'm so used to liking men who will never want me that I'm suspicious of his interest.

"Why don't we take it a little at a time?" His hand slides behind my neck as his other slips around my waist, drawing me in close.

"That sounds good." Not exactly the timeline I was hoping for, but his mouth takes mine, and I can't think of anything but his touch as he draws me against his hard, toned body.

I've been kissed before. I've even messed around with some guys, mostly out of curiosity. But when Drew kisses me, my whole being catches on fire. He slides his tongue against my lips and I part them to let him in.

A low growl in the back of his throat at my submission makes my panties wet. My pussy pulses with need. I clutch his shirt to hold myself up as my knees try to give out. When his tongue slides against mine, I whimper.

He tastes of whiskey and sin.

He pulls me in close as he devours my mouth. The kiss is carnal and needy and everything I've never had before. When he lifts me against him, I make a startled noise. He chuckles against my lips as he sets me on the counter, which helps with the height difference.

He cradles my face and nips at my lips. "You taste like strawberries, princess. I fucking love strawberries."

A shiver courses through me as I open my eyes to his darkened ones.

He trails his thumb along my jaw. Leaning in, he kisses along the sparks he left behind.

"You're better than a fairy tale." He trails kisses down my throbbing pulse.

"Why's that?" My voice is breathy, and I'm having a hard time focusing on the words he says when his lips are making me feel things I didn't know were possible. My heart pounds and that need inside me pulses, hot and achy.

When I try to press my thighs together, Drew is between them.

"You're real, princess." He finds this spot where my shoulder and neck meet and sucks and bites on it until my breath shortens and I'm tugging at his shirt to draw him closer.

When he touches my bare knee, I startle as electric fire jolts through me.

He lifts his head and his dark eyes meet mine.

"Is this okay?" He slides his hand up my inner thigh.

I nod, too lost in the fire he's stirring inside me.

He smirks as he captures my lips and his hand travels higher. When his knuckles brush the outside of my panties, I gasp into his mouth. He takes advantage of my open lips and his tongue dives in. He tastes me as his knuckles stroke over my panties.

My fists clench in his shirt. He'll have wrinkles, but I don't care as long as he doesn't stop touching me. My insides churn like a bomb is waiting to go off inside me and only he knows how to detonate it.

When he slides his finger along the edge of my panties, I catch my breath.

The doorbell rings through the house. We both freeze and turn toward the sound.

"You expecting someone, princess?" His hand slides back down my thigh.

Fuck. I blow out a breath. "No."

I release his shirt and blush when I see the wrinkles in it. He kisses me briefly, then sets me back on my feet. I straighten my skirt and touch my hair before walking over to our security system to see who's at the door.

Finn?

He grins at the camera and waves. I guess my brother isn't the only cockblock in my life.

"Sorry." I smile at Drew. "I'll get rid of him."

"No worries." Drew leans against the counter and adjusts his cock. My eyes widen at the size of the bulge in his pants. Fuck, my mouth waters, even as my insides clench.

Shaking my head, I walk to the door. When I get to the marble entryway, footsteps echo behind me. I turn and see Drew followed.

"I am a gentleman. At least, that's what they tell me." His cocky grin makes those butterflies flutter again. I have no doubts he's less than a gentleman.

I open the door and give Finn my best glare. "What do you want? Did you find out anything about Tom?"

"Manners, flower." Finn smirks and sweeps by me into the house.

"Come on in," I say sarcastically and shut the door.

"You must be the guy." Finn takes a minute to look over Drew.

"This is Drew Young." I gesture to Drew. "This is Finn Lawson, who, if he doesn't have any information about my brother, should be leaving."

"Wow, that's a long name." Drew holds his hand out to Finn.

Finn shrugs, shakes Drew's hand, and smirks. "I usually just shorten it to Finn."

"What are you doing here?" I cross my arms over my chest and glance at the door meaningfully.

"I'm checking up on you, flower." Finn tugs on a strand of my hair and turns to Drew. "Do I smell dessert?"

A mischievous smile tugs at Drew's lips. "You do."

"I love dessert." Finn walks into the house like he owns it. He did practically grow up here with Tom, after all.

"I'm really sorry. I'll get rid of him," I say softly to Drew.

He leans down close enough that his words caress my lips when he says, "It's okay, princess. We have time."

He follows Finn and I blow out a breath. This is not how I wanted this night to go.

Finn sits across from Drew. "Where are the folks and the hellion?"

My cheeks flare hot. "Out."

I'm not about to tell one of these assholes that my parents and little sister are overseas for the next month. Tom knew, which is probably why he told me to go to his best friends, but they definitely would intrude on what I'm planning to do.

I duck into the kitchen and sigh, remembering Drew's hands and lips on me. I'm guessing that's the end of that for the night, even though I ache and will until I'm alone later in my room.

I grab an extra plate and fork and take them into the dining room.

"My family owns Taranis." Drew glances at me when I enter.

Forcing a smile, I pass out the plates and return to the kitchen to grab the cake I made.

When I return, Finn's eyes widen.

"Perfect timing." He rubs his flat stomach. "Sara makes the best desserts. Have you tasted her desserts yet, Drew?"

The innuendo makes me blush fiercely.

"We hadn't gotten to that part of the evening yet." Drew smirks and I feel the heat in my cheeks.

"Hmm." Finn's nonresponse makes me glance at him. His green eyes meet mine from under a raised eyebrow like he's asking me, *This guy?*

Well, fuck him. This guy is actually the only guy outside those three that makes me feel anything. So yeah, this guy.

"Where's Peabody?" Finn glances around looking for our Pomeranian furball.

"Who's Peabody?" Drew catches my gaze and I sigh.

"Our dog, who is at the vet and will be home tomorrow." I serve the cake and Finn digs in like he hasn't eaten in years. I pick at it because all my best-laid plans are falling apart.

Finn asks Drew some more questions, keeping up the standard *I'm a rich guy, are you a rich guy* dialogue. Drew's phone buzzes and he glances down at the screen.

"Your cake is divine, princess. I need to head out." He holds up his phone as an excuse, and I can't help wondering if that excuse is another woman who doesn't have a Finn to deal with.

"Okay." I'm not the kind of woman to get jealous or demand anything from someone who I've kissed twice. Though I was definitely hoping for more tonight.

"Good meeting you, Drew." Finn relaxes back in the chair like he's got nowhere he'd rather be. Swallowing, I just hope he isn't planning to wait until my parents get home.

Drew holds out his hand to me. When I take it, he draws me into the foyer with him, away from Finn. "I'd hoped our evening would end differently."

He curls a hand around the back of my neck and glances toward the dining room before lowering his mouth to hover over mine. My breath catches, waiting to see if he's going to give me another kiss. My heart skips.

"Good night, princess." He claims my lips in a soul-searing kiss that ramps that fire back up inside me. He whispers against them, "I want to see you again, Sara. I want to see all of you soon."

My eyes meet his and the heat in his makes me whimper in need. He kisses me again before leaving. Fuck.

I lock the door behind him and turn to glare at my dining room where Finn still sits. I draw in a breath and walk in. He's where I left him, lounging in the chair with his dark, artfully tousled hair.

"Ah, flower, when do the folks get home?" His green eyes linger on me.

Fuck. "Not until late. You can go now."

He glances at his phone screen and then sets it aside. "I can wait."

Chapter 4

Unearned Interest

Finn

Sara's face is flushed and her pupils are dilated. She's turned on and it's hot. And when she glares at me, I feel all the heat left to swelter in her body untapped. Drew just left my girl high and dry.

"You can leave. I'm fine." She stacks plates and heads into the kitchen.

Tom has a theory about his sister that I don't agree with. Especially when Tom's sister looks like my flower. I've held back for years, watching her pine over Wyatt, but catching flashes of heat from her when she looks at me.

The dishes clatter in the kitchen. I could leave right now and everything would stay the same. Tom will still be missing. Dante will block Sara from getting to Wyatt. Wyatt will try to ignore the feelings he has for Sara. And I'll flirt with her and she'll turn me down out of misplaced loyalty to Wyatt.

Or...

Drew stirred the pot and now my flower needs more. I'm here. She's here. It can't hurt to take a taste. It might go against the bro code, but Wyatt will never do anything about that longing between them. He doesn't want to lose Tom as a friend.

But fuck, what they don't know won't hurt them. I down the rest of the whiskey Drew and I were sharing and walk into the kitchen.

"What's wrong, flower?" I lean in the doorway and watch her load the dishwasher.

"I was on a date." She points a knife at me and her green eyes flash. I figured my late entrance would anger her, but it gave me a chance to check on her and check out the guy she's dating.

I shrug. "He left because he's got somewhere else to be."

Something on his phone pulled him away. Personally, if I were him, I would've waited me out.

"Maybe he would have stayed if you hadn't shown up." She pushes the knife into the dishwasher forcefully.

Ouch. I hope she isn't thinking that's me she's jabbing the knife into.

"How about a peace offering?" I quirk a smile her way.

She narrows her eyes. "What are you talking about? Why are you even here? I'm a grown adult. I can be alone without needing pretty boys coming and checking on me."

She gestures toward me before slamming the dishwasher shut. She breezes past to get back to the dining room. Her orange scent lingers in the air, driving me fucking insane.

From the time she turned sixteen, she's been able to get under all our skin. The bikinis she wore in the summer to draw our attention. The cute little dresses. The sweets she made us. Watching her eat fucking ice cream cones was exquisite torture.

"Sara, did your gentleman caller leave you high and dry? Or maybe horny and wet?"

Her eyes narrow as she sets the cake back on the table. There's a moment of indecision, but then it's gone and she looks determined. Fuck, she's sexy when she's riled up.

"Frustrated. That's how he left me, Finn." She crosses her arms and glares at me. "Obviously, you aren't going to help with the problem."

Oh, flower. I almost shake my head. A challenge like that I'm not likely to refuse.

I stride her way and her eyes widen as she backs away from me until she's against the wall. I close in on her and press my body into her soft curves, tipping her chin up. Her lips are parted and her startled eyes search mine.

"Feeling needy, flower." I trace her lower lip with my thumb. She whimpers. "I know my way around a woman's body." My gaze falls to her lips. "Since I ran off your suitor, maybe I should give you what you need."

Her warm breath coats my thumb. Her voice is low when she says, "What do I need?"

That's not no.

I smile before dipping my head toward hers. "Release."

I claim her mouth like I should have years ago. So fucking sweet as she parts her lips for me and moans into my mouth. This could all go sideways fast. Tom would be furious. Wyatt would be jealous as hell, but wouldn't do anything about it. Dante, fuck, who knows with Dante. He wants her, and if he had this opportunity, I'm not sure he'd pass it up.

When her tongue strokes against mine, I groan and lift her against the wall. Her legs wrap around my waist and she cradles my erection between her thighs. Fuck. I need to calm down before I push too far.

But then again, if the lady wants me, who am I to deny her?

Sara

Finn is blowing my mind as he explores every inch of my mouth while grinding his cock against my pussy. If I was wet before, I'm soaked now. When he cups my breast and massages it, I gasp into his mouth as my breast tightens.

What the fuck is even happening? I was being a brat to him like I always am, but then he was on me. Holy crap, his cock rubbing against my pussy is the best thing I've ever felt.

"Fuck, flower." Finn rests his head against the wall next to mine. His hot breath bathes my skin. His hand slips up my thigh.

He lifts his head and his green eyes search mine. "Tell me to stop, Sara. If you don't say no, I'll make sure you're completely satisfied."

Sparks and heat flood my body. I bite my lip. This is what I wanted. This is what I craved.

I wanted it to be Drew tonight, but fuck, I'll take Finn. He's a no-strings kind of guy. I've had more than one fantasy about Finn Lawson.

"Prove it." The words spill out of me like a dare.

His wicked grin is my only warning before his fingers slip beneath my panties and thrust into my pussy.

"Oh, fuck." My pussy pulses around the invasion. My breathing is uneven as he holds them there inside me, stretching me around his fingers.

"Fuck, flower, you're so fucking wet and tight." Finn's forehead drops against mine. He draws his fingers out of me and lifts his hand before our faces. "See how wet you are for me?"

His fingers glisten with my wetness before he takes them in his mouth and sucks on them like they're his favorite candy. My pussy aches at the look of pleasure on his face.

When he opens his eyes, the heat in them makes my insides burn. "When do your parents get home?"

"Not for a while."

He leans in and takes my mouth. I can taste myself on his tongue and it doesn't bother me. I want more.

He lifts me off the wall. I cling to him as he sets me on the table. "I need another taste."

I bite my lip as he presses me to lie down. He lowers my panties down my legs and off. Oh, fuck, this is happening. He opens my thighs and his green eyes take in my bare pussy.

I made sure everything was clean and waxed before this weekend, hoping someone would be exploring it besides me.

"Flower, you're beautiful." He leans down and kisses my pussy.

My chest aches as I realize I'm holding my breath. He presses my thighs out as his mischievous eyes collide with mine before his mouth is on me, devouring me.

I moan as he sucks and nips and licks my pussy like he's licking it clean. Then he dips his tongue inside me and I'm catapulted into a new reality because fuck. My breath grows shorter as the spring inside me winds so tight.

He keeps fucking me with his tongue until I can't take any more.

The spring explodes and I cry out. I can feel his smile against my pussy as I try to inch away from the stimulation, which has become too much.

"No, flower, I'm not finished with you yet." He lifts my legs over his shoulders and feasts on my pussy. He thrusts two fingers inside me while he sucks on my clit and I'm done for.

"Oh, fuck, Finn. Oh, fuck." As my release overwhelms me, a gush of fluid flows out of me. I'm mortified at how wet it is. I cover my face with my hands.

"Fuck, Sara. That was the hottest thing I've ever seen." Finn draws me to sit up as he curls his fingers inside me. His face is wet from me.

"Is that supposed to happen?" I grab a napkin and wipe at his smiling face.

"Is that... ?" he repeats. His smile falters a little before his green eyes search mine. Whatever he finds, his eyes soften. "Yes, flower. It's perfectly normal for a fucking amazing orgasm to make you squirt."

His fingers keep brushing that place inside me that pushes me higher. His thumb rubs my clit slowly. "One more. Give me one more and we'll call it good."

"What about you?" I cup his cheeks as his touch overwhelms me again. I pant against his lips.

"I'm good." He claims my mouth as he makes me cry out another release. My heart is pounding so fast and my body clenches so hard around his fingers.

He draws them out of me and I instantly miss them.

"Taste yourself." He holds his fingers up to my lips.

Searching his darkened green eyes, I part my lips and take his fingers into my mouth. Fuck, I suck on them, moaning. He thrusts them slowly in and out. His gaze lowers to my lips. I imagine taking more than his fingers into my mouth.

How thick he'd feel inside me.

He pulls his fingers out and lifts me from the table. I glance over his shoulder at the mess. The mess I made. Fuck, I didn't even know that could happen. I mean, I've read about things like that, but I haven't experienced much.

I wrap my arms around him as he carries me through the house and up the stairs to my bedroom. Finally. He walks past the bed and into the bathroom where he sets me on the counter.

He kisses me softly before unwrapping my legs from his waist. I don't know what to do now. He goes to the sink and wets a washcloth. "You might be a little sore tomorrow."

My eyebrows furrow. He moves between my legs and washes me carefully.

"Is that it?" I fully expected the works, especially when he carried me up to my bedroom.

He blows out a breath and drops the washcloth in the sink. He rests his forehead against mine and strokes his thumb along my jaw.

"As much as I want to fuck you, Sara, I—" He closes his eyes and takes a deep breath before his mouth takes mine. He kisses me like it will be the last time. I slide my hand down to rub his cock over his pants.

"You want me," I murmur against his lips. His cock pulses against my palm.

"Fuck, I do. But—" He backs away and scrubs his hand over his face before looking at me with eyes not intent on seducing me. Something softer lingers in them. "Not tonight, flower."

I close my legs and slide off the counter to stand. "Did I do something wrong?"

"No. Fuck, no. You're perfect, flower." He cups my jaw and lifts my chin before pressing a kiss against my lips. "I just—"

He backs away and coldness draws into the space he occupied. The fire sputters as he looks a little lost.

"I can't do this, right now." He threads his fingers through his hair as he looks me over. He shakes his head. "Call me when your parents get home, flower."

He vanishes out my door and I listen for the sound of the door alarm going off and then stopping. I release my breath and finish cleaning myself up before changing into pajamas.

I'm not tired. Not after all that.

I still don't understand what happened or what it means. If it means anything. Finn finally took action. He finger fucked me and went down on me. It was the hottest thing I've ever done.

I walk down the stairs and finish cleaning up the dining room. My pussy pulses just thinking about what happened in here. I lost track of my orgasms.

But the way he rushed off, I sigh. Did I say something wrong or do something wrong? I nibble on my lip as I go to the front door to make sure it's bolted locked for the night. Someone walks across the street in dark clothes. The red glow of a cigarette is the only light over there. The hair on the back of my neck stands on end.

A chill races up my spine. It's just my imagination trying to make something out of nothing. I doublecheck the security system just in case.

Chapter 5

Going Private

Wyatt

Tom fucked us. At least information-wise. I've been trying to get into his cloud account for the past hour. He must have changed his password, which isn't normal for him. We've been friends for as long as either of us remembers. We've shared practically everything.

There's only one secret between us, but he knows it even though I've never said it.

My phone rings. When I glance at the screen, it's Talia. She's the last person I want to talk to tonight, but if I don't answer, she'll keep calling. Fuck.

"Hello."

"Come join me, Wyatt. You work too much," she practically whines. The sound of electronic music pulses in the background. I should end things with her, but she goes to events with me and doesn't seem to need more, except when she's been drinking.

We haven't fucked in months.

"I'm busy, Talia." I glance toward the door. Finn hasn't come home yet. He was supposed to check in with Sara and then check in with us. Maybe he went out afterward.

My thoughts always drift to Sara. At first it annoyed me to want my friend's sister, but now it's settled into a raw ache that I ignore as best I can.

"Too busy to fuck me?" Talia practically shouts to be heard over the music. "I could come over and do that thing you like."

"Not tonight," I yell to make sure she hears me. I've put her off for the past few weeks. She's sexy, but she's not the one I want. It's growing difficult to pretend otherwise.

"Wy-att."

I hate the way she says my name in that whining baby voice. Talia is becoming less convenient.

"Not tonight." I hang up and toss the phone onto the couch cushion.

The door opens and Finn walks in, running his hand through his hair.

I straighten, immediately worried. "How is she?"

Finn's eyes widen a fraction before he focuses on me. "Who?"

Fuck Tom for leaving us in charge of her. He's the one that always reminds me of the bro code. That our friendship is more important than my desire.

"Sara." My eyes narrow. The guys know who I'm referring to, so what's going on with Finn? Maybe she wasn't there? Maybe she's at that guy's house? My fist clenches as my insides boil.

"She's good." He blows out a breath and his hand goes back through his hair. "Yup, good."

"Any concerns about the guy?" Something is wrong, but I don't know what. Finn isn't meeting my eyes. Maybe he left her with the guy. Maybe he caught them in the middle of something.

My blunt nails dig into my palm, but I don't care. It's nothing compared to the pain of knowing someone else can have Sara.

"Drew's a nice guy." He backs away a step and grins. "She makes excellent cake. I need to clean up."

My brow furrows as he rushes for his bedroom. The door closes behind him. What the fuck is wrong with Finn? What isn't he telling me?

Dante strolls into the living room and sits with his laptop. He's been trying to trace Tom's phone. Since our company pays for it, we have access. I shake off Finn's odd behavior, but the need to check on Sara lingers.

"Did you find anything?" Dante asks, almost absent-mindedly. "His phone is off. He might have ditched it."

"He changed his password on the cloud." I set my laptop on the coffee table and walk to the bar. The whiskey is still on the counter from Sara. I grab a glass and pour some. She looked amazing this afternoon. But she's always stunning.

I take a sip. This isn't typical Tom behavior. He doesn't usually go dark. Not on me.

Dante huffs. "We don't have a lot to go on. Maybe this is about a woman. Who knows with Tom?"

Tom can be spontaneous, but he checks in with us. "Did you talk to Amber?"

Dante shakes his head. Fuck, no one wants to talk to Amber. We all went to high school together. Amber was a constant for Tom. They'd fuck for a while and then break up and then get back together, or not, but still fuck. If he isn't here in the mornings, he's sometimes at her place.

"I'm not calling her," I say. She can be a royal bitch. She's also made it clear she wouldn't mind a threesome with me and Tom. That's not happening.

"Fine." Dante sets his laptop down and pulls out his phone. He puts it on speaker and dials. Asshole.

"What?" Amber sounds angry.

"Tom with you?" Dante doesn't mince words.

"Why the fuck would he be with me? He's a fucking asshole." Amber's rage practically vibrates the phone. "Did you know he asked me for a threesome? With my roommate? Who's a woman? Like he wanted permission to cheat with my roommate by including me."

Rolling his eyes, Dante clicks the End button. "He's not there."

"You could have asked when she saw him last. That might have been right before he disappeared to make sure she didn't call him for a while."

She'll get over any perceived wrong Tom does to her. I don't understand their relationship or fuck buddy status or whatever the fuck they're doing now.

Dante arches an eyebrow and holds out his phone. "You can call her back."

"Call who back?" Finn walks out of his bedroom, freshly showered and cocky as ever. My eyes narrow on him. Something went down that he doesn't want me to know. I'm sure of it.

"Amber." Dante sets his phone down. "How's pipsqueak?"

Finn nods. "Locked inside her tower without her suitor. Drew Young. He seems serious about her and she seems into him."

Jealousy twists my stomach. I've watched Sara for years. I could tell this time was different when she mentioned she had a date. It wasn't to taunt me. She was angry her date got interrupted, but she didn't toss it into the conversation to rile me up.

"Was she mad at you?" I ask. After all, he interrupted her date again.

Finn grabs a beer from the refrigerator. "You know Sara."

That's vague. He sits on the couch and drinks from the bottle.

"Did anything else happen? Were her parents there?" It's like pulling teeth tonight with Finn. My fingers itch to check the security cameras surrounding the townhouse. Tom helped set them up, so I know the password.

"She's supposed to let me know when they get home." His phone dings. He glances at it. "Apparently, they're home."

She was home alone with her date? Fuck, maybe this one is serious. She didn't take him to a restaurant she knew I'd be at like she normally does. My heartbeat quickens. This should be good. Maybe seeing her with someone serious will finally cure me of the aching need for her.

"We should check on her tomorrow." I rub the back of my neck. Those cameras wouldn't show me her. "Either that or install fucking cameras to check on her. We don't know what Tom has gotten her or us into."

Finn shakes his head. "Nah, we don't need cameras. She's secure and Sundays are family days. They usually go to brunch and shit like that."

He's right. I'm overreacting. I need to chill. Shaking out my hand, I focus on the password problem.

"She starts with us on Monday." Dante's gaze meets mine.

I've been preparing for this since Tom told us it was happening. Three months of her showing up in our office. Three months of seeing her almost every day. It will be torture and pleasure every moment of every day.

That burning need to possess her will drive me insane as she flits around our office.

"I'll deal with her." Dante's lips thin. Tom was supposed to watch over her. If Tom was there, it would keep me in check.

"I could help with her." Finn drinks more beer. "We get along well enough."

Finn still isn't meeting my eyes. It isn't like him to volunteer to watch over Sara. Dante took on that role long ago when it became obvious Sara wanted all of us but focused on me.

"We can trade off." Dante's gaze returns to his screen. Maybe nothing is off about Finn tonight. Maybe I'm just seeing what I want to see.

Tomorrow maybe I'll go by during brunch and install those cameras, even if these two won't help me.

Sara

I texted Drew Sunday morning, but he has family obligations all day. It's weird not having the rugrat burst into my room first thing

Sunday morning. Caitlyn has way too much energy and jumps on my bed whether or not I'm ready to wake up. But she's always excited about her Sunday brunch, where she gets to pretend to be an adult at almost seven years old.

My phone buzzes. Only one person calls me.

"What's up, demon spawn?" I stare at the ceiling above my bed.

"Mom said I had to wait until now to call you." Caitlyn's voice sounds pouty.

"Mom was right. It's almost time to get up for brunch." I sit up and sigh. Last night, Finn walked me into this room and I thought finally, but then he left.

"We're at a café so Mom and Dad can have espresso. I got a chocolate croissant and hot chocolate."

"That sounds yummy."

"Are you going to go to brunch without me?" That note of homesickness in Caitlyn's voice hits me right in the heart.

"Of course not. I wouldn't dare go without you." I say it like I'm truly offended by the mere thought. "I'll just have a boring, plain old croissant at home."

"Good."

I almost laugh at the forcefulness of her *good*.

"Mom wants to talk to you."

Before I can even tell Caitlyn *goodbye*, Mom says into the phone, "You have chocolate on your cheek, sweetie."

"Good morning, Mom." I flop back in the bed. I bet she already knows about Drew.

"Are you taking care of yourself? Don't forget to pick up Peabody. Alyssa Wyndham texted me to say she saw you out with Drew Young yesterday for brunch."

"Wow, two seconds, that has to be a record." I roll my eyes. Of course Mom has heard about Drew. I'm surprised she's not already picking out wedding colors.

"Should I not be interested in my daughter going out on a date on her own, without me pushing her into it?" Mom's tone almost goes high-pitched, but she'd never lower herself to sound screechy.

I sigh.

"It was one date, Mom. Don't start the registry just yet." I pick at my sheets. He's also one hell of a kisser. My cheeks heat remembering Finn's kiss and touch. My thighs press together at the ache.

"He's perfect for you. I couldn't have picked better. We'll have his parents over for dinner when we get back. Oh, I wish I was there now so we could have that dinner. I'm sure they'll love you," Mom practically gushes. "Just don't come on too strong like you usually do. Try to be a little more coy. Guys like that."

I consider for a moment hanging up the phone and saying I got disconnected. In fact, I dream of it a little before I say, "Okay, Mom. I love you."

"Do you want to talk to Roger?"

I laugh when I hear Roger say in the background, "She doesn't want to talk to me, Bitsy."

"No, I'm good. Enjoy your vacation and don't worry about me."

"Oh, you start your internship with your brother tomorrow." Mom's words make my gut tighten. She doesn't know about Tom's disappearing act. "Tell Tom to call me. I know he won't, but I left him a message this morning."

"I'll tell him," I say before swallowing. I don't want my mom to worry, because she always does when Tom disappears. What I really don't want is for her to show up here thinking she can do something to help. I need this time alone. And they desperately need this vacation.

"Okay, sweetie. I love you."

"I love you too."

The phone disconnects and I toss it on the bed beside me. Sleep won't happen now, so I roll out of the bed and cross to my bathroom. After turning on the shower, I brush my teeth and then strip out of my clothes.

In the mirror, I catch a slightly pink mark on my neck and lean in for a closer look. Last night, Drew left a mark on me. Pleasure ripples through me as I stroke my fingers over the faint hickey. I don't think anyone's ever given me a hickey before.

As I take my shower, my thoughts keep drifting to Drew and Finn last night. My hands slide down my wet body. I'm tempted to bang one out fast, but instead I quickly finish my shower. The other nice thing about having the house to myself is no little demon spawn to race into my room, interrupting what I need to do.

So I can actually take my time.

I dry off and wrap the towel around myself while I blow-dry my hair. The ache grows the more I think of what should have happened last night. Drew in the kitchen, me on the counter, his fingers moving in and out until he replaced them with his cock, thrusting inside me until I couldn't even think as desire crashed over me.

Or Finn never stopped and, instead of lifting me off the table, eased his cock deep inside me, filling me so fucking full until my pussy clenched around him.

I set the dryer down and stare at my flushed cheeks in the mirror. And that one mark that means Drew wanted to claim me. Fuck.

I hurry into the bedroom, jerk back the covers and drop my towel on the floor. Naked, I get into bed with the covers at my feet. I stroke my hands over my nipples, imagining Drew's hands instead.

Closing my eyes, I picture Finn smirking off to the side as Drew lavishes attention on my breasts and nipples, sucking, licking, touching. My pussy clenches, empty.

Parting my legs, I slide a hand over my trembling belly and touch my pussy, imagining Finn walking over and pulling my hips to the side so he can feast on me. The slippery surface of my swollen clit sucked on instead of rubbed like I'm doing. I whimper.

Both men worshipping my body with their mouths, taking me higher. I slide my fingers back to my entrance and push inside, arching at the sensation. I can almost feel Wyatt watching me. His dark eyes watching what Finn and Drew do to me, flashing with heat, wanting to join in, but only watching.

I'm so close. Dante would ease down on the bed beside me and trail those long fingers over every inch of me. I lower my other hand to circle my clit as I thrust my fingers into my pussy, faster, harder, winding myself up until I'm ready to burst.

Something makes a sound in the room and my eyes pop open as my hands freeze. I turn my head and see my previously closed door open. Fuck.

I disengage and roll off the bed, grabbing my towel and wrapping it around myself. Next to my bed is Tom's old baseball bat. I grab that and hold it high as I walk into the hallway.

My legs tremble, but I need to check why the security alarm didn't go off. My heart races. Tom's door is open and I make myself go to it. Holding my breath, I push open the door.

A figure stands in the darkness. For a second, I think it's Tom, but this guy is so much taller and his cologne reminds me of the ocean. I drop the bat to my side and turn on the light.

"What the fuck are you doing here, Dante?"

Chapter 6

Restructuring

Sara

"Why aren't you at breakfast, pipsqueak?" Dante's deep voice makes me aware of the fact I'm standing in only a towel with my pussy wet and still aching. Did he see what I was doing? From the doorway, he would have been able to see almost everything. My cheeks heat.

It takes a moment to realize he asked me a question. A legitimate question. I bite my lip and lean the bat against the wall to give myself a moment to think. I can't let him know my parents are out of town, not with the note my brother left. There's no way I'm moving into that apartment.

"I need to pick up Peabody in an hour." I almost high-five myself for my quick thinking. And also, "What are you doing here?"

He shifts his weight on his feet. Fuck, I swear he always seems bigger in real life than in my imagination. There's always been something primal about my attraction to Dante. He's the largest, most fit guy I know. Intelligent and gorgeous.

I definitely wouldn't mind a ravishing from this particular Viking. A shiver of desire rolls down my spine. I press my thighs together against the throbbing, aching need that, instead of abating, grows more urgent.

"Checking on things." He arches an eyebrow, obviously daring me to question him. But fuck that. He invaded my privacy.

I step closer and narrow my eyes up at him. "In my room?"

He smirks. "You weren't supposed to be there, pipsqueak."

"You could have texted or called, but you just let yourself into *my* house?" I'm trying to build up my anger, but it's not working. The desire I stirred grows hotter inside. "Why are you in Tom's room?"

Mom keeps Tom's room exactly how he left it, just in case. Personally, I think she's delusional. Tom has an apartment and isn't going to come home to visit when he lives a few blocks away.

"Searching for clues." Dante steps toward me and I automatically back up. Not that I'm afraid of him. I tip my chin up at his smirk. He strokes his fingers over his jaw. "It's strange, pipsqueak..."

I glance around the room with my brow furrowed. It looks like it always does. "What's strange?"

"Your parents' room is untouched and most of their luggage is missing."

My heart clatters in my chest as he takes another step closer. This time I hold my ground though. Fuck, he knows. And if he knows, he'll make me move in with them and that can't happen. I can't do what I need to do with Drew if I'm surrounded by those guys.

And seeing Finn every day at work will be bad after last night, but having to spend twenty-four seven with the guy? And watch any of them bring other women into their beds?

No, thank you.

I'd probably go apeshit on any woman Wyatt brought home.

"So?" I try to brazen it out. After all, he doesn't know anything.

"Caitlyn's cat is gone."

Yeah, that's not a usual thing. Her stuffed cat that Tom gave her is a prized possession. Mom insists she keeps it at home. The poor thing used to be white and pink but now is more brownish pink with clumped fur.

"She must have taken it to brunch." I arch an eyebrow, daring him to challenge me more.

"Now, pip, why would she do that when that's grown-up time for her?" He closes the distance between us a little more. His heat and the scent of sunshine flow over me.

Fuck, I hate they know as much about our family as Tom does. I tighten my lips and glare at him.

"I kept wondering why Tom would word your texts and our note that way. After all, there's nowhere safer than under your parents' watchful eyes." He's not wrong. Roger is an ex-marine. "So why insist you come to us, when we're the last guys he'd want to tempt with you?"

My brow furrows. *Tempt?*

He releases a breath and it coats my bare shoulders. A shiver races down my spine.

"We have a problem, pip."

"I don't see a problem." I cross my arms over my chest, thankful my towel is tucked in tight.

"We can't protect you if you're here all on your own, but if you come to our penthouse, other issues might..." He glances down at the swells of my breast. Awareness stirs inside me. My breasts become tight and achy. His light blue eyes are a little darker when he raises them to mine. "Arise."

"I'm not coming to live with you, so we don't have a problem." Well, except the scent of my arousal filling the room. Standing this close to Dante stirs all sorts of naughty thoughts. He's so big and strong. I bet he could lift me against the wall with one hand and fuck me.

I wet my lips.

"I don't have a choice, pip." Dante shakes his head. His blond hair is pulled back in a bun, showing off the sharp angles of his face.

"I appreciate your loyalty to my brother, but there's a security system in place. We don't even know if there really is a threat. For all we know, it's some woman who Tom wants to get over him. Though why he doesn't just sic Amber on her, I'll never know."

"It would be easier with you here." Dante's gaze drops to my towel. "But Tom—"

Fuck it. I drop my arms. "Seriously, I don't want to live with you guys. I'll do anything, Dante."

He rubs his finger next to his full lips. "I'll let you stay here. Alone. Under two conditions."

I narrow my eyes. "What conditions?"

"One, you call if you need anything. Don't fucking hesitate. The littlest thing, you call me." He almost seems to get larger as he says that.

"Fine." That's easy because he won't know if I don't call him. "And?"

"Finish what you started, pip."

Dante

Sara's mouth drops open and her cheeks flush even more pink. "What?"

"Did I stutter?" I'm ninety-nine percent sure she'll back down and pack her bags to come stay with us. When I opened her door to place the small camera Wyatt bought, I never expected to find Sara naked on her bed giving herself pleasure.

My cock hardened painfully at her parted lips. The flushed heat that coated her skin pink from her cheeks to her breasts. Her fingers pumping into her pussy while she rubbed her clit.

Do I want to watch her finish? Yes, but I shouldn't and she won't. Sara is bold, but not that bold.

Her mouth presses into a thin, stubborn line. Good. Now she'll pack like a good girl and come with me. I'll figure out how to keep her from Wyatt once we get there. Maybe I'll lock her in Tom's room.

I cock an eyebrow.

"Fine." Her devious smile should have been a warning. She reaches for my hand and tugs me toward the door. "But not in Tom's room."

Uh, what? She leads me down the hallway to her room. She stops inside and scrutinizes the space, looking around for something.

"Stop playing around, Sara. Get dressed and we'll go get Peabody and head to the apartment." Peabody is another issue we'll have to deal with later.

She shuts her door with a final click. Stepping in front of me, she pushes her finger against my chest. Her pale green eyes flash with fire and heat.

"No, Dante, you gave me an option and I want to take it. I just want you to have the perfect view." She takes my arm and moves me along the wall before pushing me back against it.

"You're not going to willingly masturbate in front of me, pip." I try to sound confident and overbearing, but my cock is already hard again just thinking about it.

She turns and backs up against me. I jerk my hips back so she doesn't feel how hard I am. "Hmm, you're taller, but this should be a good view."

As she turns to face me, her dancing green eyes capture mine. With a naughty grin, she backs toward her bed. Her hands move up to the knot in her towel.

"Sara…" I'm about to scold her about being a tease, but then she drops the towel to the ground and continues to back up to the bed. My mouth goes dry as I take in every perfect inch of her body. Her freckles, that her mother always tells her to cover up, spread down her chest.

The urge to kiss every one of them and tell Sara how perfect they are makes me clench my fists to hold me in place. When my gaze dips lower, I swallow. She's shaved bare from the waist down.

My cock twitches.

She sits on the edge of the bed and spreads her legs open for me.

Fuck. I lean against the wall to keep from falling to my knees and begging her to let me worship every inch of her body with my tongue and hands before sliding into her beautiful pussy.

I lift my eyes, pausing on her tightened pink nipples, taking in her parted lips before meeting those pale green eyes, dilated with desire.

"You wanted to watch me finish." Her voice is breathless as she raises her hand to her breast. "But I need to work up to it."

Liar, but I don't call her on it. She's so wet I can tell from here that her pussy is glistening.

She cups her breast and teases the nipple. I lick my lips. She's temptation incarnate. I've kept away because of Tom and Wyatt. But seeing her like this makes me want to claim her as mine.

"Pinch it." The words come out rough, almost angry.

Her eyes collide with mine as she pinches her nipple. She gasps.

"Tug on it, pip."

She moans softly as she does what I say. "Dante."

My name on her lips is like music to my ears, but I don't move from the wall. My control is in place but fragile. I'd love to show her exactly how to take care of her needs. But for now, I've dug my grave to just watch. That's all it will be. A show.

A show that will be ingrained in my memory because this girl is perfection.

"Lift your other hand to your breast." I clench my fists to keep from stroking my hard cock.

"Like this?" She takes her other breast in her palm and pinches and tugs on her nipple. "Fuck, that feels good."

"You wet for me, pip?"

Her darkened eyes collide with mine. "Yes, Dante."

"Show me."

Her brow furrows in confusion.

"Slide your fingers into that pussy and show me how wet you are for my cock."

Moaning, she slides her hand down to her pussy and thrusts her fingers inside with a gasp.

"Pull them out and hold them up like a good girl."

She bites her lip and does what I say. Her fingers glisten in the soft light. I'm fucked. I should leave right now. Out of the house and out of her life because I'm crossing a line. Not a major line, but a line I swore I wouldn't cross.

As long as I'm not the one touching her though...

Her eyes sparkle as she opens her mouth and slides her fingers in. She moans and my cock jerks.

"How do you taste, pip?"

She sucks and pulls her fingers out. "Tangy, but a little sweet."

"Rub those wet fingers over your nipple."

Her fingers drop to her nipple and circle it. I can almost imagine how she'd taste if I drew that taut nipple into my mouth. Can she come from having her breasts played with?

"Dante, please," she whimpers, so fucking ready to move on to the next part.

"Are you ready to finish what you started, pip?" I wet my lips and she nods. "Lie back on the bed and let your knees fall out to the side."

She grabs a pillow and rests her head, so she can still see me. "Will you stroke yourself for me?"

She parts her legs and lowers her knees to the bed. I'm going to fucking hell for this. She slides her hands up and down her thighs as her breasts lift with every breath.

"You want to imagine it's my cock in your pussy instead of your fingers, pip?" I rub my cock through my jeans, and a sizzle of electricity flows through my blood.

"Yes, Dante. I want to feel your cock buried inside me when I come." She bites her lip as her fingers glide over her pussy, opening herself up to me.

For a second, I give in to the fantasy and imagine sinking my cock into her warm, wet pussy, feeling it tighten around me as I fuck her to orgasm. But I can't do that. Not to her. Not just because of Tom, but because of Wyatt too.

But I can watch her get off while I get off.

"I'm not fucking you, pip." I warn her with my eyes as I undo my belt.

"I have a good imagination." She strokes her finger over her center and makes this needy little noise that has my cock weeping.

Her eyes widen as she focuses on my hands on my jeans. I'm so fucking screwed with this girl.

"Keep your hands still, pip."

She moves her hands to her thighs.

"Good girl." I lower my zipper slowly, drawing it out to make her wait.

"Fuck, Dante." She whimpers.

I'm going to blow like a teenage boy at this rate. I free my cock and she inhales sharply.

"What's wrong, pip? Worried you can't handle it?" I stroke my hand down my large, curved cock. "Don't worry. I know exactly how to make you scream."

Her tongue darts out to lick her lips like she's imagining my cock in her mouth. I groan. Fuck me. Her hungry gaze lifts to mine.

"Use both hands. Slide a finger inside that pretty pussy while you stroke your clit with the other." I slide my hand up my cock and fuck into my tight fist as she follows my command. "Slowly, pip."

She watches my hand and matches my rhythm. Our harsh breathing is the only sound in the room as I slowly quicken my pace. She follows my strokes. A flush of pink coats her body.

"Add a finger in your pussy."

She presses another finger into her pussy for me as I smooth my precum over my cock.

"How does your cunt feel squeezing around your fingers, pip?"

"Tight. Hot. Wet." She pants and bites her lip. "I can't get deep enough."

I tsk. "I'm not fucking you, pip. Add another finger and stretch that pussy for me. Show me how much cock you can take."

She adds a third finger, thrusting them in and out. Her lips are parted. Her pale green eyes are almost black with desire as she focuses on my hand on my cock.

"Are you going to come for me, pip?" I thrust hard into my fist.

"Dante!" She thrusts her fingers in and catches in that moment of intense pleasure between breaths. Her pussy gushes her release all over her hand.

"Fuck, Sara." Groaning, I come coating my hand and jets of cum fall onto her wood floor.

She collapses against the bed. Naked with her fingers still buried inside herself, she looks like a goddess. I'm so fucked. I want more, but this is all I can have.

"Want a taste, pip?" I arch an eyebrow.

She opens her eyes and nods, licking her lips. "Yes, please."

My cock still hard in my hand, I cross the distance to her. "Keep your fingers inside yourself."

Because I don't trust myself not to ease into that beautiful, dripping-wet cunt clutching at her thin fingers. My cock twitches as I imagine those pulses around it. If she thought her three fingers were tight, what would she think with my thick cock buried inside her?

She eyes my cock, but lets me bring my cum-covered hand to her face. Her pale green eyes lift to mine as she parts her lips and sucks on my finger, licking around it.

I put my cock back in my pants and zip up as she sucks my finger clean, running her tongue along the webbing before taking another finger into her mouth.

When my cock is tucked away, I pull her wrist to bring the fingers in her pussy to my lips and suck on them. She gasps around my fingers and her eyes burn into mine.

In this moment, she's all mine. I could take her on this bed and she'd let me. I could strip naked and lose myself between her thighs over and over again until we're both satiated. Savoring the taste of her, I draw her fingers out of my mouth and take mine out of hers.

"I'll keep your secret for now, pipsqueak, but if I believe you need to be with us to stay safe..."

She presses her thighs together and pulls the covers over her naked body. "I'll be good right here."

Her red hair is spread out on her pillow. I want to rip the covers off her and cover her with my body. Instead, I walk into her bathroom and wash my hands, listening for her padding footsteps.

But when I come out, she's still on the bed. A goddess, a temptress.

Grabbing a washcloth, I clean up her floor as she watches. When I finish, I toss it into her hamper.

With my back to her, I pause by her dresser and surreptitiously set the small camera on it because I told Wyatt I would. If he catches the show I caught, I don't think bro code would hold him back. My gaze is drawn to the enchantress on her bed again. Maybe I need to tap into the feed.

Her eyebrow arches and her smile is seductive. "You can check up on me anytime you want to, Dante."

Fuck. I narrow my eyes. "Behave, pipsqueak."

Her soft laughter follows me into the hallway. I'm so fucked.

Chapter 7

Start-Up Costs

Wyatt

"Did you set up the camera?" I ask as Dante walks into the apartment. I've been poring over the recent billings to see if I can figure out Tom's secret companies. Whatever he was doing he kept it off the books, which is bad for all of us.

"Yes." He goes to the bar and pours himself some scotch before downing the whole glass in a gulp.

I raise an eyebrow. It's barely noon and Dante rarely drinks.

"Everything good?" I shut my laptop because the numbers were practically dancing in my vision. Maybe we'll have better luck this week.

"I placed your camera." His tone is gruff, but that's not unusual for Dante. When I mentioned what I planned, Dante insisted he could do it for me.

"I won't use it." The words are hollow. We both know my control when it comes to Sara is fragile. She's my weakness. Dante has played my foil to keep her from realizing how much I want her.

Because when she wants something, she's determined to get it. And at some point she decided she wants me. But I can't have her.

"Maybe we should talk to her parents tonight about Tom." I run a hand through my hair.

"That's not a good idea." Dante sets the glass down and leans against the wall behind the bar. "It will just worry them and you know how Tom's mom is."

She worries about everything. After Tom and Sara's father died, she almost bubble-wrapped the two of them. When she married Roger, she finally found some peace. If she even had an inkling that one of her children was in danger, she'd tear apart the world searching for him.

I nod. "You're right. It would just make me feel better if they knew and could watch over Sara."

"You mean keep Sara under lock and key and maybe disapprove of the new boyfriend." Dante shakes his head.

"Is he her boyfriend?" I'm curious because Dante usually knows everything about Sara, including when she's actually into someone.

"Maybe." His look turns thoughtful for a second before he shrugs. "Besides, she has Peabody."

"Fucking mutt," I mutter.

Dante chuckles. "Just because you're the only person on this earth that dog hates—"

"The feeling is mutual."

"—doesn't mean he won't potentially scare off the new guy."

"Peabody is a terror." He's a five-pound ball of fur with the attitude of a German shepherd. He adores Sara, but absolutely hates me. Can't say that I see the point of the tiny monster. He doesn't bite the other guys, but me? I must smell like kibble.

I almost needed stitches from a couple of the times he caught me unaware.

"Maybe he'll hate Drew since Drew likes Sara." Dante shrugs, but there's this tension in his jaw. Maybe he doesn't like the idea of Sara having someone either.

I'm not blind. I know both Finn and Dante are attracted to her, but she chose me to fixate on. And we can't betray Tom by fucking around with his sister so nothing will ever come of it.

"I'm going to shower." Dante gestures to his room before disappearing into it.

As soon as his door closes, I open my laptop and sync into the camera in Sara's room to see what angle he left it. The room is dim with only sunlight bleeding through the curtains. I can see her bed and the doorway to her bathroom.

A little white streak goes across the bottom of the camera accompanied by the clicking of toenails and the jingling of a bell on his collar.

"What are you doing, Peabody?" Sara walks in. Her jeans fit her like a second skin. Her light sweater falls off one shoulder, showing the strap of her camisole under it. She has her red hair drawn into a low ponytail, cascading in loose curls down her back.

I suck in a breath. No matter how many times I see her, it's always the same. My desire for her is like a punch to the gut. Or maybe lower.

"Already creeping on Sara." Finn's voice comes from over my shoulder.

"Ensuring the camera works." I shut it off and close the laptop. It's set to record to the cloud. So if something happens to Sara, we'll be able to review it.

"You better hope she doesn't have Drew over or you'll get your own porn." Finn laughs but the words settle like lead in my stomach.

It was only a matter of time before Sara finally gave up on me and found someone who could actually have her. I run a hand through my hair. Not that I can do anything about it. She's Tom's little sister. Tom's my best friend.

"It's not like she hasn't had boyfriends." Ones I enjoyed terrorizing with Tom when we were young. They never deserved Sara. No one is good enough for her. Definitely not me.

"Best prepare yourself, my friend." Finn sits on the couch in front of the TV and turns it on. "This one has staying power."

I blow out a breath and resist the urge to creep on her with the camera again. At some point, I'll figure out how to let Sara go. But right now she needs us and our protection. For once, it's okay if I fixate on her.

Sara

Peabody runs in circles outside in our tiny backyard. Normally, I'd take him for a walk, but I'll admit only to myself, the two times I saw someone smoking, seemingly spying on me, have me spooked. So a quick wee in the backyard is all Peabody is getting this morning.

"Come on, Peabody." I sip my coffee while I wait for the little speed demon to wear himself out. The dog walker will come by at ten and two. If I call, she'll come by at five too. Not that I expect to have to work late my first week, but who knows with these guys.

Peabody races up to my feet and sits with his butt wiggling.

"Such a kiss up." I reach into my pocket for his treat and bend down to give it to him. He takes it and trots into the house, straight to his bed. I close and lock the back door.

In the kitchen, I empty my mug and put it in the dishwasher before going into the half bath to check my appearance. I've got on an almost fifties-style blue dress, with a swing skirt and a buttoned-up top.

I curled my hair and tied back half to keep it out of my face. Makeup completes my look with winged eyeliner and red lips. I need all the armor I can get after this weekend. Those stolen passionate moments with Finn and Dante kept me up most of last night.

Drew and I plan to get together for lunch sometime this week, pending my schedule. But today, I have to look Finn in the eyes after he went down on me and Dante after I masturbated for him and licked the cum off his hand.

My cheeks flush in the mirror. Yeah, definitely not bringing up either of those incidents today. Did they tell each other? Did they tell Wyatt?

My heart pounds a little harder and my hands shake as I lift them to tuck my hair behind my ears. I'm not embarrassed about taking control of my sexuality, but it could get a little awkward because they're friends with each other and my bosses for the next few months.

All I can do is be bold and pretend nothing happened.

Like they both didn't shake the walls I so carefully constructed to the ground. My walls built on the foundation that Finn is a flirt who does nothing about it, while Dante protects Wyatt from me. Now I know they both want me, but neither of them took me when the opportunity presented itself.

I came, and it was glorious, but neither of them went further.

Is it all because of Tom? Or maybe it's because Wyatt feels something for me? My heart skips a beat.

Fuck.

No.

Stop. I can't keep doing this to myself.

No more mooning over Wyatt. I'm better than this. Straightening, I give myself a narrowed look before leaving the bathroom. Wyatt Hawkins doesn't deserve my time. I'm done waiting for something that won't happen.

I grab my purse off the counter and stoop in front of Peabody, balancing on my three-inch black heels.

"Be a good boy today." When I pat him, he cocks his head at me before returning to his toy.

It's weird that Mom isn't here to send me off to my first internship, but we talked about it. This is my chance to be on my own. She and Roger wanted to take Caitlyn to experience the world and have some time to themselves.

Caitlyn has a big sister and big brother. We both dote on her, but we got all that stuff when we were kids. She needs it too. If I didn't have my internship though, Mom would have insisted on me coming with.

I open the app on my phone and page my driver to come to the front of the building. After setting the alarm, I walk out onto the stoop in front of the townhouse. The road is quiet for the city, but the noise filters in from the street down the way.

I breathe in the new day. I'm going to kill this internship. My phone dings and I look down.

MADISON:

Good luck today!

HOPE:

Kick some accounting ass!

KAYLA:

Tell Dante if he needs a chick to ravish I'm available

And good luck, but you don't need it!

Smiling, I reread the texts. This is the best thing to come from the setups my mom always makes me go on. These women. I'm so glad I was honest and upfront with Noah when he showed up for our "date."

Now I have these three women in my life and we're stronger than ever.

A black car pulls up in front of my building. I glance at the driver. Seeing Brandon, I wave. He tips his head to me and faces the front.

I walk down the steps and look around the street again. Nothing moves. Nothing has changed but a chill sweeps through me. I shake it off and slide into the car.

"Good morning, Brandon. How's Gretchen and Jon?" I smile at the rearview mirror.

He meets my eyes. "They're good, miss. To work?"

I grin. "Yes, Brandon. Thank you."

Nodding, he pulls off the curb.

I return to my text messages.

ME:

And I'm off! I can't wait. Lunch this week?
Or maybe happy hour tonight?

KAYLA:

I'm in for happy hour!

HOPE:

Me too!

MADISON:

I should be good to go.

ME:

Yay!

I set my phone on my lap and turn to look out the window. Something black moves in the corner of my eye. My head turns, but whatever it was is gone. Ice trickles down my back.

It might just be my imagination playing tricks on me at this point. With Tom's warning still ringing in my ears and Dante's worry, maybe I'm being stupid for not taking them up on their offer. For not doing what Tom asked me to.

But what would living with Wyatt, Finn, and Dante accomplish besides a hardcore case of lady blue balls. If I were still trying to win over Wyatt, I would have jumped at the chance, but how much can a girl humiliate herself before she gets the picture?

He may want me, but he doesn't want to want me, so fuck him.

Drew wants me. And maybe Drew will be the only one willing to take it all the way because Tom's not his friend. I pull up my texts and shoot off a quick one.

ME:

First day of my internship. I'll let you know
what day works best for lunch.

DREW:

...

I smile at the little dots that mean he's already writing me back. That he isn't going to leave me on *read* all day.

DREW:

I can't wait to see you again. Good luck on your new job.

See, that's what a guy who wants me sounds like. My hands tremble when I realize how close to the building we are. I don't know what I'm walking into here.

If Tom were here, he'd take care of me. He'd laugh off Finn's flirtations, punch Dante in the arm when he gets growly, and steer me clear of Wyatt and tease me about my attraction in the same breath.

He'd make this easy for all of us.

Instead, I'm walking into a potential minefield. That I created. I'm the one who took Finn's challenge when I should have laughed it off. I'm the one who didn't back down like Dante expected me to when he called me out for masturbating.

But fuck, I can't regret either of them. Because that shit was hot and I can't wait to do it all over again.

The car stops and I bite my lip. It's not happening again, but if it did...

"This is your stop, miss," Brandon says. "I'll be back at five unless you page me."

"Thanks, Brandon." Taking a deep breath, I open the door. The sidewalk is busy, but people aren't rushing by. I navigate my way to the door.

A guy around my age in a suit opens the door to the building and sees me. He's a good-looking guy with blond hair. His brown eyes rake over me before he smiles and gestures to the door. "After you."

I give him a grateful smile as I pass by and keep walking to the elevators. He follows me and we both step onto the elevator to go up.

"What floor?" He raises an eyebrow as his finger presses the tenth floor.

"Ten, actually." I smile. "Thank you."

No one else gets onto and the elevator doors close.

"Client?" he asks.

"Intern. You?"

"I'm an associate." He holds out his hand. "Greg Holden. You must be Tom's sister."

I take his hand. "Sara Morris."

He points at my hair as he takes his hand back. "Your hair should have tipped me off."

Tom has red hair too. I nod. "We take after our grandmother."

"I've always been a sucker for a redhead." His cheeks flush a little as the elevator dings its arrival and the doors open. "After you."

I walk into the office space. Low cubicles that are easily seen over take up the main floor. The guys have offices with great views toward the back of the building.

"It was a pleasure to meet you, Sara. I hope we work together." Greg moves off in the opposite direction, lifting a hand to someone in the cubicles.

I walk toward the guys' offices. I don't know where they're going to put me. My heart picks up pace as I draw closer. I didn't think this through. I'll be working with Dante, Finn, and Wyatt all day.

Two of them now know how I taste. Dante's seen me naked while Finn's only seen my pussy. Yeah, great first day thoughts.

"Sara." Dante's voice sends a bolt of awareness through me.

I turn and he gestures for me to follow him. He's wearing a dress shirt with his sleeves rolled up to show his forearms. A black tattoo trails up his arm and peeks out of the collar of his shirt.

I've seen the man shirtless, in only a towel, and now I've seen his cock. And fuck, he's big and curved and thick, and I don't know if that would fit inside me, but I'm willing to give it a try.

Dante stops in front of a door and pushes it open. His eyes are back to their cool blue as he looks at me. "This is Tom's office. Since he's not here, we figured it would be best if you were close by so we could monitor you."

"Sounds good." I walk around him. Apparently, we're going to be professionals today and not discuss how he made me come so fucking hard I saw stars. Pretty sure I blacked out for a moment too. We're going to work and figure out what the fuck Tom was into.

Unlike Tom's bedroom, his office is immaculate. His desk is free from any papers. Just a monitor and a keyboard off to the side.

"So what am I going to be working on while I'm here?" I set my purse on the desk and turn to meet Dante's eyes, except his gaze was on my ass. He lifts it to mine.

I smirk as he clears his throat.

"Paperwork first." He reaches onto the console, takes a folder of papers, and hands it to me. "I'll come get you when you finish."

"Oh, joy." I walk around the desk and sit down in the chair. It feels weird to be in Tom's office without him, but I grab a pen from the drawer before opening the folder to begin on my paperwork.

Chapter 8

Detective Controls

Sara

I finish the paperwork, but Dante hasn't come back to check on me. I could go find him. His office is probably close. Instead, I open the drawer and put the pen back.

Fuck it. This is Tom's desk. I open the drawer more and rummage through of various office supplies. A couple of blank Post-it Note pads. I grab a pencil and try the whole *rub on the pad to see what was written on it* thing, but come up with nothing. That's all I get, nothing that tells me what he was working on or who he was working for.

I open another drawer and shift through the contents. Nothing stands out though. When I pull out another drawer, a piece of folded paper flutters to the floor. I glance up at the open door to see if anyone else is seeing this, but I'm still alone.

Closing the drawer, I pick up the paper. I unfold it and lay it on the desk. There's a logo on the note that has "VV" in it. Then someone with really girly handwriting has a bunch of numbers in a column with a completely wrong total on it. My brother's sharp handwriting totals the column correctly beside it.

I bite my lip. What if this is a clue? What if Tom just ran off with someone who's terrible at math? Oh, Mom would be so mad. She's been after Tom to go out with *respectable* women from good families. Yeah, Tom just blows her off, meaning Mom focuses on only me for setups.

I look at the note again and the logo.

Or maybe VV is the business he was working on that the guys can't figure out.

Fuck it. I grab the paper and step out of Tom's office to look around. The doors to the other offices are closed, but the conference room at the end has a window and I can see Finn in there.

Finn will know what to do with this. I walk over to the conference room and push open the door.

"I found something weird in Tom's desk." I hold the paper up and then look at the three faces staring at me in disbelief.

"Can we call you back, Mark?" Finn says slowly.

A voice comes from the computer. "Sure."

Oops. My cheeks flush, but this is important. This is about Tom. Finn closes the laptop and leans back. He raises an eyebrow and smirks at me. I haven't seen him yet today. Fuck, he looks good in a suit.

My panties grow damp from just the heat in his green eyes at his slow perusal of my outfit, so I turn and find Dante's cool eyes just watching me, like he did in my bedroom while he stroked his cock. That's not safe either.

Finally, my gaze rests on Wyatt. He scowls at me, annoyed that I interrupted whatever meeting they were having. Yeah, that will do it.

"This fell out of Tom's desk." I hold it up. "It wasn't in a drawer. Maybe this company has something to do with why he disappeared."

Leaning over the table. I open the note and spread it in front of them. I point to the numbers someone else wrote. "That's not Tom's handwriting. But that logo has to represent something. Especially with Tom's notes."

I glance up and catch Wyatt's eyes looking not at my face. When I tip my head to look, I notice the gaping in my dress, showing my cleavage. I lift my eyebrow and meet his dark eyes. His face is expressionless, but I narrow my eyes at him.

They're boobs. And I have nice ones, so I guess any guy would look. I ignore the little happy dance happening in my head that at least my breasts can capture Wyatt's attention.

"Do any of you know what VV stands for?" I straighten and cross my arms while my gaze moves between all of them.

Dante stands and I swallow because, fuck, he's tall and it's easier to talk to him when he's just a sitting giant. "Let's go, pipsqueak."

I back up a step and tip my chin stubbornly. "This is about Tom. I need to find out what he's running from."

"You need to learn how to knock on doors." Dante closes in on me and I move around behind Finn. We've played this game a hundred times, but I'm done with it. I'm done with being ushered off to the side.

"No, we need to figure out what Tom's worried about. For all we know, the company he was working for is this VV. I mean obviously whoever added these numbers needs help." I grab the chair next to Finn and hold it in front of me to block Dante from getting closer.

"We have work to do." Dante points to the computer. "We have a business to run. We can't sit around and play detective with you all day, pipsqueak."

I purse my lips. "I'm here for a job. Not just to fill out paperwork all day, Dante. It's not my fault you put me in Tom's office and left me there to rot."

"Tom's the one who hired you." Dante straightens and his cool eyes flare with that heat he showed me yesterday.

My insides warm, but I'm not giving in. "Tom's not here. This should be the most important thing. Making sure Tom's just doing a fucking walkabout and that he's worried about nothing. I don't know about you, but Tom has never in his life told me to seek any of you out. So why now?"

"Maybe because he knows what a huge pain in the ass you can

be." Dante's voice is loud. His words strike me in the chest. "Maybe he left so he wouldn't have to put up with you."

I actually step back like he hit me. Tears well in my eyes, but I refuse to let them fall. My lip trembles. I blink a few times and draw in a breath. Dante doesn't yell at me.

His eyes soften. "Sara—"

"No." I straighten and move to escape. "Clearly the only one who wanted me here was Tom."

"Flower..." Finn begins to rise, but I make it to the door.

"I'm sorry I interrupted your meeting. It won't happen again."

Wyatt stands, but I'm already out the door and shutting it. I make it to Tom's office and lock the door behind me. My heart pounds so hard I put my hand over it to keep it in my chest. A tear slips from my eye, but I brush it away.

Fuck, I hate it when my emotions get in the way. This is supposed to be a job. I wouldn't have done that anywhere else but here. Dante was right. I should have knocked and waited, but this isn't a normal work environment for me.

I've known these guys practically all my life. Jerking forward, I grab a tissue from the box and dab at my eyes. They want me to sit in here like a good little girl. Fine.

Drawing in a breath, I walk over to the door, unlock it, and open it a crack. At noon, I'm going to lunch. Maybe I'll see if Drew can meet me. It'd be nice to see a friendly face. Someone who actually wants to see me.

My heart is slowing as I sit behind Tom's desk and pull out my phone.

ME:

Having a shit morning. Want to meet me for lunch?

DREW:

What time is your lunch break?

Honestly, I don't know and don't care what they say it is.

ME:

Noon

DREW:

I'll swing by your office to pick you up

My cheeks flush as I look up at the door. None of them bothered to check on me. They probably went right back to work. Which is what they're here for. I sigh.

ME:

10th floor

DREW:

Got it, princess

I melt a little at that and smile. See, this guy wants to want me. So why am I letting these assholes get to me? I heart his message and open my browser. How many places could be named VV?

———

Finn

"Tom would kick your ass for making Sara cry on her first day." I lean back in my chair and resist the urge to follow after her. I've always been a sucker for her tears even when I knew they were crocodile tears. These weren't that.

Wyatt seems frozen in place, like he wants to go after her but knows he shouldn't.

"Fuck," Dante whispers and collapses into his chair. He never loses his cool with Sara, that's why he's the one that usually handles her. He can remain the ice block he usually is as he carts her away from the danger of Wyatt.

"Are you going to apologize?" I gesture to the door. One of us should check on her.

Shaking his head, he runs a hand across the back of his neck. "She needs time to cool down. She wouldn't want me to see her cry."

Ah, the legendary pride. As a little girl when she'd fall down and scrape her knee trying to run after us, Wyatt would go back to her and help her to her mom. Her lip would quiver and tears would fill her eyes, but she'd never let them fall in front of him or us. Unless she was trying to manipulate one of us, then she'd let loose these huge fake tears.

Wyatt takes a breath and grabs the paper off the table, looking it over. "What the fuck was Tom doing at Veiled Vixen Gentlemen's Club?"

I hold out my hand for the paper. When Wyatt hands it to me, I recognize the logo. We went there a few times for bachelor parties. It's a nice place.

"Didn't Amber have a friend who worked there?" I ask. My gaze strays to Dante.

The guy looks wrecked. We've never talked about our mutual attraction to Sara, but we all know. Tom knew, which is why he made us swear that we'd never date his sister. What an asshole.

"I'm sure Sara is fine." I tap the table with my knuckles.

Dante looks at me and nods. "She's strong."

Wyatt sits. "We should go to the club tonight and see if we can figure out what Tom was doing there and which stripper is bad at math."

"A strip club on a Monday night?" I laugh. "I don't think we're going to find the kind of woman Tom would go after on a Monday night."

"We can at least check out the place. Maybe that was his new client." Dante sits forward and pulls his tablet in front of him. "We need to get back to work."

I clear my throat. "Do you want me to deal with Sara and get her started on something?"

Dante stops and lifts his pale eyes to mine. "I have a list for her. At least Tom did something before he left us high and dry."

"Might want to give her something so she doesn't tear apart Tom's office." I smirk.

Dante smiles. "Serve the bastard right to leave us in charge of his sister and then abandon us."

"She'll be fine until the end of our meeting." Wyatt gestures to me. "Get Mark back on the line."

I open my laptop and resume the meeting. This note is the only thing we have to go on. Tom covered his tracks a little too well.

Chapter 9

Future Value

Sara

I've scheduled a few appointments for myself: a waxing and a mani-pedi. Made sure the dog walker got into the house okay and watched a few cat videos on my phone while waiting for the dick patrol to show up to tell me what I'm supposed to be doing.

After all, I get paid either way, so if they want to pay me to watch a video of a cat squeezing through progressively smaller holes, who am I to go disrupt their meeting to get actual accounting work. I'll get the credit for school either way, even if I don't get the experience.

"Sara."

I raise my gaze at Dante's voice and arch my eyebrow. He better have an apology ready.

"I've got a list of things for you to work on." Dante gestures with his head.

I cross my arms over my chest and glare at him with my lips firmly closed. I don't care that this is their business. That's not how he treats me.

His eyes narrow, but he sighs and comes into Tom's office. He shuts the door. "I didn't mean to yell at you, pip."

My eyebrow raises higher even as my heart races at the shortened nickname, which he's only used one other time. Like hell he didn't mean to yell.

He presses his lips together and sits in the seat across from me. His hands clasp between his knees as he leans his elbows on his thighs and looks up at me.

"You interrupted our meeting. That's not how things are done at work and you should know that."

My cheeks heat because I do, but I don't want to cave on this. "I got excited because I found a clue."

Dante nods. "It might be, but it could have waited. I'm sorry you were sitting in here with nothing to do, but we still have to work. It won't happen again. I can keep you busy all day."

Other parts of me get heated at the thought of him keeping me busy all day. I brush it off and stop thinking about how perfect his dick is.

"Fine." I stand and run my hands over my skirt. "Show me what I need to do, but I'm leaving for lunch at noon."

His blue eyes narrow on me and he says with a smirk, "Hot date?"

I smile. "Actually, yes."

His smirk disappears. "Don't take longer than an hour, pipsqueak."

"It never takes me that long, Dante." Winking, I walk past him to the door. "You know that."

His low groan merges with my laughter as I open the door and walk into the open area. Wyatt turns to look at me and my laugh dies in my throat. I swallow because there's still a part of me that longs for his attention. Craves it.

Dante's hand presses on my lower back and a shiver rushes through me. When I turn to him, he gives me a gentle headshake. Yeah, there's no problem here, so I don't need the constant reminder that Wyatt is off-limits.

Dante leads me to his office and releases me at the visitors' chairs. I sit on the edge of one and wait.

He rounds his massive desk and sits in his chair. With him behind it, the desk doesn't look as massive. There's an extra laptop on the surface. He lifts it and sets it closer to me.

"You can use the docking station in Tom's office for this." He taps on his keyboard and the printer in the corner comes to life, spitting out a paper. "We have a small company that we do bookkeeping for. Part of your duties will be to review the transactions and make sure they've been appropriately applied. If anything is out of place, make a note and we'll review it before we give it to the associate handling the account."

Bookkeeping. Good, I can do that. "Okay, what else?"

"A few special projects. A cash flow analysis of another company. We're worried that something might be left off their books. They have their own internal bookkeeping. We provide audit support, but they just let an employee go for suspected fraud, so we need to track the money to see exactly where it went."

"That sounds interesting." I'm not even lying. It does.

"You'll do some filing. I'll show you where the returned files are stacked and the cabinets they go in." Dante sets the paper on my new laptop.

"Do you want me to get you coffee too?" I tease. I scan the list, but it's all pretty standard stuff.

"That's not necessary." Fuck, the guy is back to cold Dante.

But that just makes me want to torment him.

"You'll have quite a bit of autonomy. I'll introduce you around to the other associates, but you'll work close to us. If you're leaving, for lunch or an errand or for the day, you will let me know."

"What about when I pee? Do you need to know that?" I lift my eyes to his and try to keep a completely straight face.

"No, Sara, you don't have to notify me of your piss breaks." He shakes his head and stands. "Let me show you around."

I roll my eyes, but grab my laptop and paper. He leads me back to

Tom's office where I set my things down. When we come out, my gaze strays toward Wyatt's door. It's closed.

"Come on, pipsqueak." Dante guides me into the other half of the company space.

I meet so many people so quickly that the only one I can remember is Greg. Dante shows me the file room. The returned files, which is a large stack that I can't imagine adding more to without it falling over. The breakroom. The bathrooms, though the guys have their own bathroom that I fully intend on using.

He points out Finn's and Wyatt's offices when we return. He stops at Tom's door.

"If you need anything, ask me first. If I'm not available, ask Finn."

"And if he's not available, ask Wyatt?" I assume.

"No, just wait." Dante tips my chin up with his knuckle. "You'll keep busy, pip. If you run out of things to do, we'll find you more. We're looking into Tom's clients. You don't need to look for clues or Nancy Drew this mystery."

I arch an eyebrow. "Nancy Drew?"

His smile softens and his thumb rubs against my jaw, sending tingles chasing through my blood. "You need anything. Just ask."

My blood is boiling when he backs away and I'm pretty sure he scrambled my brains because I don't have a quick comeback. *Can I have another orgasm* would have been the top of the list though.

I go into Tom's office and get to work on my tasks.

———

Drew

It's five to noon when I enter the building that's surprisingly close to our corporate headquarters. The elevator is quick. When I walk into the offices of Stone, Lawson, Hawkins & Morris, the receptionist straightens.

"Welcome. How can I help you?" Her brown eyes rake over me and her smile deepens.

"I'm here to pick up Sara Morris." I give her a grin because smiles make everyone more willing to help.

She blinks twice before looking down at her chart. Her gaze drifts in the direction I assume Sara is. "I believe she's in Tom's office. I don't have her cell phone number yet. If you want to wait—"

"I can find the way. Thanks." I leave her with her mouth gaped open. I'm sure she'll sound the alarm and one of Sara's brother's friends will appear like at dinner. Protective bulldogs.

When I turn a corner through the open door, Sara sits behind a desk with a pen in her mouth as she concentrates on the numbers before her. Fuck, she's beautiful. I don't want to fuck this up.

I've let others move me like a chess piece around the boards of their lives, but now, I've found a queen that I want to capture. Unfortunately, this queen is just looking for someone to fuck, which normally I'm good with, but not with her.

She makes my pulse race, and unlike some women I've dated, she actually wants to be with me. She sought me out. I'm afraid once we fuck that will be it for her, and I don't want that. Not this time.

I lean in the doorway and put my hands in my pockets as I watch her. Her eyes flit from the paper to the screen and her forehead scrunches briefly. My phone lets out a soft chime on the hour and she looks up, startled.

Her face softens and she smiles when she sees it's me. No one else has looked at me the way Sara Morris does. Like I could be a knight in shining armor. Her knight.

"Hey, is it time for lunch already?" She sets the pen down and taps a few keys before shutting her computer. "Have you been there long?"

"No, just admiring the view."

She turns and looks at the closed blinds before her cheeks turn pink. "We should get going. My boss is very strict about lunch."

"I know just the place." When I hold my hand out, she slides hers into mine with a smile.

She arches an eyebrow. "Is it a surprise or should I guess?"

"Let's make it a surprise this time." I love how she practically glows when I say things that imply a future. I'm just going with how I feel, and Sara makes me feel hopeful and afraid at the same time. Those other women couldn't hurt me, but Sara... Sara might have the ability to break my heart.

I don't think she'd do it intentionally.

"Oh, just a second." She pulls away and leans into the doorway next to hers. Her hands on either side of the door. "I'm heading out to lunch, boss."

"One hour, pipsqueak."

I step behind Sara and look into the office to see Dante Stone. I've seen him at events. He's a hard guy to miss. He's taller than everyone I know, has long blond hair, icy-blue eyes, and a chiseled jaw.

I catch Sara around the waist and draw her against me. She makes a little surprised sound, and Dante's eyes flare with a hint of jealousy before he hides it. Interesting. I saw the same in Finn's eyes when we had dessert.

Her hand covers mine and I put my chin on her head.

"Any word on Tom?" I ask.

Dante shakes his head. "Nothing yet. He seems to think whatever made him run will have some kind of backlash for Sara."

My arm tightens around her waist. What kind of backlash?

"Sara didn't mention that." I give him a nod to let him know I'll keep her safe when I can.

"Sara doesn't mention a lot of things." Dante lifts his pen and nods. "See you in an hour, pipsqueak. Not a minute later."

"It's not like you'll punish me for being late." She steps out of my arms and takes my hand.

"Don't count on that, pip."

I cock an eyebrow at Dante. Sara said she was getting over Wyatt, but there's something here with Dante too. And I didn't miss the way Finn watched her. I need to be careful because any misstep will let them swoop in.

"Let's go, Drew." Sara tugs on my hand and I let her lead me out of the office. When we near the elevator bank, I rest my hand on her lower back to guide her.

When we enter the crowded elevator, I move her into the corner so I can protect her and feel her body pressed against mine. Her breath catches as she looks up at me.

Using my thumb, I slide a strand of hair back behind her ear. Her hand squeezes mine. I lose myself for a moment in those pale green eyes. The elevator dings and everyone gets off, except us.

"Are you getting off?" some guy says, standing next to the elevator door.

"Not yet," Sara murmurs as she leads the way out.

I smile at the guy as I stay close to her. Definitely not yet, but hopefully soon.

It's a quick walk to Silver Honeybee Bistro. A small lunch spot I found a year ago that I like to frequent. We walk in and Sara's gaze darts all around the space. Her eyes widen and her smile grows as she takes in all the little details. It's like a fairy garden with all the hidden nooks and crannies.

"Your table, Mr. Young?" The hostess picks up two menus and leads us deeper inside.

After we sit down, Sara grins at me. "Your table?"

I shrug. "I like to eat here. They like me. I tip well."

She laughs lightly. "Women fall over themselves to serve you wherever we go. Have you slept with all of them?"

Her question isn't biting or jealous, just curious. It's that easiness that draws me to her. She isn't looking for a rich husband or an heir to save her family name. All she sees is Drew Young.

"Not all of them. No." I take her hand and slide my fingers along her palm. Her eyes are already dark from the dim lighting back here, but they darken further and she licks her lips. "Do you need a list or a number from me, princess?"

She shakes her head. "I know it's more than three. That's good enough as long as you're safe."

"To be honest, it's been about a month since I last hooked up. But

I get tested regularly and always use a condom." I lift her wrist to my lips and kiss her pulse. "What about you, princess? How many knights have climbed into your chamber?"

She laughs and her cheeks flush with color.

"What can I get for you today?" The server stops at our table and looks from me to Sara with a smile on his face.

Sara draws her hand back and picks up the menu. I take a few minutes to give him my order before she looks up, obviously ready with hers.

After we order, he takes our menus. "I'll be right back with your drinks."

She watches him go. Then she sighs when she turns back to me. "Is the number important?"

I shake my head. "No, as long as you're safe and get tested, it doesn't matter if you've been with fifty knights or two."

Her cheeks deepen in color. "I'm safe."

I can't help but wonder if she's embarrassed because the number is high or because it's low. It doesn't matter to me either way. I'm just glad she thought of me.

"Good." I take her hands across the table. "We can go as slow or as fast as you like. But I want to keep seeing you."

Her eyes twinkle as she meets mine. "I want to keep seeing you too."

Chapter 10

Reconciliation

Sara

My lips tingle from the kiss Drew gave me outside the building. I can't wipe the smile off my face as my fingers touch my lips. I didn't think it was possible to fall for someone else. But Drew caught me off guard.

I'm not in love, but the potential is there.

I wasn't looking for someone else. Honestly, I figured he'd fuck me and we'd have a great weekend, maybe a week together, and that would be it. But the butterflies in my stomach are writing a whole different story.

A very confusing story when it comes to Drew, Dante, and Finn. Because I want them all and don't feel any shame about experiencing pleasure with the other two while I'm dating Drew.

I'm not this woman, but fuck, it's freeing to not worry about how one guy might feel about my actions.

I practically float back to Tom's office. When I step across the threshold, my feet come crashing back down to earth. Wyatt sits in Tom's chair. My breath catches. He raises his dark gaze and all those lovely butterflies Drew stirred go into hyperdrive.

It's not that I want Wyatt more. Maybe it's that I've wanted him longer. He was my hero growing up until things changed. He stopped touching me, stopped hugging me. I became a nuisance instead of someone he cared about. His indifference drew me, made me want more, made me want the Wyatt I loved back.

When Wyatt focuses on me, my insides spark like an overcharged engine, revving to go.

"Where did you find the paper?" His deep voice haunts my dreams.

I clear my throat and point to the left side. "Second drawer down."

I'm afraid to step into the room, afraid to get close to him and let the stirrings he causes spin me in dizzying circles. Waiting for him isn't an option. He doesn't want me. I won't fall back into the helpless romantic I was.

The doorframe holds me as he searches the drawers. His dark hair falls over his eyes. It's a little longer than he normally lets it get. He's always been handsome, almost dignified. But he's also always been Tom's best friend.

After I turned sixteen, Wyatt stopped touching me entirely. If I stumbled, he wouldn't reach out to stop me from falling. He stopped caring for me like he used to. I didn't know how much it'd meant to me until it was gone.

It hurt, but I think I understand it better now.

It's painful to want something I can never have. It's hard to have him this close and know he'll never feel the same. That no matter how much I want him, he doesn't want me.

If he touched me, I might break.

I wrap my arms around my middle and release my breath.

"If you're going to be long, I can go do some filing." I gesture with my hand, but I don't want to leave. I want to bathe in his presence, because apparently, I enjoy the pain it causes.

"I'm done."

He stands and I almost take a step back as his dark eyes meet mine. Fuck, the sparks I feel from him are more intense. Is it because I can't touch him? Or that I know what it feels like to be touched by someone who wants me now?

If he touched me that way, would I explode on contact?

My hands shake as he comes closer. I grab onto the doorframe behind me as his woodsy, leather scent overwhelms me. I've tried to find his cologne, but it's not the cologne that makes my insides soften. It's the way it smells on him. I stop myself from drawing in a deep breath to hold it in my lungs like a caress.

He pauses, close enough I could reach out and touch him, but far enough away that just a hint of his warmth reaches me, teases me, torments me. "You'll tell me if you need anything?"

Oh, fuck, the things I need from this man. I've dreamt of the day he finally touches me. When he realizes I'm the only one he could ever want. But those are the daydreams of a girl. I can't keep waiting on a daydream that won't happen.

"Sara."

I suppress the whimper wanting to escape at my name on his lips. Instead, I hold my breath and nod jerkily.

His eyes narrow, then his gaze drops to my lips. I swear my whole body lights up like he's kissing me, finally. He makes an acknowledging noise and sweeps past me.

The breath I held releases as he shuts the door to his office. Yeah, I'm so not over that guy. His scent lingers in Tom's office, making me want to close the door so no one can see how much I enjoy it. If this wasn't my brother's office, I might even get off to that scent.

But that's a little too ick for me.

I push my obsession to the side and dive into the projects Dante gave me until I notice the time. It's almost five. I'm meeting the girls at six at McAvoy's Bar. I have to let Peabody out before that and I might change into something more comfortable.

Closing down the laptop, I text Brandon I'll be down in five minutes. I'm putting away a pen when something under the drawer brushes my knee. What the hell?

Pushing back my chair, I kneel on the floor and look under the desk.

"What are you doing, flower?"

Startled, I bonk my head on the drawer. "Ow."

Closing my eyes, I lift my hand to my aching head.

"You okay, flower?" Finn's footsteps grow closer and his hand touches my elbow.

When I open my eyes, his green eyes are right there. They're deep and sparkle like emeralds with flecks of gold. It's so easy to get lost in them. He's kneeling beside me. His hand smooths over my hair.

"No lump." His gaze follows his hand.

My heart slams against my chest remembering his lips on mine. My pussy pulses with an aching need. I've never come so much in my life. Definitely not like that. Heat floods me.

His gaze collides with mine and his lips tip into his flirty smile. "Want me to kiss it better?"

Oof, I almost nod because hell yeah, I do. Instead, I see the slip of paper hanging from the drawer. It's a Post-it. I peel it off and study the sequence of letters and numbers.

"A password?" I turn it but that changes nothing.

"Could be. Tom has a horrible memory." Finn stands and holds his hands down to help me. Of the guys, Finn is the shortest, but he's still over six feet which, even in my three-inch heels, makes me feel pretty small.

He cups my jaw and trails his thumb over my cheekbone. "You good?"

I nod, staring at his lips, wanting to feel them against mine again. He kisses like he wants to consume me whole and I'm definitely on board for that.

"Finn," someone else says.

We almost jump apart as we turn toward Dante standing in the doorway. His eyes narrow suspiciously, but I don't owe these guys anything. Neither of them was anything more than a way to get off.

Neither of them offered me more. That doesn't stop the flush from taking over my chest, neck, and cheeks.

"I found another note under Tom's desk." I hold up the slip of paper.

Dante strides into the room and stops behind me. With both of them surrounding me, I resist the urge to fan myself from the heat accumulating under my skin. Dante doesn't take the paper but reads it over my shoulder.

Finn arches an eyebrow at Dante, since I'm literally between them. I'm trying to maintain my cool but losing it by the minute to the flood of desire drowning me. They're both close enough to touch me. To press me between the two of them.

"Password?" Dante's breath teases the hair beside my ear. A shiver races through my body.

Finn's grin widens as he lowers his gaze to mine. "Possibly."

My hand shakes slightly from the tension brewing. Dante slips his hand over mine, steadying it, and I almost lean back into his warmth.

"You don't mind if I take this. Do you, pip?" His fingers touch the small of my back and a jolt of sparks rains down over me. My lips part.

Finn chuckles. "I don't think she minds at all. In fact, she wants you to have it. Don't you, flower?"

My gaze lifts to Finn's mischievous green eyes. My tongue darts out to wet my lips and he moves in a little closer. What's happening here?

Footsteps sound outside the office door and they both step away from me. I'm still flustered and aroused when Wyatt stops in the doorway.

"Heading out?" His dark eyes linger on me.

I swallow and nod. "I found a potential password under Tom's desk."

Wyatt steps in and my knees want to give out. The three of them are too much for my system to handle. I set the paper on the desk and grab my purse.

"I need to let Peabody out." I glance at the other two and feel the sexual tension from each of them. Biting my lip, I stop a couple feet in front of Wyatt who's blocking the door. My voice is softer when I say, "I need to go."

Wyatt cocks his head as if seeing me for the first time today, or like what I said didn't make sense. But then he moves out of my way. I don't look back as I edge around him and leave the office.

I don't know what that was, but I'm not quite ready to be that bold.

I tied my hair up in a high ponytail and changed into jeans and a light sweater. I reapplied my favorite red lipstick and made sure Peabody ate his dinner and got some outdoor time before I left.

The car stops in front of McAvoy's Bar.

"When do you want me to return, Miss Sara?" Brandon meets my gaze in the rearview mirror.

"I'll catch a ride home. Have a good night." I grab my phone and clutch and step out onto the curb. When I open the bar door and step inside, the car pulls away.

The bar is dark, but fairy lights add some much needed light to the room. I spot Hope sitting at the bar talking to her brother Jason. He's a large guy with a bald head and the same bright blue eyes as Hope.

I wrap my arms around Hope from behind. She startles before she realizes it's me.

"Hey." She turns on her stool and smiles. "How was the first day?"

Jason sets a strawberry daiquiri on the bar in front of me. I give him a grateful smile.

"Long. Weird without Tom there." I set my clutch down and draw the daiquiri over for a drink. "Mmm, I need this."

"And I need this." Kayla sits down next to me and bumps my arm. "Do you know how many good-looking men work at my new branch?"

"A lot?" Hope asks and takes a sip of her daiquiri.

"Not one." Kayla holds up a hand toward Jason, but he sets a daiquiri in front of her with a wink. "At least your brother is hot."

"Seriously?" I ask. "How is it I'm surrounded by gorgeous men and you get the orc edition of *Lord of the Rings*?"

"Not to worry. There are hot women, who unfortunately are straight." Shaking her head, Kayla takes a drink of her daiquiri.

"It's probably best not to dip your pen in the company ink anyway," Hope says. "It doesn't always turn out like Madison's guys."

"Now I'm even more depressed." When Kayla raises her hand, Jason sets a bowl of peanut M&M's in front of her. "I mean, why couldn't I get propositioned for more than work on my first day?"

"It wasn't the first day." Madison takes the other bar stool with a grin. "They told me when they hired me."

Madison holds her hand out to me with her palm up. I put my hand in hers and squeeze.

"How was your first day?" she asks.

"Good. Long. Kind of lonely, honestly." Now that I think about it. I was mostly in my office all day with no need for contact with anyone else.

Kayla frowns. "That's not good."

"It's how most of my days go," Hope says.

"I found something that might be a clue about Tom." I grab a napkin and pull a pen out of my purse. "Some woman wasn't good at numbers, but there was a logo on the piece of paper."

I draw the VV logo from memory and show the girls.

Hope and Madison give me shakes of their head, but Kayla snorts a laugh.

"Do you know what it is?" I stare down at it. "I couldn't find a business with VV in the name."

"Oh, I know it. Been a few times. It's the Veiled Vixen Gentlemen's Club."

"Wait!" My eyes widen. "Like a strip club gentlemen's club?"

"Only the best one in the city." Kayla takes a drink and eats a couple M&M's. "The girls there are gorgeous. It's clean. Good establishment."

"We should go." I pick up the napkin. "We can talk to the strippers and see if one of them knows my brother."

"I'm in to go talk to strippers." Kayla smirks. "My day just got a whole lot brighter."

"I can't." Madison gives us a little pout. "I promised Seth I'd be home early."

"I can't either." Hope shakes her head. "But you two should go."

"Maybe we can wait until later in the week." I stare at the logo. "Are strip clubs even open on Monday nights?"

"Vixen's is." Kayla smiles. "Don't worry it doesn't open until eight, so we have some time to discuss your first day with the smoking-hot Viking."

I haven't told them about what Finn and Dante did to me over the weekend. I'm not sure I'm ready to share that. "I had lunch with Drew."

"Now if I had to put together a harem of men, Drew would definitely be in it." Kayla pops an M&M in her mouth. "And Coop because holy hotness. But I wouldn't just go for dicks."

"I'm pretty sure Madison is in a unique position. I'm not sure many men would want to share their girl." Hope runs her hands over her jeans. "After all, those guys all grew up together and then decided before her to share women."

Madison laughs. "I'm just lucky those other women didn't put them off it entirely."

"There was this moment today." I grab an M&M. "When Finn

and Dante surrounded me. I almost couldn't breathe, imagining what it would be like to have them both touch me."

Madison's eyes soften and she gets this far-off look. "Yeah, that's the best."

"Damn. I want that." Kayla sighs. "I'd be happy with just one guy or gal."

"I'm good on my own right now." Hope takes a drink and her blue eyes lift to mine. "It's hard to let a guy near me even to hug me."

I rub my hand down Hope's back. She was kidnapped and held for days. They cut her arm but didn't assault her in other ways. The fear of that and possible death must have played with her in that dark basement. Both of the bastards that did it are dead.

I shiver and put my arms around her.

She leans into me and releases her breath. Her arms round my shoulders and she returns the hug.

"How's therapy going?" I say when we draw back.

She tucks her hair behind her ear. "It's okay. I don't know if it's helping though."

I nod, because I don't know the right thing to say in this case. What she went through was traumatic and not dealing with it would be worse, I imagine.

"Okay." Hope smiles even though it doesn't quite reach her eyes. "Tell me about something good that happened today."

We fall into our normal patterns of talking and laughing and not diving into the deep stuff again. The hour passes quickly and Madison is the first to leave. Seth shows up and draws her into his arms. The way he looks at her reminds me of Drew.

We stay for another half hour with Hope.

"You guys should go." She grins and pushes away her empty glass. "See some strippers. If you don't find out anything, we'll all go another night."

"I'm all for going to strip clubs whenever." Kayla's eyes are a little glassy as she finishes her third drink. "They even have a ladies' night. They find the hottest dancers."

I give Hope a hug. "Take care."

She hugs me back before Kayla gives her a hug and a kiss on the cheek.

"If you and I are still single when we're forty, we'll shack up." Kayla chucks Hope under the chin. "I'll show you that chicks are more fun than dicks."

Hope laughs. "Sure. Forty is a ways away."

"I need to sow my wild oats. So off to the strip club." Kayla grabs my arm and pulls me toward the door.

I wave to Hope and use my phone to get a car for hire. "It's going to be five minutes."

"Oh, I need to pee." Kayla veers off to the ladies' room, leaving me near the doors. I stand in the vestibule, outside the bar but still inside, with windows showing me the people laughing inside and the dark street out the other windows.

For all I know, Tom went to the strip club and started talking accounting with a woman there. It might not be a clue, just a note that fell into his desk. Abandoned.

Checking my phone, I see our driver is about three minutes away. I lift my head to look around the bar. Hope and Jason chat in the corner we just left. They're close siblings.

Tom and I are close too, but not like those two. We carved our own paths in school. He had his friends and I had mine. Of course, mine turned out to be untrustworthy, backstabbing bitches. His ended up his best friends.

Something catches my eye at the other end of the bar. A large guy is hunched over the bar drinking. His coat is black. I'm not sure what caught my eye, to be honest. He looks like anyone else sitting, drinking alone.

He twists his head. His dark eyes lock on me. A chill rushes through me. I suck in a breath at the intense gaze.

Kayla grabs my arm. "Let's go. I need to see some tits and ass."

Chapter 11

Surprise Audit

Sara

The drive across the city doesn't take long and we're let out at a nice-looking building. No one mills around outside. There's nothing obvious that says this is a strip bar or even a happening nightclub. The only thing is the logo from the napkin on the door.

Kayla takes my hand and threads our fingers together. "Okay, just follow my lead."

I arch an eyebrow. "I'm sure I can handle myself in a strip club, Kayla."

"This isn't a dive bar, honey. This is a classy joint with a lot of high rollers." She grins and looks me over before nodding. "Just play along and we won't attract a bunch of old dudes trying to get in our pants."

"Play along with what?"

She doesn't answer, just leads me to the door and knocks three times.

A guy in a black suit opens the door. "You lost, ladies?"

He eyes us like he's taking our measure. Straightening, I wish I had on something sexier. I'm glad I put on my red lipstick at least.

"Not lost. We're on the list. Kayla Wagner plus one." Kayla wraps her arm around my waist and draws me against her. She's soft and warm, but a lot different from Finn, Dante, and Drew. Definitely not any sparks, but I lean into her because she said go with it.

Which means I guess we're a couple tonight to keep creepy guys from hitting either of us up. But what happens if a creepy guy wants to join in? Or just watch? I don't think she thought this through.

The bouncer looks at his phone, scrolling with his finger.

Nodding, he opens the door for us and Kayla leads me into the space. There's a small entryway with black tile and black walls. The guy closes the door and gestures to Kayla who releases me and holds her arms out.

The guy pats her down. Oh. I swallow. No one's ever patted me down before. He didn't touch Kayla inappropriately, that I could tell. Is this why she wanted us to be a couple? To make sure he kept his hands in appropriate spots only?

He turns to me and gestures with his head for me to assume the position. Okay, I can do this. I spread my arms out.

Someone knocks on the door before he touches me.

"Stay there," he says before he goes to the door and opens it.

"You didn't mention a pat down," I whisper yell at Kayla. It's not like I have anything illegal on my body for him to find. It's just that I wasn't expecting to get felt up this evening. And definitely not by a strange man.

Shrugging, she leans into me to say, "It's the best part."

"How did you get on the list?" I ask with one eye on the bouncer.

"My friend. I texted her and she got us in." Kayla acts like it's no big deal to get into an exclusive club in this city. Maybe it isn't for her. I'm actually impressed.

"Flower."

My shoulders tighten at his voice. I turn and watch them come through the door. Finn grins, Dante cocks an eyebrow with a disapproving look, and Wyatt... His dark eyes narrow on me.

"Wait here," the bouncer tells them before approaching me. He nods and I reassume the position.

"Don't touch her," Wyatt growls. My blood heats as my gaze jumps to him. "She's with us."

Protective older brother vibe? Dante steps forward and pulls me from the bouncer before I can react.

"Hey." I try to step away from him, but he's too strong.

"Rules, gentlemen. Everyone who gets in gets checked." The bouncer reaches for the radio at his hip.

If these guys ruin this for me, I swear I will ruin their day tomorrow. I don't know how yet, but probably something with their coffee.

"She's leaving." Dante draws me toward the door. Oh, hell no.

"No, *she* isn't." I jerk my arm away. "I have every right to be here."

His cold eyes tell me not to mess around, but fuck him. Just because we masturbated together doesn't mean he owns me. I'm not taking orders anymore. Not outside of my job.

Walking over to stand in front of the bouncer, I say, "Go ahead and check me."

I tip my head up as he pats down my sides. It's quick and efficient. He doesn't even touch my breasts. When he finishes, he nods toward a door.

"Ladies, have a good night."

Linking my arm with Kayla's, I ignore the guys.

We walk through the door into a whole different world. The club is decorated in reds and blacks. It's dimly lit, but the stage is bright. The music is loud enough to make it difficult to hear conversations from the others, but I can hear the server as I pass by her. The servers have on short black dresses that barely cover their asses and show off a considerable amount of cleavage.

Kayla was right. Every woman here is gorgeous, in all shapes and sizes.

The tables are set apart from each other. The stage runs down the middle of the room. No one is throwing dollar bills or stuffing them into the women's G-strings. The dancer performs her routine to the pulsating music without any interference from the audience. It's as if she isn't the main entertainment here.

The men all watch as they talk. Everyone is dressed in business suits or nice clothes. It's a place to make deals and discuss strategy. Just with a veritable buffet of beautiful, barely clothed women walking around.

A woman in a dress that leaves nothing to the imagination walks over to a man sitting at a table and takes his hand. Her eyes sparkle as she leads him down a hallway.

Another woman leads another man back to one of the other doors in that hallway.

"What's back there?" I ask Kayla softly.

"Private rooms." She leads me to an unoccupied table in the corner and we sit down. "The guys pay for whatever the dancer is willing to do."

Oh. I didn't think about that. Isn't that illegal? "So more than stripping happens here?"

"Not technically." Kayla coughs and leans forward. "If those women choose to do more, that's up to them, not the man. He can only pay for a dance with no touching. The charge for the room goes to the house, but the strippers keep whatever they make in there."

Fascinated, I nod. The woman on stage takes off her top with a flourish before running her hands over her breasts and stomach. She's attractive, and her body is toned and sculpted to perfection.

I swallow and glance back toward the door. Where did the guys go? Are they watching this? Is that what they want? Women like that? I'm not shy about my body. I take care of myself and work out, but even I'm not that well-constructed.

Seeing the guys here has me all flustered, but they haven't come in yet. Maybe they won't get in. That would make this all easier.

"Those guys were your three bosses?" Kayla presses against the table, eagerly.

I meet her green eyes. "Yup."

"Who was the growling one?" Her eyes widen and her grin is huge.

Shivers race up my spine just thinking of that growl and the almost possessive tone of his voice. "Wyatt."

"I see the appeal." She leans back.

Maybe it wasn't so much possessive but more protective older brother. That hopeful part of me sits back down, because every little inch Wyatt gives me makes me think this could be so much more. Until I waste my life waiting for a man that doesn't want me that way.

A waitress stops by and takes our drink orders. When she walks away, I lean into Kayla. I need to get this back on task. We're here to figure out what Tom's gotten into.

"Okay, we're looking for someone who can't add very well. Like really bad."

"It seems like we're on the same mission." Finn drops into the seat next to me and wraps his arm around my shoulders. I tense, wondering what fresh hell they'll create for me. "Crazy to see you here, flower."

Kayla's eyes widen as Dante sits on my other side and Wyatt leans against the wall in front of me. His gaze is on the center stage though.

"Finn, and you are?" Finn holds out his other hand to Kayla.

"Kayla Wagner." Her gaze takes him all in. "Aren't you a gorgeous piece of man candy?"

"I like her." Finn grins. "Don't you have other friends as well?"

"They couldn't come." I resist the urge to push his arm off my shoulders. While it would work on the other guys, Finn just comes back stronger with every little rejection. I turn to face him. "You knew what the logo was when I showed it to you, didn't you?"

Finn laughs. "Do I know the best gentlemen's club in the city? Of course, I do, flower. Don't worry, I only come here for the articles."

Kayla chuckles. When I arch my eyebrow, she shrugs. "What? It was funny."

"You shouldn't be here, pip." Dante leans down, so he's speaking directly into my ear. Little shivers course through my veins.

"Last time I checked, you guys don't control my hours after work." I straighten because this is the hill I'll die on.

Dante's hand slides over my knee and squeezes. I press my knees together at the ache that spirals up between my thighs. Quietly so only I can hear him, he says, "You and I had an arrangement, pip."

I turn so that my face and his are only a hair's breadth away from each other. My eyes search his pale blue ones. We shared a moment, but we barely touched. His exhale fans my lips and that ache increases.

"You wanted me to call if I needed anything." I wet my lips and glance down at his hand on my knee before returning my gaze to his. "I don't need anything, Dante."

Heat rages in his eyes as he narrows them. His fingers clench my thigh. My breath catches wondering if he'll do more. If he'll finally claim my lips with his.

The server stops and sets our drinks down, breaking the tension between us. The guys' attention shifts off me as they give her their drink orders and replace my card with Wyatt's. I draw in a relieved breath.

I lift my gaze to Wyatt's. His head is cocked as he studies me. His eyes remain as distant as ever, but there's a curiosity that hasn't been there before. Maybe he's wondering if I've really moved on.

The server comes back and holds the card out to Wyatt. "Drinks are on the house. The owner would like to see all of you in his office."

She sets down the guys' drinks and tells Wyatt how to get to the owner's office.

"That's weird, right?" I ask Kayla. "Why would the owner want to talk to us?"

"Weird." She nods but her gaze remains on the stripper on stage.

She sips her drink. The brunette is tall and leggy. Her brown eyes are locked with Kayla's as she removes her lingerie to reveal her breasts.

"Come on." Dante stands and takes my hand but I stay seated.

"Kayla." When I tap her arm, she turns. I gesture for her to come with us.

She nods and heads for the stage instead. I stand with Dante as the stripper leans down to listen to Kayla with a cocky grin. Kayla winks at the woman before coming back over to us.

"I have a private dance later. I'll make sure to ask about Tom and his stripper." Kayla bumps into me and I smirk.

"Do I get to go into the room with you?" I'm curious what that would look like. I'm not sheltered per se, but I don't usually get to do anything like this. My high school friends wouldn't have wanted to and the few people I know in college are acquaintances at best. I live off campus at home, so I don't have many friends.

"No." Dante wraps his hand around my hip and pulls me in against him. Fire lights beneath my skin as I glance up at him and swallow. He shakes his head. "No going into private rooms, pipsqueak."

Now I really want to go into that room with her and the stripper. Unless she's paying for extra, then maybe I shouldn't get in the way. Kayla winks at me as she links arms with Finn.

"You know, you could join me and Amethyst in the private room." She bats her dark eyelashes at him. "She wouldn't mind and I'm always game."

Finn smirks. "Maybe if Sara comes too."

When my gaze jerks toward him, he wets his lips. As I remember that tongue between my legs, my panties grow even wetter.

Kayla chuckles as I turn to face front. Wyatt leads the way through the club and down a darkened hallway. At the end is a wooden door. He knocks and we all wait.

"This seems a little sketch." Kayla leans into Finn.

I was just going to say that.

He pats her hand. "We'll be fine. Maybe they know where Tom is. Maybe this is the client that Tom was worried about."

My eyes widen. What if we're walking into a trap? "Maybe we should—"

The door opens. Drew stands there with a huge grin. "I never figured you'd all end up at my club, but come in."

Chapter 12

Control Risk

Wyatt

I've never minded Dante redirecting Sara, but something's changed between them. He's more possessive than protective. And Finn is more overtly flirtatious with her. Maybe it's her though. She seems more open to both of them.

"You must be Wyatt." The owner holds his hand out to me. "Drew Young."

He gives me a hearty handshake before gesturing for us to come in. This is the guy dating Sara? He owns a strip club? If Tom knew about this, he'd explode.

Everyone walks in. His office is huge with a couple large couches. The desk at the back is also large. He's probably compensating for something. I glance down at his slacks and wing tip shoes. Or hiding something. With the way he's flaunting his wealth, he can't be suitable for Sara.

"We haven't officially met." Kayla steps away from Finn and holds out her hand. "Kayla Wagner. I've heard a lot about you."

Drew takes her hand and kisses her knuckles. "Hopefully all good things."

He winks and she chuckles.

"All good things, of course." She winks right back.

"Dante, Finn." Drew looks at each man before his warm eyes settle on Sara. His voice changes when he says, "Sara."

Fuck, this isn't someone who's playing with her. He wants her. He holds his hand out and she takes it without a moment of hesitation. Fuck, she wants him too.

"Please sit. It seems like we have a lot to talk about." He draws Sara over to the couch and they sit next to each other. I join Finn and Dante on the other couch, while Kayla sits next to Sara.

"You own this club?" It may seem obvious, but I want clarity.

"Unofficially." Drew relaxes and puts his arm across the back of the sofa behind Sara. He strokes his fingers over her shoulder and my hands clench into fists. He's allowed to touch her. "I'm pretty skilled at finance. Everything I earned, I turned into more. I wanted something outside my family's business. This suits me. I like the elevated feeling here."

I watch Sara's face. It's obvious she didn't know this, but she's not repulsed by it either. It's not a deal breaker. It's a fucking strip bar dressed up as a gentlemen's club. Tom would hate that she's with this guy.

"My brother came here. Some woman who couldn't do math talked with him." Sara glances at the three of us before turning to Drew. "We were hoping to find out more about who Tom might be hiding from."

Drew smiles and rests his knuckle under her chin. My insides twist, but I keep my expression blank like I have for the past six years.

"Crystal." Drew laughs. "Do you know she charged someone fifty-eight thousand dollars instead of four hundred?"

Sara shakes her head.

"Her boyfriend didn't like her stripping. She quit last week. I don't know what Tom was doing with her, but I could go back through security footage."

Sara perks up and grins. "That would be great."

He rubs his thumb across her jaw and she leans into his touch. Fuck. I'm not going to be able to handle this. Him touching her when I can't.

When Drew stands, he looks each of us in the eye with a curious expression. When he meets mine, his lips tighten and he nods slightly. "This might take a minute. I'll call in a server to refresh your drinks, unless you want to return to the bar to watch the entertainment."

"I'm good here." Sara lifts her drink to her lips and looks over the rim at Finn and Dante. She always used to seek me out. But not lately unless I catch her staring and then she can't seem to look away. Neither can I unfortunately. It's better if she doesn't focus on me.

But it doesn't ache any less when she acts like I'm not here.

Kayla leans into Sara. "Do you mind if I duck out? I've got that meeting to attend."

Sara smirks. "Have fun. I want to hear all about it."

Standing, Kayla straightens her shirt. "How about it, Finn? Want to watch a gorgeous woman give me a lap dance?"

Finn laughs. "I'm good right here."

His gaze flicks to Sara, whose cheeks grow pink. What in the hell is happening around here? When I stepped into Tom's office earlier, tension filled the air. Something had been happening and Sara couldn't wait to leave. The guys haven't said anything, but I can tell they're keeping something from me.

"Suit yourself." Kayla waves to Drew. "Be good to my friend."

Her green eyes roam over me and Dante before she turns to Sara. "If you need me, text. I might be a while."

Kayla leaves and the room falls quiet except for Drew's typing on the computer.

"Do you know when he might have been here?" Drew glances up.

"There wasn't a date on the napkin and I don't have it with me." Sara turns to us.

"I have a picture of it." Dante goes over to stand next to Drew, showing him his phone.

"First strip club?" Finn asks with a smolder at Sara. Nothing new for Finn. He's always flirted with her, and she's always ignored his flirting.

But this time her cheeks tinge pink again. "Yes."

"We should spend some time here. Maybe pay for a private dance of your own." Finn chuckles and takes a drink.

Sara's eyes flash with heat and she arches her eyebrow. "Did you see anyone you'd like to watch me with?"

Fuck, my dick twitches. I don't have enough strength to watch another woman grind on Sara. I'm hanging on by a thread. Only my promise to Tom keeps me from claiming her, but maybe it's already too late.

What if she's moved on and doesn't want me anymore? Our eyes catch and that fire that's always on simmer burns inside me. But I can see it clearly in her eyes. That want, the desire, but she looks away first.

I'm not supposed to encourage her, but she's always been mine. She chose me. I couldn't claim her, but she's always been mine. Even though I can't have her, I burn for her.

I down the last bit of my whiskey.

"This is it." Drew walks over and Dante sits on the other side of Sara.

Her heated gaze meets his before she returns her attention to Drew. What the fuck is happening?

A TV turns on and the music from the club plays in the room. Dante leans in close to Sara's ear and says something. A secretive smile plays on her lips.

"Sorry." Drew hits a button and the sound shuts off. He glances at Sara and she gives him an encouraging smile. Not a fake smile like she gave all those guys she used to try to make me notice her. But a genuine smile that eats away at my soul.

"There's Tom." Sara points to the screen.

I focus on the mission. Fucking Tom, leaving me with this mess. If he were here, he'd put an end to all of this and Sara would be safe again.

Tom sits at a table with a blond woman who has barely any clothes on. They hunch over a napkin as he explains the numbers to her. Pointing at things with his pen.

She grins and hugs him. Stiffening, he shakes his head and looks behind him.

"Can you back this up?" I lean forward, trying to determine if he knew someone at that table or just glanced that way to avoid looking at the woman's breasts. The latter isn't likely.

"Sure." Drew rewinds it. There's a lot more of Tom explaining the basics of addition to who I assume is Crystal. Until he backs across the screen and talks with a guy in black at that table before backing away to the door.

Drew hits play when Tom comes into the room and we watch him walk to the table. He pauses and talks with one of the guys before he talks with the big guy who gestures toward Crystal. Tom glances at her once before he nods and heads over to her.

They shake hands and sit down with napkins and a pen.

What the hell is Tom doing? They could potentially be the mystery client he brought in. But none of them look familiar.

"Do you know those guys?" Dante points to the table of men.

Drew blows out a breath. "Not off the top of my head. I have a manager who deals with the day-to-day operations. I can look up members, but we don't have facial recognition software."

"I don't recognize them." Finn glances at me.

"What exactly is happening with Tom?" Drew sits down and leaves the video playing in the background.

"He just up and left after sending a bunch of texts telling me to let the guys protect me." Sara watches the video like she's going to pick up on a clue.

"He left us a note saying to watch out for Sara and their family." Dante watches the video with the same discerning eye.

"Do you know why?"

Finn shakes his head. "He's had a new client he was secretive about, but that's nothing new with Tom."

"Neither is running off." Sara stretches forward to reach her glass.

"What makes you think this napkin has anything to do with his disappearance?" Drew asks.

"It fell out of his desk at work. It wasn't in his drawer, but hidden." Sara takes a drink. How many is that for her? She seems fine, but the color never leaves her cheeks and her eyes are a little glassy.

"Or it fell between the drawers and he didn't open that drawer." I blow out a breath. "What date was this?"

"About two weeks ago." Drew presses a button and a server comes in with refills on all our drinks. "I don't know what to tell you. He wasn't here to see me. I don't think I was even on the property when this took place."

Drew smooths his hand over his jaw and I notice Sara watching him, how she used to watch me. A muscle in my jaw ticks. We need to look into this Drew. Tom isn't around to do the usual background check.

I don't trust this guy and definitely not with Sara.

"I wish I could help you more." Drew wraps his arm around Sara's shoulders and draws her into his side.

I wish I had a reason to lay this guy out, but I don't. She isn't mine. She can't be mine.

Sara smiles up at him as she sighs.

Fuck. I'm not ready to deal with this. Tom should be here. He'd do what he always does and run this fucker off.

"We should go." When I stand, everyone looks at me like I've grown a second head. I have and it's fucking green as hell.

"We're already here." Finn gestures to the room. "It's a comfortable space with free liquor. We can get to know Drew a little better to make sure he's a decent guy for Sara. Do the due diligence Tom would have done if he'd known she was dating someone."

"We have time." Dante shrugs. Dante is usually the voice of reason. The one who makes sure I'm not about to go unhinged.

Drew meets my eyes and smiles. "If this space doesn't suit you, we could move out to a private booth in the club. Or even one of the private rooms, if you'd like a more personal show."

It's like he's trying to take my measure. But I'm not the one to worry about when it comes to Sara. My hands are bound and she's completely off-limits. Maybe another woman giving me a lap dance will clear my head. Or maybe it will be enough to push Sara to go home.

"Fine. Let's get a room."

Chapter 13

Negotiation Strategy

Sara

My eyes widen and my gaze jerks to Wyatt's, but he isn't looking at me. He's looking at Drew.

Wyatt's head tips down in challenge. He wants to get a private room?

My stomach churns. Am I about to watch a woman do to Wyatt what I'll never be allowed to do?

Or is this his little trap to get me to leave?

Make me uncomfortable so I insist we go. Yeah, fuck that.

"Sounds good." Standing, I hold my hand down to Drew.

He smiles at me like I'm precious, but I don't want to be precious to these men. I want to be filthy and naughty and completely taken.

"I think I have the perfect woman for you." Drew turns to Wyatt as he squeezes my hand.

Fire blasts through me, thinking of Wyatt with another woman. Finn and Dante look at each other before glancing at me with concerned eyes. Yeah, fuck them too.

With his arm around my waist, Drew guides me out into the hallway and back to the club. The woman on the stage wraps herself around the pole and spins all the way to the floor. I'm impressed. That's not easy. I took one of those pole dancing classes with a friend from college during the school year.

My ass was sore for a week from the workout.

"Do you want to pick out a woman, princess?" Drew whispers in my ear. A rush of arousal spreads through me. "Or maybe you want to be the woman?"

My breath catches, but his dark eyes aren't jealous. Just curious.

Drew smirks. "I'm not blind, princess. You feel some way about each of those guys. Pretty sure the feelings are mutual, but something holds you and them back."

I don't know what to say. He leads me down the hallway to the private rooms.

"You don't have to say anything and I won't either, but I'm a fairly open-minded guy." His fingers stroke up my side beneath my sweater, sending sparks through me. "I'm willing to do whatever you want."

My eyes widen as I look into his dark eyes. We're stopped in front of a door. I'm about to go into a private room with Finn, Dante, Drew, and Wyatt. They're all waiting for Drew to open the door.

He wants me to admit to my deepest, darkest fantasies? To have them all.

I step in closer to Drew and go up on my toes to reach his ear. "Not tonight. We can talk later."

Before I can lower back down, Drew catches me in his arms and kisses me. Not a friendly little peck, but a full-on *make my knees weak* kiss that steals my breath away.

That growl sounds again, making me wet. Drew chuckles against my lips before drawing away. Not releasing me, he turns with a grin toward the guys.

"You know how it is. It's hard to resist a beautiful woman, especially when she tastes like strawberries."

I don't look at the guys, avoiding their reactions. Trying not to care what they think about me kissing Drew after what I did with them. I'm not dating any of them. I don't owe them anything.

Drew opens the door and we walk into what looks like a luxury suite. There's a huge bed against one wall. At the other end is a stage, much smaller than the one in the main room, and armchairs surrounding it.

"Make yourselves at home." Drew gestures to the space.

I drop into one of the chairs as the others walk in. A server follows us and goes over to Drew, who stands next to the bar on one side. His brown eyes never leave me and I can feel his kiss still. My heart pounds as the guys sit in the chairs next to me.

I drink my cold drink to try to cool off. My mind is a little sluggish with all the alcohol I've had tonight. How many drinks have I had? I should ask... Kayla. "Oh, fuck."

"What's wrong, flower?"

Glancing at Finn, I pick up my clutch. "I need to tell Kayla where we are."

"Not to worry, princess." Drew comes over and takes my hand, pulling me out of my seat. My head spins a little, but he holds me tight against him, centering me. "The server will let her know. I also ordered another round of drinks. Our entertainment will be here in fifteen minutes. Plenty of time to get to know each other."

Drew sits in my chair and pulls me down onto his lap. Okay, maybe he's a little possessive. Or maybe he just wants to show off to the other guys. He's allowed to touch me, kiss me, hold me.

"She'd be more comfortable in her own chair," Dante grumbles.

"Would you, princess?" Drew pulls my legs over to one side of his. The high backs of the chairs give me support. It would lower the tension in the room if I moved. But fuck that.

Dante yelled at me this morning. Finn left me after giving me many amazing orgasms. And Wyatt... Yeah, I'm not going to think more about him.

"I'm perfectly fine here." I wrap my arm around Drew's neck and take a drink, only to find I've emptied it. Is that two or three since we got here? The daiquiris at the bar earlier just kept showing up too.

Drew plucks it from my hand and sets it on the table. "You all grew up with Sara?"

"Tom's our friend." Finn leans back in the chair and, with hooded eyes, studies the way Drew holds me. "We've always watched out for Sara."

"Why a gentlemen's club?" Wyatt leans his elbows on his knees with his glass of scotch held between them. He swirls the amber liquid. His dark eyes don't shift to me but stay on Drew. "Your family business is in what? Textiles?"

Drew sips from his drink and raises an eyebrow. "Can you think of anything more boring than textiles? It's good and we've found our niche, but I can only talk about fabric for so long before I want to gouge my eyes out. I appreciate our business and will run it with the utmost care when it's mine, but this club..."

He gestures with his drink to the lush room. His eyes sparkle when he meets Wyatt's. "This is something all my own. Not directed by my parents. I make the decisions about what happens within these walls. Who to let in. Who to keep out. It's my own little empire."

Finn nods. "I can see the appeal." He indicates the bed. "Do you partake in your empire?"

Drew laughs. "No. I don't pay for sex and I only hire dancers. What they do within these walls or how they use the room is their business and no one else's."

"Do all the rooms have a bed?" My gaze keeps straying to the luxuriously appointed bed at the far end of the room. My thinking may be slowed, but the thought of all these men on that bed with me makes my breath and pulse quicken. I press my thighs together.

"This is our special suite. It's only used by VIP members." Drew draws his finger along my jaw, spreading sparks through my veins. "It's perfect for the fantasy, even if no one uses the bed."

I can't imagine this world. The decadence... and the underbelly.

These women must get propositioned constantly, but they decide what happens.

"How do you protect the women?" I've had too much to drink if I'm asking that out loud. It's really none of my business. I'm here as a guest. Wait, no, I'm here as a customer.

Drew's serious eyes meet mine. "There's always a bouncer outside the rooms, but if the dancer doesn't feel safe, he can be inside with them. I'm not saying it's a perfect system, but it works. And if a dancer complains about a client, he's banned from the rooms for three months. If he gets a second complaint, he's no longer a member."

That's good. The server walks in and hands out drinks.

Dante grabs mine before I can lift it to my mouth.

"Hey!" I reach for it, but he holds it away.

"You've had enough, pipsqueak."

"I'm fine." Okay, that came out a little slurred. "You all won't let anything happen to me." I wiggle my fingers and give him a coy smile. "Please, boss, may I have my drink?"

Drew chuckles against my neck and a shiver rolls through me. Dante gives me a stern look before passing it over.

"We're driving you home, pipsqueak."

I smile over the rim of my glass at his heated blue eyes. "Whatever you say."

The door to the suite opens again and a woman walks in. She's dressed in red silky cloths that wrap around her tight body. Her dark hair is tied into a braid hanging down her back. Her eyes are dark and she smiles at me.

She lifts her gaze to Drew.

"Good evening, sir. How may I entertain you?" Her voice is smooth like hot chocolate. It's a shame Kayla isn't in here. This woman is smoking hot. Fuck, if I went for women, I'd be asking her to take me to the bed. My arousal spreads as I imagine these men watching her with me. Damn, maybe I should stop drinking.

My gaze wanders to the others. Finn takes in every inch of her and wets his lips. Dante leans back and studies her. I swallow before I look at Wyatt. But he's not looking at her. His dark gaze collides with mine.

My heart hammers in my chest. What the hell is going on? Has he been watching me this whole time? I haven't been looking his way because I didn't want to see the censure for flaunting my relationship with Drew. Not that he ever hid his string of women from me.

"I think we'd all appreciate a dance tonight, Maya." Drew repositions me on his lap so I lean back against him, facing the stage, breaking my stare down with Wyatt.

Dark liner edges Maya's brown eyes that seem to glow amber in the dim light. "It would be my pleasure."

She walks over to the stage and climbs the stairs. Fuck, even that she does seductively. I'd probably trip my way up to the stage. I take a drink and glance out of the corner of my eye at Wyatt.

He's drinking his scotch and turned toward Maya now. Maybe I imagined it. Maybe my fantasy life has me imagining things that could never happen.

She claps and the lights go dark. A haunting strain of music fills the room. A light finds Maya as she sways on the stage. She draws off a silk from her arm and dances with it before it flutters to the ground. The music is soft and sensual.

Fluidly, she moves around the stage, slowly removing every scrap of fabric until all that's left are the ones holding her breasts and some around her waist and hips. She's fascinating to watch. Drew slides his hand up and down my thigh, heating my blood and making my pussy wetter.

He slips his hand beneath my sweater, skating his fingers across my bare stomach.

I lean back against him, feeling his hard length pressed against my backside. His breath is hot against my ear. Awareness floods me.

"What if I carried you back to that bed and fucked you while these guys watch Maya finish her striptease?"

My breath catches as his fingers slide beneath the waistband of my jeans, teasing the edge of my panties.

"Do you think they'd be watching her or watching you, princess?"

I bite my lip, waiting for him to slide his hand lower and find out how wet I am for him. To touch me in front of the others because he can. My desire makes me dizzy.

"They'd watch you. They'd want you and know that I have you. Do you think they'd be able to hold back any longer if they saw you spread out naked before them?"

I whimper as sensual images of Dante and Finn flood my mind.

The music pulses faster as Maya loses more of the silks.

"Do you know how bad I want to touch you, Sara? Sink my finger deep into your wet pussy until you scream my name?"

"Please," I whisper, because I don't have control anymore. I've given it all to this man and I want what he's offering me. I want him to show these men what they're missing. What they could have taken and had for years, but didn't.

He undoes my button and slips his fingers down until they slide against my pussy. The music covers my low moan.

"Shh, princess." He pulls his hand out and straightens my pants. "Soon, I promise. But I don't want your bulldogs to beat me to a pulp tonight."

He puts his finger in his mouth and sucks on it. I can't tear my gaze away as my pussy aches with desire.

The music stops and there's a smattering of applause, jolting me back to where we are. Maya lifts to her feet with only a patch of silk covering between her legs. Her breasts are spectacular. Firm and round. Frankly, I'm jealous. Her dark eyes land on me and she smiles.

Her eyes never leave me as she walks down the stairs. She carries four silks, draping one over Finn's shoulder as she passes. Then one over Wyatt's. Then one over Dante's. When she reaches me and Drew, she holds out her hand.

"Come," she says.

I finish my drink and set it down, taking her soft hand. Not questioning what she wants me to do.

She drapes the final silk over Drew's shoulder and leads me back on stage with her. The stairs are a little tricky with how tipsy I am. She makes me stop in the light, holding my hips from behind. I can't see the guys anymore, just the light, but I can feel them out there. Watching, waiting.

"Do you know what I see when I look out into the crowd?" she whispers in my ear. She lifts a silk and runs it over my throat. It's soft and tickles, and it's strangely erotic knowing those four men are out there watching me and her. Does this turn them on?

Seeing me with this beautiful creature?

I want to peel off my clothes and give them a show. "The light?"

"The desire." She lifts my arm and holds it in a dancer's pose, elongating my body. My sweater lifts to expose the skin above my jeans.

"You're very beautiful," I concede. I can feel their desire for her.

"Not for me. For you." She draws the silk down my side. "These men want you. Their desire is palpable, but it's only for you."

A shiver rushes through me, but I've drunk enough that her words mesmerize me. Like she's weaving a spell around me and I'm helpless to resist.

"Your brother worries about them and how much they want you."

The fog of desire lifts from me.

"Tom?" I spin to face her and hold out my hands to steady myself. The room sways with the music, but this is important. "You know Tom?"

"Tom likes me. He always asks for me." Her brown eyes sway before me, but I'm not sure she's dancing still. "He talks about them."

The whole floor shifts from under my feet and then the lights go dark.

Chapter 14

Volatility

Dante

I'm close enough I can hear everything the dancer says to Sara. Including that she knows Tom. I also realize the moment Sara starts to faint off the edge of the stage.

I catch her body as her knees give out.

"Lights!" Drew yells.

I hold Sara tight against my chest as I walk to the bed and lay her down on it. She's pale, but her chest rises and falls. I shouldn't have let her have that last drink.

"Wet towel?" I smooth my hand over her forehead, which feels normal and not hot. Good. My hand trembles as I draw it away. She could have been really hurt.

Drew sits on the other side of the bed and holds her wrist. "Her pulse is steady."

Finn hands me a towel and I wipe the back of her neck with it. She doesn't budge. I glance over and see Wyatt standing at the end of the bed. His hand is wrapped around the post so tight his knuckles are white.

"She just had too much to drink." I hope. She's always been a lightweight when it comes to alcohol. And she met her friends at a bar before this.

Maya sits on the edge of the stage, wrapped in a silk robe that must have been available in the room. I want to question her to see what she knows, but I'm not willing to leave Sara's side until I know she's okay.

Finn sits next to Drew on the bed and we all wait.

She lets out a little snore and rolls toward me, curling around my arm. I brush some strands of her hair that escaped her ponytail back out of her face.

Drew chuckles. "She's fine."

I don't trust him yet. The instinct to pull her into my arms and away from him is strong, but I resist it. I put my hand on her shoulder and try to shake her awake.

"Five more minutes, Mom." Sara rolls from me, grabs a pillow, and pulls it to her chest.

The tension leaves my shoulders, but I keep my hand on her as I meet Drew's eyes.

"Your dancer knows Tom." I narrow my eyes. What the fuck is this guy's game?

Drew smiles and shrugs. "I thought it was a possibility. It's why I asked her to come in. When she paid attention to Sara, instead of the obviously wealthy men sitting around the stage, it confirmed my suspicions."

Finn nods to me and stands. He strolls over to Maya. After a few minutes of talking, he leads her back to us. He turns a chair around for her to sit in.

"How do you know Tom?" I ask.

"He comes to watch me dance." She strokes her fingers along the collar of the robe down between her breasts. "He told me about her."

Her gaze lands on Sara's sleeping form. Then her gaze lifts to Finn. "And you." Her gaze slides to me. "And you." It settles on Wyatt. She tilts her head as she looks him up and down. "And you."

"Did he ever talk about his work?" Finn asks.

She smiles coyly. "Tom wasn't focused on work when he was with me, but his clients would sometimes interrupt us. They come here. Not regular. I haven't seen them since he disappeared."

Sara rolls back toward me and grabs my thigh, pulling herself against it like she held the pillow. I swallow before lowering my gaze to her. She presses her forehead against my hip. This girl. I'm so fucked.

"I told Maya Tom took off this weekend. If I show you some videos would you be able to identify the clients that interrupted you?" Drew asks, already rising from the bed. He takes in Sara, but I don't see tension or jealousy because she's wrapped herself around my thigh.

He looks sure of himself and his place in her life. Curious. They haven't been dating that long.

"Most likely." Maya shrugs. She stands to follow Drew out of the suite. Finn trails behind them. When she reaches the doorframe, she stops and glances sideways, not at any one of us. "He knows you want her. He knew putting her under your protection would make things difficult, but he wouldn't do that if he thought she'd be okay on her own. So if he's gone, she must be in danger or he never would have intentionally put her in your path."

Finn turns to look at me and Wyatt, but who the fuck was she saying that to?

She slips from the room. Finn shakes his head and follows them.

Wyatt steps away from the bed and turns back to look at her. "She's good at home, right? We're doing the right thing."

I draw in a breath and release it. Telling Wyatt she's by herself would mean he'd have to bring her under our roof. If he did that, all hell would break loose. I haven't missed the way she's looking at Finn or the way she's looking at me. Wyatt probably hasn't missed it either.

I crossed a line with her that I shouldn't have. It wouldn't surprise me if Finn did too.

"She's safe at home for now," I say.

For now. She squeezes my thigh and my gaze drops to her. The security system works. And this keeps her safe from us.

"Dante," she murmurs without opening her eyes. She shifts her legs together. My cock hardens even more than it already was. I don't acknowledge my name or my arousal.

Wyatt arches an eyebrow. He's not stupid, but he's got a huge blind spot when it comes to Sara that I'm banking on.

Fuck. If he figures out what happened between us, it could ruin our friendship.

"Maybe Drew will take her in if it gets bad." I don't want to push her away like that, but I don't really have a choice.

"Absolutely not." Wyatt stalks away before turning around. "That guy is a fucking joke. Tom would never approve of him."

I sigh. "It doesn't matter if Tom approves or not. It matters what Sara wants. She likes him."

Wyatt thrusts his hand into his hair and tugs on it. "Fuck."

"What?" Sara almost sits up but doesn't open her eyes.

I rub her back. "Go back to sleep, pip."

Wyatt stills as he watches me with her. I let my face go blank. We've always taken care of Sara. She was our little shadow when we were growing up. Her mother never felt safe letting Sara play on her own, so Tom kept her with him.

"She'll be fine. I'm sure Tom is overreacting or he has something figured out to fix this."

Wyatt approaches the end of the bed but doesn't get too close. "She needs us."

I nod. "We'll take care of her at work. We'll check out the new guy to make sure he's not a serial killer or with the mafia."

If anything, Drew likes to stir up trouble, from what I can tell. But Sara likes him in a way I haven't seen her like any other guy she's gone out with.

She stirs again, and this time stretches, drawing her sweater up to show her slender waist and pale skin. I've seen every inch of that skin bared and beautiful before me, but even this glimpse makes me want to tuck her away so no one else can have her.

She rolls on the bed and blows out a breath.

I smile and shake my head. "She's a little bit of a mess."

"She's always been a little bit of a mess." Wyatt's closer. His gaze remains on her with that soft look he hides from her.

Tom is our friend. He doesn't want us with her for whatever reasons. That's his choice. We all want her, which has kept us away. How could I stand by and watch her be with Finn or Wyatt? How could I have her and keep them? I'm sure they feel the same way. Add Tom into that equation and the way she focused on Wyatt... It made it easier to ignore the need to possess her.

But if Sara wants me, I don't know that I can continue to resist her.

Finn

The dancer sways her hips in front of me and gives me sly looks over her shoulder. Fuck if I can tell what she really knows and what she's just guessing. Do I feel guilty for eating Sara out on her family's dining room table?

Yes, I do.

Would I do it again? In a fucking heartbeat.

I haven't been able to get her off my mind, and now with her in the office... Fuck, I took a few extra "coffee" breaks today. I think Dante's up to something too, but I can't quite figure it out. He's always been protective of her, so it might be that vibe I'm picking up on.

Drew opens his office door and we all enter again. "Let me pull up the video."

He rounds his desk and hits a few keys.

"So you and Tom..." I give her my best winning smile. "He never mentioned you."

Shrugging, she pulls on the belt of her robe. "No reason to mention me. I'm cheaper than therapy."

I highly doubt that. But she glances up, and with those dark eyes fixed on me, I can see why Tom would spend time and money with this woman. She's just his type.

"Got it." Drew comes around and presses a button on the remote.

Maya studies the guys at the table that Tom talks to. "It could be them. It's hard to tell."

I squint at the screen. It's not the best quality. I don't know, if I saw any of these guys, if I would recognize them from this video.

"Can you let me know if they come in again?" Drew asks.

Maya nods. Her gaze shifts to me and she smiles seductively. "Do you want a lap dance?" She walks around me and rubs her breasts against my back. "I could help ease that pressure she inspires in you."

"I'm not sure what you're talking about." I step away from her. "But I appreciate the offer. You're a beautiful woman."

She fake frowns and then her smile returns. "If you need me, I'm here."

"Thanks, Maya." Drew turns off the video and sets the remote on his desk.

Maya finger waves and leaves.

"Want a drink?" Drew walks over to the bar on the side of the room and pulls out a top-shelf whiskey.

"If you're buying, I'm drinking." I sit on one of the stools. "So, you and Sara just fucking or is this serious?"

Drew smiles and sets a glass in front of me to pour. "We haven't fucked. Not that it's any of your business. But she's definitely someone I want to be serious with."

I can see that. Nodding, I lift the glass to my nose and smell the peaty, woodsy aroma before drinking a sip. "I know about that shit you pulled with Elizabeth Hartfield and Leighton Porter."

He smirks. "So does Sara."

I huff out a laugh. It figures that's why she'd be drawn to him.

"We talked about it on one of our dates." Drew leans against the bar and swirls his whiskey. "It's actually how we met. She was at the dinner where it all blew up."

"I heard you were the one that blew it up."

He chuckles. "The guys wanted me to, and who am I if I don't entertain at a dinner party?"

"Sara's not like those others." I look him over.

"I know. That's why I want her." At least he's not ashamed to say it. That's better than any of us.

"Are you exclusive?" I arch an eyebrow. This guy plays the field. It's well-known.

"She hasn't asked for it." He drinks a sip and meets my eyes. His face completely serious. "But I'm giving it to her because I know not to fuck this one up."

Makes sense. "But she isn't exclusive to you?"

His grin slowly reappears. "I haven't asked for it. She's entitled to whatever pleasure she seeks out. But I'm in this."

I nod in acknowledgment and hold my glass out for him to add more whiskey. When he sets the bottle down, I lift my glass to him. "May she get all the pleasure she deserves."

He chuckles and clinks our glasses together. "I'm all for that."

Sara

My pillow is hard and not very comfortable, but it smells absolutely divine. Male voices penetrate the fog of my sleep. What in the hell is happening?

I lift my head and stare at someone's leg. Not someone. Dante. I'm wrapped around his thigh like he's my pillow. I sit up and look around, but I don't recognize the room at first. It's definitely not my bedroom.

The stage at the other end with red scarves scattered over it makes my brain catch up. Oh, shit. I passed out at the strip club. I'm also on the bed with Dante, who's sitting upright. What the hell did I do?

"What'd I miss?" I straighten and meet Dante's amused gaze.

"You gave us a striptease that put the dancer to shame." Finn laughs as my gaze jerks to him. "You should have plenty of dollar bills shoved in your panties."

I pat myself and find I'm still clothed. I pick up a pillow and fling it at him, hitting him square in the chest. "Not funny."

"It definitely wouldn't have been funny at all, princess." Drew stands over at the bar, sipping an amber-colored liquor. "But it would have been sexy if you hadn't passed out."

My cheeks flood with heat. I rub my head. How much did I drink?

Wyatt sits in a chair with his hands clasped between his knees. His dark eyes find mine and I'm caught like a moth to a flame. The others all hold my attention, but Wyatt pulls at me, makes me want so much more.

Closing my eyes to break the connection, I flop back on the bed. "Where's Kayla?"

"She said to tell you she'd hit you up in the morning for details." Finn laughs. "I like that one."

"You can't have her. She's my friend." I put my hands against my forehead as I stare up at the mirror above the bed. I didn't notice it earlier, but why would I? It's on the ceiling. "So, this mirror? Is it actually useful or do you just catch yourself at really weird angles?"

I prop up on my elbows and look around the room, figuring one of them would know.

"Anytime you want to play in here, princess, you let me know and I'll make it happen." Drew winks.

I grin and wink back.

"Not tonight." Dante stretches next to the bed. Fuck, he's one hundred percent gorgeous. I'm lying on a bed with the four guys who star in my dreams nightly surrounding me. How can I make this happen?

I'd have to be bold and just start stripping. Maybe put on a show of my own.

"Come on, pipsqueak. We should head home. You've got work in the morning." Dante reaches his hand down to me.

I blow out a breath and take it, letting him help me up from the bed.

Drew steps over to me and pulls me into a hug. "I'll text you later."

"Thanks." I'm still a little groggy and definitely still drunk.

He cups my cheek and kisses me softly. He whispers, "Behave, princess."

His brown eyes search mine and he gives me another kiss.

I sigh as he pulls away. I could just pull him down to the bed and find out what happens. It's tempting, but also probably the wrong move right now.

"What happened to Maya?" I almost forgot. "She knows Tom."

"We know, flower." Finn wraps his arm around my shoulders and leads me to the door. "She was a little helpful, but not really."

I turn to look at Wyatt. His face is as blank as ever, but there's heat in his eyes as he looks at me. If it weren't so hopeless, I'd totally make a play for him. But he doesn't want me. Not like the others do.

Finn leads me through the club. It's a little darker and grittier now. I don't know what time it is, but it must be late. How long did I sleep?

He opens the door for me and we step out onto the sidewalk. A black car waits for us. Wyatt slips into the front seat while Dante and Finn sit on either side of me in the back.

Hello, awkward. I lace my fingers together in my lap. Neither of them has brought up this weekend. I don't think they've even told each other what happened. I'm definitely not up to confronting what happened in Tom's office. That tension that lingers. The longing that sparked. I'd love to be caught in a Dante-Finn sandwich any day.

When I shiver, Dante shrugs out of his jacket and drapes it over my shoulders, surrounding me in the fresh ocean scent that clings to him like I wouldn't mind doing. Though apparently in my sleep I have the balls to grab onto him and not let go.

"I'm coming in with you, pip," Dante says quietly.

The others don't know my parents are out. It's probably late enough that they'll assume my folks and Caitlyn are asleep. This one is nonnegotiable so I don't fight it. I just nod.

I'm still tipsy and sleepy, so having him with me will make it easier to fall into bed quickly. Yes, I'd love to pull him into bed with me, but that can't happen. Not tonight. Maybe never.

I sigh and rest my head on Dante's shoulder.

"Sad thoughts, flower?"

I turn to Finn. "Just thinking of what will never be."

"Never say never." He strokes his finger along my jawline, sending a fever rush through my blood.

"Some things will never be." I glance into the front and see Wyatt's eyes in the mirror watching me closely. I drop my gaze to my lap. No matter how much I wish things were different.

That doesn't mean I don't want the others and what they're offering.

Chapter 15

Yield Curve

Sara

When the car stops at the townhouse, Dante gets out and holds his hand down to help me. Once I'm on the sidewalk with him, he wraps his arm around my waist. His warmth covers me even through his coat as we hurry up the stairs. Quickly, I let us in and turn off the alarm.

Peabody barks from the kitchen.

Dante holds my arm and stops me. "Wait. I want to check out the first floor."

I nod and huddle in his jacket as it swallows me whole. He disappears into the house, not turning on many lights, just enough to get me to the kitchen.

Peabody makes excited noises as Dante reaches the kitchen.

"Hey, mutt."

I grin, knowing Dante is probably squatting down to let Peabody give him kisses.

"Come on in, pip."

I walk into the kitchen and sure enough Dante is almost on the floor with the little furball.

"Take him out and I'll check upstairs." Dante straightens and I shiver as awareness flows through me.

He heads to the stairs while I take Peabody into the backyard. Peabody runs in a few circles before doing his business and racing back to me.

"Okay, we'll go to bed." I open the door and Dante waits for me inside. He's so large and imposing. He rarely smiles, even less than Wyatt. While Wyatt took care of me when I was young, I think I annoyed Dante when I followed them around.

And then I seemed like a pest that he needed to keep far away from Wyatt.

Now? Fuck, now he's hot and I want another taste.

Realizing I spent too much time staring, I clear my throat. "Thanks for checking."

"Are you okay to get yourself to bed?" He tips my chin up and studies my eyes.

"Are you offering to take me to bed?" The smile I give him is a little sloppy.

He shakes his head but the corner of his lips tilts up. He reaches into the refrigerator to grab a bottle of water. He holds it out to me and I take it.

When he scoops me into his arms, I let out a shriek. Liquid heat flows through me from where our bodies meet.

"What are you doing?" My arms wrap around his neck as he carries me up the stairs.

"Making sure you make it to your bedroom and don't end up on the couch all night." He nudges my bedroom door open with his foot and sets me down. "Wouldn't want you to be late for work."

Peabody comes running in and Dante lifts him up and puts him on the bed, where Peabody circles and lies down.

I take off Dante's jacket and hand it to him. "Thank you."

"Are you good, pip? I could come by later..." His words trail off. That would be a very naughty idea. And I wonder if that's what he wants. To come over and crawl into bed with me. The idea of

Dante curled around me makes my insides float like champagne bubbles.

"Dante?" I meet his eyes. "Do I get a kiss good night?"

"Sara." His tone is a warning, but his cold eyes flash with a hint of heat that only encourages me.

Smirking, I arch an eyebrow in challenge. "Just a peck. Simple. It would help me sleep."

"Only good girls get kisses." He shakes his head, but lowers his mouth to hover over mine. His breath caresses my lips and my whole body buzzes with anticipation. "I'm not sure you've been a good girl."

"I've been a good girl for a very long time, Dante." I grab hold of his shirt. "It didn't get me kisses."

I go up on my toes and press my lips against his. He grabs my shoulders and I'm afraid he'll push me away. I part my lips and slide my tongue against the seam of his lips. He groans in surrender and draws me in close, opening his mouth over mine and kissing me back.

I feel like a light bulb with too much energy, glowing so bright inside as he tastes my mouth and draws me even closer. Lifting me off my feet. I wrap my legs around his waist and his hard cock presses against my pussy with far too many layers between us.

He walks with me and lowers me onto my bed. Finally. I want to cling to him and draw him down on top of me, get him to burn with me. But the others are waiting in the car just outside. If they come in, they'll know my parents aren't here.

"Fuck, pip." He lifts off me and runs a hand through his hair.

Smiling, I raise up on my elbows. "You can come back later, boss, and finish what you started."

"Not tonight, pip. Maybe not ever. Fuck. I can't. It's you." Dante shakes his head and those shutters fall over his eyes. Disappointment rolls through me, but I'm getting to him. "I'll see you at work tomorrow. Call if you need me."

The door closes behind him. I roll over and grab my clutch.

Opening my phone, I pull up my text messages.

ME:

I need you.

DANTE:

Be a good girl

ME:

I'll be your good girl

DANTE:

Sleep it off, pip

I bite my lip and blow out a breath. Fuck. I want to kiss all of them and have all of them kiss me and do so much more.

Dante. Finn. Drew. Wyatt.

I touch my fingers to my lips, still tasting his scorching hot kiss. I'm playing with fire. These aren't guys who want to share a woman. It's impossible and I'm going to end up the one hurt in the end. But what a fucking ride it will be in the meantime.

I take an extra long shower in the morning, trying to push through my hangover. A part of me is tempted to call in sick, but it's my second day of work and they all know what I was up to last night. I'm sure Finn or Dante would show up to bring me in.

The other part of me wants to hide in a hole. Did I honestly kiss Dante Stone? And tell him I was sick of being a good girl. First off, way to go drunk me. Second off, I have to face that man this morning. It was bad enough after the self-pleasuring incident.

He must think I've lost my damned mind.

Maybe I have. While I let Peabody out in the backyard, I fill a large, insulated tumbler with coffee. It's going to take a whole pot to make me feel alive today. When I let the idea of Wyatt go, I figured this would be easy.

I'd find someone who wants to fuck me, aka Drew, and finally be able to move on with my life. But then Finn kissed me. My gaze is drawn to the dining room table. I swear my knees get weak thinking about his tongue.

And then Dante. Holy fuck, Dante. Getting off with him was spectacular. And that kiss... Fuck, I'm melting just thinking about it.

Drew doesn't seem to mind me being with anyone else, but is it really possible?

Peabody rushes back inside and dances around my feet, waiting for his snuggle and treat.

I scoop him into my arms and give him kisses. Setting him down, I put the gate up. "Tonight I'm staying in. Promise."

He barks and goes for the toy filled with peanut butter.

As I get ready to leave, the doorbell rings. I don't even glance at the security camera, figuring it's Brandon. When I open the door, Drew gives me a smile I feel all the way to my bones.

His light brown hair falls over his mischievous brown eyes.

My mouth opens, but I don't know what to say.

"Good morning, princess." He holds out a cup of coffee from a popular coffee shop. Awareness shivers through me. "I thought you might need coffee this morning and a ride to work."

"I—" I shake my head with a smile. "Sorry, you caught me off guard. I don't know what to say."

"Say yes." He runs a hand through his light brown hair, mussing it a little, but it still looks really good. His smile is confident as he closes the distance between us. "You're busy with work and so am I, so let's squeeze in something before we go out Thursday night for dinner."

I take the coffee and sip it. Oh, fuck, that's good. A mocha latte.

"Is that your way of asking me to dinner on Thursday?" My gaze takes in his blue tie. He's dressed in a suit with a cream shirt. It's cut and fit perfectly to him. He's attractive in everything he wears and pulls me in like a magnet.

When I return my gaze to his, he gives me a cocky smile that makes my knees draw together. "Do I have to ask, princess?"

He offers me his arm and I sigh. I've never had someone come at me with such determination. Honestly, I don't hate it.

He leads me down the steps to the car idling on the curb.

"Wait." Stopping, I hand him my coffee and my thermal mug. When he takes them without question, I pull out my phone to text Brandon that I don't need a ride this morning. I slide it back into my purse and look up into his chocolate brown eyes.

"Good?" He hands me the mocha but keeps my thermal mug.

I take a sip and nod. "Yes."

He opens the door to the back and holds my hand to help me down into the car. It's a luxury sedan with leather seats and the dividing glass already raised. When Drew slides in the other side and closes the door, the dark tinted windows enclose us in a very personal space.

Sparks zing through me as I remember last night when he slipped his finger inside me. My pussy throbs. I sip my coffee and set it in the holder as the car starts.

"How's your head?" Drew leans back in the seat with a smirk.

"Better." I look at him through my lashes. "So Thursday?"

"Yeah." He grabs my hand and pulls me closer. My breath catches. "I want to see you this week and things are a little hectic."

I arch an eyebrow. "Stripper business or textiles?"

"Both." He smirks and tugs me to straddle his lap. My fingers wrap around the back of his neck where his silky hair brushes it. His gaze drops to my lips and a corresponding wave of desire crashes over me. "I won't lie, Sara. I want you."

"Are we going out or staying in for dinner?" I bite my lip, kind of hoping he'll say staying in, but also a little afraid at the same time.

He groans. "Going out. Because if we stay in, all I'll want to do is fuck you and we need to get to know each other better."

I straighten the skirt of my light green dress so I can settle a little better on his lap, pressing my pussy against his hardening cock. I bite my lip at the solid press of him there.

He squeezes my hips and leans in to take my lips. No hesitation.

No moment of worry. He requests entrance with his tongue and I open for him. He drinks me in, consuming me like a fine wine. Maybe I should feel some shame about having kissed both Finn and Dante, but those thoughts scatter in Drew's kiss. My blood hums with warmth as his hands slide down my thighs.

When he reaches my bare skin, he trails his hands under my skirt to the junction of my legs. He draws away from the kiss and when I open my eyes, he's right there waiting for me. His eyes are dark and filled with heat.

"We don't have time for much, but I want to make you come, princess." His thumb skates over my damp panties.

My breath catches, but I nod. Last night I thought about masturbating, but I wanted so much more than my own hands and fingers.

Drew smiles. "I wasn't lying when I said I wanted to fuck you in front of those guys, show them what they're missing out on."

I could tell him now about Finn and Dante, but his fingers slip beneath my panties and slide over my pussy. Desire spirals inside me, making me hot and needy.

"I would have finger fucked you to orgasm right in front of them, but then they would've gotten to see what I can do to you before I did." Drew slides a finger inside me and rubs his thumb in circles over my clit.

I try to picture it. Me in that chair watching the stripper as Drew slides his finger in and out of my pussy, pushing me closer and closer to the edge, while the guys remain oblivious to what's happening.

"And I don't want to share my first glimpse of your face when you shatter, princess." A second finger slides in with the first.

The stretch makes me moan and grip his hair.

"Fuck, you're so tight, princess." Drew's breath caresses my lips as I begin to rock with his thrusts. "This time is for me. All mine. But if the moment takes us next time, I won't hold back. I don't care who sees you come after this. In fact, I want them to know how I make you feel. How I'm willing to give you the release you need so badly."

"Drew," I whimper as everything inside me tightens with every word.

He curls his fingers. "Open your eyes, princess."

I hadn't even realized I'd closed them. My forehead rests on his as his fingers work magic over and in my pussy. His dark eyes smile.

"Come for me, princess." His words spark the match and I explode.

I cry out, not caring who hears me, so caught up in experiencing every inch of pleasure that bursts through my bloodstream. Our gazes remain locked as he works me through it, prolonging my release until it becomes too much.

When I try to squirm away because I'm too sensitive, he smirks and shakes his head. "No, princess, that one is mine too. Give it to me. Come all over my hand, so I can smell your sweet scent all day long."

He thrusts a third finger inside me and I scream as the flood takes me under. My pussy pulses and throbs around his fingers buried inside me. I sag against him. My forehead rests on his shoulder as I work to slow my breathing.

His other hand rubs my back and he doesn't pull his other fingers from me, but he doesn't move them either. If I were bolder, I'd return the favor, but there isn't enough time. My pussy tightens around his fingers in an aftershock.

"Fuck, princess. I can't wait to taste you and feel you throb around my cock." He slips his fingers out and lifts them. "Watch."

I tip my head to the side to see how wet his fingers are. He slides each one into his mouth, sucking off my wetness, one by one. My pussy pulses again.

He reaches over and pulls out some wipes. He uses one on his hand and then slides another between my legs. My thighs tremble.

"As much as I want them to know how good you smell aroused, I want you to be comfortable." As he cleans me up, he presses his lips against my temple. "You good, princess?"

I smile because yeah, I'm so good right now. My legs are like wet noodles and I really want to feel both his tongue and dick inside me, but I realize the car isn't moving anymore.

Straightening, I remember I have to work. "Fuck."

"Shh, you're okay." Drew helps me arrange my clothes and picks up my coffee, handing it to me.

I take a sip. When I swallow, he kisses me, soft and gentle.

"Have a great day at work."

My cheeks flare with heat as I grab my thermal cup and my purse. My gaze drops to his cock straining against his pants. I wet my lips as I meet his chocolate eyes.

He smirks and draws me back in for a kiss. He searches my eyes with an intensity I'm not used to seeing from him. "We'll have plenty of time to get to all that. You don't want to be late on your second day."

"Thank you for the coffee and the ride." I startle when the door opens and a tall, bulky guy holds it open for me. The driver? "Have a great day at work."

"I will. And princess, I can't wait for Thursday."

Neither can I.

Chapter 16

Deferred Interest

Sara

As I walk into the lobby with my sunglasses on and my afterglow lighting me up inside, my phone buzzes. My whole body still tingles with what Drew did in the car. What a way to wake up. I sip my mocha and sigh.

I'm paying attention and noticing a lot more since I gave up on Wyatt. And what Drew offers is a really good time. Suddenly, Thursday can't come around fast enough.

Stopping at a bench, I set down my thermal mug to get my phone out.

> **KAYLA:**
>
> Tell me you scored with at least one of those guys last night

> **ME:**
>
> I'm so hungover, all I got last night were kisses *sad face emoji*

> **KAYLA:**
>
> *shocked face emoji*

Damn I figured with the bed and the mirror...

If I'd known I'd left you with good boys, I would have stuck around.

We should go to Veiled Vixen more often. That way you can see your boyfriend.

ME:

> He's not technically my boyfriend. We're just seeing each other.

Definitely not official with Drew. Well, not exclusive. Not after kissing Dante and Finn. Seeing Drew on Thursday night seems forever away. A little rush races through me. It's only Tuesday. Fuck, I can't wait to be back in his arms.

Will he go down on me like Finn did? I bite my lip.

KAYLA:

> Drew might as well have peed on you to claim you last night

ME:

> Ew. No. Yuck.

KAYLA:

> Not literally. *eyeroll emoji*

> Unless you're into that kind of thing

It's way too early in the morning to think about golden showers. An involuntary shudder rolls through me. Nope, that's a hard pass. And the thought killed my buzz.

I need to get her on another topic so I can go back to dreamland. Besides, I missed a lot last night by passing out.

ME:

> How was your lap dance?

KAYLA:

Girl. Amethyst is a legit artist. I asked for her digits

ME:

Did you get them?

KAYLA:

Of course

I smile. Good for Kayla. I pocket my phone and grab my thermal mug to head to the office.

Time to face the music.

When I take a sip of my coffee, my hand shakes. My bosses are waiting for me upstairs. We all enjoyed an impromptu strip show together, but we didn't learn much last night, except I can't hold my liquor. And I really want to have sex in that suite with someone so I can figure out if the mirror is helpful or a hindrance.

Or with all four guys and that mirror. It would definitely be stimulating to watch. A shiver rushes through me. Imagining their hands all over me. Their mouths. Their cocks. The thought of all of them is enough to make me ache.

Oof, I need to focus on work.

As I near the elevator bank, one is closing. I rush forward and squeeze through before the doors close. Ha, I didn't have to wait for an elevator, which means I won't be a minute late.

I straighten and reach to press the button for my floor, but it's already lit. I take off my sunglasses and turn to see who else is in the elevator.

Wyatt leans against the back of the elevator watching the numbers go up. My insides explode into bright colors of warmth. He shouldn't have this effect on me. For fuck's sake, Drew just got me off not even five minutes ago. My pussy aches from his fingers. I'm still bathing in the afterglow.

What if Wyatt can tell? My face grows hot.

"Good morning," I mumble and move to the other side of the elevator.

Wyatt nods but doesn't speak.

I take a sip of coffee and look up at the numbers. Halfway there. Fuck, a year ago I would have been excited to be in an elevator alone with Wyatt. The opportunity to have his full attention would have sent me spiraling. Now?

I don't know how to feel. There's something here, but I'm not game to act on it anymore. I'm done pushing. I'm done trying to make something happen that just won't.

"How's your head?" His gravelly voice startles me and I nearly choke on my coffee.

As I cough and sputter, he steps toward me.

Backing away, I raise my startled eyes to see the hurt in his. "I'm good."

It was an instinct because I know if he touches me I'll be lost again. He hasn't so much as held my elbow since we were little.

Nodding, he runs his hand through his hair and leans back against the wall. "Hangover?"

"A little." My cheeks heat.

Is this where I get a lecture about drinking? Or maybe about sitting in men's laps? Or maybe just being at a strip club in general? After all, Tom isn't here, and that means Wyatt has to fill in as my surrogate older brother like he always does.

When he opens his mouth, I hold up a hand. Fuck it. He's not Tom and I don't need a fucking lecture.

"Save it. I don't want to hear it this morning." I pop up a finger. "Strip club. Fuck you, I'm twenty-two years old and don't need or want your or anyone else's permission to go to a strip club. If I want to go, I'll go. If I want to climb up on stage and strip for dollar bills, that's no one's business but mine."

Wyatt's eyes narrow.

"Two." I hold up another finger. "Drinking. Again old enough and the only one who has to pay the consequences is me, so that's another fuck you."

"Sara—"

"Three." I hold up another finger and step closer. "Save me your thoughts on Drew. I'm not your problem. I've never been your problem. You didn't want me to be your problem. So yes, I'm seeing Drew, who, while the owner of a questionable establishment, is a hard worker, and he fucking likes me. So fuck you, Wyatt Hawkins."

The elevator doors open and I sweep out, not waiting for him to chastise me. Fuck, that felt good. My insides buzz. I feel ten feet tall, like I could do anything.

I walk into Tom's office and get around his desk before the door closes. My startled gaze jerks up to Wyatt's dark eyes.

He's just as controlled as he always is. I used to fantasize about making him lose that control. What might happen? Would he sweep everything off the desk and bend me over it? Pull my panties aside and thrust deep inside my pussy? A tiny shiver works through me.

Fantasy that will never happen.

I sit in my chair and cross my legs. "How may I help you?"

He draws in a breath and steps forward. I arch an eyebrow and set my elbows on my desk, lowering my chin to rest in my hands, just waiting. Because whatever he's going to say should be good.

"Tom is gone." He's so fucking still.

What would he do if I started stripping off my clothes? I almost laugh out loud at that thought, because the last thing Wyatt wants from me is anything sexual. His control is locked firmly in place.

"Yes, he disappears all the time. Do you need any help with business today? Or are you just here to tell me things I already know?"

"Fuck, Sara." He runs his hand through his hair and steps forward again.

The closer he gets the harder it is to keep up the nonchalance and breathe.

"You're not my sister—"

"I never have been." I lean back and fold my arms over my chest. See? This is his problem. He sees me as a sister.

"But I'm responsible for you." He looks like he's in pain.

Fuck that. I stand and walk around him to the door, pulling it open. "No, you aren't, Wyatt. The only one responsible for me is me. So if you don't mind, I'd like to get to work."

Wyatt

Her citrus scent fills my nose as she passes me. I'm holding on by a thread here. I watched her last night. The way she responded to Drew's kiss. The way Drew claimed her on his lap. The way her eyes grew wide seeing the stripper and wondering how we all saw the woman.

How she could have been hurt when she fainted if Dante hadn't caught her. The way she clung to Dante's thigh on the bed. The curiosity in her gaze as she asked about the mirror.

I don't know how much of her flaunting this newfound independence I'll be able to take.

Or how much watching the others touch her when I can't I can handle before I break.

She clears her throat behind me. Her voice is snippy when she says, "Are you lost?"

She has no idea how lost I am. I turn and fire fills her pale green eyes. Her toe taps on the hardwood floor. Her dress flows over her curves, hugging them softly.

Everything inside me wants to pick her up, toss her down on that desk, and fuck her until I'm all she thinks about. All she needs. But I can't.

It's not only a promise to Tom. It would rip us all apart. Finn, Dante, and me.

Sara can never belong to one of us without destroying the other two. Maybe it's best that she's with Drew.

Even as I think it, my insides burn, remembering his possessive touch. She's not his. She'll always be mine, even if I can't do a damned thing about it.

I close the distance between us and she sucks in a sharp breath. Her eyes are wild as they search mine. The air between us is charged, electric. One more step and I could touch her soft curves. Kiss her plush lips. Taste her. Touch her. Own her.

My blood flows hot through my veins. She wets her lips, drawing my gaze, and for a minute, I want to give in to the urge. To say fuck it to the universe and take what's mine.

"Sorry to interrupt." Finn's voice makes both our heads turn. He smirks. "Wyatt, we're supposed to go over the Addison file?"

Sara slips back into her office, taking her warmth from me. Taking my urges with her. They still burn inside, but the immediacy has lessened.

Nodding to Finn, I turn my back on her. I wouldn't have lectured her in the elevator. I just wanted to check in to see how she was feeling. But then she popped off about how much of a grown-ass adult she is.

Like I need a reminder that she's ripe and ready to be plucked.

My plans didn't include following her into her office and closing the door. But I did. Almost like I couldn't help myself.

I'm wound too fucking tight. I'm going to do something I shouldn't if I don't do something else to release some of this tension.

Finn follows me into my office and closes the door while I go around my desk.

"Do I want to know what was happening there?" Finn sinks into a chair and plucks a pen from my desk. He spins it in his hand as he studies me.

"No," I bite out. Fuck. I pull up my phone and look at the texts Talia sent me last night. She wants me to take her out, show her off. Maybe that's what I need. Talia.

I just need to find a release, and that's what Talia will do for me.

Even as I type, I cringe, knowing this isn't what I want. She isn't who I want.

I want red hair spread on my pillow with pale green eyes blazing up at me while her small body writhes on my cock. Fuck.

ME:

Thursday dinner?

TALIA:

Will we be having dessert?

I rub the back of my neck. She's not who I want, but she's not off-limits. She'll take care of the immediate need so I can focus on what's important. Tom's disappearance and keeping Sara out of danger.

ME:

Plan on it.

I set my phone away from me on the desk and lift my gaze to Finn's concerned green eyes.

"You know she wants you still. If you want her, you could have her." He rubs his jaw. Sara. "Tom would get over it."

Finn doesn't understand. He thinks it would blow over. He believes Tom would be angry for a while, but then everything would go back to the way it's always been. Except it wouldn't just fracture me and Tom. It would fracture all of us.

This isn't just some woman we all want. This is Sara. The little sprite who followed us around. The young woman who tried to get us to pay attention to her. The grown woman who makes me long for her at night, when I'm alone in my bed, stroking my cock to the memory of her lips, the fire in her eyes, the curves of her body.

"It can't happen." I shake my head to rid myself of my dirty thoughts. It hurts too much to think about what can't be. "Let's focus on work."

My phone vibrates, but I don't look at it.

Finn leans over and glances at the screen. He flinches. "Talia? Is that really smart? I thought you were shrugging her off. She'll just dig her claws deeper into you if you play with her again."

I shrug. She'll help me clear my head so I don't do anything stupid like kiss Sara, because once I kiss her, there will be no turning back. She'll be mine.

Chapter 17

Bottom Line

Sara

This week has been moving so fucking slow. It's Thursday morning so at least I have something more exciting to look forward to tonight than going home alone, eating alone, and going to bed alone.

Peabody is good company, but he's not very talkative.

At least I haven't seen the smoking guy hanging around outside. Maybe I was just imagining it last week. Overactive imagination caused by Tom's cryptic messages.

I look over the column of numbers I've been struggling to make sense of for the last twenty minutes, but whatever is wrong is still eluding me. I glance at the time on my computer.

Dante and Wyatt left for a meeting. So I can't ask Dante. I could ask one of the other associates. It's not like they're off-limits, but they don't treat me like one of them. I've tried striking up conversation in the breakroom, but they act like I'm one of their bosses and not another worker bee.

And every time I see Greg, he looks about ten minutes from asking me out and I don't want to deal with that.

I unplug my laptop, walk over to Finn's office, and knock on the door. It's been a long week because I've been avoiding the others since that incident with Wyatt. It left me feeling raw and vulnerable.

He was so close that it felt like he was finally going to act on this attraction between us. What would've happened if Finn hadn't shown up?

I draw in a breath. It doesn't matter because tonight, I'm going out with Drew and hopefully taking him home to my lonely house, or maybe to his place. Butterflies swell within me, beating a nervous pace with their wings.

"Come in, flower." Finn's muffled voice comes through the door.

I turn the knob and step into his office. That sinful cologne of his is heavy in here and makes everything inside me soften. I clear my throat.

"I'm having an issue with a spreadsheet. Could you help me figure out what I'm doing wrong?" I feel like a little girl asking him to help me with my homework.

Finn waves me inside. "Close the door."

He returns his gaze to whatever he was looking over before I came in. His office is as big as Tom's, but he has a small seating area with a couple of comfy-looking chairs and a table. I sit in one of the chairs and set my laptop on the table.

Finn's office is decorated in rich colors, from the mahogany of his desk to the deep green of his walls. He finds pleasure in pretty things, which makes sense. A beautiful woman on his arm. The best suit, fitted perfectly to his body.

When he finishes whatever he's working on, he stands and stretches. I swallow, remembering his lean, toned body pressed against mine as he savored my lips. I cross my legs against the ache building within.

His long legs eat up the length of his office as he approaches me. When he settles into the chair, his green eyes focus on me. My breath catches and a throb of desire flows through me.

"What can I help you with, flower?" He wets his lips. Fuck, he's potent.

"Don't you think you should find something besides *flower* to call me?" I pull my laptop toward me to have something to do with my hands. I'm not usually nervous around Finn, but right now, even my hands are shaking. "I was eight when you started calling me that."

He smirks. "Trust me, it's evolved since the cartoon skunk you loved."

I arch an eyebrow. I had a thing for *Bambi*, namely the skunk. Finn found it amusing and has called me *flower* ever since. Which when I was little was another way of calling me *stinker*. "How so?"

His eyes sparkle. "I'll tell you, but it'll cost you."

"What will it cost me?" My pulse skips and everything inside me tingles in anticipation.

He stands and walks to the door, flicking the lock. When he holds his hand down to me, I take it, curious as to what he has in mind. He lifts me out of the chair. For a heartbeat, I'm pressed against his chest. His hard body close to mine.

When he sits down, I'm confused for a half moment before he pulls me down to straddle his lap, arranging the skirt of my dress around him. My face is hot, but he locked the door, meaning no one will interrupt us.

"Is this really business appropriate?" I tip my head to the side as I settle my hands on his shoulders and sit in his lap.

His smirk lights me up inside. "Since when do you care what's appropriate, flower?"

I shrug. "How has *flower* evolved?"

"This isn't the cost. I was just getting us comfortable." His fingers skim up and down my thighs over my skirt.

My breath hitches as his fingers trail closer and closer to my pussy.

"I'm going to ask you a question and I want an answer. A truthful answer." Finn smiles softly.

"Okay." I squirm, wondering what question he wants to ask.

His hand slides around the back of my neck and I'm grateful I put my hair up in a bun today, because his fingers touch my bare skin and light me on fire inside.

"First, I want a taste." He leans in and our lips collide. It's just as heavenly as the first time he kissed me. His other hand wraps around my hip and draws me forward until his hardening cock is pressed against me intimately.

I moan into his mouth and he deepens the kiss. Fuck, Finn is a great kisser. His lips, his tongue. The way he sucks on my lower lip. It's perfection and all I want to do is ride his cock right here. Right now.

"Fuck, flower," he whispers against my lips before his hand slips beneath my skirt. He takes control of the kiss again, and his hand slides up to my panties. That fire rages hotter as his fingers slip beneath my panties and lightly caress my pussy.

I gasp into his mouth and my hands tighten on his shoulders.

"So fucking wet for me," he murmurs against my lips.

My fingers thread into his hair and I take control of the kiss, exploring his mouth as he groans and thrusts his finger inside me. Fuck. He pumps his finger in and out as his thumb presses on my clit. I rock my hips with his fingers, falling into his rhythm.

He takes over the kiss, pushing me higher and higher. Until I can't go any higher. Suddenly I'm falling. I shatter around his finger, moaning long and deep into his mouth. He draws away and I open my eyes to his darkened green ones.

"Tell me, flower." Finn thrusts his finger in deep and an aftershock rolls through me. "Do you want me?"

"Yes," I whisper, pressing my forehead against his. "Yes, Finn, I want you."

He removes his finger and rights my panties, then brings his finger to his mouth and sucks it. My pussy pulses in need. He makes this pleasure-filled noise as he cleans the taste of me off his finger. It's so hot it almost makes me come again.

His green eyes hold me captive as he draws his finger out and leans in to kiss me. I taste myself on his tongue as he strokes it against mine. Fuck. My fingers twitch in his hair. I could undo his pants, slide my panties to the side, and feel him inside me, filling me.

Finn pulls back and rests his forehead against mine. His breathing is deep, but his eyes are focused on me. "I'm not the only one you want though."

"No." I bite my lip and shake my head. "You aren't."

"That night in the suite at Veiled Vixen..." His finger slides against my lower lip. I part my lips, take his finger into my mouth, and suck on it while meeting his eyes. "Fuck, flower."

He pulls his finger out of my mouth and kisses me, grinding his cock up into my pussy. My hands slide down his chest. His muscles twitch beneath my fingertips. When I reach his buckle, I work on releasing his belt.

He pulls away and holds his hands over mine. My eyes open to his and the muscle ticking in his jaw. "You wanted all of us that night in the club. Am I right?"

I nod as my fingers rub the leather of his belt, waiting for him to release my hands so I can free his erection that presses against my pussy.

He lifts my hands and returns them to his shoulders. "I'm not going to fuck you in my office, flower. Not the first time."

My cheeks flush with heat.

His eyes narrow slightly before they clear. "As you grew, you continued to blossom. *Flower* changed from the funny name of a skunk to a term of endearment for the beautiful woman you've become."

My heart melts a little.

His gaze drops to my lips and he shakes his head. "I can't kiss you again."

It's more to himself than to me. So, I lean in and take his lips, kissing him until he opens and takes over. A knock sounds on the door.

"Fuck," Finn whispers. He lifts me to my feet, but I'm unsteady on my heels after what we just did. He catches my hips and supports me.

"Sit in your chair like a good girl." His green eyes demand my submission.

I reach up and wipe my lipstick from the corner of his mouth. Then I run my hands through his hair to straighten it. When I finish, I step back and sink onto the chair, grabbing my laptop and trying to look like I'm concentrating.

He shakes his hands out before opening the door.

"Hey." Dante's voice fills the room. "I was just wondering if you—"

I feel it when his eyes land on me. Fuck, I hope I don't look a wreck. I close my laptop and lift my gaze to Dante's ice-blue eyes.

"Sara, I need you to work on a file right away." Dante jerks his head in the direction of the office. "Come on."

I stand and straighten my skirt.

"If you still need me later, flower, you know where to find me." Finn's green eyes capture mine.

As I pass him, I brush the backs of my fingers against his, enjoying the sparks. I don't know why he wouldn't let me touch him, but I do know he wants me. And now he knows my fantasy. Drew implied he did too at the club.

I don't think I could ever admit it to either Dante or Wyatt, but somehow knowing that Drew and Finn know makes this all so much sweeter.

The rest of the day was a blur of numbers. I buckled down and got the work done. When I returned home, I let Peabody out and gave him his food. Honestly, having an orgasm at work made the rest of the day tolerable.

I walk into my bedroom and step into my closet to pick out a dress that will make Drew's mouth drop open. Tonight I have every intention of having sex. I pick a dress my mother would never let me buy, let alone wear on a date.

It's perfect. It clings to my curves, shows off my cleavage, and still flares out at the hips. Drew won't know what hit him. I grab some skimpy panties and forgo the matching bra. A quick shower and a change and I'll be ready for my date.

When I walk through my room toward my bathroom, something catches my attention on the dresser. I set my dress and panties on the bed. When I reach my dresser, I lift the quarter-sized black box and see the lens.

The only person who has been in my room lately is Dante. I set it back down and glare at it. Seriously? Is he watching me? I mean, it could be for security purposes. Maybe he'll only watch it if something happens to me. Or maybe he's watching it now.

Smiling, I set it exactly how it was.

Leaving my dress to change into after my shower on the bed, I step away from the camera to make sure, if he is watching, he gets an eyeful. I reach behind me and undo my zipper, letting the fabric of my dress fall around me and onto the floor.

I turn to face the camera and give it a wink before releasing my bra and sliding it off. After I lower my panties, I blow the camera a kiss and go into the bathroom to take my shower. Just the thought of Dante watching me undress for him gets me hot and bothered.

Quickly, I finish my shower and turn off the water. As much as I want to get off, I'd prefer to make sure Dante gets a good show.

Wrapping my towel around my body, I walk out to the bed and move some pillows so I can watch the camera and make sure he has the best angle.

I drop the towel and lie back on the pillows with my knees up and my legs spread, giving him the perfect view of my pussy. A little pregame would be nice before tonight anyway. Though Finn gave me a very good pregame earlier.

It isn't hard to imagine Dante standing where the camera is with his long, thick cock in his hand, lazily stroking it. My mouth waters remembering the salty taste of him. I hold my pussy open with one hand and slide my other fingers over my clit, making sure to maintain eye contact with the camera.

I don't know if he's recording this or taking in the live show, but fuck, just the thought of him watching makes me so fucking wet. I slide my finger inside myself, imagining his voice telling me what to do, how to fuck myself for him.

My breathing quickens as I cup my breast. I toss my head back as I ride the waves threatening to take me under. It's like they're all here in the room watching me. Dante. Finn. Drew. Wyatt.

Wyatt

I'm an asshole, I freely admit it, and a piss-poor friend. But that doesn't stop me from turning on the camera in Sara's room every day as soon as I get home from work like some junky who swears he can stop at any time.

I've got my laptop open in my bedroom as I get out of my shower and go to my dresser to grab some boxers to get ready for my date tonight. Normally, Sara moves about her room and changes in her bathroom. It's not exciting to watch for any normal person.

But it soothes me to see her and know she's safe.

Sara wears only a towel as she arranges the pillows on her bed. I put my hands on the edge of my dresser, working to figure out what the hell she's doing. Her eyes lock on mine for a second and I swear a shiver runs over me.

She must have found the camera. I should tell Dante. But then Sara drops her towel. Her hair is pulled up in a bun, but her body is beautifully bare. My fingers clench painfully around the edge of the chest of drawers as my cock swells beneath my towel.

Fuck. Every inch of her is just as I always imagined. The camera doesn't do her justice, but her breasts are handfuls with tight nipples begging to be sucked. Her stomach swells gently into her hips.

She lies back on the bed and opens her legs, baring her smooth pussy to me. I should look away, but I can't make myself. I jerk my towel from my waist and grab my pulsing cock. Fuck.

It's one thing to fantasize about her when I jack off. It's another to have her spread out before me while she gets herself off. I couldn't look away if I wanted to. I don't want to.

Her eyes remain locked with mine as she parts her pussy lips and glides her finger over her swollen clit. I stroke my cock as she works that little bud. My mouth waters wondering what she tastes like. How her clit would swell against my tongue as I push her over the edge again and again.

She slips a finger inside her entrance and I groan, stroking my cock in time with her glistening finger working her tight little pussy. I smear my precum down my cock as I fuck my fist, wishing it was her.

She cups her breast and I can imagine how soft her skin must be, how full she'd feel in my palm. The tight tip brushing against my fingertips until I pinch it slightly. A low moan fills the speaker.

When she tips her head back, I watch her throat work as her lips part. She lowers her hand to work her clit as she thrusts two fingers inside her pussy.

"That's it. Show me how you make yourself come," I whisper, keeping pace with her fingers, watching them sink into her pussy over and over until she arches. Her legs close around her hand.

Cum rushes out of my cock and spills on the floor. "Fuck."

She pulls her fingers out and meets my eyes as she sucks them into her mouth. Fuck me. My cock jerks in my hand.

Wiping her fingers on her towel, she walks over to the end of the bed and puts on a skimpy pair of panties. She dons a dress that makes my balls tighten and my cock harden again.

Fuck. She moves in front of the camera and leans forward, shoving her hand down her neckline to pull her breasts up. When she straightens, she releases her hair and shakes it out a little before winking and puckering up at the camera.

She walks into the bathroom and closes the door.

My cock aches with need again. I clean up my floor with the towel. I need to get laid, but there's only one person who gets me hard. And she's apparently going out tonight.

Chapter 18

Dinner Receipts

Sara

Drew picks me up at exactly six forty-five. When I open the door, he sweeps me into his arms and kisses the hell out of me. My knees go weak. Just as I'm sinking into the kiss, he lifts his head.

"Fuck, I missed you, princess." He cups my cheek and checks over my lips to make sure he didn't smear my lipstick. "If we didn't have a reservation, I'd ravish you right here and now."

When I open my mouth to say I wouldn't mind, he chuckles and kisses me again.

"Lock up." He steps back and holds out his hand. "I promised to feed you, so we're doing that before anything else."

After setting the alarm, I close the door and lock it. When I take his hand, Drew pulls me down the stairs and to the rear door of his car. He helps me into the street side before rounding the car to get in beside me.

The privacy panel is raised and my whole body shimmers with anticipation. Drew tips my face his way and he takes me in. The desire in his eyes is palpable.

"Have I told you how beautiful you look tonight?" He kisses the corner of my lips before kissing the other side.

"No, you haven't." I smile, loving the attention. It's nice not having to beg someone to want me.

"You're gorgeous, princess." He pulls away and looks down at my dress. "And this dress, fuck, you're going to get me in trouble tonight."

"You don't like it?" I give him a fake pout.

He grabs my waist and pulls me to straddle him. I squeal at the sudden move and put my hands on his shoulders. Finn held me just like this today. And then I got off for Dante on the video camera. I'm having fun, but what if I'm hurting Drew by doing those things with the others.

We haven't really discussed some very important topics.

"Where'd my smile go?" Drew rubs his hand down my back, sending shivers of desire through me. I don't want to be a bummer, but...

"We should talk."

"More ominous words have never been spoken." Drew wraps one of my curls around his finger. "What's on your mind, princess? Besides my cock."

I don't fight the smile his words bring out. Especially as I settle a little more on his hard cock with just my panties and his dress pants separating us. But this is important.

"We're not exclusive, right?"

Drew laughs and tugs me closer. "Did one of those bulldogs pull his head out of his ass?"

Heat floods me. "If he did?"

"Let me guess." Drew doesn't look taken aback at all. "Finn seems like the kind to get a little handsy. Did he make you come, princess?"

I bite my lip and nod. He seems okay with it, but what if he's not? What if he tells me to stop? Can I make that promise to him? If Finn kisses me again, could I pull back? Will I still ask Dante to kiss me?

I've been so focused on getting Wyatt's attention that I never pushed the other two, but now, I don't think I'm able to end what's happening between any of us. And I don't want to.

"What are we talking? Tongue, finger, cock?" Drew's hands slide beneath my dress and grip my bare ass. "Fuck, princess, what are you wearing under here?"

His fingers find the lace of my thong. He grins like a boy in a candy shop.

"Not much," I admit. Swallowing, I meet his golden brown eyes. I have to be honest with him. "Last weekend, he kissed me and used his tongue and hands to make me come. Today, he kissed me and used his fingers."

"Mmm. I would have liked to see that." Drew slides his fingers lower to glide over the silk between my legs, covering my pussy. Little sparks build beneath his fingers.

"You aren't mad?" My words are a little breathy as he stirs the desire inside me with every flick.

He relaxes against the seat, slowly building the need for more. "We haven't had this talk. I was hoping to get you off before the restaurant, but it can wait."

I'm sure I pout, making him chuckle.

"This is important. I don't care how or with who you chase your pleasure, princess." He slips his finger beneath my panties and pushes inside me.

"Drew." I clutch at his shoulders as he thrusts in and out, pushing me higher and higher.

He pulls his finger out before I find my release and sucks on it. "Consider that an appetizer."

I bite my lip, wanting to ask for the full meal now. But there's something I've been hesitant to ask. Because even if I don't want to be exclusive on my side, I'm not ready to hear about the women he's sleeping with. "So we're not exclusive?"

"I didn't say that, princess." He leans back and runs his fingers over the neckline of my dress, chasing little thrills along my skin. "I'm not planning on straying, but I know your bulldogs are itching to play with you."

When I ease to the side to return to my seat, Drew catches my hips and frowns. "Hey, I'm not saying it's wrong. In fact, I wouldn't mind playing with you with them if the chance arose, but this is your decision. I want you to feel free to explore what could be."

I search his eyes and all I see is sincerity. How is that possible? When I met this guy he was sleeping with two women, actually three. "You don't want more?"

"I'm done messing around and juggling multiple women at a time." He cups my cheek and strokes his thumb along my jaw. "I've watched you at benefits with dates and never seen you as comfortable as you are with those three and me. I've seen the way you look at them and the way they look at you. I'm all in, princess. You want me, I'm yours. You want them too, I'm still yours."

He presses a soft kiss to my lips. "Now, I'm not into guys, so that would have to be your thing, but like I said, watching them fuck you? I'd be into that. I enjoy being on either side: audience or performer."

I squirm on his lap as my panties dampen. "I don't think that will happen."

Drew grins. "You'd be surprised what a beautiful woman can make a man do. Or many men do."

The car stops.

"Dinner first." Drew kisses me again, soft and tender.

When we walk into the restaurant, I feel much better about what I'm doing. The hostess seats us right away at a small table toward the back. My mind is so occupied with what Drew said I barely notice where we are until I look at the menu.

When I realize what restaurant we're at, I laugh.

"What's funny, princess?" Drew takes my hand on the table.

"This is where I always brought my dates to make Wyatt jealous." I shake my head. "I thought if he saw someone else who desired me, he'd finally make a move. But that ship has definitely sailed."

"Maybe he realized you didn't want any of those guys, so he thought it was safe to turn a blind eye." Drew brings my hand to his lips and presses a kiss to my knuckles. Butterflies launch inside me. "Trust me, I think he's noticing now."

Tuesday morning there was a moment when I swore Wyatt would kiss me, but then Finn interrupted. I shake it off.

"Trust *me*. He doesn't want to want me like that." I set my menu to the side and can't stop myself from looking at the table he always brings his dates to. It's currently empty.

"*I* want you like that, princess." His words are filled with awe.

My gaze finds Drew's golden brown eyes and something settles inside me. It's one thing to have Finn and Dante want me, but not want to do anything about it. It's another to have Drew, who wants me and isn't afraid to show it.

I lean in and kiss him, because I can and I know he won't reject me. His hand goes to the back of my neck and holds me to him while he deepens the kiss.

I've always shied away from relationships because of Wyatt.

But life is too short to wait for someone who doesn't want me. Or won't act on that attraction. My insides soften and suddenly I wish we weren't here at this restaurant. I wish I'd been courageous enough to drag him into my house.

He pulls back and his eyes tell me he feels the same.

Clearing his throat, he sits back and smiles this knowing smile that rushes down my spine and fills me with need.

"Good evening." The voice startles me. The server stands beside our table, waiting for us.

How long has he been there? My cheeks warm.

"May I get you some wine while you decide on your meal?"

Drew orders an expensive bottle of white wine for us. I smile at the server like I wasn't just making out at the table like a teenager. When the server nods and moves away to fill our order, a giggle falls out of me.

Drew's eyes sparkle as he strokes his fingers down a strand of my hair. "You should laugh more often, Sara."

"Then I'm exactly where I need to be." I release a happy sigh.

Tom's still missing, but things seem settled. Maybe he exaggerated the whole thing. Maybe there wasn't any danger and he just needed a vacation.

Who knows with Tom. I love my brother, but he disappears sometimes when he gets overwhelmed. Mom worries, but I don't. But he doesn't usually leave me and the guys with cryptic messages. Maybe he's bored and wants to shake things up.

The server comes back with the wine and pours a little in each of our glasses. I take a sip and sigh. Good wine.

Drew gives me a questioning look and I nod slightly to let him know it's good.

The server fills our glasses, and after we both order and the server steps away, Wyatt's favorite table fills my view.

Where Wyatt currently sits with his blond date.

My heart catches fire and crumbles like a stone into my stomach. My breath hitches and I can't seem to release it. Wyatt's on a date. Not just any date, but one with the same blond bimbo he's been out with multiple times before.

Okay, maybe she's not a bimbo. That's judgmental of me. But how can he be with her when he could have me?

Drew takes my hand.

"Hey, princess," he says quietly and turns my chin his way. His eyes are knowing and concern swims in them.

Or maybe it's the tears in mine that make his swim. Fuck. I blink back those traitorous tears. I'm not still pining over Wyatt Hawkins. I'm here with this really great guy who deserves all my attention.

"Do you want to leave?" Drew brushes his thumb my cheek.

I draw in a deep breath and shake my head. "We've already ordered and this is our first dinner date."

I smile even though my heart is settled somewhere in the pit of despair right now.

Drew kisses me and rests his head against mine. "It's okay to feel, princess. If he can't pull his head out of his ass, it's his loss and my gain."

Drew's spicy cologne fills my senses and my heart doesn't feel so heavy. I open my eyes to his and he smiles, and some of the ashen remains of my heart reform.

"That smile. Fuck, princess. It makes me feel warm all over." He pulls away and holds his glass out to me. "To a future without regret."

I lift my glass and touch his. The sparks he lights within me are exactly what I need and want. "To a future without regret."

We both take a sip and set our glasses down.

"How has your first week at work been?" Drew gives me his full attention ,which makes those butterflies rise. Here is this great guy and I'm stuck on an asshole who used to be nice to me as a kid. I need to focus on the right man.

"With the exception of Tom going AWOL, pretty decent." I take a sip and refuse to let my attention stray to Wyatt and his date. That's not my life anymore. We talk about my work and Drew's work at his family's company.

By the time dinner arrives, Wyatt is just this nagging little tickle at my consciousness.

I take a bite of my lobster frittata and moan.

"Good, princess?" Drew raises an eyebrow.

"So good." I eat another bite and moan again. "Do you want a bite?"

"Not of that." His eyes sparkle with mischief and heat pours through me. He lifts the wine and tips more into my glass. Is that two or three times he's refilled it while we were talking?

"So what exactly will the main course you promised me entail?" I lean toward him. I'm not drunk, but definitely tipsy.

His smile grows. His gaze shifts for a moment before he returns his focus to me. Under the table, his foot draws my chair closer to him.

"You remember how I told you that first one was for me." He wets his lips as his hand settles on my knee right below the hem of my skirt.

"I remember." The car and how he got me off twice on the way to work. A man who brings me coffee and orgasms is definitely a keeper.

He leans in until his lips press against my ear. "This one is for the guy who's too stupid to take you."

A shiver ripples through me. "Here?"

"Right here, princess. Continue to eat and act like nothing is happening." His fingers slowly sneak up my thigh. "Relax and open your legs for me."

Oh, fuck. I'm helpless to stop him because I want it. I crave it. The white table cloths drape to the floor, hiding everything under the table. Parting my legs, I take another bite of the delicious dish as he rubs my pussy through the silk of my panties. Heat rises up my neck.

He takes a bite of his steak and a drink of his wine, while his eyes never leave me. "Still good, princess?"

I nod and try not to squirm to get his fingers to press harder. Sparks sizzle through my veins. "How's your other business going?"

He smiles at the tremor in my voice. "The Veiled Vixen? It practically runs itself. Though I have been reviewing the tapes looking for those men, and my manager is keeping an eye out as well."

The men that Tom talked to.

"Hmm, maybe I don't want to discuss something to do with my brother. Right now." I widen my eyes at him.

He huffs out a breath. "Would you rather discuss how we can use the suite next time you visit me?"

His fingers push my panties to the side, leaving my pussy bared. Anticipation floods me. I take a bite of the decadent lobster and his fingers glide over my wet flesh, sending shivers through me. This isn't appropriate for public, but I don't want him to stop.

No one will know. It'll be our secret. And if it happens to be a little revenge against Wyatt, all the better. Even if he won't be jealous, if he knew, he'd be that mad overprotective asshole.

"Ideally, I'd have your bulldogs with me. Finn is an easy ask."

I meet his eyes and tilt my head in question.

"Finn likes games and he'd be all in to play with you. He doesn't have some of the hang-ups the others seem to." Drew rubs my clit and my lips part on a pant at the building pressure inside me.

"Finn doesn't want to fuck me," I bite out and clutch the table-cloth with my free hand. Neither he nor Dante have tried to fuck me. They like playing with me, but maybe fucking is a step too far.

Drew chuckles and thrusts his finger into me. I whimper at the feeling.

"He wants to fuck you, but there might be a line he's still not willing to cross. I'm pretty sure the big guy would fuck you hard." He adds another finger and begins thrusting them slowly in and out of my pussy.

"Dante," I whisper. His kiss. Fuck, I could live a hundred lives and not get enough of his kiss. It was passionate, fiery, and claiming, so unlike the coldness in his eyes.

"Hmm, yes. He's hanging on by a thread. When you clutched his thigh, there were definite possessive vibes there." Drew adds a third finger and I moan around my next bite of food. "I'm guessing he's packing some serious heat in there, so having someone stretch you out for him will be essential."

I give up the pretense of eating as Drew rubs my clit with his thumb while curling his fingers inside me. I'm so close and I don't know if I can be quiet about this. What he's building to is going to be messy and so fucking good.

"Princess, look at me."

Fuck, when did I close my eyes? I open them to his darkened gaze. The sounds of other diners filters through the pleasure Oh, hell, everyone in this restaurant is going to know exactly what he's doing to me beneath this table. Instead of pushing him away, the idea makes me even wetter.

"Are you with me?"

"Mmhmm." I'm desperately trying not to roll my hips with his thrusts and to appear calm and collected like he isn't fucking me with his fingers currently, maddeningly. I'm not sure I'm being convincing.

"There's one more." Drew's eyes sparkle. "He's the hardest to make cross that line. He can't even touch you he wants you so much."

I can't help it. My gaze strays to Wyatt and collides with his dark, narrowed eyes. I bite my lip as my orgasm rolls through me, pulling me higher.

I want to cry out and moan and pant, but I keep it all under wraps, focused on Wyatt's eyes as Drew works my clutching pussy through my release.

"That's it, princess. Show him what he's missing. Show him what he won't be able to resist."

My lips part on a gasp at his words and the shimmering aftermath of my release. Wyatt's eyes drop to my lips and an aftershock rips through me. I moan softly, unable to stop myself.

Chapter 19

Deferred Payment

Sara

Drew withdraws his fingers and straightens my panties, but I can't tear my eyes away from Wyatt. It could be seconds or minutes that we stay locked together as my release fades.

"How is everything?"

My cheeks burn as my gaze darts to the server. And the realization that I just came in a very public place that my mother's cronies might tell her about. Fuck.

"Everything's wonderful." Drew takes my hand and squeezes it. "I think we'll skip dessert tonight."

The server nods and walks away.

"Excuse me. I need to use the restroom." I blush, realizing how damp I am between my legs.

Drew stands and helps me to my feet. He leans in to my ear. "No spot on the back, princess. You're safe."

I breathe a *thank you*. I would have worried the whole walk across the dining area if he hadn't said anything. The bathroom is blessedly empty and I clean up as best I can.

Fuck. What the hell am I thinking? I'm so wrapped up in Drew and the guys that I can't see clearly or just use common sense. My mother's friends are always having dinner here, or know someone who is.

Everything I do gets back to my mother.

This month was about exploring being on my own. Trying new things. Dating someone I actually like. Not coming in a restaurant filled with my peers while meeting Wyatt Hawkins's eyes.

Is Drew right? Is that why Wyatt stopped touching me? He wants me as badly as I want him? This is fucking with my brain.

Wyatt

I tip my glass at the waiter as Sara disappears to the bathroom. There isn't enough alcohol in the world to erase the image of Sara coming at the table across from me. I might not have known what that looked like if I hadn't been a perv on the wall in her bedroom an hour ago.

"Wyatt, do you think the pink or the white is better?" Talia holds her phone out to me, showing me pictures of fingernails.

Fuck, what am I doing? I could try to get it up for Talia tonight, but the reality is, I'd close my eyes and see Sara. Her red hair spread out on the pillow. Her pink lips parted as she comes around my cock.

Finn is right. I can't keep doing this. Even Talia deserves better.

The waiter brings me a fresh glass of scotch and I sip it. Drew gives me a nod as he lifts his glass and takes a drink. He casually brings his fingers to his nose to smell her.

Fuck, I shouldn't be envious of *that* guy. Even though I've seen her come, I haven't felt her pussy convulse on my fingers or tasted her on my tongue. I don't know what her arousal smells like.

But Drew knows. Sara has to be serious with him. She wouldn't do that with just any guy. She doesn't use guys the way I use women to try to get over her.

This should be for the better. Sara's moving on. She's finding someone who's free to love her the way she deserves.

I should be happy for her, but my insides roil like a stormy ocean. I toss back the rest of my drink.

"We're leaving." I can't be here anymore. I can't watch her be happy with another man.

"Someone's anxious to get to dessert." Talia smiles and grabs her clutch.

"You're going home alone." Standing, I pull her chair out.

"But, you said..." Her red lips press into a line. Her bright blue eyes narrow on me. Her disappointment clear.

I'm done playing with her. This should've never happened. I should've never asked her out again. I could tell her *this is a me-not-you thing*. The woman I'm obsessed with is moving on and I can't handle it.

"I need to use the ladies' first." She strolls off to the bathroom before I can stop her.

I shouldn't have responded to Talia's text, but with Sara in the office, without Tom, is too much of a temptation. She works quietly and doesn't beg for my attention, but I can feel her there. Just out of reach but so fucking close.

Lowering into my chair, I pull out my phone. Maybe I'll call Talia a car. It would be easier than dealing with her octopus arms when I drop her off. When I get home, I'll drink myself into a stupor so I don't feel anything.

"Hey." Drew gestures to a chair at my table, like we're fucking friends. Not like he's my worst nightmare.

I nod, because otherwise everyone will wonder why I'm snubbing Drew Young. Fucking gossipmongers.

"No hard feelings, right?" Drew leans back in the chair like he has every right to be with Sara. The thing that really pisses me off is, he does.

"About what?" My scotch glass is empty so I take a sip of my water, feigning nonchalance when I want to throttle this man for taking what's mine.

"Making your girl come when you can't touch her." Drew glances toward the bathroom door. "She's still not over you."

"What are you hoping to accomplish?" I lean my elbows on the table and glare at him. He's like a used car salesman in a nicer suit. Sara deserves better than him and better than me.

"That you'll recognize what an ass you are." Drew's devil-may-care smile slips and his eyes drill into me. "You didn't see her when she realized you were here. With a date."

"She wasn't supposed to be here." Not that it mattered that she was.

"It's like all the happiness died inside her." He ignores my statement. His eyes soften as he looks toward the bathroom again. "You did that. You took away the brightness from her pretty green eyes, so I gave it back to her."

Fire blazes inside me, knowing he's had his fingers on my girl—fuck—Sara. She's not mine. But I've been taught not to react in public. So I narrow my eyes on him and wait until I have his full attention. "Sara is—"

I can't fucking say it. I can't say that Sara isn't mine. She is and always will be, no matter who puts a ring on her finger and claims her as his own. She'll always be mine.

"The best thing that's happened to me, man." Drew grins. "I want to give her *everything* she desires."

My brows furrow because I'm not sure he just means sexually. "She deserves the best."

Drew nods. "I couldn't agree more. When you realize what she actually needs, call me."

He tosses a black card on the table before me. A number is printed in gold.

"I'm sure you'll figure it out sooner or later." Drew nods. "Or you could just ask her. She's an honest woman and doesn't hide her feelings. I like that about her."

I make a noncommittal noise as I tuck his card into my suit jacket. It might be useful to have.

Drew leans in close. His words only loud enough for me. "Stop fucking things up though. That Barbie doll you paraded in here can't be what you want. But you know that hurts her, don't you?"

"Sara wasn't supposed to be here." I glare at him.

"It wouldn't have mattered if she wasn't. It still would have hurt her."

His sincerity shines through. If anything, this guy isn't a bullshitter.

"I can't tear my friends apart." I rub the back of my neck.

Drew chuckles as he leans back. "Maybe you should check in with your *friends* on how they feel about Sara."

My brow furrows. What the fuck does that mean?

He rises. "Don't fuck this up, man. Pretty sure the only way this works out is as a package deal."

Sara

I'm finishing touching up my lipstick when Wyatt's blond walks into the bathroom.

My gaze follows her as she saunters to the counter next to me. Her eyes meet mine in the mirror.

"Oh, Siren Red, my favorite." She points to my lipstick and smiles. "It goes really well with your complexion."

I slide it back into my clutch. "Thank you."

"I've seen you around." She touches under her eye like her perfect makeup was trying to get out of line before she swings her bright blue eyes to me. She scrunches her lips and taps her finger over them. "There aren't that many natural redheads around. Are you related to Tom Morris?"

"Yes, he's my brother."

Her eyes brighten more, if possible. She reaches out and grabs my arm. "Tom is Wyatt's best friend. I'm surprised we haven't met. I'm Wyatt's official plus one, Talia."

She releases my arm and holds her hand out to me. Her fingernails are long enough that she can't do much work and there are sparkling gemstones in each of her rings.

I take her hand and shake it. "Sara."

"Who are you here with tonight?" She leans in conspiratorially as if she's digging for gossip.

"Drew Young." I really don't want to talk more with this woman, knowing she'll be sharing Wyatt's bed later.

"Oh, I've been meaning to call him. He's quite the catch." She wiggles her eyebrows. "Good on you, girl."

"Wyatt is quite the catch." I don't choke on those words.

Talia laughs. "He's fantastic if you can convince him to sleep with you. I was hoping tonight, but..." She gives me a fake pout that makes my heart feel lighter.

"You aren't..." I don't know how to finish that statement.

She shrugs and gives me a mischievous grin. "He asks me out from time to time and early on he'd fuck me, but lately, he doesn't return my calls or come out with me."

Fuck, I'm feeling better by the minute.

"He was game when he texted me the other morning, but now—"

"Which morning?" I need to know.

"Tuesday. I swear, I can't get a read on that man. Hot and cold. He was definitely ready to fuck me when he texted." She smiles at herself in the mirror. "Maybe he drank too much scotch and can't get it up. No one wants to admit that. If you know what I mean."

I don't, but Tuesday morning was when we had that moment. Fuck, was he just particularly horny then and I caught the byproduct of it? My heart bursts into a shower of burning confetti, falling right back into my stomach.

"Have a great night." I back away from the mirror, suddenly wanting to be anywhere but here.

"Don't worry. I've got a guy on backup if Wyatt doesn't put out.

Sometimes, us girls need a few guys just in case one doesn't satisfy us." She smirks. "But from what I've heard about Drew Young, you enjoy that ride while it lasts, girl."

"You've been quiet. Did I push you too far in the restaurant?" Drew squeezes my fingers. We're in the back of his car heading to my place. Earlier, I was excited about inviting him in tonight, but now, my head is a mess.

"Hmm." I turn from blindly staring at the passing lights out the window. "I'm sorry. I'm distracted."

He nods. "I've noticed."

"It's not you." Facing him, I squeeze his hand back. "Just a lot on my mind."

"If you don't want me to do things to you in public, princess, just tell me. I can behave." He lifts my knuckles and presses a kiss against them.

My heart flutters, but it still feels really battered and bruised. I sigh. "Would you be upset if I didn't invite you inside tonight?"

"Not at all." He holds my hand against his heart. Its beat is strong and steady. "I'm willing to wait as long as you need."

"I just don't understand anything anymore."

He pulls me into his side and wraps his arm around my shoulder. "You're in this tricky situation that could go sideways really fast or spin so out of control you wind up on your ass. But you know what?"

"What?" I glance up at his face in the dim interior of the car.

He smiles and kisses my temple. "I'm on this ride. You can try to shake me off, princess, but this time, I'm not going anywhere."

I draw in a breath and lean into his side. "That helps."

"Good." He rubs my arm. "I'm just glad I got to give you a little pleasure tonight."

My neck heats. "I've never done anything like that."

"I'm not surprised." He tips my chin up and I can just make out his features in the dim streetlights. "Was it okay? Because I can keep things more tame when we're out and about."

I slide my hand around the back of his neck and draw his lips down to right above mine, holding his hair to keep him from claiming them. I search his eyes as best I can.

"If you like it, I like it. Though I'm hoping my mom doesn't hear about it." I bring his mouth down to mine. We make out the rest of the way to my house until I'm a half second from inviting him in anyway.

He walks me to my door and stops a step lower than me, bringing us closer in height with my heels. "I had a lovely time tonight."

I grab the collar of his suit jacket and pull him in to kiss him again. Every kiss lights me up and makes me feel better about this whole night. He slides his hands over my ass to draw me in against him.

"When can I see you again?" I look into his golden brown eyes, seeing how much he wants me.

"How about in an hour?" He captures my lips again and sucks on my lower lip.

When he draws back, he moves his hands to my hips.

"I'm pretty sure I could fall for you, princess." He brushes my hair behind my ear and sighs. "If I didn't have plans this weekend, I'd spend the entire time making you mine."

I bite my lip as he steps down a step.

"What kind of plans?"

He lifts my hand to his lips and winks. "Secret plans."

Pressing a kiss to my hand, he draws me down a step and kisses me senseless again.

"If you aren't coming in, you'll need to go soon or the neighbors will talk." I half hope he offers to come in.

"Fine, but let them talk. My intentions are honorable, princess." He brushes his lips over mine and turns me toward my door. "Now get inside before we make a spectacle of ourselves."

He slaps my ass as I move. I cover my offended cheek and give him a glare.

He chuckles and winks. "We'll play slap and tickle another time."

I shake my head as I go to the door. After I unlock it, I turn toward him. "Wait, when will I see you again?"

He never answered my question.

"How about brunch on Sunday?" He goes down a few more steps with a boyish smile that makes my heart spin.

"What's with you and brunch?" I push the door open behind me and hear the beeping of the alarm system.

"Brunch is the perfect meal, princess. Everyone can get exactly what they want. Now go inside so I can go home and imagine you in my bed." He steps down to the sidewalk.

The temptation to ask him in is on the tip of my tongue, but my insides are all tangled up.

"Good night." I step through the door.

"Good night, princess. Sweet dreams."

Chapter 20

Unbalanced

Sara

Something heavy drops on the floor, waking me from a deep sleep. I bolt upright, completely disoriented. Peabody barks furiously into the darkness.

I'm on the couch. Fuck, why am I on the couch?

"Peabody," I whisper yell.

"Fuck." A man's voice has my heart racing.

I fumble for the light, and for a moment, it blinds me.

"Call off the little bastard." Wyatt's voice calms my heart. Peabody makes enough noise to wake the dead.

"Peabody, leave Wyatt alone." I rub my eyes, trying to remember what the hell happened.

Peabody jumps on my lap and growls in Wyatt's direction.

"Peabody," I scold, but he just settles on me, never taking his eyes off Wyatt.

I finally look up at him. He's wearing jeans and a t-shirt. There's a small table on its side behind him.

"What are you doing here?"

"Why are you down here?"

We speak at exactly the same time. Peabody growls until I pet him. I don't know why Peabody doesn't like Wyatt. Tom always encouraged it though.

"What do you mean why am I down here?" I smooth my dress down. After Drew left, I watched some TV and I must have fallen asleep. It's been a while because the TV shut off.

"You weren't in your room." He points to the staircase.

My eyes narrow on him. Something isn't lining up. "How do you know that, Wyatt Hawkins?"

I stand and Peabody growls on the couch next to me as I step closer to Wyatt. The only way he'd know is if he could look in my room. There's only one way to look in my room currently.

Some of the anger leaves Wyatt's face and he actually looks chagrined.

"Wyatt, how do you know I wasn't up in my bedroom?" I take another step and poke him in the chest with each of my next words. "Answer me right this minute."

He backs up and runs his hand through his hair. "It's my camera."

I take a step backward and cover my mouth. Heat fills my neck and face as I realize what I did. What he might have seen. "Oh, fuck."

"I had Dante set it up so we could check it if something happened to you."

Which sounds reasonable until you factor in earlier today. And the fact I was out with Drew.

"Were you checking to see if Drew spent the night?" I step forward again, trying to ignore the tingles that race through me at the thought of him watching my "show" earlier.

"I was making sure you were okay." He straightens like I offended him. "You wouldn't have a guy spend the night if your parents were home."

I want to throw in his face that my parents aren't home and that if I wanted Drew to stay the night, he could have. But that would open up a can of worms I'm not ready to deal with.

"I was fine until someone broke into my place." I cross my arms over my chest and suddenly remember he knows I'm not wearing a bra.

His gaze drops for a split second and I groan.

"Wyatt, that's an invasion of my privacy."

"Tom's gone and he's worried something will happen to you." He takes a step closer. "*I'm* worried something could happen to you."

"So you watched me in my *bedroom?*" A wave of heat rushes through me. He saw me masturbating, and I mean, he saw everything. When I thought it was for Dante, I was taunting him. He'd already seen everything anyway. "That wasn't for you." The words burst out of me.

Wyatt closes in on me again, forcing me to look at his chest or tip my head up to maintain eye contact. "Who was it for, Sara?"

I narrow my eyes and purse my lips. "Fuck you, Wyatt. You don't get to invade my privacy and act all self-righteous about it. You need to leave."

His hand lifts and my breath catches. Will he touch me? I still can't believe I poked him in the chest, but if he touches me, all those walls I've built around my heart will crumble.

"Leave, Wyatt," I say quietly. For a second, we both just breathe, so close to touching but not.

He lowers his hand and his head and backs away. "Be safe."

Dante

It's still early when Sara storms into my office and sets the little camera on my desk. "My bedroom is off-limits."

I take a breath and stare at the camera. "I left it where you could find it."

She turns and looks at the door. She crosses the room and closes it before coming forward and putting her hands on my desk.

"Wyatt came by last night because I wasn't asleep in my bed." If she could shoot daggers from her eyes, she would.

"Where were you sleeping, pip?" I'm not sure I want to know.

"Not that it's any of your business, but I fell asleep on the couch."

"The camera was for your own good." I set my pen down on the desk and rock back in my chair.

"My own good?" She looks about two seconds from blowing up. "You put a camera in my *bedroom* and I knew you were the last one in there. Trust me, when I found it yesterday, I gave you one hell of a repeat performance."

She pushes off my desk and crosses her arms.

Fuck, it's early and I haven't had enough caffeine to deal with this. "Repeat performance?"

She glares at me. "Seriously?"

Slowly, it registers. Oh, fuck. I laugh. Fuck, I don't mean to, but it bursts out of me. All those years of keeping her away from Wyatt and then I basically set a ticking bomb between them.

"This isn't funny, Dante." She looks livid. If looks could kill, I'd be dead and buried.

"No, you're right. This isn't funny." I straighten in my chair and can't help but imagine exactly what Wyatt saw. I saw firsthand, and she puts on an amazing show. He's been in denial about his feelings for Sara forever.

"If Tom were here, I'd tell him what you two did and what Wyatt saw." She's gone stubborn now but she didn't say what I saw, only what Wyatt saw.

"Good thing Tom isn't here then." I rub my chin.

Like all the energy goes out of her, she drops into the chair across from me and puts her face in her hands. "What am I doing?"

"Living?"

She lifts her green eyes and returns to glaring at me. I hold my hands up in surrender.

"Seriously, pip. For years, you put yourself on hold for Wyatt. Now you're actually living. I have to admit, I like this side of you."

"Of course you do. I give a really good masturbation show," she says grumpily.

"You do." Fuck, I'll admit it's been my go-to memory to get off to recently. "But you have this spark that I've been watching die for years and it's back."

Sighing, she drops her hands onto her lap. "I don't know what I'm doing, Dante. I'm dating Drew and he seems okay with the fact that I've been kissing you and Finn—"

"Whoa, pip. Me *and* Finn."

Her cheeks blossom pink. "Um, yes."

With fresh eyes, I look her over. She does seem more confident. More in possession of herself. More tempting than she ever did before. I'm not surprised Finn noticed.

The misery clicks. "But not Wyatt."

She shakes her head. Of course not.

"Do you want him too, pip?"

She blows out a breath and throws her hands up. "I don't know what I want anymore."

I lean my elbows on my desk and study this woman I've known practically my whole life. It's weird that things are changing, but I'd be lying if I didn't say they changed years ago. This unspoken agreement between the three of us to not go after Tom's sister went into effect and we all decided a hands-off approach was best.

Tom kept her away from us as much as possible and then I got tapped to run interference when she decided to charge headlong in Wyatt's direction. Wyatt was the first to back away from her because his obsession with her was too much.

"Whatever you choose will be right, pip, if it's right for you."

Her pale green eyes collide with mine. "What if I don't want to choose?"

173

Sara

After my outburst in Dante's office, I sequestered myself in Tom's. I even ordered lunch in. I asked my dog walker if she could keep Peabody for the night.

Even though I haven't decided what I want to do, I'm tempted to call the girls over to hang out and get their read on things. But I still hesitate to text them.

I could text Drew and tell him what happened. He'll give it to me straight, but part of me just wants to be alone and veg on the couch with some *Bridgerton*.

"Quitting time, flower." Finn stands in my doorway, casually leaning against the jamb like he's on the cover of a magazine.

I blow out a breath. I'm not ready to confront any of them yet.

Once I shut down my laptop, I put away my stuff.

"You okay?" Finn steps into the room and puts his hands on the back of a chair. His dark hair falls over his green eyes.

"Yeah, it's just been a long week." I grab my purse from the drawer and put it on the desk. "Lots to think about."

He nods. "We'll figure out where Tom went soon, flower."

Tom is the furthest thing from my mind right now. I want to know what happened to him too, but so much is happening with me. Confusing stuff that I've just been letting brew.

"You want company tonight?" He raises an eyebrow and desire pours through me, thick and heavy.

I could lose myself in him, but that wouldn't be fair. "I think I'm just going to veg at home."

"If you change your mind, text me." He gives me a wink and leaves.

I haven't seen Wyatt all day. I'm not sure I want to see him. The whole situation is a fucking mess. I wish I could say I'm embarrassed that he saw me do that, but I'm not. Part of me wishes I'd been bold enough to do it years ago. Maybe things would be different now.

But something tells me this collision course was set before I even knew about it. It's not like Finn and Dante just noticed me. There have been moments over the years. Heart-wrenching moments when I knew I could make a decision and lean in one way or the other, but somehow it wasn't the same without Wyatt.

Purse in hand, I text Brandon that I'm ready to go.

When I step into the hallway, a throat clears and I look up to meet Wyatt's dark eyes. I sigh and wait, because he's the one who showed up at my house. He's the one who needs to apologize.

"I'm sorry." His tone is gruff but his eyes are sincere.

"Okay." I don't know what to say besides that. He tipped my world upside down last night. I thought I was getting over him. But then I saw him with Talia and it burned me deep.

"Sara, I—" He steps forward.

"I can't." I flinch away from him slightly. "I'm sorry, but it's been a long day and I just can't deal with this anymore. I want to go home, maybe have a bath, and just think about this week. Maybe something will pop up that I missed with Tom. But I really just want to go home."

He backs away a step. "I didn't mean to upset you."

I sigh, because that's the problem. "Trust me, I know."

He rubs the back of his neck.

"You were trying to protect me because Tom asked you to. You went about it in the wrong way, but I'm..." I take a breath. "I'm grateful you're looking out for me."

Pretty sure I manage a small smile too, but I'm so done right now.

"If you need anything this weekend..." He lets it trail off like he always does.

I ignore the tears choking my throat. It's never him that will help me. It's always Dante or Finn.

"See you Monday," he says quietly.

I hurry to the elevator and catch it just as the doors are closing.

"Hey, Sara, how was your first week?" Greg smiles. He looks friendly, but I've caught his eyes checking me out.

"It was great." There are plenty of others in the elevator so I just pay attention to the numbers as we descend.

When I step into the lobby, Greg says, "Have a great weekend."

"You too." I lift my hand and give him a tight smile.

I get to the car without any other distractions and lean my head back as we make our way to the house. What am I going to do? It's not like I'm hurting anyone by messing around with the others. Drew doesn't care. Dante doesn't seem to care. Finn doesn't care about Drew, but doesn't know about Dante.

My heart pinches and I put my hand over it. Then there's Wyatt.

Talia implied he wasn't going to sleep with her last night. And he was at my house late. I can't do this dance again. I can't keep beating my head against the same wall and hoping for different results.

For whatever reasons, Wyatt doesn't want me. That should be the end.

"We're here, Miss Sara," Brandon says.

"Thank you." How long was he parked before he told me?

"Are you going out again?" He meets my eyes.

"Not tonight." I slide out of the car, walk up my steps, and open the door. The alarm begins its beeping so I wave to Brandon and duck inside. After I turn off the alarm, I head into the kitchen, almost forgetting that Peabody is at the sitter's.

My head is not on right. I just want to change into pajamas and stuff myself with junk food and romance shows. I pull up the pizza app and order a medium on the way up the stairs.

When I open the door to my bedroom, I freeze. Every drawer, every surface has been tossed onto the floor. I back into the hallway.

My phone is in my hand and without a second thought, I dial a number.

"Yeah?"

"I need you."

"Are you safe?"

"I don't—"

"Sara, are you safe?"

I turn and run to the hallway bathroom and lock myself in. My hands shake. "Come quick."

"I'll be there. Two minutes."

Chapter 21

Just-in-Time

Dante

I'm out the door with Sara still on the phone. I can hear her panicked breathing. Sweat rolls down my body, but the gym is only a few blocks from her townhouse. I don't hesitate to run over there. On the way, I notice the cell must have disconnected.

She wouldn't call me unless it was an emergency. But it wouldn't matter if it was just a spider in her bathtub, I'd still come running for her. Though from the tone of her voice, it was something far worse than a spider.

I punch in the code for the door and fling it open. "Sara!"

The alarm is set so I walk to the panel to stop it from beeping. I glance around to see if anything is off. Anything that would make me think someone was still in the house.

Lifting my phone, I redial her number.

"Dante, I'm upstairs in the hallway bathroom. Someone was in my room." Sara's voice is quiet, like she's whispering into the phone.

Fuck, if Wyatt hadn't been a dick to her, that camera would still be there and we could have checked out the playback to see who it was.

"Are they still here? Did you see someone?" I grab an old baseball bat out of the umbrella stand.

"I didn't see anyone. Please hurry."

"I'm here, pip. I'm coming." Putting my phone on speaker in my short's pocket, I make my way through the first floor. "Where's Peabody?"

"Pet sitter." Her voice is small and tinny, but I hear it.

"Good." I check all the windows and doors as I pass them until I reach the staircase. "I'm on my way up."

"Okay." The terror in her voice is real.

I blow out a breath and hold the bat up, ready to swing if someone comes at me. The fourth stair up creaks, so I step over it. When I get to the upstairs hallway, I hold my breath.

No sounds come from anywhere up here. If someone is here and wants to get out, they'll have to go through me.

The first door is her parents' bedroom, which is untouched. As is Caitlyn's bedroom next door. But Sara's looks like someone tore through it. Tom's isn't much better. Fuck. I pick my way through the wreckage to check the bathrooms and the closets. But there isn't anyone in any of the rooms.

Setting the baseball bat to the side, I make it to the hallway bath and knock "Shave and a Haircut." The door flings open and Sara bursts out. Her arms wrap around me so fucking tight. Her whole body trembles as I fold my arms around her.

"What if Peabody had been here?" Her voice is muffled in my shirt.

"He wasn't." I draw my phone out and disconnect our call. I have to make sure we're all safe. I dial Finn.

"Why would someone do that? And the alarms were active when I came home. Nothing suspicious at all. They could've still been here and I would've walked right in." Tears fill her voice and my chest aches for her. I know I'm not letting her out of my sight again.

No more outs. She's coming back to our place.

"Shh, pip. Let me talk to Finn."

"Hey." Finn's voice comes through the phone.

"Are you home?" I keep one hand between Sara's shoulder blades, holding her close as she clutches me. Her fingers are wrapped in the back of my t-shirt. The tremors are fading and hopefully the tears too.

"Yeah, where are you?"

I'm not answering that right now. "Check Tom's room."

"What?"

"Just go to Tom's room and tell me if anything is out of place."

Sara sighs against me and rubs her face in my damp shirt. Fuck, I must stink. I'd been working out and then the run here. Sweat rolls down my back. My cock is definitely getting the wrong idea with her soft body against mine.

"Strange, but okay." Finn opens a door. "The only thing missing is Tom. Now, what's this about?"

"Thanks. I'll tell you later." I disconnect and tuck my phone back in my pocket.

"The house is clear." I rub my hands down her back. "But you can't stay here."

"I'm not moving in with Wyatt." Her tone is firm.

Fucking Wyatt. Of course he had to blow up everything. But I can't stay here with her all the time. The house isn't secure. Whoever is after Tom or Sara has proven that. I can't believe I'm about to say this. "What about Drew?"

"He's busy this weekend." Sighing, she rests her cheek against my chest. "It's too soon anyway. We haven't even slept together."

A little wave of relief flows through me. I shouldn't care if she's slept with him or not.

There's no other solution. She's coming with me if I have to drag her kicking and screaming. I won't be at ease until she's in our apartment, under lock and key. Our building has a doorman that every guest has to go through before even accessing our floor.

I'm not sure how they got around the alarm system, but I'm definitely setting up more cameras in here.

"Then you have to come to our apartment, pip. I can't leave you here alone."

She releases a sigh of defeat. "Not tonight."

She lifts her red-rimmed, pale green eyes and I'm lost. Something shifts inside me, just a little. I've always cared for Sara, but she's never been mine. In this moment, she's mine and all I want to do is protect her.

"I can't leave you alone—"

"Then don't, Dante." She takes a deep breath. "Stay here with me and I promise I'll go with you in the morning. I know I can't stay here alone, but I can't be near him. Not yet."

Wyatt. Nodding, I glance toward Tom's door. Tom's clothes will fit me as long as whoever ransacked the place didn't tear everything up. Destruction didn't seem to be their goal.

"I ordered a pizza." She steps back and looks me over. "Were you working out?"

"Yeah, my gym isn't far." My shirt clings to me from the sweat. "Fuck. I need to take a shower and see if Tom has any clothes left here."

She nods still a little dazed. "Roger might have something too."

"Tom's more my size." I take her hand to keep her with me as we go to Tom's room. I release her when she freezes in the doorway. Her face gets paler as she looks around at the mess.

"Who would do this?" She picks up a trophy and sets it on the shelf like putting one thing back will make this all better.

"Whoever Tom is running from is my guess." I grab a shirt and shorts before returning to Sara. I tip her chin up so I can search her eyes. Still there. Good.

"You can yell through the door or I can set up our phones while I shower." I move down the hall back to the bathroom she just escaped. After I place the clothes on the counter, I turn as the door shuts.

Sara shakes her head. "I don't want to be alone in the house. Not again."

I nod because I'll do whatever it takes to make her feel okay right now. "Do you want to turn around?"

Reaching into the shower, I turn on the hot water. She laughs behind me.

"Feeling prudish?" Her voice is closer and I glance to find her leaning on the counter across from the glass door of the shower. She shrugs. "I've seen your cock."

"Just trying to read the room, pip." I pull off my shirt with one hand and toss it toward the door.

She bites down on her lip as her heated eyes take in my chest and abs. I step forward and brush my knuckle over the corner of her mouth. "You had a little drool..."

"I did not." She bats my hand away.

I chuckle because she's going to be fine. I check the water and adjust the temperature. "How long until your pizza arrives?"

"Forty-five minutes to an hour."

I take my shorts and boxers off and they join my shirt.

She hisses in a breath, but all she's getting is my back right now. Of course, my ass is nicely toned. I take the time to treat my body right. My cock is already hardening knowing she's watching me, taking in every inch of me.

I step into the water and consider for a moment whether I should turn the dial to cold.

Sara

Someone was in our house. Someone violated Tom's and my rooms. It swirls in my head, but something else takes precedent. Dante's ripped back and that ass I could bounce a quarter off of.

And his cock. Fuck, it's not even fully hard and it's massive. Not that I have a lot to compare it to.

He steps into the shower and the water flows over his body, tracing every single inch of him until I can't stand it anymore. I unbutton my shirt and slip off my skirt. They both flutter to the floor silently as I undo my bra and shimmy out of my panties.

I can't get the smell of him out of my senses. Like a dark ocean in a storm. I want to be swept away by him.

When I open the shower door, he doesn't seem to notice until I touch his shoulder. His muscles tense against my hand and he freezes.

"What are you doing, Sara?" His voice is strained as I press against his back.

Oh, fuck, that feels so fucking good. His skin is hot and wet. Every inch of my skin tingles with anticipation. "Taking control of my life, Dante."

Everything has been spiraling out of control. Work. Tom. The guys. But right here, right now, I'm making a choice. I'm taking something for me. I'm giving something in return.

"Pip."

His voice has a warning in it, but I'm not listening to warnings anymore. I'll return to his apartment with him in the morning. I'll see Wyatt and know he saw all of me and still doesn't want me. But I know Dante wants me.

And I want him.

I glide my hands over his hips and he blows out a breath. The water is warm as it slides between the two of us.

"I don't want to think anymore." I move my hand over his thigh. My fingertips brush his now-hard cock. "I just want to stay in this moment. With you."

He turns slowly, giving me every opportunity to say *just kidding*, but I'm not.

"I won't fuck you when you're vulnerable, pip." His hand cups my jaw and his light blue eyes search mine with a fierceness I admire. Dante isn't afraid of what he feels, but he holds back a lot.

I don't want him to hold back anymore. "Then let me take care of you, boss."

I turn my head in his hand and part my lips around his thumb, sucking gently while watching the fire burn in his eyes. He wants me and I want him.

"Sara." My name on his lips is a surrender. It buzzes through me, but he's still not touching me.

I pop off his thumb and kiss his chest. My hands smooth over his hips. I've never had this opportunity to explore a man with my hands and mouth. I'm sure some guys wouldn't have minded, but I didn't want them.

Not the way I want him.

"You don't have to fuck me, Dante." I lick his salty skin. "I just want to explore."

His hands press against the tile on either side of my head. "Whatever you want, pip."

A thrill goes through me as I kiss his chest. Finding one of his flat nipples, I open my mouth around it and flick the hardened tip with my tongue. His breath rushes out, so I do it again.

I suction my mouth over it and run my hands over his hard ass, pressing my breasts against his hot skin. His body tenses against mine and I grow wetter between my thighs as my nipples harden against him.

His cock presses against my stomach. I want to touch it, but I want him to feel that anticipation the way I do. So, I work my way over to his other nipple and flick it with my tongue, before sucking on it.

"Sara." It's a plea. A worshipful word that makes me giddy. I want to worship him in a way I've never wanted to with anyone else.

My hands move between us and I lift my chin so I can watch his face. His head hangs. His wet, blond hair is bound in a bun with tendrils escaping it. His lips are firm, and if I could reach, I'd kiss them, tease them, part them with my tongue and taste every inch.

I wait there. His eyes are closed. My fingers massage his hips, waiting.

His eyes open and meet mine. I gasp at the heat in them. The restraint. Fuck, I want to unleash Dante. Unravel this perfect man.

I lean back against the tile, taking my skin away from his. I miss it as soon as it's gone, but I want to watch this and I want him to see.

I lower my eyes to his cock, jutting proudly from his hips. So thick and long. Honestly, it's beautiful. I drag my fingers over his hip bone and along his abs, feeling the muscles twitch beneath my fingertips, until my fingers brush his shaft.

My gaze shifts up to his face as I slide my hand around him. His lips part as he watches me tentatively stroke down to where his cock meets his body and then back up, stopping at the ridge of his head.

His eyes darken and my insides burn with need.

I return my gaze to his cock and trace my fingertips over the ridge and through the precum gathering at his tip. I bring my finger to my lips, tasting it. Salty and earthy.

He groans above me, but he's no longer trying to stop me. His light blue eyes remain focused on my hand. My pussy throbs, thinking about how it would feel to take him inside me.

To have him fill me with his cock. Stretch me to fit him. I lift my other hand to cup his balls.

"Fuck, pip."

"How does that feel?" I'm curious. Am I doing it right?

"Good." He lifts his eyes to mine and his arms tense against the wall.

I glide my fingers down the underside of his cock before dragging my nails lightly back up. How much control will Dante have before he breaks? It's an interesting problem I'm determined to discover the answer to.

He's so tall that if I dropped to my knees, I wouldn't be able to reach him with my mouth. So I bend at the waist and lick the tip of his cock.

"Fuck," he hisses. "Sara, you don't have to—"

Lifting my eyes, I meet his so he can see exactly how I feel. "I want to. I know how you taste. I want to feel you come inside my mouth."

Without waiting for him to try to talk me out of it, I lean and take his cock into my mouth, swirling my tongue around the head and tasting his precum. I hum at the solid feel of him before taking him deeper.

Wrapping my hand around the base of his cock, I stroke as I try to take him farther into my mouth.

"Pip, I'm going to come if you keep doing that."

I don't care. I want to feel this, to bring this man to his knees for me. I want control over my life. Wyatt saw me at my most vulnerable. I don't regret doing it or even that he saw it, but it wasn't meant for him.

The reason I did it, to drive *this* man insane. Because Dante wants me but never takes me.

His fingers thread into my hair and I worry he's going to pull me away. Instead, he brushes my hair to one side and strokes his fingers over my cheek.

"Do you like the way I taste, pip?"

I clench my thighs together as his words make me ache with need. I hum around his cock.

"You can take me deeper. Just breathe through your nose." His large hand cradles the back of my head as he pushes me down more. I moan around him, feeling him so deep inside my mouth that he's nudging my gag reflex.

"Swallow, pip."

When I do, he makes this pleased noise that rushes over me like warm rain.

"Do you want me to fuck your mouth? Take you hard and fast until you're filled with my cum?" His fingers relax on my head.

Fuck, I want that. I press into his hand and whimper. His other hand reaches down to cup my breast, holding it, molding it. When his fingers caress my nipple, sparks ignite throughout my body.

"I'll make sure you get what you need like a good girl." He threads his fingers through my hair and draws me almost all the way off his cock. "Use your tongue. Slide it through my slit and clean up the mess you're making of my dick."

My knees feel weak as I do what he says, tasting more precum.

"Good girl. I'll go slow at first." He presses my head, pushing his cock deeper into my mouth, past my gag reflex, and holds me there when I try to come off. "It's okay. Just swallow, pip."

My eyes tear up. I swallow and try to relax and breathe out my nose, but there's not a lot of air getting through. He draws me back and I gasp around his dick. My eyes lift to his and he's watching me with such tenderness.

When he pinches my nipple, I moan. My knees weaken as he pushes back into my throat. He gives me a moment to adjust each time, until he pushes in and I relax around him.

"Good girl. Faster now and then I'll fill you with my cum. You're going to swallow like a good girl, right, pip?"

I moan around his tip in my mouth, remembering the way his cum shot out of his cock in my bedroom. I press my hot pussy against the tile, wishing I was taking him deep inside me instead.

He begins to thrust his hips and move my head while tugging at my nipple. It's too much and not enough at the same time. His pace quickens as his breath comes out in sharp bursts. I suck on him, hollowing out my cheeks.

"Sara!" he bellows as his cock jerks against my tongue and hot cum fills the back of my throat. I swallow, trying to capture it all. I'm wound up and my pussy aches. But this is fulfilling in its own way.

Dante is here for me.

Chapter 22

Disclosure

Sara

Dante pulls my mouth off his cock and lifts me against him, claiming my lips with his. I wrap my legs around his hips as he presses me against the tile. My arms latch around his neck, clinging. Our bodies slide against each other. His skin scorches mine.

I burn for him and every touch just inflames me more. When his tongue demands access, I part my lips.

He holds my hip as he explores my mouth with his. His other hand slips below and his finger teases my entrance. A moan escapes me into his mouth and he smiles against my lips.

When his thick finger slides deep into my pussy, I gasp at the intrusion. I never thought we'd be like this. Naked in a shower after I sucked his cock. So close to doing so much more.

His icy-blue eyes are like the inner flame of a fire, hypnotizing.

"So fucking tight. Warm. Wet. Fuck." He thrusts his finger in and out as his gaze meets mine, making me whimper.

I want to beg him not to stop, to keep going. Make me his. But the words choke off in my throat. He already said he wouldn't fuck me.

"Tasting my cock turned you on, made you want more." His lips brush mine. "Do you want to come on my fingers, pip?"

"Yes, boss." I tighten my legs around him. My pussy presses against his abs. I need more. I want to fly with him. His fingers in me, his body pressed against mine.

Slowly, he adds another finger and eases them both inside me. It's almost too much.

"Dante." My eyes squeeze shut as he kisses me.

"Shh, pip, you can take it. You can take all of me like a good girl."

His fingers are long and thick, stretching me, making my pussy pulse. Need claws at my insides. I pant against his lips as he works them in and out of me, driving me insane. When he curls them, touching a part of me that makes me ache, I moan. I want to cry and beg and make him give me what I so desperately crave.

"Dante." My voice is ragged. This aching need inside me will destroy me, burn me into ash, if he doesn't release me.

"What, pip? Tell me where it hurts." His dark voice causes my pussy to clench around him.

I'm so on edge. I can't answer him. Words escape me, leaving me a mass of need in his arms. He could do anything to me and I'd let him as long as he gives me what I need.

His thumb smooths over my clit in slow circles, winding me even tighter. My breath catches. He presses against it, pulsing in time with his thrusts. His lips tease mine. "Tell me, pip, so I can make it all better."

My head falls back against the tiles as the pressure builds inside me, winding tighter and tighter. I'm a slave to the throbbing. My hips rock with his fingers thrusting in and out while his thumb torments my clit. I can't think. Can't breathe.

"So many things to do, pip. We could spend all night exploring each other and I still wouldn't get enough of you. Tasting you. Fucking you." He drags his lips down my throat before sucking where my shoulder meets my neck. He pumps his fingers in and out of my pussy in time with my heartbeat.

My breasts press against his chest and the taste of him still fills my mouth as the first wave takes me under.

For a second I don't breathe as ecstasy races through my veins. I'm aware of my mouth opening and his fingers driving in and out, but I'm lost in a haze of bliss.

"That's it, pip. Take your pleasure like a good girl. Squeeze my fingers like you want to squeeze my cock." Dante's words make me shatter again and I cry out as I drench his fingers with my release. "Good girl. So fucking wet and tight. I can't wait to feel you come on my cock. You'd like that, wouldn't you?"

"Dante," I breathe out. His fingers haven't stopped and that ache inside isn't easing, but building again, hotter, faster, threatening to consume me whole. It's too much and not enough at the same time.

He lifts his head. "Open those eyes, pip. Tell me who's fucking you."

"Dante." I open my eyes and stare into his confident gaze. His cocky smile pushes me over the edge. When I cry out as my release crashes over me, his mouth claims mine as he works me slowly through the orgasm, easing me back down.

My pussy stops convulsing as he holds his fingers still within me. When he withdraws them, I rest my head against the tile and stare into his eyes.

I'm still wrapped around him, naked. Fuck. Maybe he'll fuck me after all. I blow out a breath. He could pretty much do anything to me after that and I wouldn't protest.

He lifts me against him and walks us both under the water. I sputter a little and he laughs quietly. "Time to let go, pip."

My gaze jerks up to his, but he's just saying to release him so he can shower. When I loosen my hold on his waist, he lowers me to the ground. His cock is hard between us again.

I wet my lips and Dante chuckles.

"My eyes are up here, pipsqueak."

I lift my chin. He smiles down on me softly as he hands me the soap.

"No more play time. Get clean. We have a lot of work ahead of us."

————

After washing ourselves and drying off, Dante goes to my bedroom and grabs a pair of pajamas for me while I braid my wet hair. After we're both dressed, we walk down the hall and stand in the doorway to my room.

"Should we call the police?" I mean, we could've done it before the shower. Just looking at the mess they left overwhelms me. Everything that wasn't nailed down, they spilled all over my floor. I don't even know where to begin putting my life to rights.

"They entered with the alarm activated. Someone with that skill wouldn't leave behind prints." Dante picks up a picture frame. "We have no idea what Tom was into and what may trigger them to escalate. They didn't bother hiding they were here."

His gaze falls to the picture. It's of us one summer when we were kids. Tom, Dante, Finn, and Wyatt all have their arms around each other's shoulders, and I have my arms wrapped around Wyatt's waist and a huge grin on my face for the camera.

I should feel guilty about what I'm doing with Dante, but something about being with these men feels right. Finn and Dante, they're a part of my life. Drew is like a bonus I never expected to find. I don't want to stop with any of them.

"But if we call the police, they'll know to keep an eye out on my street." Even I know that a breaking and entering in the middle of the day may get an occasional patrol car drive-by, but it won't necessarily stop whoever did this. Not if an alarm system didn't.

"And they'll probably call the owners. We aren't filing an insurance claim." Dante picks up a diamond earring off the floor and shakes his head. "They weren't here for money. Let's focus on cleanup, pip. How do you want to tackle this?"

"I don't." I have to be honest. "Right now, it seems like too much. I don't want to tackle it at all."

Dante threads his fingers through mine and draws me back into the hallway, shutting the door behind us. "Then we won't."

Relief floods me. I should go through it, but I'm glad he's here. I'm not alone.

He leads me downstairs and into the kitchen. When he grabs my waist, I squeal as he lifts me onto the counter. Releasing me, he chuckles and opens the fridge.

"Drink?" He glances my way and heat fills me. With what happened in the shower, I need to be honest about something, but I'm not sure how he's going to take it.

"I think there's a bottle of white in there." I bite my lip. If I want this to go further, I need to come clean.

He grabs the bottle and holds it up. "Just the thing to go with pizza."

"I don't know if I ordered enough for both of us." I shrug. "Thought it would be just me, but I went with a medium because it was a long day."

"I'm sure I can find other things to eat." His smirk makes my panties melt, leaving my imagination to run wild with what his lips would feel like on my pussy. He sets the wine bottle on the counter and grabs the corkscrew. "What do we need to do to make you comfortable at our apartment?"

That's a difficult question because it's not me I'm worried about. It's *him*. I don't know that I'll be able to keep up the lie that I no longer want Wyatt. Sure, I'm moving on, but deep down, there's a part of me that will always belong to him.

But there are a few logistics to discuss if I'm staying in Tom's room.

"I'll need to wash Tom's sheets and bleach every surface." I shake my head because I know my brother is sexually active and I can only imagine the stains on his bed.

"Already done. With new sheets." Dante pulls the cork, flexing his bicep in the process. Fuck, he's all man. Every inch of him is lickable. And there's so much of him.

When I swallow, he glances at me with a smirk. "I had it cleaned after he left, but we have a service that comes twice a week."

I reach into the cabinet beside me to pull out two wineglasses and set them on the counter.

The smile that curves his lips tantalizes me. It's small and secretive like we share something now. We do, but he doesn't know that.

"I might have Drew over." I test the waters as he pours the wine.

"I wouldn't expect you to put your life on hold for this, pip." He holds out a glass to me and my fingers graze his, sending electric shocks through my system.

"You don't care that we just did that..." I point in the direction of the bathroom. "And I'm talking about having another guy over."

"No." Dante lifts his glass and clinks it against mine before leaning on the counter across from me. He's studying me and it makes me uncomfortable.

Do I want him to care? There's this tiny part of me that craves a little jealousy, a little possessiveness. Especially with what we just did.

I take a sip, refraining from gulping down the whole glass. "I'm not used to this."

"What's that, pip? Being with multiple guys?" Dante drinks his wine.

My cheeks burn as I think about what I've done and who I've done it with. But that's not what I'm talking about, at least not all I'm talking about. "You know I've had a crush on Wyatt forever."

Dante nods and cocks a grin. "I noticed."

"Yeah, I wasn't subtle about it." I swallow a few mouthfuls of wine. "So, I didn't really go out with guys I actually wanted to date, because I didn't want anyone else."

This is hard, but this is all stuff he probably figured out a long time ago. Dante always seemed to be there to lead me off or distract me if I got too close to Wyatt.

"This isn't new information, pip. I could tell you didn't like any of those men. And I can tell you like Drew." He swirls his wine. His pale blue eyes capture mine. "Are you worried about staying away from Wyatt?"

I shake my head and set my glass on the counter. Fuck, I don't know how to say this without saying this. I cover my eyes with my hands.

"I've never done what I did with you." Yup, confessing while not looking at him is much easier. Maybe I could just text him and make it even easier than that.

His wineglass clinks as it settles on the counter. His warmth closes in on me and his hands wrap around my wrists. I let him draw my hands down.

His eyes are soft. His thumbs trace the back of my hands, sending tingles through me. "Which part, pip?"

I groan, not wanting to admit it, but knowing I should. "All of it. I mean, I've kissed other guys."

His brow furrows as if he's trying to make sense of something. "Are you saying... ?"

I'm not saying it. I don't want to say it so I press my lips together.

Dante shakes his head. "No. There was that guy in high school. The jock that slept with practically the whole senior class." His eyes lock with mine. "You dated him."

"Dated, yes. He was an asshole. Pretty much thought he deserved it, so I punched him in the dick and told him I'd tell Tom if he tried to claim anything else happened."

He snaps his fingers. "You liked that one guy your first year of college."

I snort out a laugh. "Ethan?"

"Yeah, curly hair."

"He's gay." I lift my shoulder. "He was a lot of fun to bring around because he thought you all were hot too, so we would go to events and talk about you guys the entire time. I was sad when he coupled up."

He was my first best friend after my friends betrayed me in high school, but he moved for school and his man. We still text occasionally, but until Madison, Hope, and Kayla came into my life, I didn't have a best friend like him.

Dante's hands squeeze mine. Slowly realization crosses his face at what I'm trying to tell him without telling him.

"You're a..." It's like he can't wrap his head around the concept. "But you've been with Drew and Finn."

"I've *kissed* Drew and Finn." I blow a stray hair out of my face. My cheeks heat. "Finn went down on me and Drew has fingered me."

"Fuck." Dante tries to take his hands off me, but I wrap mine around his, holding him close. I need him to understand me.

"Just because I've never had sex doesn't mean I don't want to or that I don't think about it." I wait for his blue eyes to lift to mine. "It's gotta happen sometime. But I guess all those years, I was saving myself for Wyatt. I didn't want to do that with anyone else."

"Sara—"

I charge on. Now that it's out, I want it all out. "I gave up on Wyatt ever seeing me as anything more than an *annoying little sister* type. Honestly, I thought Drew was the perfect guy to do the job. He's kind of a man whore and he's good-looking. I really thought we'd have a weekend and it would be done with. I wouldn't be a virgin anymore and then I could truly get over Wyatt." Shrugging, I chuckle a little, defeated. "Who knew that Drew Young would want an actual relationship with me?"

Dante cups my cheek and his eyes sparkle with something I can't read. "Anyone would be lucky to have a relationship with you."

"Except Wyatt." And that's the issue. "Maybe I'm the problem."

Dante kisses me. His lips are soft on mine and when he parts his lips, I open for him, wanting more, but not trusting anything right now. I don't breathe as his tongue glides along mine. My insides shimmer with anticipation, but I'm still holding back.

He lifts his head and rests his forehead against mine. "I want you, pip. Your Drew wants you. Finn wants you."

I wait for him to tell me Wyatt doesn't want me.

"But I told you earlier, I'm not going to fuck you tonight and I mean it. You're not thinking clearly." His thumb traces over my lower lip. "We'll eat some pizza, drink some wine, watch a movie, and in the morning, we'll pack your stuff and head to our apartment."

Chapter 23

Co-Mingling

Dante

While we eat pizza at the dining room table, we talk about the week. Afterward, we move into the family room. Sara picks her comfort movie for the night, *Happy Death Day*.

When I settle on the couch, she sits beside me, but I pull her against me. Wanting her close, needing the connection. We've shifted a few times and now my back rests in the corner while she leans on my chest with the popcorn bowl on her lap.

As far as big reveals go, Sara being a virgin isn't one I was expecting.

My fingertips trail along her upper arm. I keep wondering if I should have known, but at no point did I feel she was that inexperienced.

Fuck, I shoved my cock into her throat.

Tom's going to kill me.

If Wyatt doesn't kill me first.

If Wyatt knew how deep her devotion to him went, he would have claimed her long ago. There's no way I can take that from her and him. Not even if she thinks that's what she wants. She may be mine now, but she's always been Wyatt's.

A friend of Sara's is in a relationship with four men. It was a publicity nightmare for a few months, but things have settled since they went public. They go out on dates all together. I've seen them. She gives them all attention and they all clearly adore her.

Could I imagine sharing Sara with Finn and Wyatt? Honestly, it's not hard to envision. Will Tom murder us all in our sleep? Probably. But add in Drew? Where the hell does he fit in? He's not one of us.

But if he means something to Sara, can I look past that? Because she doesn't seem to want to let go of any of us and no one has asked her to choose yet.

Wyatt doesn't know about any of this but Drew... He might be the tipping point for Wyatt.

Sara squirms on my lap, making my cock harden. Fuck, I wasn't lying about being able to go all night with her. The things I've imagined would make her blush. And that just makes my cock ache more.

Imagining showing her all the ways I can make her come.

When she squirms again, I draw her closer.

"What's wrong, pip?" I angle her chin so I can see her beautiful, frustrated eyes.

She wets her lips. "I'm... restless."

Her thighs shift together. When I grabbed her pajamas, I didn't realize they were a tank top without a built-in bra and shorts that bared her legs. After the kitchen discussion, I tried to keep my thoughts neutral and ignore her hardened nipples poking against the soft fabric.

The girl on the screen screams. I arch an eyebrow.

"Do horror movies turn you on, pip?" The backs of my fingers graze the side of her breast as I trail them down her arm.

She sucks in a breath. "No. But apparently Vikings do."

I chuckle, but she presses her ass back against my erection. "What do you want to do about it?"

She shivers against me and her legs fall open. Her hand slips beneath her shorts, but I grab her wrist.

"No, pip." I can't watch her fuck herself again. My self-control barely made it through the first time. "Let me take care of you."

I draw her arms up and wrap them around my neck, stretching her body over mine.

"Yes, please," she whispers and my cock jerks.

I skim my hands over her breasts. The cotton tank is soft to the touch, but I need to feel her skin. I gather the hem and slowly drag it up to reveal her breasts. I tug it off over her head and drop the tank on the floor.

Her fingers grab my hair tie and pull it loose, freeing my blond hair as she settles back against me. She slides her hands into my hair, sending little bolts of lust through my veins.

I move her slightly so I have the best view of her perfect breasts. In the shower, I held one and she pressed them against my back and chest. On her bed, they lifted with her every breath. But here and now, they're finally mine to explore and admire.

They fill my hands as I take their weight. She gasps softly. Her nipples are pink and small, pebbled into two peaks, begging for my touch, my tongue. I want to suck them into my mouth, but I don't want to move her again. Not yet.

Holding my finger in front of her lips, I whisper in her ear, "Suck on it, pip. Make it nice and wet for me."

She moans and takes my finger into her mouth, sucking, licking it to perfection. Her thighs shift against each other. I draw my finger out and rub the wetness around her nipple. She whimpers and arches into my touch. I hold my other finger in front of her mouth and she takes it in, sucking it, while I play with her nipple.

I remove my finger and use her saliva to slide around her other nipple. She releases a small moan. Her legs move restlessly as she squirms on me. When I pinch her nipples, she gasps at the sudden bite of pain.

"Tell me, Sara," my voice low and soothing, "what does a good girl do?"

She moans as I torment her nipples. "Whatever you want, boss."

"Mmm, good girl." I slide my hands down her sides and push her shorts down.

"I want to be your good girl." Her fingers dig into my hair.

I lift her hips and slide her shorts and panties off, dropping them with her tank on the floor. Her breath shudders in and out of her.

When my fingers slide along her wet pussy, she sucks in a harsh breath.

"I want to taste you." I kiss her temple as I shift with her. "Ride my face, good girl."

"Dante," she whimpers as I shift us into a position that will work.

I'm flat on the couch when I lift her and turn her. Dragging her up my body, I find her mouth with mine, while my hands explore her breasts between us. Her tongue slides against mine.

My shirt rode up when I shifted her so her bare pussy caresses my abs. How easy would it be to push my shorts down and slide my cock into her warm, wet heat? How good would she feel? So fucking tight. Fuck.

I drag her the rest of the way up until that pussy is right above my mouth. She kneels over me in the corner of the sectional and leans her arms on the back of it.

"You're so wet, pip." I part her pussy lips to look at her. Fuck, pink, glistening, beautiful. "Give me a taste."

I grab her hip and pull her down so my tongue can swipe along her pussy.

"Ahh." She tries to lift off me, but I grab her thighs and growl against her pussy. "Dante, oh, fuck."

I latch on with my mouth, suctioning against her clit. Needy little noises come from her throat as I circle my fingertip around her entrance before sliding inside, thrusting it in and out. She finds a rhythm, grinding against my face.

Needing more of her, I draw my finger out and slide my tongue into her pussy, taking her essence. She's heady, like a drug, and I want so much more.

"Oh, fuck." Her hand clutches at my hair as her first orgasm bears down on her.

I return to sucking her clit and thrust two fingers deep into her pussy, shattering her around me one more time. She cries out as she rides my mouth and fingers. I lick her clean while she comes down.

Dragging her down on my body, I find her mouth with mine and kiss her, letting her taste herself on my tongue. When her hips begin to rock, I break away from the kiss and lower her head to my chest.

"Just relax, pip." I stroke my hands down her bare back as she cuddles into me. I grab the blanket off the back of the couch and cover us.

Sara

Light hits my closed eyelids and something hard pokes into my hip. I blink open my eyes and see Finn sitting in the armchair. I fell asleep. On top of Dante. Naked.

Heat floods my face as I realize what this looks like. A blanket at least covers me.

"Good morning, flower." Finn's green eyes smile.

Dante grabs my ass cheek and grinds his erection up against me. I moan as awareness floods my body and my pussy grows wetter.

I lift to look down at Dante's sleeping face.

"You might want to wake him, flower." Finn gives me a flirty look. "He's likely to forget himself and plunge into your pretty little pussy."

"Fuck off, Finn." Dante shifts beneath me, making me acutely aware of how naked I am and he's not at all.

"That's not very nice. After all, I brought you both coffee and sweets, but I see you've already sampled the sweets." Finn reaches down to the floor and plucks up my pajamas and panties. "Yours?"

"Yes," I whisper.

"I take it Wyatt is the odd man out of who's seen you naked?"

My mouth opens and closes. "Technically, you and Drew haven't seen me naked."

"Care to change that, flower?" Finn's green eyes are alluring and I want to fall into them, but I'm also still a little sleepy and need to use the bathroom.

"Maybe after breakfast?" I pull the blanket around me and slide off Dante. I pause in front of Finn and hold out my hand.

"There's a fee." He lifts a dark eyebrow.

I roll my eyes but open the blanket. His gaze takes in every inch of me and I know Dante is watching. Fuck it. I drop the blanket entirely and hold out my hand for my pajamas.

Finn's darkened eyes meet mine. "Very nice, flower."

A shiver ripples through me, but he doesn't touch me. He holds out my pajamas and I take them and head into the bathroom. It's only a half bath, but Mom keeps spare toothbrushes and paste in there so I freshen up after I dress.

When I walk out, Finn and Dante both sit with their hands clasped between their knees and their heads practically together.

I clear my throat. "Am I interrupting?"

"No, pip." Dante stands and towers over me. His hand caresses my ass as he makes his way to the bathroom and closes the door.

"Come here, flower." Finn holds his hand out to me and I take it.

I've stopped trying to overthink this. I like each of these guys and I'm attracted to all of them, so who cares if I want to see where this can lead.

He pulls me down to straddle his lap. His thumb grazes my jawline as he wraps a hand around the back of my neck. "I heard something rather interesting. Something I suspected, but didn't have proof of."

I set my hands on his shoulders and tilt my head at him. "What's that?"

He smirks and gestures for me to come in for a secret.

I blow my hair out of my face and lean in.

He tips my chin to the side so his mouth touches my earlobe. A little shiver chases through me along with the tingles his touch causes.

"You didn't tell me you've never had sex, flower." He catches my earlobe in his mouth and sucks on it.

I gasp and squirm in his lap at the aching throb in my pussy.

He releases my earlobe and whispers, "Tell me, was I the first to put my tongue on your pussy?"

My breath catches and I whisper, "Yes."

The sound of approval he makes ruins my panties. "Good girl."

"You said you brought coffee." Dante's voice makes my cheeks flush as I turn my attention to him.

"Yes, we should have breakfast and help our girl pack." Finn helps me stand before rising and tipping my face up. His green eyes search mine. "To be continued, flower."

He captures my lips in a soul-searing kiss. Fuck, he's an excellent kisser.

Finn lifts his mouth from mine and groans. "You make me want to behave badly."

I laugh. "Isn't that how you always behave?"

He grins and tugs me into the dining room. Dante holds a coffee out to me.

"Mocha latte."

"Mmm, my favorite." I take it and sip with a little moan. My eyes widen at the box of pastries and my stomach growls. I pick a cinnamon scone and sit at the table.

Finn appears with a few plates and slides one under my scone. He returns my smile before sitting next to me and grabbing his own pastry.

Dante grabs the remaining pastries and puts both on his plate, taking the seat on the other side of me.

"So you're finally moving in with us?" Finn sets his coffee down, tears off a piece of his chocolate croissant, and pops it in his mouth.

I swallow my mouthful of coffee and blow out a breath. "Looks like."

I'm still not sure how this is going to work with Wyatt. Working with him is hard enough. Seeing him all the time, knowing I can't have him. What if he has a woman over? What if any of them have women over?

"So..." I pick at my scone and glance at Dante and then Finn. "You know what would make me more comfortable about moving in?"

"What, pip?"

I swallow. "If we have a no-women policy?"

Chapter 24

Inside Information

Sara

Fuck, they'll never go for this. A no-women policy. I don't really want to stay here by myself either though. Someone was in my house, and knowing they could return at any minute? While I'm sleeping? No, thank you.

Finn smirks. "Does that mean you can't be there, flower?"

I sigh. "I don't want to..."

Neither of them says anything.

"Fuck it. I don't want to see women come out of any of your bedrooms. If that's a deal-breaker, then I'll figure something else out." I take a bite of my scone. I'm messing this up.

"We'll have to run it past Wyatt. We weren't planning on having women over, but I can't speak for Wyatt. If it's your safety, we'll do it." Dante's blue eyes hold mine. "There's no way you're staying here alone, pip."

"But Drew can come over?" I've already asked and Dante's already said yes, but then the couch happened. I'm not sure what I'm doing, but I don't want to stop seeing Drew. Finn and Dante might just be toying with me, for all I know.

"If that's what you want." Dante doesn't drop his gaze. My insides burn again because what I'm asking for is ludicrous. It's their apartment. I'm a guest.

"So how far have you gotten with Drew, flower?" Finn leans back in his chair sipping his coffee. My lips press together.

"He's had his fingers in her pussy." Dante takes a bite of his pastry as he watches me. "I assume he made you come?"

I nod. This is so fucking embarrassing.

"Did you know she squirted for me?"

My gaze darts to Finn, who is talking only to Dante.

"Not surprised. She definitely came all over my face last night when she rode it."

"Oh my god!" What the actual fuck?

"She did get over her gag reflex pretty quickly though." Dante takes a sip of his coffee like they're discussing the latest football stats. "Took me beautifully down her throat."

Finn's heated gaze shifts to me and awareness courses through me. "Was his dick the first you sucked, flower?"

Licking my suddenly parched lips, I nod again. Need aches between my thighs.

"Dante isn't small. That's impressive." Finn arches an eyebrow. "Want to go for two?"

My mouth opens to say... what? I have no idea. So, I say, "You want me to suck your cock?"

What the hell is happening in my life? My nipples harden as arousal swells inside me.

"You want four guys, pip."

My brow furrows. "Three."

Dante just smiles and shakes his head. "Let me make you feel good while you make Finn feel good. Maybe you won't like having two men making you come at the same time."

I can hear Hope and Kayla and even Madison yelling at me to just do it. It's not like it will change anything. I've already had both of them go down on me. I want them both and don't want to pick one over the other.

Sipping my coffee, I look them over. I've flirted off and on with Finn over the years, but I never took him seriously. Dante, fuck, Dante shakes the foundations of everything I ever thought I wanted. I genuinely thought he didn't like me at all.

They're serious about this and so am I.

I arch my eyebrow at Finn. "Show me."

His grin is wicked as he undoes his belt and stands to undo his jeans and lower them to the floor. He's wearing black boxer briefs that do little to conceal his huge hard-on. My mouth waters and I take a sip of coffee as his dark hair falls over his green eyes.

They never leave mine as he lowers his boxers. I swallow and look down. Dante's definitely bigger, but not by much. Fuck. I press my thighs together.

Finn strokes his cock. "What do you think, flower?"

"I'm trying to figure out logistics."

"We've got you, pip." Dante takes my cup from my hand and lifts me onto the table. When he presses on my shoulders, I lie back on the cool wood. My breath shudders in and out of my lungs. Nothing like this has ever happened in my life.

I never imagined something like this *could* happen. Not with Finn and Dante.

Dante draws my shorts and panties off my legs, leaving me bare from the waist down.

"Wouldn't this work better on my bed?" Pretty sure Mom wouldn't approve of me using her dining room table to get off with two of my brother's best friends.

Before I can call the whole thing off, Dante shifts me so my head hangs off the edge of the table. Finn's hand cradles my head. His cock bobs in front of my face.

"You need me to stop, you tap on me three times." Finn's green eyes focus on mine. "Repeat it, flower."

"If I need you to stop, I'll tap three times."

His thumb traces my lower lip. "We'll do this in stages."

Nodding, I feel warm breath against my pussy and grow wetter. Finn slides his hand down my neck.

"Stage one, flower."

Dante's mouth closes over my pussy and I arch on the table as pleasure courses through me. Finn's hand holds me down as he slides it under my tank and over my breast.

"You have spectacular tits." Finn's touch is different than the way Dante touched me last night. But so is the way Dante licks and sucks on my pussy.

My shirt is tugged away and suddenly Finn takes my breast into his mouth and sucks. Moaning, I curve into him. Dante splays my legs out to the sides and sucks on my clit. It's too much and I shatter into a million pieces.

My breath freezes in my chest as I slowly come back to myself. Finn kisses his way to my other breast.

"Very nice, flower, but we want you to scream this time."

I barely take a breath before he takes my other breast into his mouth. Dante eases his finger inside me as he licks and nibbles on my clit. It should be a slow build but suddenly I'm right back on that edge.

"Fuck," I whisper as Finn does something with his tongue against my nipple while Dante sucks on my swollen clit. It tips me back over the edge. I cry out and my release gushes over Dante's finger. My breathing is ragged as Finn kisses up my neck, stopping to suck every now and then.

Dante slowly thrusts his finger in and out of me. His hot breath scorches my wet pussy, but he's not licking me, not sucking me.

"Stage two, flower." Finn kisses my chin before straightening.

He lowers my head and the smooth tip of his cock touches my lips. I open and he slides inside. My tongue glides over his cock as he keeps going deeper and deeper. When his abs press on my nose, I swallow around him.

He draws back until just his head is still in my mouth. Closing my lips tight, I suck.

"Fuck, flower, that feels good." He thrusts forward, deep again. A shiver works through me and my pussy pulses.

Dante's finger slowly moves in and out of me. His thumb slides over my clit and fire scorches me. Finn rocks back and forth in my mouth as I suck on him. This angle opens my throat more than when I took Dante last night.

But Finn's not going as deep.

"Stage three." Finn's fingers trail down my chest until he cups my breast while he fucks my mouth and Dante's finger slides in and out of me. Finn pinches my nipple and an explosion of pleasure flows through me.

I moan around his cock and Dante's mouth closes over my clit, pushing me over the edge, fast and furiously. I cry out around Finn's cock before he pushes it deep into my throat.

Dante adds a second finger, stretching me, and I'm falling apart at the seams. As one, they begin to fuck in and out of me, Finn in my mouth and Dante's fingers in my pussy.

I don't think I come down from my orgasm, just keep rolling with the same one as they continue to work my body. Finn's fingers pluck my nipple.

"I'm going to come, flower. You ready?" His voice is tight and I can feel his cock thicken in my mouth.

I hollow out my cheeks and suck on him.

"Fuck." He groans as his cock pulses hot cum into my throat. I swallow as much as I can. When he draws his cock out, I finish swallowing his release.

"You're spectacular." He lifts my head and kisses me upside down. His tongue sweeps through my mouth, tasting himself on mine.

Dante's fingers stretch me until my pussy convulses, tightening around them. "Good girl, pip."

"Catch your breath, flower, we're not done playing with you yet."

Finn's voice is dark and makes me shiver. I'm ready for whatever else they want to do to me.

Finn helps me sit upright on the table as Dante draws his fingers out of my pussy.

"You okay, pip?" Dante cups my cheek with his other hand. My pussy still pulses around nothing.

I nod as he searches my eyes.

He leans in for a kiss and I pull back.

"Finn..." I offer as explanation.

His blue eyes smile as he wraps a hand around the back of my neck. "I don't care, pip. Kiss me."

His lips claim mine and I open as he draws me against him. His shorts block his hard cock from touching my bare pussy, but the feel of him against me is divine. I moan into his mouth.

"What do you think, pip?" Dante lifts his head and once again his eyes search mine. "You good with two guys?"

"I could get used to it." I turn to find Finn watching us. There's no jealousy, just pleasure. "Have you two shared a woman before?"

Finn shakes his head. "No, flower."

Warmth blooms in my chest. That means this is a first for them too.

"We could take it further." My words are soft as I look up through my lashes at Dante.

"We will, but right now, we need to get you packed and moved into our apartment." Dante steps away. His cock is hard.

I move to the edge of the table and slide to the floor. I grab the waistband of his shorts and draw him closer. "Let me take care of you."

His hand slides into my hair. "You don't have to—"

"I want to." Sitting in the chair behind me, I draw his shorts down to expose his cock. I lick from his balls to his tip, never dropping my gaze from his.

Parting my lips, I take him inside my mouth. My pussy throbs with aching need.

Dante steps to the side and I feel hands parting my knees and drawing me close to the edge.

"Focus on Dante, flower. I'll take care of you." Finn's mouth closes over my pussy and I moan.

"Fuck that feels good." Dante caresses my cheek before his hand slides down my neck and over my breast. "Do you like it when Finn sucks your clit?"

Finn thrusts a finger inside me, in and out as I move on Dante's cock in the same rhythm. I'm so close to exploding again, but Finn draws his finger out of me and slides it back, circling my asshole with his wet finger.

Dante pulls out of my mouth as he caresses my breast and watches Finn. "Still good, pip?"

It feels weird to have Finn touching me there, but it's not bad.

"Good, boss."

Dante groans. I smile up at him, but Finn slides his finger into my puckered hole.

I gasp. "Oh, fuck."

That doesn't feel bad at all. He drags his finger out and slides it back in, slowly fucking my ass. Everything inside me sizzles. Finn's darkened eyes meet mine and he grins before leaning over and running his tongue over my clit. My lips part as he thrusts his finger deeper into my ass.

He latches onto my clit and sucks while he moves his finger faster inside my puckered hole.

I cry out as it becomes too much and I come all over him, my ass squeezing around his finger. Dante tips my chin his way and I part my lips to take him inside again, wanting to suck on him, needing to suck on him.

Finn doesn't let up. He slides two fingers into my pussy and thrusts them in time with the one in my ass. I moan around Dante's cock and his hand slides into my hair.

"Want me to take over, pip?" His blue eyes burn into me. I relax into his hand and his smile tips me into another release as he begins to fuck into my throat.

Finn sucks my clit and I'm lost in a haze of pleasure, tumbling into release, as they take my body higher. Dante groans as he comes in my mouth. I swallow him, taking everything inside, while coming again around Finn's fingers.

Dante withdraws his cock and Finn pulls away from me. I'm in a fucking daze. Literally. I think they fucked my brains out.

Dante lifts me into his arms and carries me upstairs.

Finn starts the shower running as Dante removes my tank top and his shirt. He lifts me back into his arms and walks me into the shower with him. When he lowers me, I lean against him, feeling completely boneless.

Finn steps in behind me and pulls me against him. I turn in his arms and hold on to him. His hand smooths down my back. "It's okay, flower. We've got you."

I sigh, because I know they do.

Chapter 25

Return on Investment

Wyatt

I'm desperately hungover when I wake. My mouth is dry. I look around completely confused. Where the fuck am I? I'm in some loft apartment on a leather couch. Fuck, what did I do?

"Coffee?"

I turn to squint at Drew Young in a kitchen I've never seen before. My head throbs. "Where the fuck am I?"

"My place. I couldn't let you crash at the club and didn't know if anyone was home at yours to make sure you didn't vomit all over yourself and die. Pretty sure my princess wouldn't like that."

Fuck. The smell of coffee perks me up and I open my eyes to a cup in my face.

"Hope you like it black." He sits down on a chair across from me.

"She likes cream in her coffee." I take a sip because my mouth tastes like ass. Not literally. I don't think.

Drew smirks. "I know."

Fucker. "What am I doing here?"

"You showed up at my club last night. Security called me. I came.

We drank. You were in no shape to get yourself home, so I brought you here." Drew takes a drink of his coffee.

"Why don't I remember any of that?" I rub at my head and Drew tosses me a bottle of pills. I catch them and wait for his answer.

"You were already drunk when you showed up at the Veiled Vixen. Kept saying you needed to see me." Drew gestures to himself. "You're lucky I was there last night or they might have called the police."

"Fuck." I set the coffee down, take two pills out of the bottle, and swallow them with another mouthful.

"What's going on, Wyatt?" Drew leans back with his cup. He glances at his watch, but doesn't seem in a hurry.

"You said to check with my friends on how they feel about Sara." Some of the fog is lifting from my brain. "The other night."

"Been stewing on that, have ya?" Drew chuckles. "Did you ask them? Did you ask her?"

"No." Fuck, no. I don't want to hear them say they have feelings for her. We all do. It's why none of us have crossed that line. "They wouldn't—"

He laughs. "I'm afraid you seem to be the only one upholding your neutrality agreement."

"You don't know—"

"Sara told me. She told me she's kissed both Finn and Dante."

My heart stops. My breathing stops. That can't be right. They wouldn't. They know what she means to me. Why I've pushed her away for so fucking long. Because of them. For them. So we would never have to make a choice.

Her or them.

Drew leans forward and pats my knee. "If it's any consolation, I haven't slept with her yet."

My mouth opens and closes. What the hell is happening in my life? Tom is missing and suddenly Sara is dating Drew and kissing Finn and Dante? Part of me wants to growl and snarl and claim what's mine.

But what if it's too late? What if she doesn't want me anymore? Not that I can have her. I take a drink of coffee. She was angry at me for watching her. She doesn't try to touch me or be near me anymore.

"Fuck, man."

My gaze jerks up to Drew. He shakes his head.

"Whatever you're thinking is bringing *me* down." He smirks. "What's going on?"

"She's mad at me." I run a hand through my hair. "I fucked up."

"So apologize." He shrugs like it's that easy. "Sara's a pretty chill woman. Beautiful. Open. Sexy as hell."

"Thanks." I wave off him telling me things I already know.

"Whatever messed-up chivalry thing you have going on, get over it." Drew leans forward. "They kissed her after I started seeing her. I know because she was worried about me and her being exclusive."

I narrow my eyes.

He chuckles. "Don't worry I didn't lock her into anything. At least not on her end. If she wants to explore more, who am I to stop her."

"You could be her boyfriend." I don't know why I say it. I don't even know why I'm here talking to Drew Young, of all people, about Sara.

He smiles. "Maybe, but Sara doesn't want just me."

The coffee and the pills are working on the pounding in my head, but my brain still isn't functioning fully.

"What's that supposed to mean?"

"It means she's been hung up on you for so long that she can't possibly know what she wants. Though it's getting clearer." Drew sits back and takes a drink of his coffee. "She wants me."

I scoff but it's true. I've seen it and my insides squeeze with the pain it causes.

"She wants Finn."

My gaze jerks up to his smiling eyes.

"She wants Dante." He shakes his head. "But she also wants you."

"What does that mean?" I'm not sure what game Drew is playing, but it's confusing when I'm hungover.

"It means, why are you here at my place when you could have the girl of your dreams?" He stands and walks into the kitchen.

"Sara isn't—"

His laughter cuts me off. "Fuck, even you don't believe that. She sure as fuck doesn't believe it. So make a move. Join the fun."

"Sara isn't just fun." Acid pours through my veins.

"You're right. She's someone I want to hold onto, but unless she gets over you, that's never going to happen. But if I'm on board with her being with you and being with me, then at least I get the girl."

I set the coffee mug down. I don't trust this guy. "What game are you playing?"

"No game. Not this time." He looks at his watch and grimaces. "However, I do have plans today. Feel free to rummage through my apartment to discover any hidden secrets. The door will lock when you leave, but I've got something I have to do."

He walks over to the chair and grabs his suit jacket from the back of it. Shrugging it on, he looks me over and sighs.

"Take a shower. Sober up. Have another cup of coffee. Make yourself an egg. Ask yourself why you came to me when you should have gone to Sara." He ruffles my hair and grins. "I have the feeling you and I are going to be best friends."

He goes to the door and salutes me before ducking out. Best friends, my ass. I lean back against the couch and look around. It's a nice apartment, but I'm not surprised. He did say I could check things out.

I blow out a breath and drink some more coffee. My phone is on a charger near me. When I lift it, the time says eight forty-five. I rub my hand over my eyes.

There are a few missed texts from Dante. From an hour ago.

DANTE:

Sara's coming to stay with us in Tom's room

Her parents are out of town

Someone tossed her and Tom's rooms at
the townhouse

FINN:

I can come help pack. Wyatt didn't come
home last night.

My heart slams against my chest. Fuck. The urge to go to her right away makes me rise, but Dante has her. Dante who I've always trusted to keep her safe when I couldn't.

I have access to some of the cameras in the house, but she took out the one I had in her bedroom, which would have shown us who was in there. Fuck.

We don't know who's after her or Tom or what they might be looking for. But Sara is in danger. I need to get home to see if we can figure out who was in the house.

My shoes are at the end of the couch. I pull them on and then snoop enough to find the bedroom, the primary bathroom, and a small half bath. I scrub my face and use a new toothbrush he left out to brush my teeth.

Pausing, I meet my eyes in the mirror. I've put my feelings for Sara on the back burner for so long. But what if my actions could have gotten her hurt? What if she didn't want to move in with us because of me?

I hang my head. If only it was just about that perceived boundary, but there's more to it. A reason Tom doesn't want me with his sister.

Fuck.

I glance around. I should really look through this guy's stuff and figure out what makes him tick. Especially if he's going to be in Sara's life. But I need to get home and see if I can find out who was in the house.

When I turn, Drew's desktop computer is right there. I bump the mouse and the screen comes on. It's not password protected.

He did say to make myself at home basically. I'll use his computer to check the feeds on the other cameras. That way Sara doesn't find me spying on her again.

Sara

By the time we find most of the things I need for at least a week and clean up a little, I'm tired and ready to crash. Brandon picks up Dante, Finn, and me and drives us to their apartment. After we unload the car, I let him know I won't need him this week.

"You call me if you do, Miss Sara. Anytime." He clasps my hand between his.

"I will."

He goes back to his car and leaves me standing outside Tom's building. A little chill goes through me. That creeping feeling of someone watching me rushes through my veins. I look around, but no one stands out. I shake it off and go inside.

Finn is at the front desk, adding me to the list and getting me an access card since Tom took his with him, wherever he disappeared to. I sent him a text this morning to let him know about our rooms. I even mentioned the creepy guy I saw.

But nothing. I don't even know if the messages were received.

I walk up to Finn and rest my head on his arm. At my touch, he slips his arm around my shoulder.

The doorman gives him a card and me a smile. "Welcome to the building, Ms. Morris."

"Thank you."

Finn leads me to the elevator and we ride up again to the apartment. Wyatt either isn't home or is in his room. I'm not brave enough to go looking for him. Dante told me he informed Wyatt about me moving in. So that should be fun when he shows up.

I didn't bring much. When we walk into the apartment, Dante looks up from the refrigerator. I had a little food that we brought too.

His smile is soft and makes my insides flutter. I don't know what any of this means. Are we going to do that more? Are we going to do more than that? Or will it all end because Wyatt is here too?

I drop onto their sectional and kick off my shoes. "What next, boss?"

Dante walks into the living room and sits across from me. "You want some lunch?"

Finn sits beside me and grabs my hand, entwining our fingers. My heart skips a beat.

"Lunch sounds good." My tongue darts out to wet my lips and I meet Dante's blue eyes. His hair is back in a bun, but it was silky between my fingers last night.

"Where's Wyatt?" I need to know.

"He didn't come home last night." Finn shrugs like it isn't a big deal.

My heart clenches. Did he go home with a woman? Is that why he isn't here? Because he's with her?

He isn't mine, but it still feels like a knife to the gut.

I lean my head on Finn's shoulder.

"Will it ever stop hurting?" The words are little more than a breath, but Dante and Finn exchange a glance. I'm messing around with three guys, but there's still someone I want and can't have.

Neither of them says a word. What can they say? I've known for years that Wyatt doesn't want me, even as I pursued him recklessly. The only person I was hurting with my obsession was myself. Tears sting the backs of my eyes.

Fuck. "I'm going to go unpack."

Finn helps me to my feet. I go into Tom's room and shut the door behind me. A tear escapes and I brush it away. What a fool they must think I am. I'm still not over Wyatt. Even though he's never been mine.

Maybe I should find a therapist. This isn't healthy. I don't understand it, but there's this pull I can't seem to shake. I know this obsession isn't good for me.

I draw in a shaky breath and open my suitcase. Acting on instinct, I put things away, not focusing on anything in particular. Knowing that at any moment Wyatt will come home from his night out.

Will he smell like her? Will he brag to his friends about the woman he went home with? That sounds worse than seeing her come out of Wyatt's bedroom.

I lie down on the bed and curl into a ball. I can't go home and I have nowhere else to go. I need my little furball.

Fuck, Peabody!

I'm off the bed and out in the living room in a heartbeat. Finn stands.

"Everything okay?"

"Peabody." I grab my phone and text the sitter. She responds and lets me know she dropped him off at the townhouse ten minutes ago. My shaking hand covers my mouth.

"What is it?"

"I have to go." I glance around for my purse. Fuck, did I leave it in Tom's room?

Finn grabs my shoulders. "What's wrong, flower?"

"The sitter left Peabody at home. What if they come back? What if they hurt him?" I'm close to tears again. Fuck.

"I'll go." He brings me around the couch and sits me down. "Dante should be back shortly. He went to pick up lunch. I'll go get Peabody."

"I can go with you." When I try to stand, he keeps me down.

"No, Sara. Let me go and take care of this. Stay here."

I swallow and he cups my jaw.

"I've got this." He kisses me gently before grabbing his keys and heading out the door.

I stand and pace, unable to sit still. How could I forget about Peabody? Maybe because I was wrapped up in two guys giving me orgasms?

It was so easy to just let them take care of everything. To let them sweep me into this life with them. Fuck, I haven't even told Drew that I'm living with them now. What will he think?

Probably nothing. He doesn't seem to have any hard limits when it comes to me. But still, I should let him know.

ME:

Can't stay at home. Moved in with the guys.

DREW:

Are you safe?

ME:

Yeah.

DREW:

Good. Brunch tomorrow?

ME:

Yes please

DREW:

Send me your address

I blow out a breath and some of the heaviness lifts from me. Drew is easy. I like that about him. I text him the guys' address and set my phone to the side.

Damn, it's quiet. I've never been in their apartment alone. I perk up. I'm *alone* in their apartment.

Standing, I rush over to the other doors. Which one to pick first? I push open Dante's door and step inside. It's neat as a pin. His king-sized bed is made with crisp white sheets. I'm tempted to jump on it and mess it up.

The whole room is big with dark wood furniture. He has a desk in one corner and a huge bathroom with an extra large shower, no tub.

The scent in here is divine and I spritz his cologne in the air to smell it. It's nice, but it smells so much better on him.

I make sure not to leave anything disturbed and go into the hallway. This time I pick Finn's door. I step inside and his cologne hangs heavy in the air. His dark sheets and comforter are rumpled on the bed. Clothes overflow his hamper.

He has books and notes all over his nightstands. I pick up a few and read the backs. Finn won't mind if I'm in his room and he probably won't be able to tell if I move anything. His bathroom is a jumble of stuff on the counter.

It fits him.

I walk out into the hall and stand in front of Wyatt's door. The others didn't feel like an invasion but Wyatt's does. Until I remember the camera in my room.

Pushing open the door, I wait for a second. After all, he could be in there. But when nothing happens, I walk inside. His cleanliness is somewhere between Finn and Dante. The bed is made, but not as neat as Dante's was.

His room is tidy, but there are little things out of place that tell me he lives in it. I drag my fingers over the red bedspread and open his nightstand drawer. I didn't go through the others' drawers.

Glancing over my shoulder at the open door, I purse my lips. I'm supposed to be a guest, but Wyatt put a video camera in my bedroom. I sit on his bed to see what's inside.

If he wants to play the invasion-of-privacy card, I have a trump card for that. There's a box of condoms. New. Bottle of lube. Also new. I set it on the nightstand and find a black box. I pull it out and put it on my lap. Curiosity rages inside me as I lift the lid off and stare at the toys inside. Sex toys. Fuck.

They're beautiful. Made of stone and glass. It's like art, but dildos. I trace my finger over a jade one. The stone is cold, smooth, and firm beneath my touch. My pussy throbs thinking of what he would do with these or how they would feel inside me. I gently return the box to the drawer along with the condoms.

It's possible he's used those before. Some lucky woman that he actually wanted to fuck. I sigh and head into the bathroom.

I'm picking through his cologne and aftershave, when the front door bangs open. My heart hammers.

"Finn! Dante!" Wyatt yells, but they aren't home yet.

I step out of his bathroom, but hesitate to reveal myself. He sounds pretty fucking mad. Maybe I should hide in the closet and hope this passes or one of the others gets home.

I take one step and lift my gaze at a movement by the door. Wyatt stands there.

Fuck, I'm caught.

Chapter 26

Risk Management

Sara

My heart lodges in my throat at the almost feral look in Wyatt's brown eyes. Tension races through me.

"Where's Dante?" He steps into the room and it feels like it shrinks.

"Getting lunch." Swallowing, I'm trapped. I'm in his room. I shouldn't be in here at all.

"Finn?"

"He went to pick up Peabody." My hands are shaking, so I clasp them together. Something about his energy and the way his eyes never leave me makes me nervous. Wyatt doesn't look at me, ever. But right now, his focus is fixed on me.

"I should—" I gesture toward the door and step that way, but Wyatt stalks in my direction. My brain glitches because this isn't what Wyatt does. Is he angry because I'm in his bedroom?

I draw in a ragged breath and pull up my big girl panties. I won't cower before him.

"You saw my bedroom so I figured it was only fair that I saw yours." I put my hands behind my back so he can't see the trembling and tip my chin up in defiance.

He stops right before our bodies collide. The room smells divine with him in it. My insides soften even as I try to hold tight to that little bit of anger and hurt clawing within.

He didn't come home last night.

"Where were you last night?" I ask. Even my voice trembles because Wyatt is so close and all my hormones are on high alert.

"I went to the Veiled Vixen." He reaches out and grabs a lock of my hair, rubbing it between his fingers. Everything in me goes on high alert. Wyatt doesn't touch me.

A shiver races through me but I try to ignore it. I'm ignoring the fire burning within me for an entirely different reason and focus on my anger. "Did you take advantage of their rooms?"

"I woke up on Drew Young's couch." His dark eyes focus on mine.

Fuck, the intensity of his gaze is almost too much. Until his words finally register. Drew? "What?"

He tugs on my hair slightly, making me gasp. His gaze drops to my mouth. My lips part at the heat in his eyes. Suddenly, all I can think about is his lips on mine. My breath quickens and anticipation grabs hold of my body.

I'm at war with myself. Part of me wants to collapse into his arms and beg him to take me. The quiet, fearful part of me wants to run, to avoid this confrontation, to avoid more rejection. And another part of me is so fucking confused by his attention.

"He said I should ask you about something." He lifts his gaze to mine and I'm lost.

"What should you ask me?" I breathe, so far gone that I almost sway into his heat, let it consume me. He's still only touching my hair. But his full focus is on me and it's intoxicating.

"What have you been up to, trouble?"

Suddenly I'm captured in his gaze unable to look anywhere else. *Trouble?*

"What do you mean?" I search his eyes, trying to figure out what is happening right now. He's so close. Awareness of his heat sends my body into overload.

"You're dating Drew." He looks at the strand of hair between his fingers.

That wasn't really a question. "Yes."

His eyes flare with heat. "And Dante?"

My cheeks burn. "I'm not dating Dante."

"Then why did you give him a show, trouble?"

When I masturbated for the camera, I thought Dante was watching and Wyatt must have figured that out. Anger floods through me. Fuck him and fuck this.

"What do you want, Wyatt? Do you want me to confess all my dirty little secrets to you so you can tell my big brother when he gets home?" I narrow my eyes.

The heat pouring off him sizzles through me. "You're playing with fire, trouble."

Don't I know it. I'm burning from the inside out.

"That's my choice. If I want to fuck every man I meet, that's my choice. My brother doesn't control me. You don't control me." Fuck, it feels freeing to say that.

He closes in on me and I back away. The only one that could truly burn me is Wyatt. I'm already singed from him. My back hits the wall and he puts his hands on either side of my head.

His breath fans my lips and a little gasp escapes me. Every inch of my body longs for the heat of his. The anticipation of his touch is killing me, but I know he won't. I don't know why, but Wyatt doesn't touch me.

"Is that what you want, trouble? Someone to control you? Someone to put you in your place when you're being a brat?" Wyatt rubs his nose against mine.

My breath rushes out of me as awareness floods me. Do I want that?

Barking fills the silence between us and then a growl. Wyatt yelps.

"Fucking terror." Wyatt steps back and shakes his leg to free himself of the little white furball.

"Peabody!" I squat down and hold open my arms for him, and he rushes to me, proud of himself for biting Wyatt. I glance up at Wyatt and he runs a hand through his hair. My breathing and heart race.

Finn pops into the doorway and his wide green eyes bounce from me to Wyatt. "Hey, sorry. He's a little beast when he wants to tear into Wyatt."

I scoop Peabody up and shoulder past Wyatt into the living room. His scent is too intoxicating in there. I hand Finn Peabody and then turn to face Wyatt.

"Sit." I point to the couch and Wyatt arches his dark eyebrow. "I need to look at your leg."

He walks around the couch and sits. Finn brushes my arm. His eyes search mine.

"You okay, flower?"

I draw in a deep breath and nod. Some of my control returns as I walk around the couch and sit on the ottoman to face Wyatt.

The door opens and Dante walks in with a bag. His eyes take in everything as he sets the bag on the table. He walks up to Finn where Peabody is wiggling for Dante's attention.

Dante pets Peabody. "We forgot about you."

Peabody licks Dante's hand.

I focus on what I can do. "Give me your leg."

"It's nothing." Wyatt's back to being a closed-off asshole. Fun.

"Just give me your leg." I roll my eyes. All that fire and heat he stoked within me is still there, but I've got it carefully banked.

He lifts his leg to rest on the ottoman beside me. I push his pant leg up to see the tiny teeth marks. They barely bled but I should put something on them, so they don't get infected.

I head for Tom's bathroom where I know there's some Band-Aids and ointment.

"So are you all fucking now?" Wyatt's words stop me cold.

"What?" I turn and stare at him like he's a stranger.

"I saw the video." His eyes narrow on Finn and Dante. "I thought I might find out who broke into the townhouse. I didn't expect to see you two fucking Sara on the dining room table."

"More cameras?" I let my outrage be heard, because fuck this guy. "Wyatt Hawkins, what right do you have to put cameras in my house?" I put my hands on my hips.

"He's just trying to protect you, pip." Dante steps forward. Always trying to stop me and Wyatt from doing anything. Whether it be fighting or something else. I'm done with it.

"By watching me in my bedroom? He didn't even know my parents weren't home—"

"What?" Wyatt stands and closes the distance between us. His anger radiates off him. "I thought they just left."

"They've been in Europe for a while." I cross my arms and glare. "Not that it's any of your business. None of this is."

"Of course it's my business. You're my business. You're in fucking danger and you were alone in that house. What if the guy broke in when you were there?"

A chill races through me. "One, we don't know it's a guy. Two, he didn't."

"Fuck, Sara, you could have been hurt. Why didn't you just stay with us?" Wyatt yells those words. In another tone of voice, I might have felt chagrined or embarrassed.

"Because of you!" The words fall in the room like a fucking bomb.

He winces but doesn't back off. Anger still laces his words, but there's something else there too. "You could have been hurt."

"I'm fine." I don't let him see the trembling of my hands, because all those thoughts went through my head. They could have broken in at any time. While I was sleeping. That guy across the street who watched me through the windows.

But why break in now? What changed? They could have gotten in at any point. The only difference was…

"How secure was the camera in my bedroom?" I turn to Dante since he was the one that planted it. "Could someone else have accessed it?"

"It's always possible, pip. But we had it secure."

Finn lets Peabody down. Peabody jumps up on the couch before sitting to glare at Wyatt. That's my dog.

I swallow, trying to think through everything. This is easier to focus on than the angry man standing near me. "But was there a way for them to know it was there even if they couldn't access it?"

"Possibly." Finn sits down next to Peabody. "You think they knew the camera was gone from your room?"

"It makes sense." I bite my lip. Wyatt is still glaring down at me.

"They could have seen you bring it into the office." Dante leans his shoulder against the wall, watching me and Wyatt with a quiet intensity.

Maybe. Bracing myself, I look up into Wyatt's dark eyes. "Who I fuck isn't any of your concern."

"Flower—" Finn sounds reasonable.

"No. He's made it perfectly clear he doesn't want me." I can't meet his eyes. "That gives him no right to say anything about my life."

Dante's lips press into a fine line. Finn runs a hand through his hair.

"Sara…" Wyatt's voice isn't angry and his hand lifts as if he's going to touch me.

I back away because I'm not that fucking strong. I can act strong and believe I'm strong, but I have a weakness. And he's standing in front of me.

"I don't have to explain myself to you." I steel myself and look up into Wyatt's eyes. "You're not my brother. You're not my boyfriend. Hell, you're not even my friend anymore."

He winces and runs a hand through his hair. "You're right."

Tears choke me, but I hold them back. I don't want to be right. I don't want him to not want me.

"I've been an asshole." Wyatt returns to the couch. "Fuck."

Finn and Dante shift their attention between the two of us. I straighten and go into Tom's room, needing the break and to grab the stuff for Wyatt's leg.

Dante

When Sara disappears into Tom's room, I go into the kitchen and pull lunch out of the bags. This was bound to happen. I'm so proud of Sara for sticking up for herself, but at the same time, I know what's between them is deeper than attraction.

If it was just attraction, they would have gotten past it long ago. She wouldn't have saved herself for him. She's been willing to give herself to Finn and me, but we need to sort through this before it goes any further.

"We need to talk." I grab some plates.

Wyatt's eyes narrow on me. "Yes, we do."

"You need to chill out." Finn stands and walks over to me. Peabody growls at Wyatt before jumping down and flouncing over to us.

"I just watched you two fucking Sara on her dining room table. How am I supposed to chill out?" Wyatt growls.

"We didn't technically fuck her." I know it doesn't make it better for him. This is the girl he's been wanting forever but keeping at arm's length. But there is a solution for this.

Wyatt joins us at the table. His fists clench at his sides. "Are we really going to get into semantics here?"

"Yes, we are." I put my hands on the table and meet his eyes. "Because she means something to all of us. We all put our attraction on the back burner. Because she threw everything into wanting you. Now she's realizing she wants all of us."

"You know there's an easy way to solve this," Finn says quietly as he grabs a plate and fills it. "She doesn't seem opposed to sharing."

His green eyes flick up to mine and then to Wyatt's before glancing toward Tom's door.

"And you think Tom would be okay with that? He'd never be okay with me." Wyatt hisses. "He may be gone, but eventually he'll come back. It's one thing if one of us is fucking her, but if all of us are..."

I glance up as Sara walks into the room. Her lips are pressed into a firm line. How much did she hear?

"You do know that Tom fucked your girlfriend behind your back in high school? It's not like he has an honor code." She pulls a chair out and glares at Wyatt. "Give me your leg."

Wyatt sits next to her and pulls his jean leg up. "Are we having this discussion?"

"Appears so." Finn takes a seat and so do I. Dishes are passed around until everyone has lunch, while Sara applies antibacterial ointment and a Band-Aid to Peabody's most recent attempt on Wyatt's life.

He's just lucky Peabody isn't a German shepherd.

Wyatt watches her with soft eyes as she works on him. This won't work unless we're all on board. It's time we discussed the real reason Tom doesn't want Wyatt with his sister.

She washes her hands and then returns to the table. We all begin to eat.

"Sara hasn't properly fucked anyone." I'm just going to start this out with a bang.

Wyatt's dark eyes lift to mine in shock and then turn to Sara.

Her cheeks flush pink. She arches her eyebrow at me and I shrug. If we're going to talk about sex, then that's where this has to start.

"That doesn't mean I'm inexperienced." She doesn't meet Wyatt's eyes. "It just means—"

"You haven't had a cock buried in your pussy." Finn winks at her and her flush deepens . "Or ass."

Wyatt remains still. I can't tell how he's processing this information. We all assumed she's had some sexual experiences. Not that we dwelled on it or discussed it, but she's twenty-two years old.

Her lips press together and her eyes narrow. "I don't see how this information is pertinent. Especially since Wyatt doesn't want me. He just wants to control me."

"Oh, Wyatt wants to do more than control you, pip." I sit back in my chair and cross my arms over my chest. "There's a reason Tom doesn't want Wyatt with you."

Her brow furrows as she looks at each of us. Her gaze finally lands on Wyatt and she cocks her head to the side. "Why would Tom not want you with me?"

Wyatt glares at me before he stands up and walks away. His hand combs through his hair as he stalks back toward us. "Because he knows my sexual proclivities."

Her lips part and she wets them. She leans forward a little and I can see the interest in her pale green eyes as she studies him.

"What kind of sexual proclivities?" Fuck, our girl is more than curious. I bet she's wet just thinking about him having a kink. She clears her throat.

When Wyatt shakes his head, I know that bastard isn't going to tell her. And as much as I want to, it's not mine to tell.

Chapter 27

Nonexclusive Basis

Fuck if I'm not curious. Wyatt still hasn't said that he wants me. I'm afraid my attraction might be one-sided, especially after all these years.

Finn leans back. "Honestly, I think Sara would be perfect for what you want."

That sends a little shiver through me. I've been aware of all these men since they returned to the apartment. But right now, my focus is on Wyatt.

Wyatt sinks back into his chair. "That's not for me to decide."

"Okay, let's backtrack and table that for a few minutes." Dante steeples his fingers against his lips. "Whoever Tom is afraid of might be after Sara too. However, we know they had access and didn't use it to get to her."

"Yet." Finn takes a bite of his sandwich.

"They made it obvious they'd been there and didn't trip the alarm system. It was a warning. A threat." Dante's blue eyes meet mine. I swallow. How many nights did I sleep there alone, possibly unaware of the danger lurking?

"There was this man I saw a few times."

All their attention shifts to me and I squirm in my chair.

"It wasn't obvious he was watching me." I pick apart my bread to focus on something besides the guys. "I saw him at the bar. And outside the coffee shop. And then that one night on my street outside the house."

"Why didn't you tell me?" Dante surges forward. "Fuck, Sara, you could have—"

"I'm fine, and really it could've been a coincidence." I shrug. "And I'm telling you now."

"Did you know her parents were out of town?" Wyatt's voice is quiet, but there's that energy behind it again.

"Yes." Dante rubs the back of his neck.

My cheeks flush, remembering how I got him to let me stay there on my own. When I smirk at him, his cheeks stain pink.

"You should have insisted she come and stay with us." The fear in his voice is raw.

I've been avoiding looking at him, but now I shift my attention to him. His hands are fisted on the table. On instinct, without conscious thought, I put my hand over his.

Everything freezes in place. There's just Wyatt and me for the space of a breath. Tingles burst through me at the contact. I snatch my hand away and time speeds back up. Wyatt's dark eyes capture mine with their heat and feral need.

Awareness splashes over me, leaving me hot and achy.

"She didn't want to come here." Dante clears his throat. "She didn't want to be around you."

Wyatt's eyes widen and his attention shifts to Dante. I suck in a breath. Fuck.

"What's that supposed to mean?" Wyatt asks.

I find my voice. "It means that I didn't want to watch you flaunt women in front of me. You can't begin to understand how I've felt for years. Watching you with other women, knowing it would never be me. And then to be forced to live with you and watch women rotate out of your room and having to smile and act like it's not shredding my heart into pieces. Fuck that. It means I didn't want to want you more than I already do."

My heart pounds in my chest. It takes me a second to comprehend what I just let out into the universe. I sit back in my chair, semidazed.

It wasn't a secret. Not really. I was never subtle, but I never came out and admitted it before.

Finn takes my hand and entwines our fingers, giving me his support. I don't draw away from him. He doesn't burn me like Wyatt does. Finn and Dante and even Drew light me on fire, but none of them hurt as much as Wyatt does.

The way I feel about Wyatt is an ache I can't shake off.

Wyatt takes a breath like he's going to explain everything to me.

"No." Dante leans forward and looks at both Wyatt and me. "We're not getting into that just yet. We need to figure shit out before we open that wound."

It does feel like an open sore already. At least for me. The wound never scabs over. It never heals. It just festers with every breath.

I squeeze Finn's hand and release it. Right now I need to stand on my own.

"I didn't want to move into your apartment and work with you too. It seemed like overkill, so I asked Dante to not tell you."

Wyatt's gaze lifts to Dante.

Dante shakes his head. "I was doing what was best for all of us. The minute she entered this apartment, things would change. No one was ready for that."

"And now we are?" Wyatt runs a hand through his hair.

Dante stands. He gathers the leftovers from lunch and cleans up the table. "We are. And we will."

It seems like a natural break so I walk over to the couch and wait for Peabody to climb on my lap. The guys finish putting everything away. When Dante comes over, he hands me a glass of white wine and sits beside me.

Peabody stands and goes to sit on his lap. The little traitor.

Finn stops at the bar and pours scotch into three glasses. Wyatt sits on the edge of the couch like he wants to be able to bolt at any minute.

Dante drapes his arm around my shoulder and I lean into him, grateful for his warmth and comfort. This weekend just gets more stressful by the minute.

"Drew should be here." Finn sits and glances at the other two before his green eyes focus on me.

"He's busy. I have brunch with him tomorrow." Taking a sip of my wine, I watch Wyatt over the rim.

"I saw him last night and this morning." Wyatt rests his head against the couch. "He had somewhere to be today, but whatever you guys want, he's probably all in."

Wyatt's gaze locks with mine, but I look away. I'm okay as long as we stick to the mystery of Tom.

"Did you ask him if he's found anything out about Tom?" Dante's fingers sweep across the back of my neck and little shivers trickle through me.

"No. Apparently, I went there to confront him about Sara."

My eyes bounce up to his, but he's looking away.

"Why apparently?" Dante asks.

"Because I don't remember. I drank too much last night." Wyatt runs a hand through his hair again, making it stick out every which way. It makes me want to run my hands through it to smooth it back down. To run my hands over him and smooth him back down.

He sighs and drinks most of his scotch, then leans forward with his elbows on his knees, dangling the glass between them. "He spoke to me at the restaurant on Thursday night."

That's news to me.

"I told him I couldn't tear my friends apart, and he said maybe I should check with you guys." Wyatt lifts his dark eyes to Finn and Dante. "When I asked him what he meant this morning, he told me you'd both kissed Sara. And that if I wanted to know what Sara wanted, I should ask her."

That makes sense.

"He also said he's sure we're a package deal." Wyatt's attention lands on me and my breath catches. Drew has made it clear to me that he's open to me being with more than just him.

But with Wyatt's attention on me, it makes me squirm. It works for Madison, but is that really what I want? The full focus of four men on me?

I slip back to the memory of this morning with Dante and Finn. My panties dampen at how good it felt to be with both of them. Wyatt leans toward me, holding my gaze.

"Is that what you want, trouble? Four men ready to service your every need?" His dark eyes hold me locked in time. This is one of those questions that could change the direction of my life.

I know the answer, but that fear of his rejection still stains my heart.

"Am I what you want?" My voice shakes but I hold my head high. I'd rather him be honest with me now.

He reaches out and captures a lock of my hair. "You're all I ever wanted, Sara."

My heart hammers in my chest, but I see the moment he withdraws again. A stone sinks in my gut.

"I don't know that I can be what you need." He finishes his drink and sets the glass on the table before retreating to his room. Tears well in my eyes.

"You should talk to him, pip." Dante squeezes my shoulder.

I shake my head because, as much as I want to take charge of my life, Wyatt is the one thing I can't have. And to let myself believe again that he wants me and I can have him just to lose it all over again would break me.

When Wyatt left the conversation, the conversation stopped. Finn turned on a game and I went into Tom's room to put away my meager belongings. Peabody finds a spot on the corner of the bed where he can watch me.

The room is spotless like Dante promised. Instead of Tom's bedspread, a set of crisp white sheets and a pretty, subtle floral duvet rest on the king-sized bed. The pillows all look new too.

It takes me less time to unpack than it did to pack everything. I sit on the edge of the bed next to Peabody and sigh. I'm not sure what to think anymore. What to feel anymore.

Wyatt's worried that he can't be what I want, but how would he know if I don't even know what he needs? I lie back on the bed and Peabody gets up and snuggles against me with a loud sigh.

My phone buzzes and I reach out to pick it up.

KAYLA:

I'm bored. Want to go to the strip club again?

ME:

I might be on lockdown

I don't even know anymore. Is it safe for me to go out with my friends? It's not like someone will run up and grab me and carry me away.

MADISON:

Your brother?

HOPE:

Where?

ME:

Someone went through my and Tom's rooms last night at the townhouse

> I'm staying with Dante, Finn, and Wyatt in Tom's room

KAYLA:

> You could've stayed with me

HOPE:

> I have room too

I think about repacking and moving to their couches, but this morning and that look in Wyatt's eyes makes me want to stay here and figure this out.

ME:

> Thanks, guys, but I'm settled

MADISON:

> How about a movie night?

Madison lived for school and her career for years, so we've been educating her on what she missed. I get up and go to the door, opening it to see who's still out in the living room. It's just Finn and Dante.

Dante works on his computer while Finn watches the game.

I clear my throat to get their attention.

Dante glances my way and his blue eyes soften, making my insides buzz softly.

"You need something, pip?"

Okay, those words shouldn't make me want to grab him and drag him into this room. Fuck, things are complicated now.

"I was hoping to go over to my friend's to watch a movie." I feel like I'm fourteen again and have to ask permission to do anything.

"Sure, I can make sure you get there and back." Dante glances at his computer screen. "What time, pip?"

I hold up a finger and text the group. The response is quick.

"An hour?" I ask.

"I've got you, pip."

My insides buzz from him and his words. But then my gaze goes to the closed door across from mine and some of that fades. Maybe my friends will help me understand this. Maybe there's a way to have them all without it being a struggle.

Chapter 28

Clean Opinion

Sara

"Marvel or DC?" Kayla asks as she scrolls through the listing of movies.

"I prefer Marvel." Hope stands next to the microwave in Madison's personal living room, waiting for the popcorn to finish popping. "Less dark and gritty."

"Which is the one that has Thor?" Madison brings a bottle of wine and four glasses over to the couch.

"Marvel," Hope and I say at the same time.

This is exactly what I need. I feel like I can finally breathe here. The confrontation with Wyatt has my emotions reeling. His intensity still pulls at me though. The way his dark eyes searched mine. I put my hair back because every brush of it on my neck reminded me of his touch.

"Perfect." Kayla selects the movie but doesn't press play yet. "Okay, let's get the dirt first, because the way those guys were at the strip club had me thinking you were going to get your own special show."

Blushing, I settle into the corner of the couch with my wineglass.

Hope comes around with the popcorn and Madison passes a glass to her.

"It's complicated." I blow out a breath and drink my entire glass of wine before holding it out. More wine is definitely the answer.

"Very complicated." Madison nods and gives me a refill.

Swallowing, I look into my drink for courage.

"I've messed around with Dante and Finn." I can't go into details. It's not that I don't want to share with these women. It's just too new and I want to keep it to myself. Dante and Finn. Their hands and mouths... I've never felt anything like it before. I want more.

"You're still dating Drew?" Hope pops a piece of popcorn into her mouth and pushes her glasses up.

I nod and groan. "And then Wyatt was all growly earlier, but then nothing. Like I really thought he might at least kiss me. Peabody bit him. And apparently, Drew thinks they're all a package deal for me."

My cheeks heat. I want to understand what that looks like. I've seen the way Madison and her guys are around each other, but I don't know if I can see myself with four guys. That would mean only picking one of them. But when it comes to choosing which one, my brain melts.

Madison smirks. Hope's mouth drops open. Kayla grins.

"Hell yeah. That would be a sweet group of guys to fuck." Kayla clinks my glass and takes a drink.

"Yeah, well I haven't fucked any of them." *Yet* lingers on my lips. I will get at least one of them to fuck me eventually. "But there's something going on with Wyatt. He says he can't be with me because of his sexual proclivities."

"Proclivities? Who uses a word like that?" Kayla taps her finger against her lips. "Like a kink? Or is he into men?"

"I think kink?" I sigh. "Tom apparently knows about it and doesn't approve. Wyatt doesn't think he can be what I need, but how the hell would he know if I don't even know what I like?"

Kayla's eyes widen slightly. "Whoa, whoa, whoa. Back it up a minute. How would you not know what you like?"

Shrugging, I confess, "I've never been with anyone. At least not fully."

I've been around these women for a few months. I think everyone just assumes that someone my age will have at least fucked someone. And I have had offers, just none I wanted to accept. But now, with these guys, suddenly it's all I think about.

Madison takes a drink. "So your only sexual experience has been with these guys?"

"Yes." I swallow because I don't know about Hope, but Madison and Kayla are a lot more experienced than I am. I never said anything because I expected to be that experienced some day. And never thought I'd be having this talk with them.

Drew was supposed to fuck me and get it over with, but instead he turned into the rallying cry for the others. I touch my lips and smile. Who knew?

"Okay, so what kind of kinks would make a brother not find a guy acceptable for his sister?" Kayla thinks for a moment, but then she gets a wicked grin. "Why don't we ask a brother?"

"I don't think—" Madison stops as Kayla is already out the door. She looks up at the ceiling and says mostly to herself, "I'm going to get punished for this later."

"Blake, we have questions." She knocks on a door.

Madison just shakes her head as Blake Wagner follows Kayla into the room. He's a big guy with muscles. His dark hair contrasts with his green eyes, the same shade as Kayla's. He's got on a t-shirt and jeans.

"Ladies. What's going on?" Blake's gaze settles on Madison and softens.

"We need a brother's opinion." Kayla grabs a handful of popcorn. "If you had a best friend who wasn't already fucking your woman—Wait, let's say Coop wanted to fuck me." She grins. "And Madison didn't exist because otherwise I'd be breaking up your happy home.

But if Coop wanted to fuck me and was really kinky, what kind of kink would make you tell him not to pursue me?"

Madison laughs behind her hand.

"No, on imagining Coop. I would never forbid anyone from pursuing you. I would enlighten them to your personality and maybe tell them for their own safety to run for the hills." Blake leans against the doorframe with a smirk.

"That's not very nice, but accurate." Kayla smirks back. "Fine, pretend you need to look out for me."

Blake rubs the back of his head. "I mean, there are kinks that border on abusive that I wouldn't be happy about unless you were definitely into that."

"Like what?" I can't help asking.

"There are a lot of sadomasochistic practices that might make a loved one fear for your safety. There are people who crave the pain. As long as you are safe, consenting adults, I wouldn't have a problem with my sister participating. But if one person takes advantage of the other, it can get into a gray area." Blake meets each of our gazes.

Kayla smiles. "Aw, my big brother cares about me and my needs."

He sighs. "I've given up. You are who you are. If someone tried to do you dirty, you'd make them pay."

"That doesn't help me." I take a handful of popcorn. It still doesn't answer the question.

Blake's attention shifts to me. "Honestly, with you, your brother might be concerned with any kink. I don't know Tom personally. He may not want to think of his sister being involved in something more than vanilla. I have little choice with mine."

"And you love me for it." Kayla preens.

"If you need anything, tiger, let me know." Blake steps into the room and leans down to press a kiss to Madison's lips before leaving.

"Thanks!" we say as he closes the door.

"So it could be anything, like spanking or bondage." I pick at my pants. "Neither of which sounds good or bad, but I'd be willing to explore to figure out if I could like them."

"Maybe you should just ask him." Hope shrugs. "The worst he can do is not tell you and then you still don't know."

"I say you go for it. Just strip down naked for the guy and say do your worst." Kayla winks. "You'll have a really great time and figure out if his kink is for you. Win-win."

Both ideas have merit. Though it would be better to know what I'm getting myself into than to tell him *do your worst* and end up running screaming from the room.

We laugh and chat a little before starting the movie. Kayla tells us all about her worst kink experience with a guy who didn't actually know what he was doing. The conversation continues during the movie, as does the wine.

"Mmm, we should walk Hope to her brother's bar." Kayla smiles. "Your brother has the prettiest blue eyes."

"We have the same blue eyes." Hope laughs and shakes her head. "And please don't date my brother. I like you and don't want you to disappear when he does you dirty."

"I just like looking at those eyes." Kayla cups Hope's cheeks. "That's why I like looking at you too."

I glance at my phone. It's still early and I really don't want to deal with whatever is waiting for me at the apartment. "I'm in."

"Me too." Madison puts on some shoes.

The walk to McAvoy's from the office building that Madison's apartment is in is short. We talk and laugh the whole way there. When we enter, it's busy.

"Come on, I'll get us a seat." Hope weaves us through the crowd until we end up at the bar. She catches Jason's attention and soon a few people get up, leaving room for us.

Jason smiles at Hope as he goes to get us drinks.

We drink and talk about the future. We're making plans to eventually work together after we get the experience we need. After a while, I have to use the restroom.

"I'll be back." I slip off my bar stool and catch myself as a wave of dizziness comes over me. Oof, too much to drink between the wine at

Madison's and the cocktails here. The crowd isn't any less thick, so I work my way to the bathroom and wait in a short line.

After washing my hands, I take a breath before facing the crowd again.

When I open the bathroom door, the noise overwhelms me. As I make my way slowly through the bar, a tall man steps in front of me.

I look up and it's some guy around my age. He smiles. "Hey."

"Excuse me. I'm trying to get back to my friends." I gesture behind him, hoping he'll move out of my way.

"I could be your friend." His gaze drops to my cleavage in my V-neck t-shirt with a dirty grin. Ew, no.

"Not today. Thank you." I go to move around him but he blocks the way.

"Come on. At least give me your number." He gives me a pouty face that does absolutely nothing except annoy me.

"Look, I have someone." Actually, three and a potential fourth. Not really looking to add to that number. How would that even work? My brain stumbles on it, but then I make myself return to here and now.

"I don't see him." The guy grins and puts his hand on my arm. "I'm here."

"There you are, sweetie." An arm wraps around my waist and I'm drawn into the side of a really tall, really good-smelling beast of a man.

The guys in this bar are grabby tonight.

I try to pull away. "You must have me—"

"Yes, I must, darling. But later." He kisses my temple and I once again try to pull away. "Excuse us."

His attention is on the guy in front of me. The guy with his arm around me is dressed in a business suit with a black shirt unbuttoned at the collar. He has a closely shaved beard, wavy brown hair, and stunning blue eyes.

"Sorry, man." The guy backs off without an apology to me. What an asshole.

The business man doesn't release me as he maneuvers us through the crowd. When I see he's taking me in the direction of the girls, I give up and let him lead. After all, he did save me from that guy, and he slices through the crowd like a hot knife through butter.

"Mr. Duncan." Madison straightens as we reach her. Oh, good, someone she knows and not some random stranger.

"Heath, love." Heath removes his arm from me and smiles. "I found this one being accosted by a young stud. Figured I could be of service. Last time I saw her was on the arm of your Noah."

Heath Duncan. The name is familiar, and now that I look at Heath, I recognize him from social events. He always has some vapid, gorgeous woman clinging to his arm.

Madison blushes. "This is Kayla Wagner, Blake's sister."

Heath takes her hand and kisses her knuckles. "A pleasure."

"Indeed." Kayla winks at him.

His laugh is loud and boisterous.

"Hope Williams works at Morrigan with me." Madison presents Hope.

"Williams?" Heath takes her hand and holds it for a second before glancing at Jason behind the bar. "Those blue eyes. You wouldn't be one of Troy's kids, would you?"

Hope blushes and tries to draw back her hand, but he holds it. "Yes, Troy Williams was my father."

He grins and lifts her hand to his mouth. "Huge fan. He was one of the legends of boxing."

He kisses her knuckles. His gaze never drops from hers.

She nods and finally gets her hand away. His gaze remains fixed on her for a few seconds longer than normal. There's an intensity that makes me uncomfortable.

Madison introduces me. "Sara Morris, Heath Duncan."

Heath takes my hand and kisses my knuckles. His blue eyes sparkle. "A pleasure to meet you, Sara."

"Thank you for the assist." I smile. Heath's an attractive man, but he does nothing for me.

"You're welcome. It was good seeing you, Madison. Tell Coop he owes me a call. I've got business to attend. Ladies." He inclines his head and moves to the other end of the bar.

"That was weird." Shaking my head, I climb onto my bar stool.

"I don't think I've seen Heath here before," Madison mentions as she sips her drink. "But usually I'm here with you guys and don't pay as much attention as I probably should."

"You didn't tell us your father was a famous boxer." Kayla's green eyes focus on Hope.

"He's been gone for a while now." Hope takes a drink, and it's an effective way to cut the conversation short.

Heath is talking to a guy in a black suit. The other guy looks somewhat familiar too, but I can't place him.

My phone buzzes, distracting me. I lift it.

DANTE:

Let me know when to come get you

ME:

At McAvoy's

Ready when you are

Chapter 29

Negotiable

Wyatt

Sara's been out of the living room for a while, so I come out of my room. Finn has the postgame shows on and Dante has his laptop open. I walk into the kitchen to look for something to drink. Today has been a shitshow since I woke up.

"She's not here." Finn turns the channel. "You don't have to slink off to your room again."

I know Dante wouldn't let her go anywhere she wouldn't be safe, so if he's here...

"Is she with him?" Trying to keep the jealousy from my tone, I grab a bottle of beer and twist the lid off. It didn't sound like she was going to Drew's, but after this afternoon, I wouldn't be surprised.

Maybe she'll decide to stay at his place.

"No, she's with her friends in the Morrigan Technology Group building." Dante sets his laptop on the coffee table and leans back. His full attention is on me now.

Both these guys betrayed me with Sara. How long has it been going on? When she masturbated for my camera, that was for Dante.

"You missed her giving you a show." I sit on the couch and take a swig of my beer. I sound fucking bitter because I am.

Dante smirks. "I caught her masturbating when I went in to plant the cameras. That's when I found out her parents weren't home. I told her I'd let her stay if she finished for me."

I arch an eyebrow.

"Honestly, I figured she'd back down, but not Sara." Dante chuckles.

Every challenge we threw at her as a little girl she'd do. Climb to the top of that rock. Pick up that spider. Eat the mud pie she made. That one got us in a lot of trouble when she was sick for days afterward.

"That was the first time?" I have to ask. For years, he's distracted her to keep her away from me. What if that's how he always distracted her. My insides twist.

"Yes." Dante blows out a breath. "I never touched her. Not until the night we dropped her off after Veiled Vixen. She asked me to kiss her."

I down more beer. Fuck. This isn't easy to hear. This woman I've held myself back from for years out of loyalty to Tom and loyalty to them.

I turn to Finn.

He grins. "I ate her out after her date with Drew. Kissed her too. Been thinking about it ever since. Would have fucked her, but suspected she was a virgin. Really didn't expect that."

I shake my head in denial. That can't be right. "There was that jock she dated in high school."

Tom wanted to tear that guy's head off. I would have been right there with him.

Dante laughs. "Yeah, I asked, but apparently she kicked him in the junk and threatened to tell Tom if he said anything."

"That sounds like Sara." Finn stands and grabs a beer from the fridge. "She hasn't fucked Drew either."

"He told me." I run a hand through my hair. "So, where does that leave us?"

"That's up to Sara." Dante rubs the back of his neck. "She wants us all. We always figured she'd choose one of us. And for a long time that would've been you."

"Tom made that impossible." It would never make sense to Sara that her brother stood in the way, but he's my best friend. We know too much about each other. And I know Sara. "Besides, Sara would make a lousy submissive."

"You don't really want someone to give in to your every whim." Dante leans back and smiles. "You'd be bored with a woman who gave in."

"That's true." Finn sits on the arm of the couch. "You remember Hannah?"

Fucking Hannah.

Dante laughs. "That girl was practically a lapdog."

Peabody glances at me from Dante's lap.

"She knelt. She begged. She followed your every order, and she lasted, what?" Finn glances at Dante for confirmation. "A week?"

She was the perfect submissive. Always did everything right. Boring as fucking hell.

"Five days." Dante pets Peabody. "You don't want a fucking mouse of a companion. You want Sara."

"You think she wants me to do those things to her?" I walk into the kitchen and throw away my empty bottle. "Punish her. Mark her porcelain skin with my strikes. Make her bend to my will."

Fuck, just thinking about it makes me hard. But that's not who Sara is.

I pull out another beer. "She wants a guy like that kid she dated in college. Edgar?"

"Ethan was gay." Dante laughs.

"See? Completely harmless. That's what she wants. Someone nonthreatening."

"She knew he was gay." Dante ruffles Peabody's fur. "She wants you. Fuck, you saw what we did to her in the dining room. She wants to be taken. She wants to be fucked."

Collapsing onto the couch, I lean my head back, remembering those images burned into my memory. Finn's cock in her mouth. Dante's mouth on her bare pussy. Her body arching and coming for them.

I roll my head to narrow my eyes at Dante. "Did you forget about the camera in the dining room?" I have to ask because he had to know I'd look.

Dante smirks. "Honestly, it wasn't the first thing on my mind when I had Sara bare and spread out before me like a fucking buffet."

I take a swig of beer and hold the bottle between my knees. "Are we talking about this? Is this really something we can or should do? Share Sara?"

Dante looks to Finn who smiles. "She wants us. If you can pull your head out of your ass and apologize for making the girl feel like you didn't want her. But you need to decide whether this is something you want to do, because it's happening with or without you."

I rub my hand over my face, pausing on my scruffy jaw. "Tom will kill us."

"Tom left her in our care," Finn helpfully points out. "He didn't hire a security firm. He gave her to us."

"Not to fuck."

"That's not his decision." Dante's expression is flat. "The only one that can *give* her is Sara, and she's been trying for years to give herself to you. You never told her about your kink because you never wanted to scare her away. Part of you wanted to keep her as obsessed as you are."

He's not wrong. Fuck. "Fine. So what we take turns? Go at her as a group? Do we invite Drew over to fuck her whenever he wants to? How is this not complicated?"

"Sara leads."

I arch an eyebrow at Finn and he laughs.

"Yeah, sorry. I know that's not usually your thing, but in this case, she holds all the power until she decides to hand it over to us." Finn slides down onto the couch. "She can decide how she wants all of us, but I guarantee she likes at least two at a time."

"Fuck." I don't even know what to do with all this.

"Just talk to Sara." Dante looks at his phone. "Tell her what you want from her. Give her the consent talk and show her what you want to do to her. Let her make the decision for once instead of making it for her."

He's right and I know it. For years, I've pushed her away. She was too young. Too innocent. Tom didn't want to think of his sister with someone like me. Someone who would hurt her to make her feel pleasure.

"I've got to go pick her up." Dante stands and Peabody grumbles as he moves onto the couch. Dante chuckles and pets the dog. "Don't worry. Finn will protect you from Peabody."

"Ha ha." I glare at the small dog, who growls in the back of his throat before tucking his head into his body.

"Hey, maybe if you win over Peabody, you'll win over Sara." Finn laughs.

Dante

Sara giggles as she slips and I catch her again.

"How much did you have to drink, pip?" I wrap my arm around her to hold her up. My hand rests on her ribs right below her breast.

"A bit." She giggles again as we enter the building.

The night doorman nods at me as we walk past.

When we get in the elevator, her eyes are mischievous. "Dante, where are you going to sleep tonight?"

She grabs my belt to tug me to her, but ends up stumbling into me instead. Her nose hits my chest. "Oof."

Looking up at me, she rubs at her nose. I shake my head and draw her against me, letting her lean into my warmth. Things have gotten complicated. Wyatt wants to be on board, but he's hurt Sara with his disinterest for too long.

Neither of them will be happy until they have each other. She still wants him, but she's afraid to go for it.

She kicks off her heels and presses against me. Her fingers creep up my thigh.

"Dante. Can I play with you again?"

Sara's hand strokes my cock, which is hardening with each touch. Fortunately, the elevator arrives at our floor. Grabbing her shoes, I help her out into the hallway.

The door is unlocked, so I lift her and carry her across the threshold.

Her arms wrap around my neck.

"I'm not drunk, Dante. I just know what I want." Her fingers stroke the back of my neck, sending little jolts of desire through me.

"And what is that, pip?" I close the door and turn the lock. "What do you want?"

Wyatt and Finn stand as they see Sara in my arms. I have her shoes in my other hand.

She glances at the others and grins. "Oh, yes, please."

"Is she drunk?" Wyatt steps forward.

Finn smirks. "I'll play with drunk Sara."

"No one's playing with Sara tonight." Even though I really want to. "Drunk does not equal consent."

"I consent." Her hand tugs on my bun. Her pale green eyes collide with mine. "I'm so ready to consent. Fuck. You'd think it'd be easy to lose your virginity, but man, it's like no one wants to buy a new car."

My brow furrows as I look down into her discontent face.

"I'm practically giving it away and yet no one wants it. I've offered it to you and Finn, but no. And Drew. Fuck, the first date I basically told him I wanted to fuck him. But then he always has to be somewhere else." She blows out a breath. "What does a girl have to do to get laid around here?"

Her pale green eyes lock with mine. She's definitely had too much to drink, but she's not slurring her words. How much of this is just frustrated, tipsy Sara?

"When you're sober, we can discuss it, pip." I set her down on the couch and she pouts up at me.

"Sober or drunk, it doesn't matter if no one wants you."

Peabody crawls onto her lap and settles. Her fingers sink into his white fur.

Sara rests her head on the back of the couch with her eyes closed. "I'm sure if I offered to suck a cock that would be presented to me, but spread my legs and absolutely no takers."

Wyatt arches an eyebrow at her. Yeah, this is a side of Sara we should have expected. When she was younger, she loved to pull a guilt trip on us when we wouldn't do what she wanted. And we always caved.

Because it was Sara.

"There was this one guy at the bar. He definitely wanted to fuck me, but do I want to fuck him? No. Of course not. That would be too fucking simple." She sighs and pets Peabody.

Shaking my head, I go into the kitchen and grab a bottle of water and a couple of pills.

Finn settles next to Sara on the couch. "If you could choose right now who to give your virginity to, who would it be?"

"Don't answer that." I hand her the water and the pills and glare at Finn.

Her eyes are full of mischief. "Why not? Aren't you curious, Dante?"

She straightens. Her gaze takes in every inch of me before moving on to Finn and then to Wyatt. She taps her finger against her lips.

"We're down one." She passes Peabody to Finn and stands. "It's not really a fair question though. See Kayla probably had the right idea."

Sara's smile turns wicked as she faces me. "She said I should just get naked. Which isn't a big deal because all of you have seen everything already."

She arches her eyebrow at Wyatt before meeting my eyes.

I swallow as she pulls her V-neck t-shirt off and tosses it at Finn. Her bra is lacey and her nipples are hard points, barely concealed. I explored them last night, but not enough. To have her for a whole night would be amazing.

"Maybe you should go to bed." Wyatt's voice sounds strangled.

She grins at me and turns to face him. Her hands go behind her back as she releases the catch on her bra. "Why would I do that, Wyatt? I'm having a good time. And this time I want you to look."

She drops her bra on the floor next to Finn. He just sits back and watches, but he loves chaos. Lives for it. I like order, and Sara is currently out of control.

She unbuttons her jeans, shimmies them down, and steps out of them. Her panties are the only thing left on her.

Fuck, she's gorgeous. She lifts her arms to release her red hair and shakes it out behind her.

"See, Kayla thinks I should just tell Wyatt to do his worst, but something tells me this will go like every other time we collide." She closes the distance between Wyatt and her.

His dark eyes watch her every move. He's a fucking bomb ready to go off and she's already lit the fuse.

"What do you think, Wyatt? Should I pick which one of you gets to do the deed with me tonight? Is that the game we're playing now?" She stops right before him. Her pretty face tipped up to search his eyes.

"Sara," I try to warn her, but it's too late.

"Do you want to know why I've said no all these years?" Wyatt's jaw ticks.

I start toward them.

She cocks her head. "You mean why you've rejected me for years. Why at every point in my life when I would've said yes, you acted like I didn't exist. I could have fallen at your feet and you would have stepped over me. So yes, please tell me why now. When I stand naked in front of you, waiting for something, anything to happen."

Her eyes shimmer in the light.

"If I tell you, are you going to run back to Dante to protect you?" His hand threads through her hair behind her head.

She shakes her head. "No. I'm done being protected."

His eyes meet mine. He's under control and he's telling me to let this happen. I stop. Fuck it, they need to figure this out. It's time.

He tightens his fingers in her hair and she gasps at the bite of pain, but she doesn't back down.

"Do you think you can be what I need, trouble?" He lowers his head and brushes his nose against hers.

A shiver sweeps through her. "What do you need?"

"Tonight, I need to taste you." His lips brush over hers.

She whimpers and her hands clutch his shirt. "Wyatt."

"When you're sober, we'll talk. Because what I want from you won't be pretty. It won't be chocolate and flowers. I want you fully aware of what you'll give me and what I'll take from you."

Her lips part on a gasp before he claims her mouth. I expected to feel jealousy. I didn't earlier with Finn, but Wyatt was always Sara's end game. But as I watch them, I want more. I want to see him fuck her. Watch the way she comes for him.

I want to overwhelm her with touch and taste and fill her with our cocks until she begs for more. Make her squirm for us. Fill her with us so she never feels unwanted again.

Wyatt breaks the kiss and leans his forehead against hers. He lifts his gaze to mine and then Finn. He wants that too.

"In the morning." Wyatt trails his finger over her swollen lower lip.

She whimpers and he tugs her hair, making her gasp again.

"Sleep tonight, trouble. Dream of what we can do to you. Tomorrow, we'll make your dreams come true."

Chapter 30

Assertion

Sara

My brain stopped functioning around the time Wyatt pulled on my hair. And then he kissed me. Like end-of-the-world kissed me. My whole body lit up like a carnival that I most definitely want to attend.

As if I could sleep after that.

Dante ushered me into Tom's room—still almost naked—kissed me on my head and hurried out before I could even take a breath.

Did I have a few too many really yummy daiquiris at McAvoy's Bar? Yes. Am I horny as fuck right now with three men within striking distance? Also yes. Should I do anything about it?

That's where my brain stalls out. They obviously aren't going to take advantage of me. And I really want to know what Wyatt's going to tell me in the morning.

I grab a t-shirt nightgown that barely covers my ass and tug it on.

I go through my nightly ritual in Tom's bathroom. It's large and clean. I put out all my toiletries and fill up the shower with my stuff. I'm not sure where Dante stored Tom's things, but it's like Tom doesn't even live here.

When I finish, I sit on the end of my bed, well Tom's bed, to figure out what the hell is going on while I drink my bottle of water. My fingers touch my lips. My brain is slowly working through it.

Wyatt kissed me. Everything inside me burst into flames. I realized we would combust on contact but, fuck. That was so much better than I could've imagined.

I got naked in front of them. Dante, Finn, and Wyatt. Sure they've already seen me naked, Wyatt only on camera. They may have been behaving, but that was lust in their eyes. Lust for me.

Fuck, I wanted to shatter their control and for once make them forget themselves. Forget the little girl I was and realize I'm a woman now. Ready for the taking. Begging for it. I want to be ravished.

Flopping back on the bed, I know I could take care of the aching need between my legs. It would be good. I could imagine Finn's or Dante's tongues pressing inside me. Wyatt's grip on my hair as his cock slides into my mouth. I groan and roll to the side to grab my phone.

I'm so sick of imagining.

Drew wouldn't have left me hanging. He wouldn't have sent me off to bed desperate for release.

ME:
Are you still awake?

DREW:
Is this a u up text?

I smile and sit up. I love that he's always right there to text me back.

ME:
More like an I miss you and am thinking about you text

DREW:
Fuck, princess. I wish I could be there

ME:
What are you doing?

DREW:

You wouldn't believe me if I told you

He owns a strip club. I'm prepared for anything he could throw at me.

ME:

Try me

DREW:

At a bar mitzvah

ME:

Seriously?

DREW:

Yes, but I'd rather be wherever you are

I sigh and lie back on the bed. I hope I get the story about why he's at a Bar Mitzvah. That's part of what I like about Drew. I don't know everything about him. He's a mystery, but I enjoy uncovering more.

ME:

I wish you were here too

DREW:

Line dance, be back

I set my phone to the side and glance at the door. Are the guys even still awake? Last night when I was restless, Dante helped me. My toes curl thinking about how he helped me.

Maybe someone is still up. Finn seemed more than willing to play with me. Besides, where's Peabody? He's not in here with me. I should check up on him. Though if I know the little traitor, he's probably curled up with Dante.

Not that I can blame Peabody. Dante makes a very lovely bed and I'd love to curl up on him too.

I shove off my bed and creep across the room. It's not like I don't have free rein of the house. I'm not under house arrest.

Opening the door, I step into the hallway. A little shiver trickles through me at the darkness. I've never been in their apartment at night. Wyatt's door is right there. I could open it and crawl into bed with him.

Fuck, I could crawl into bed with any of them. Bet that would be a surprise.

After that kiss with Wyatt, I want more. I blow out a breath. I've waited this long. I guess I can wait until morning after we have our talk.

Yay, a talk.

Why does everything have to be so complicated?

Can't we just fuck now and talk later?

I walk into the living room and check for my little furball, but he's not on the couch. He's in with either Finn or Dante. Wyatt would look like a pin cushion in the morning if Peabody could gnaw on him all night.

I chuckle to myself as I reach the kitchen, grab a glass from the cabinet, and fill it with water. Taking a drink, I turn to study the darkened room. What happened tonight and how could it have gone differently?

Would it have gone differently if I hadn't drunk so much?

It didn't feel right without Drew here, though. Which is an odd thought to have. These guys I've known all my life. I've known Drew for a few months. If anything, I should be excluding him now that Wyatt wants me.

A little thrill goes through me.

Yes, Wyatt definitely wants me. I felt his hard cock pressed against my stomach as he kissed me. But that doesn't mean he's a sure thing. Besides, I would have been insulted if I was naked and he didn't have an erection.

There's going to be a *talk*.

Probably where Wyatt tells me all the reasons he can't be with me. I'm sure my innocence will be the top thing on the list. Then there's his friendship with Tom. And whatever his kink is that he thinks I won't be able to handle.

I haven't even had time to contemplate those dildos in his drawer. They seemed high quality. Maybe a collector's thing. Maybe he likes to use them on himself?

I shake my head at the thought. If Wyatt were gay or bi, someone would have told me by now. Fuck, Tom would have told me to get me to stop pining over his friend. And that kiss. A shiver works through me. Definitely attracted to me at least.

That doesn't mean he doesn't like to use them on himself though. Which would be weird and kinky. I turn and refill my water glass. A door opens and I set my glass down on the counter. I've been caught.

I remind myself there's no reason I can't be out of my room.

The jingle of Peabody's tags fills the room as he trots over to me. I squat down next to him and stroke my hands over his face.

"Hey, buddy, where have you been?"

I lift my gaze to a pair of legs in pajama pants and keep climbing to reach the face of my Viking.

"Everything okay, pip?" Dante holds a hand down to me.

I take it and feel that now familiar zing of electricity between us as he lifts me to my feet. "Just wondering where Peabody was and getting some water."

Dante looks less than convinced, but his eyes drop to the thin fabric covering my breasts. They grow heavy and my nipples harden beneath his gaze. I bite my lip and press my thighs together at the growing wetness.

He gives me a wary smirk. "Feeling needy, pip?"

Fuck, those words make everything inside me burst into flames. I wet my lips. "I was needy earlier too, boss."

His hands go to my waist and he lifts me onto the counter. "Fuck, what are you wearing? This barely covers you."

I shrug as his hand skates up the inside of my thigh. I place my palms on his bare chest. He's warm and solid beneath my hands. My fingertips buzz.

"Will you kiss me again?" I whisper, like we could be caught at any moment. Because we could. Part of me really wants to be caught and the other part wants to see how this goes. Just him and me.

He captures my chin and tips it up. His pale blue eyes search mine as his thumb trails over my lower lip. Sparks light through my veins.

"Even though you might finally have Wyatt, you still want me, pip?" His head lowers.

My breath catches in anticipation. "Yes, Dante. I want you. I want all of you. Please, kiss me."

He kisses me and brushes his fingers over my damp panties. I gasp and slide my fingers into his hair. His tongue grazes against mine as he explores every inch of my mouth. He sets me on fire.

He jerks my panties to the side so he can touch my bare skin.

"So wet for me, pip."

He presses his fingers inside me as his thumb glides over my clit. His fingers curl against that spot and rub. A hum of electric lust flows through me. My lips part and he smiles against them.

"That's it. Feel that right there, Sara? That's the spot that's going to make you see stars." He slides his fingers out and presses them back in, hitting that spot again. I moan at the buzz.

"Dante." I can't move the way he has me pressed on the counter. My knees are on either side of him. My butt is on the edge. I want to rock my hips. I make a frustrated noise in the back of my throat.

"No, pip. I'm going to make you come and send you off to bed with a huge grin on your face." His lips take mine again as he keeps his hand moving inside me, stroking me, pushing me higher.

I run my hands down his chest and hard abs to dip into his pajama pants. I grasp his hard, thick cock and he groans. Now it's my turn to smile into our kiss. I stroke his length with both hands, spreading his precum down over his smooth skin.

"Fuck, pip," he whispers into my mouth.

He curls his fingers again and thrusts harder and faster until I can't hold back anymore. Needy noises fill the room around us. His mouth closes over mine as I cry out and shatter in his arms. As promised, stars burst behind my eyelids. My toes curl as the delicious orgasm runs through me.

Part of me longs to guide his cock to my entrance, to feel him press inside me and fill me, stretch me. To pulse around his thickness instead of his fingers.

Instead, I work his cock with my hands, twisting around and sliding them up and down, until he groans into our kiss and his hot seed coats my hands.

We break apart, both of us panting. Catching his eyes, I bring my hand to my mouth and lick his cum off. His eyes darken. He captures the back of my head and kisses me deeply, like he's trying to taste himself on my tongue.

An aftershock courses through my pussy, clutching around his fingers.

"You know anyone can walk into the kitchen." Finn's voice makes both of us freeze.

Dante removes his fingers from my pussy and straightens my panties. I take my hand out of his pants as he backs away. He lifts me off the counter and lowers me to my feet.

I flash a smile at Finn before turning to wash my hands in the sink. He's holding Peabody. Dante grabs a paper towel.

"Someone got bored waiting for you two and scratched at my door."

Dante wraps his arms around me to wash his hands in the sink. Our hands tangle and a desperate longing for more rushes through me. I lean back into his warmth, feeling much more content than before. He dries his hands and turns to Finn. Peabody lets out an excited yip and I figure that means Dante took him.

As I dry my hands, warmth coats my back and Finn wraps his arms around my waist.

"I could have helped you, flower." His lips brush my ear, sending a delightful shiver through me. His body presses tight against mine and I can feel how much he wants me.

My insides tighten with need. I can imagine doing the exact same thing with Finn, but he'd make it different. It wouldn't be like Dante. That's what makes this exciting.

They're all different. They all make me want them, but every touch is new and electric. Every kiss is exactly what I need.

Finn's hands trail up the outsides of my thighs as he kisses the nape of my neck. My breath comes out in pants. I drop my chin to my chest as his tongue slides up my spine and his hands slip under my nightgown.

He hooks his fingers into my panties and drags them down until they flutter to my ankles.

I draw in a sharp breath. "Finn."

"Shh, flower. Dante got a taste. Now it's my turn." He leans into me, pressing me down to the counter. His hard cock rubs against my pussy with only his boxers between us. He whispers, "I could slide inside you right now."

I whimper because part of me is desperate to feel that. To have his thick cock deep inside me.

"But we'll figure that out later, flower." His hands spread my ass cheeks and he grinds his cock against my pussy. "Soon. I'm going to thrust inside you and take you so fucking high you'll never want to come down."

I gasp out a breath at the fire raging inside me. Finn wraps his hand around my hip and his fingers rub over my clit. My heart pounds in rhythm with the throbbing need between my legs, but he doesn't push his fingers into my pussy.

His cock grinds against me, hard and thick. His boxers are in the way. I want his skin on mine.

"You're soaking my boxers, flower. You need a thick cock in your pussy, don't you?" He dips his other hand between us and thrusts his finger in and out quickly.

I rock back against him, seeking more, wanting more.

He pulls his finger out and I groan. He chuckles as he drags his finger up to my asshole.

"I can't wait to take you here, flower." He eases his wet finger into my puckered hole.

I moan at the sensation of his finger penetrating me there. It's different, but so fucking good. He presses his hips against me, pushing me into the counter, sliding his covered cock against my pussy while his finger works my clit and his other finger is buried in my asshole.

"I want to take you here." He thrusts his finger in and out of my ass as his hips rock his cock against my pussy. He sucks on my nape, sending sparks scattering through me. "I want a cock in all of your holes, flower. Dante in your sweet pussy. Me in your ass. And Wyatt in your mouth. Can you handle that, flower?"

"Finn," I whisper as the image pushes me over the edge. I bite my lip as I come around his finger.

"That's my good girl." He sucks on my neck, pushing me higher again and I shatter. "You're going to love being fucked, flower."

My fingers clench on the edge of the counter as he keeps fucking my ass with his finger and grinding against my pussy. He's keeping me wound so fucking tight that every time I fall, he lifts me back up.

His hand leaves my clit and he lowers his boxers. His cock slides between my pussy lips. Will he finally take me?

"I want to feel your pussy on my cock when I come," he whispers into my neck before thrusting his cock back and forth over my clit. His finger follows the same rhythm in my ass. I'm not coming back down. I'm so high, pushing back against his finger, seeking more, craving more.

Crying out, I come. He groans against my neck and his warm cum hits my thighs.

"Fuck, flower." He draws his finger out of my ass and grabs a paper towel to help clean up the mess as I stay in place, trying to catch my breath.

Dante chuckles. "This would be less messy with a condom."

"But also less thrilling." Finn reaches around me to wet a paper towel and cleans me thoroughly, his mouth following behind to kiss and suck my ass cheeks. I lean my head on my hands on the counter.

He draws my panties back up.

"We definitely need to discuss fucking her bare." Finn pulls me up against his front and wraps his arms around my waist. "She's never been with anyone. We've been tested. And if we're fucking Sara, I'm not fucking anyone else."

"Interesting proposal."

I turn toward Dante's voice. He sits at the table watching us. This should be weirder than it feels. But somehow these two feel right, being together with them.

"Makes for a messier experience though." Dante lifts his eyebrow at me. "And we don't know if the others will be on board. You on birth control, pip?"

Nodding, I sigh and suddenly I just want to go to sleep. As I lean back against Finn, I close my eyes.

"You wore her out." Dante chuckles.

"Good. She'll sleep then." Finn lifts me and I release my breath. Safe and secure in his arms.

Chapter 31

Operating Lease

Sara

I wake up alone in Tom's bed. Stretching, I stare at the ceiling. Last night feels like a dream, but I know it wasn't. None of it was.

I grab my phone from the nightstand where someone put it on the charging block.

There are a few new texts from Drew.

> DREW:
>
> Still up, princess?
>
> Guess not.
>
> Got an interesting invite to do brunch at the guys' apartment.
>
> See you soon.

That's news to me. What the hell is going on?

I stumble into the bathroom and take a quick shower. When I look through the clothes I brought with me, I look over the pale green dress I'd planned to wear this morning to my brunch date with Drew.

I guess I still have a brunch date with Drew, it's just being taken over by the guys I'm living with. A smile touches my lips. Wanting to be prepared, I slip on a sexy pair of panties and leave my bra off. The dress wraps around me.

After I put on a little lip gloss, I curl my hair. If I'm not going out, I'm not doing a full face of makeup. I make a note to call my mom later today. Caitlyn needs to fill me in on everything she's seen and done overseas.

Taking a deep breath, I look at myself in the mirror. I'm ready for whatever they have to throw at me this morning. Wyatt might be into something really weird that I can't get on board with. If so, what will that mean?

I don't want to think about losing him entirely. I don't even know if we're talking about a relationship or just fucking. Damn. I should know that.

Finn and Dante haven't been talking to me about dating, just fucking. Drew wants to date me. I'm not sure where Wyatt's head is at. So I need to know which side of the fence I'm on. Do I need a relationship with these men or do I just want to fuck them and figure it out later?

When I asked Drew out, I wasn't looking for a relationship. But all these years I was hoping for one with Wyatt. Can I boil this attraction down to just sex? Can I experiment with these four men and come back with my heart intact?

I guess there's only one way to find out and it's through that door.

After straightening my skirt and pushing my hair behind my shoulder, I open the door and step barefoot out into the living room. The smell of bacon and eggs makes my stomach growl. The sound of men's voices stops as they all turn to look at me.

Dante, Drew, and Wyatt sit on the sectional with coffee mugs in their hands, while Finn stands at the stove making breakfast.

"I was just going to send in a search party, flower." Finn winks before turning back to the stove. "Breakfast is almost ready."

Drew stands and sets his mug on the coffee table. He walks toward me with a smile.

"How are you, princess?" His hands settle on my upper arms and he draws me in for a brief kiss. His brown eyes search mine.

"I'm good." Why would I be bad? Did they tell him I was sick? Or just how drunk I was last night?

"You look beautiful this morning." He holds me back as he takes in my dress. His eyes burn with heat when they meet mine. "I thought about you last night."

My cheeks flush, knowing the others hear his every word. "Thank you."

He leads me over to the couch and Finn brings me a cup of coffee. He leans in and kisses me before I have time to anticipate his move. My eyes widen, but his green eyes just twinkle mischievously.

"Morning, flower."

"Finn." I don't know what else to say. He's kissed me in front of Dante before, but not Drew and definitely not Wyatt. I lower to the couch, not meeting anyone's eyes.

Dante sits on my other side. He brushes a lock of hair behind my ear, sending little shivers through me. Walking out that door I thought I knew how this would feel. But, wow, was I wrong.

I glance up at Wyatt through my lashes, but he's sitting back taking it all in. Last night, he said he wants me. I don't know if he still feels that way this morning. He leans forward and grabs something off the coffee table.

He moves in front of me. "Creamer, trouble?"

My gaze jerks up to his as my mouth falls open in an O. Whatever conversation they had this morning must have been a good one.

He smirks as he adds some creamer to my mug. His dark eyes hold mine.

My heart tumbles over itself. I don't know what to think or what to say. When Wyatt resumes his seat, I take a sip of my coffee.

"All done." Finn claps his hands.

I stand and walk around the guys to the table before anyone else can kiss me. Not that I don't want their kisses. It's just really early and I wasn't ready for this kind of attention. Finn holds out a chair for me.

"Thank you." When I sit, he pushes me in.

The others join me at the table and Finn brings over the eggs, bacon, potatoes, and toast.

"Sorry it's not a full brunch spread, but I was making do with what we have." Finn takes his seat and passes the potatoes to Drew.

"This smells and looks great." Drew passes me the serving dish and I put some on my plate.

Before long, I have a full plate and it's time to eat. I should lead this discussion. After all, it's my body. But also I'm the person with the least amount of experience at this table. How do I even start this?

Drew's hand stills my bouncing knee. "So I assume everyone is now on board with giving Sara exactly what she wants?"

He casually takes a bite of his egg as he looks at everyone else while I stare at him. A slow smile spreads on my face. I knew I liked Drew Young for a reason. He makes everything so easy and simple.

Finn coughs to cover his laugh and my gaze darts to his green eyes. "Mostly we need to discuss what our expectations are."

"Especially if we're all in on this," Dante says.

I tighten my thighs at the thought of all of them in. I should have talked more with Madison about exactly how this works with four guys. Are there positions or stretches I need to know or do ahead of time?

Wyatt clears his throat and I lift my eyes to his dark ones. His focus is on me again and it's disconcerting. My heart throbs and my hands shake on my utensils.

"There are things we need to discuss and have clarity on before we can start." His gaze sweeps to Finn and Dante. "From the sounds coming from the kitchen last night, I'm sure you two warmed Sara up nicely."

My insides heat and I squirm on my seat. I'm sure my face is red by now.

"She gets restless." Dante smirks. "She can't sleep without a good orgasm. Or a few."

Finn chuckles.

"What all have you done, trouble?" When Finn opens his mouth, Wyatt holds up his hand. "This is the time Sara talks. If we're going to have any kind of sexual relationship, both of you said she needs to lead. So Sara, what all have you done?"

I cross my legs under the table and put my utensils down. Now isn't the time to pretend to be shy. I put my elbows on the table and join my hands. "I've masturbated with my fingers. Oral sex, given and received. Also, both at the same time. Been finger fucked."

I tap my lips trying to think of what else.

"Oh, I've jerked Dante off."

Finn chuckles again, but Wyatt gives him a stern look.

"Anyone besides the guys at this table?" Wyatt cocks his head a little.

I shake my head. "No."

He lifts his coffee to his lips and takes a sip while holding my gaze. It's intense and disarming. It's everything I always wanted from him.

When he sets his mug down, he turns to Drew. "If we're all sharing, that means no sex outside this arrangement. The three of us have discussed it, but is that what you want?"

I turn to look at Drew. He promised me he was only interested in me, but that was before this all came out. Maybe he feels differently now that he knows they're willing to cross the line. I swallow.

Drew turns to me and cups my jaw. "I'm all in, princess. However long you need to be ready."

Fuck, I'm ready now. For a second, I contemplate pushing everything on the table off and offering myself to them, but this conversation is just beginning.

"Good." I give him a smile before turning back to Wyatt.

Wyatt leans forward and his gaze dips down to my cleavage before returning to my eyes. My breasts grow heavy with desire.

Please don't be into pony play. I really don't think I could pretend to be a horse for him.

Maybe? I mean, it's still sex play.

"We need to discuss kinks, because I'm not the only one with a kink that will play with you." Wyatt glances at both Dante and Finn.

My eyes widen. Oh. But everything we've done is so vanilla. Besides both of them at the same time and watching each other. Which are kinks in themselves.

Drew laughs. "You look so surprised, princess. You shouldn't be. There's a reason we're drawn to you and it isn't your innocence."

"Then why?"

"You're curious and open. Frankly, I'm surprised you didn't experiment more in high school and college. But I can tell you were holding out for more." His gaze flicks to Wyatt before returning to me. "You already know I like to play in public. I also like to watch."

Falling into his brown eyes, I wet my lips.

"I'm open to most kinks." He takes his phone out and taps on a few things.

My phone buzzes from where I left it in the living room. Finn's phone buzzes too.

"There's an app. It's pretty extensive, but it goes through a consent form. You can choose what you're curious to try and what your hard limits and soft limits are."

Suddenly, I want to run to my phone and figure it out.

"We should all enter our information into it. It's a good way to confirm the arrangement." Drew glances around. "I only have Finn's number so he can send it to both of you."

"After breakfast." Finn points to my plate. "Eat, flower."

"We should still discuss our kinks." Wyatt arches an eyebrow at Drew, who just smirks back at him. "But going through a list would be helpful, if Sara had experience."

I bite my lip. "That shouldn't be an issue though."

"It just means you'll have a lot of *curious about* and may not know what your limits are until you're in the moment." Wyatt takes a bite of his bacon.

"Which means your safe word is going to be the most important thing we need to know." Dante draws my attention. He's mostly been quiet, listening. "There are other methods to stop, pause, or ensure you're doing good. But a safe word brings everything to an end."

Finn nods. "The stoplight method. Red means stop. Yellow means pause. That can be for anything, from something is uncomfortable and you need to change positions. Or you need to pause to go to the bathroom. Or you're okay with the scene but need a break, physically or emotionally. Green means all is good."

"You need to pick a word that isn't no or stop as your safe word. Some scenes we play might include you saying *no* and *stop* but not meaning it." Dante winks, and curiosity burns inside me.

I draw in a breath. "Okay, I'll think about that. But are you going to tell me your kinks? The things you want to do?"

The guys all look at each other.

"If we tell you, it might influence how you answer the questions, pip." Dante takes my hand in his.

I laugh. "If you don't tell me, I might put *curious* about everything."

"I like restraints." Finn glances around before focusing on me. "Tying you up. Using a swing. Even a little consensual nonconsent and role-play."

My panties are wet just thinking about that. I swallow. "So you want me to act like I don't want it?"

"Within the parameters of the scene, yes." Finn's green eyes hold mine. "We would discuss the scene prior. Including what I want to do so that you're aware of everything beforehand. Until we get to a place where we know each other's limits."

I shift in my seat and drink from my mug. The way he held me down that first time in the dining room flows through my mind. My cheeks heat and my pussy pulses in aching need.

"I'm also not afraid to get you naked. To take your panties and make you walk around wet all day without them." Finn winks.

Drew's hand slides up my thigh. "I like the idea of watching him take you like that, princess. Of participating. Of watching you come so hard you scream."

My breath quickens. I turn to Dante. "You?"

His smirk makes me hot. "Oh, I'd participate in that too. But you know I like to give orders. I wouldn't mind giving you and the others orders and watching you fall in line. I don't mind playing in public. Making you come with everyone watching and not knowing that's what's happening."

I grab my glass of ice water and take a drink to cool me down. Fuck. Pretty sure I'm into all this. My gaze catches Wyatt's.

He leans forward on his elbows and captures my full attention. "I'm what's called a Dom."

"Like leather and spanking?" I cock an eyebrow.

His lips tip into a little smile. "Like overpowering you and giving orders. Like hair pulling and chasing and pinning you down as I take you."

My heart beats harder and my breath quickens. Awareness lights along my skin. "You want a submissive."

His grin makes me squirm. "In a way. You aren't really built to be a true submissive, trouble. We all know that."

My heart stops. Does that mean he's going to tell me no?

"But I don't want someone to give in to my every demand. I want the challenge. I crave making you submit to me, punishing you when you disobey. But it has to be your decision. You'll have a safe word to pull us out of whatever we're doing."

"Will you always want it like that? Rough, taking?" I wet my suddenly dry lips. Am I crazy to want that too? What if I don't like it? What if it's too much for me?

His brown eyes soften. "No, trouble. Sometimes it will just be sex, but it's part of who I am. If it's not something you want to try or feel comfortable with, this won't work for either of us."

I take a deep breath and look down at my half-eaten food. "Tom knows you like rough sex? That's why he doesn't want you with me?"

When I lift my gaze to Wyatt's, he nods.

"But if I'm okay with it?" My breath catches waiting for his answer.

"If it's not something you want to try, I won't force you, Sara." His words almost make me laugh. Everything he said was about forcing me to submit to his will. If I was still a teenager, I might have succumbed to him easily. But now, I like the idea of fighting back, of making him chase me for a change, of making him earn it.

"None of what you told me has me running screaming. Yet." I straighten and look each of them in their eyes. "More logistics?"

Dante laughs. "Yes, a few other details to work out. Group sex?"

He looks at Wyatt, who nods. Then Finn. He smiles and nods, sending me a flirty wink. Then Drew.

"I'm good with group, though it may take a while to get our dynamics down." Drew squeezes my thigh under the table.

Fuck, I'm so wet right now. I turn to Dante.

"You have the power, pip. Do you want to do this as individuals only or are you okay with groups of us?" Dante's blue eyes search mine, digging in deep to find my truth.

"I'm good with both." My cheeks heat. "I like it when you and Finn play with me together. I like the idea of all of you being there, touching me, taking me."

Dante tips my chin up a little. "We had a chat before you came out, but you need to make the final decision. We've all been tested. You're not at risk. If you want us to use condoms—"

"No. I got an IUD earlier this year." Swallowing, I look at all of them one at a time. "I'm protected. If we're doing this, I want to feel you."

Chapter 32

Consensual Contract

Sara

Fuck, that feels freeing as hell to say. I meet each of their hungry gazes.

"The other thing to get out of the way." Dante pushes his empty plate back. "How do you want to lose your virginity, pip?"

"Oh." My cheeks flush. "Yeah, that."

Drew chuckles. "We should make it special."

"I'm just so ready to be rid of it." It spills out of me. "Do you know how hard it is to get rid of when you finally decide to get it over with?"

My gaze collides with Wyatt. His eyes are intense. Does he know I saved it for him?

I suck in a breath. Suddenly, I don't want to make this decision. "What if I don't know who does the actual deed and you all fuck me for the first time?"

"Is that what you want?" Dante's calm voice draws my attention. I meet his light blue eyes and a calmness falls over me. I know he'll take care of me.

"Yes, boss. I don't want to choose. That's what this whole thing is about, right? Me not having to choose between you four. About me getting to have all of you and you all having me."

Glancing toward the bedrooms, I grimace. "But maybe not on Tom's bed for the first time? It just seems a little too much."

Especially when he was the one who kept us apart all these years.

"How about the suite at my club?" Drew offers. "We have all the essentials in the room. Lube, toys, rope, anything else you can think of. A bar to help with nerves for all parties. And neutral ground, so you don't have any potential hang-ups about being in it."

It's also memorable. Though I don't think we'll need any of that stuff for the first time.

I give him a smile. "That sounds good."

He leans in and kisses my lips softly. When I try to deepen the kiss, he backs away.

"Consent form first, princess. We'll play after." Drew gets out his phone. "I'll make the arrangements with the club. Is there somewhere I can make a call?"

Dante stands and gestures for Drew to follow him back to the office.

Finn nudges my plate. "Eat, flower, you need your energy."

My stomach clenches with nerves. This is actually happening. Oh, fuck, this is actually happening.

Wyatt stands and comes to sit next to me. "Breathe, trouble."

His hand rubs my back in soothing circles.

He looks me in my eyes. "We can wait—"

I grab his other hand and shake my head. "No, I don't want to wait anymore, but it's just... real now."

He tips my chin up. "At any time, if you want to stop, we'll stop."

I swallow as my gaze drops to his lips. He kissed me last night. I can still feel that explosion of desire inside me.

"Trouble." He captures my lips and it's not a simple touch like the others. I gasp and he takes full advantage, pulling me closer as he explores my mouth. He tastes of coffee and bacon and this darker something that can only be Wyatt.

I'm too far away. I need to be closer. We move together. I rise and he draws me onto his lap as I straddle him on the chair. His hand threads into my hair and pulls as a growl rumbles in his chest.

Fuck, I burn for him. When I shift closer, his erection presses between my legs. My pulse throbs. My tongue strokes against his and he leans into me, pressing me back, making me rely on him to hold me. I grab onto his hair and tug even though, if he released me, I'd fall back into the table.

Everything I've wanted is within my reach. Including Wyatt. But what happens if I don't live up to his expectations? What if I'm not what he wants?

His kiss softens. He cradles my head as he pulls away and touches our foreheads together. We share each other's panting breaths.

"What's wrong, trouble?" His voice is deep, sending shivers through me.

"I can't believe this is happening," I whisper, like saying it out loud will make it all disappear. Like I'll wake up alone in my bed at home.

"I'm sorry I hurt you all these years. Sorry I made you feel less desirable. I thought it was for the best. That I was doing it for you." Wyatt's words are soft and they sink into my chest and make my pulse quicken.

"I'm scared you'll pull away again." I have to put that out there. Beating around the bush isn't my style. Yes, I tried everything to get him to notice me, short of showing up naked in his bed. But that fear of his rejection held me back.

"We talk at all times, flower." Finn's voice makes me turn to see him watching Wyatt and me. Wyatt's hand is spread in the middle of my back, holding me. "Communication is the thing that makes this work. If something isn't working, we talk. If you're worried about something, we talk. If you hold it in, this will fall apart."

"I won't reject you, Sara." Wyatt's eyes hold mine again. "I'm done running away. I'm done holding you at arm's length. I'm all in."

Something broken inside me feels like it's healing. It's still not quite whole, and it will never feel the same as it did before it cracked, but I can bear the little shards left from the break.

"You aren't mad that I want them too?" My fingers slide through his hair to hold his neck.

He blows out a breath. "You've always been mine, but I couldn't claim you. Not on my own. Not without hurting the people I love most in this world."

My heart skips a little.

"But with them, maybe we can figure out how this can be more." Wyatt's words make me almost giddy, but I don't want to put too much weight on them. We've agreed to have sex, not buy a house and move in together.

Though I've already moved in with them, even if it's temporary.

"Trouble?"

I blink and refocus. "Yes, Wyatt?"

He sits back in the chair, allowing me to straighten. "Let me make you come."

That fire inside roars back to life, not that it ever really went down.

"Yes, please."

He smiles as his hand roams down over my hip. Slipping under my skirt, his fingers tease my thigh and my breath catches. His dark eyes search mine and that intensity is right there.

"I can be gentle, trouble, but it's not in my nature." His gaze drops to my lips.

Anticipation swells inside me. "It's not?"

He shakes his head and tugs on my hair, just enough to let me know he still has ahold of it, that he's still controlling me. A rush races through me.

"Am I making you wet?" His hand slides up my thigh. The anticipation is killing me. His touch is firm and not as teasing as Finn's. His dark eyes are mesmerizing, holding me to him.

"Yes." I swallow and wet my lips.

"I'm going to enjoy punishing you, trouble." His fingers reach the apex of my thighs and they tease the edge of my panties. My breath catches, hanging on that moment before he claims me.

"Punish?" My heart thunders so loud I barely hear him, so focused on his touch, on his warm body against mine.

"You strike me as a naughty girl. Someone who won't make it easy for me. Am I wrong, trouble?" He tips my head back a little farther and slides his fingers beneath my panties to my wet, pulsing pussy.

At his first touch, I moan.

"Maybe you'll be my good girl and I won't have to punish you." His fingers part my pussy and he drags one from my entrance to my clit.

My shaky breath releases as my insides tense, ready for him to push me over the edge.

He tilts his head as he studies me. "Does it hurt, trouble?"

"Does what hurt?"

"The throbbing need between your legs." He kisses my jaw and I suck in a breath. "This aching thing."

He presses down on my clit and a rush of wetness flows out of me.

"I heard you last night, trouble. Sneaking out of your room. Letting Dante fuck this pretty little cunt before Finn took his turn. He made you scream, and that made my cock ache like this tight pussy."

"Did you find your release?" I whisper, seeking his mouth, but he holds me away from it.

"Did I jerk off to the sound of you coming like I did when I watched you on the video? When you made yourself come?"

"Oh, fuck." I need him to move his fingers. I'm right here on the edge waiting for him to topple me over.

He pulls my hair a little more, making me arch into him. "Is that what you want to know, trouble? If the sound of you coming is enough to make me explode?"

I whimper as his finger slides along my clit to my entrance, gathering my wetness and dragging it to my clit. "Please, Wyatt."

"Mmm, I like the way you beg, trouble." He nips my jaw and trails kisses down my neck. "I can't wait to make you cry."

He thrusts two fingers inside me and I shatter. His words, his touch, the rich leather scent of him all around me. It's all too much.

He tsks. "No one said you could come yet."

Finn chuckles darkly as my pussy convulses around Wyatt's fingers. Like I have any control over the need for release. Wyatt drags them out and takes his hand out of my panties.

When I make a sound of denial, he tightens his hand in my hair.

"Clean my fingers, trouble." He lifts my head and his dark eyes search mine as he holds his wet fingers in front of my mouth.

I arch an eyebrow and press my lips together. It would be so easy to give in. After all, I don't mind the taste of my come, but my submission isn't what he wants, right? A light sparks in his eyes and a grim smile forms on his lips.

He shakes his head slowly. "Open your mouth."

The minute I say anything he'll thrust his fingers into my mouth. I'm not really opposed to sucking on them, but right now, I want to test if what he said is true. Does he want me to fight, to question his authority, to make him bend me to his will instead of giving in?

He swipes my wetness over my lips and brings me in close so I have to look in his dark eyes. "When that consent form is finished, I'll see to your punishment, trouble."

He licks his fingers and smashes his lips to mine. When he yanks on my hair, I gasp, and his tongue thrusts into my mouth, making me taste myself on his tongue and lips. I moan, holding him closer, sucking on his tongue to get all the taste, wanting to come again in his arms.

He breaks off the kiss and holds me away from him. He looks me over as if I'm trouble. Fuck, I love it. He pulls the neckline of my dress to the side to reveal my bare breast.

"No bra?" It's like another thing I've done wrong.

"No."

He makes that tsking sound and then leans in and closes his mouth over my nipple, sucking almost gently.

A needful noise emanates from the back of my throat.

"Her breasts are so beautifully sensitive." Finn's voice is right there. His hand cups my other breast through my dress.

Wyatt's teeth scrape my breast before he nips at my nipple.

"Ah." I can't move away with how he's holding me.

He sucks on me to make it better, sending pulses to my pussy. He releases my nipple and meets my eyes. "Maybe I'll make you come again on the way to the club. If you're a good girl."

I bite my lip. Finn tips my chin his way and claims my mouth. Wyatt's fingers dig into my hip as Finn's tongue sweeps through my mouth.

"I love the way you taste," Finn whispers against my lips.

My eyes find Wyatt's again. There's no jealousy there. Just curiosity and desire.

Finn stands and helps me off Wyatt's lap. As I straighten my skirt, Wyatt smacks my ass. I yelp in surprise.

Finn laughs. Wyatt smirks.

"There's more where that came from."

I don't know what to think about that as Finn leads me to the couch and hands me my phone.

"Get busy, flower." He sits beside me on the couch as he opens the app.

My phone buzzes. There's a new group chat with Drew, Dante, Finn, and Wyatt. The link to the app is the only message.

I click on it to download.

While I wait, I look at what the app has in it. It has a way to consent to your partners so that you both have confirmation of consent to have sex. Then there's a menu with options for sex. They don't show everything on the page, but the list includes headings like kissing, fingers, oral, vaginal, toys, anal.

I'm not sure how long this is going to take. Wyatt sits across from me. As his phone downloads the app, he watches me.

Fuck, maybe I don't want to be a good girl, because right now I want to make Wyatt do something, anything to me. My breathing quickens and my nipples tighten. Now that I have his attention I crave the interaction. Good or bad doesn't matter, just all of it.

"We're all set up." Drew comes out of the office with Dante. "The suite is reserved for us all day and night."

I press my thighs together against the ache building there. I'm going to have sex with four guys today. The temptation to text my friends rides me, but I want to see where this goes before I get ahead of myself.

The app finishes downloading and I set up an account.

"If you have any questions, flower, just ask." Finn's fingers tease the hem of my dress.

Dante sits on the other side of me and answers the questions too. I desperately want to peek at what he's putting in there.

Drew kneels before me and grabs the backs of my knees, pulling my ass to the edge of the couch.

I gasp in a breath. "What are you doing?"

He grins at me as he hikes my dress up. "Keeping myself busy. I've filled it out. Once you complete it, we can exchange consent forms, but until then, I can think of better things to do."

He grabs the sides of my panties and slides them down and off my legs. "You mentioned receiving oral sex?"

I nod. His grin grows. My pussy aches at the desire in his dark eyes.

"Good. I've been dying for a taste of you." He drapes my legs over his shoulders. His breath caresses my bare pussy.

"Now?" I have to ask because the others are right here. They're all filling out their forms but they can clearly see everything he's doing.

"Now, princess. Fill out your form." His tongue swipes from my entrance up to my clit.

I inhale at the sparks lighting up my insides. I don't know how I'm going to fill out the form if he's going down on me with the others right here.

Chapter 33

Mutually Beneficial

Sara

My gaze collides with Wyatt's before he glances down between my legs. My breath catches. Drew sits back and spreads my pussy open wide as they both look at me. I duck my head against Finn's shoulder.

"You have a beautiful pussy, flower." Finn kisses my hair.

I glance up into his green eyes as Drew's breath grazes my thighs. Then his tongue is there again, exploring and taking his time. Meanwhile my insides are boiling, and I'm not sure how I will concentrate on filling out the questions.

"Need help?" Finn takes my phone from my hand. "Let's see the experience part should be easy. We'll work on that. It's the limits and interest part that's important."

Drew sucks on my clit and a wave of heat rolls through me. My lips part.

"So let's stick with, yes, I want to try that. No, I don't want to try that. And for some things, you can say absolutely not." Finn reaches down and unties my dress. "Being naked in front of a group? You've definitely done that. I'm going with yes on that one."

Drew slides his finger inside me while his tongue dances on my clit. My breath catches. Dante lifts my wrap dress, pulling the side open, while Finn draws open the other side, baring me to the room.

Drew sits back and takes me in. "Beautiful, princess."

His finger glides in and out of me before he adds a second. I bite my lip and he gives me a wink before leaning back in to suck again. A haze of desire falls over me.

"Blindfolds?" Finn strokes his finger over my nipple, making it tighten more before he pinches it.

"Yes," I gasp and arch my back, needing more. I'm getting so close.

"You want me to bind you, don't you, flower?" Finn cups my breast and teases my nipple. "Tie you up."

Drew keeps fucking me with his fingers and sucking on my clit before licking it. My hips rock in time with his thrusts.

"Yes, bind me."

"Good girl. Gags?"

Drew quickens his thrusts.

"I don't know." As my legs tremble against Drew's shoulders, I cry out. I'm so fucking close.

"Try. Got it." Finn takes my nipple into his mouth.

I arch into his mouth as my release overwhelms me. Drew doesn't stop pushing me higher though, and someone pinches my other nipple. I shatter again, coming around Drew's fingers as bliss fills me with warmth.

"Fuck, princess. I could do this all day." His mouth is on me again, but the break lets me come down a little. Until he begins to work me over again.

Finn releases my breast and straightens. "Spanking with and without things."

"Things?" I open my eyes to Wyatt's heated gaze taking in my flushed body. Fuck, I can't wait to feel him touching me again. His phone remains forgotten in his hand.

His darkened eyes lift to mine. "Like paddles, flogs, belts, leather straps, canes, wooden paddles. Anything I'd like to use to mark your creamy pale skin."

"Yes," I cry out as Drew pushes me over the edge.

Drew sits back. His face is wet from me. He smiles as Dante runs his hand over my hip and slides his finger against my sensitive clit. I bite my lip and moan as I turn to meet his gaze. His blue eyes are heated with desire.

Finn clears his throat. "You liked my finger in your ass, right, flower?"

Dante smirks as he pinches my clit, sending a burst of pain and pleasure through my system.

"Ah, yes." I hold Dante's gaze as he slides his finger down to where Drew's are still sliding in and out of my pulsing pussy.

"I'm just going to mark all the anal *try*. You don't know if you like it until you try it." Finn clicks on my screen a few times.

Dante wets his lips and I moan at how much I want them all.

"Definitely willing to try." My voice is a little breathy.

"That's what I like about you, pip." Dante slides his finger in with Drew's, stretching me. My lips part at the thickness and fullness. "Always willing to try."

My head presses back as I shatter around their fingers. Euphoria floods my limbs.

"Fuck, how many times has she come?" Wyatt asks as he sets his phone aside.

I can't breathe let alone tell him. Besides, I haven't been counting.

"Double penetration?" Finn asks.

Drew slips his fingers out of me as Dante thrusts three fingers into my pussy before Drew's press against my puckered hole.

"Yes?" Drew asks.

I open my eyes and find his darkened eyes watching me carefully. I love that he wants to check in with me. That he was willing to wait and is willing to do this with me and them.

"Yes," I whisper and he eases inside my ass slowly. It's too much with Dante's fingers gliding in and out of my pussy, stretching me.

Drew's progress inside stops as I come, clutching his and Dante's fingers. My moan fills the apartment as my insides burst like fireworks.

"Triple penetration. Oral, vaginal, anal?" Finn tips my face his way and I open my eyes to his green ones. "You want someone's cock in your mouth while we take your cunt and ass, flower?"

His thumb trails along my lower lip and I flick my tongue out to taste it. I'm already so full with Drew's and Dante's fingers, but I want more. I want to please all these men.

Just imagining them replacing their fingers with their cocks pushes me right back to the edge. Finn presses his thumb into my mouth and I suck on it as Drew and Dante fuck me with their fingers, shooting me off into the stars again.

My body feels liquid from my releases.

"Yes." Finn draws his finger out of my mouth.

The others ease me down before withdrawing completely. I draw in a breath and Drew gives me a smile before heading into the kitchen. Wyatt kneels before me with a washcloth. Our eyes lock.

"Just to put you back together, trouble." He wipes me down before picking up my panties and putting them in his pocket.

I raise an eyebrow, but he just gives me a smirk. He stands and draws me up with him before fixing my dress. I glance at my bedroom door, but he tips my face back to his.

"No panties, trouble." His dark eyes hold me captive. My pussy clenches. I feel vulnerable without them.

"The next section is on submission." Finn's voice breaks the tension between us.

My eyes search Wyatt's. What does he need from me? "Go ahead."

"Following orders?"

"Interested."

Wyatt's gaze drops to my mouth. Desire pulses inside me. I inhale his leather and woodsy scent. It intoxicates me. *He* intoxicates me. Today he's finally going to fuck me and I can't fucking wait.

"Forced servitude?"

"What?" I blink. "What does that mean?"

"Some Doms prefer a slave-and-master scenario." Wyatt's thumb brushes my jawline, sending little sparks cascading through me. I'm still not used to him touching me. "Some subs like to give their Dom complete control over them."

"Do you want that?" My voice sounds breathy. I'm not sure I would enjoy that, but for him, would I be willing to try? Fuck, I might be willing to try anything if I can have him.

"No, trouble. I'm not interested in you waiting on me hand and foot." His gaze returns to mine. "Though I can't wait to have you on your knees."

Oof. I'm tempted to drop to them right now.

"I'll just mark that one as a no." Finn makes a reading noise. "Restrictions from your Dom?"

When I cock an eyebrow, Wyatt smiles softly. "Limits on your behavior. Usually in a scene, but I would give you restrictions on when you can masturbate and other things that might control your behavior. We would discuss them beforehand, including the punishments if you break the rules."

His eyes flare with heat when he mentions punishments and breaking the rules. Noted.

"Okay."

"Consent can be withdrawn at any time, trouble. If you find you don't want to do something you said you'd try, you can make it stop with your safe word. But we'll always talk after a scene to check in." Wyatt strokes his thumb over my lips. "If your mouth is occupied, you can hum a song or tap on whatever you can reach three times."

"I want to try," I say softly. "I don't know what I'll like or what I won't."

Maybe I should have experimented with some of the guys who were interested, but I didn't want any of them the way I want these men. I've never wanted anyone the way I want these four.

"There are things we aren't into that you don't have to worry about, flower." Finn draws my attention as he clicks *no* on a few things. "Sorry, if you're into golden showers or knife play, we'll have to find a fifth person."

"No, we won't." Dante runs his hand up the back of my thigh, sending sparks coursing in my veins and making me hyperaware of my lack of panties. "Four is plenty for Sara. If she craves something, we'll see if we can make it happen."

"I'm good." I clear my throat of the thickness my desire caused.

Wyatt's gaze drops to my lips again. "It's hard to remember why I fought so hard against this."

He dips his head and his lips capture mine. Finally. I press up on my tiptoes to get closer until he scoops me up into his arms, lifting me so our lips are level with each other. My feet dangle in the air and I wind my arms around his neck.

"If we're all good." Drew's voice pulls me back down to earth, but Wyatt doesn't relinquish my mouth and I'm not about to give him up.

"Pip needs to find her shoes." Dante chuckles. His fingers scrape the bottom of my foot and I jerk away from Wyatt's mouth.

"On it. And panties." I blush as Wyatt lowers me down to my feet.

"No panties." Finn hands me my phone. "You agreed to forgo panties in public when required."

"It does not say that and you didn't ask that." I take my phone and try to look through the app for the nudity clause.

Finn pushes my hair over my shoulder and runs his fingers down my neck, sending shivers coursing down my spine. "I might have taken some liberties with your consent. After all, you don't know what you like or what you hate until you experience it once. So live a little, flower. And maybe Wyatt will let you come on the car ride to the club."

Finn boops my nose and I honestly don't know what to say to that. He's right. I don't know what I'll like, but I'm sure there's things I'd rather not be in the middle of and have to say my safe word.

Dante puts his hand on the small of my back and leads me to

Tom's room. "Put your shoes on. Panties are the least of your worries. You can doublecheck Finn's answers later. I'll make sure you're taken care of."

I look up into his pale blue eyes. This is really happening. He bends down and brushes his lips over mine. My heart pounds loudly in my ears. Anticipation is a living thing inside me, buzzing and needy.

My hands tremble as I slip on a pair of shoes and quickly pack a small bag of things I might need after. A pair of panties and some comfortable clothes.

When I walk out, Dante takes control of me and leads me out of the apartment and into the elevator with the others. Before anyone says anything, Finn backs me against the wall and kisses me. My hands go to the back of his neck and his cradle my ass. Fuck, he's such a good kisser that I completely zone out what's happening around me.

When he draws away, he smiles. "I can't wait to be inside you."

The fire he lit blazes into an inferno.

Dante guides me out of the elevator and into a black car waiting for us. It's not a limo but it's definitely a larger car, with enough room for all of us in the back.

I've completely lost track of time, so I'm surprised when I look at my phone and it's only noon. When we leave the underground garage, sunlight brightens the interior through the tinted windows.

"I've synced everyone's consent forms with yours, flower." Finn nods to my phone. "You should read it over."

Nodding, I pull up the app. I'm not expecting any surprises. They've told me their kinks and I'm on board. I like being watched. The heat in their gazes as someone else fucks me is undeniably sexy.

I want to take all of them. Being overwhelmed with their hands and mouths is just a precursor to the actual act. Am I nervous?

Fuck, yeah, but I doubt there will be much pain. There are hundreds of ways for a hymen to tear or break. I'd be shocked if mine is intact, especially after their fingers have been inside me. I'm sure I'll be ready for whatever they decide to do to me.

The first time I'll definitely let them lead, but I want to be an active participant. There are things I'm dying to try on them. Things I've denied myself because I didn't want anyone else.

"Have you been a good girl, trouble?" Wyatt trails his hand down to my bare knee and plays with the hem of my dress.

My breath rushes out of me as I lift my eyes to his. He promised to make me come in the car if I was good.

Dante presses a button and the privacy screen goes up between us and the driver. My pulse quickens as I meet their hungry gazes.

"I'm not wearing panties, which is pretty much the only order I received." I meet Wyatt's darkened eyes. I'm wet and so fucking ready to get this started.

His hand slides beneath my skirt to my thigh. Drew's on my other side and he lifts my knee over his to spread me open. Wyatt does the same.

"Lift your dress, pip."

I glance at Dante. The confidence these men instill in me is exhilarating. I grab the hem of my dress and pull it up. Finn touches his lips with his fingers as his green eyes focus on my pussy.

"You wet, flower?" He lifts his gaze to mine and the heat in it makes my breath catch.

"Yes." My voice is softer than usual.

Wyatt's hand clenches on my thigh. When I turn to him to see if he's in control, I sink into his dark eyes. I want him out of control with lust . For years, he's closed himself off to me. I want whatever darkness he has.

"Will you make me come?" I ask.

"Are you going to wait for permission this time, trouble?" He cocks his eyebrow as his hand trails up my inner thigh, sending tingles to where I want him the most.

I bite my lip and nod. I'll try, but if I come, I still win.

"If you come before I say, you'll be punished, trouble. Do you understand?" His fingers are almost to my pussy, and my brain is melting with the attention of all these men and their scents blending into a heady concoction I'll never be able to resist.

"Punished how?"

He runs his finger down my pussy to my entrance and thrusts in. I gasp.

"I'll put you over my knee and spank you with my bare hand on your bare ass until the imprint of my hand burns on your skin." He holds his finger inside me.

I get wetter with his words and my pussy pulses with need around him.

"Do you understand the consequences, trouble?" He draws his finger out before thrusting back in deep.

"Yes, Wyatt."

"Yes, sir." His eyes hold mine captive as he continues to slowly fuck me on his finger.

"Yes, sir." I'm already so close, and having the others watching does something to me, edging me closer and closer, heightening every touch, every ache.

I meet Dante's eyes and he reaches down to adjust his cock. Images from my bedroom and the shower hit me. It happens so fast, I couldn't stop it if I tried. I cry out as I soak Wyatt's hand.

My wide eyes turn to Wyatt. He just shakes his head with a solemn look as my pussy continues to convulse on his finger.

The car comes to a stop and turns off.

"We're here," Drew announces.

Chapter 34

Fiduciary Responsibility

Sara

As we walk into the Veiled Vixen, my heart thumps like a rabbit's. My thighs are still wet from coming. Wyatt's hand is on my low back, guiding me as the others surround me, with Drew in the lead.

Wyatt's going to spank me. I knew he'd punish me eventually, but spanking? It's humiliating to think of him turning me over his knee in front of the others, but also hot to imagine his hand on my bare ass. I'm curious but also worried that I might not like it.

"Alan." Drew nods to the bouncer and Alan opens the door for us without so much as a *Have you got anything illegal on you?*

There's a small crowd and a few dancers working the room as we pass through. But this time it's a quick walk before we're at the door to the suite. Drew unlocks it and we step in. It's just how I remember it.

"You aren't actually going to spank me, right?" I draw away from Wyatt but he follows. Anticipation flutters through me.

"You earned it, trouble." His eyes sparkle as I back away and he keeps pace with me.

"I can't control when I come." I cross my arms over my chest and hold my ground, glaring up at him even as everything in me wants him to punish me. To see how it feels.

"You need to learn to obey." He tucks my hair behind my ear. "We'll need to have a full discussion about what I need from you. Each of us, privately, will talk to you. But for now, we need your safe word."

I bite my lip and look around the room. A word that will stop them no matter what. Finn arches his eyebrow when I meet his green eyes. He used to tickle me when I was little. I take a breath and my gaze locks on Wyatt's.

"Mercy."

Finn chuckles, but Wyatt nods.

"I hope you never need to use it, trouble. But if you do need it, use it." Wyatt wraps his hand around the back of my neck. Oh, hell, he thinks I might need it right now.

My startled gaze lifts to his. "Wyatt—"

"Three, trouble." He draws me over to the couch beside the bed and he sits down. "Only three spanks. You can take that."

Swallowing, I glance over at the others as they sit in the chairs to watch. Like I'm their entertainment. I suppose I am. Especially today.

It doesn't matter. I like the attention.

"Fine." I meet Wyatt's eyes defiantly. I can take this. "How do you want me?"

"Face down over my lap." When I move to lie across him, he holds up his hand. "Take off your dress."

I arch an eyebrow, but untie the bow at my waist and shrug out of my dress, letting it pool on the floor at my feet. I straighten and slide my shoes off. "Anything else, sir?"

I might have said *sir* with attitude. The room is warm but a shiver still ripples through me as their eyes take me in.

"That's five now, trouble. Looking for more?"

"No, sir." Maybe. I don't know why it's so fun to press his buttons.

"Move it, trouble. So we can get on to other things." Wyatt leans back like I'm holding up everything.

When I hesitate, Wyatt holds his hand out to me and I take it. He guides me down and I can feel the flush of heat rising from my chest to my face. He positions me so his leg supports my hips. His hand rests on my ass and I suck in a breath.

This position is so undignified.

"Count them."

I hold onto his leg as his hand comes down on my ass, filling the room with a loud smack.

"Ah, one."

"One, what?" He presses against the sting.

"One, sir." I'm not sure what to think of the pain.

He smacks my ass again in the same spot.

"Ow, two, sir."

He slides his hand down between my legs and rubs my pussy. "How does that feel?"

"It still stings." I gasp as he eases his finger inside me and uses my wetness to stroke my clit. I try to widen my legs so he can reach better. My breath quickens as my desire swells.

He pulls his hand away and smacks the same spot on my ass.

"Ow." I try to rise up, but he holds me down.

"Trouble," he says as a warning.

"Three, sir." My words are a little belligerent as he rubs my ass cheek.

"Two more." He spanks me again.

"Four, sir." My skin burns.

He slips his hand between my legs. Pleasure and pain mixes, intensifying both. I moan softly as he rubs my clit.

"One more, trouble."

He draws his hand away from me and I brace as he brings it down on my sensitive skin.

"Ah, five, sir." I sag on his lap, relief that it's over floods me.

"Good girl." He thrusts two fingers inside my pussy and fucks me hard and fast with them.

I bite my lip to stop from coming. He chuckles and slows down. His thumb gently strokes my clit. Fuck, that's even worse. I'll be coming in no time if he keeps that up. Moaning, I ache for release.

"Please, sir." I can't move in my current position, but the need to come is almost overwhelming.

"Come for me, trouble." He adds a third finger and gently fucks me with them while stroking my clit. I'm so wet I can hear his fingers as they slide in and out.

I cry out as my orgasm drags me under. Slumped over his lap, I try to get my breathing back to normal as my pussy flutters around his fingers.

He draws his fingers out and rubs my tender ass. "You okay, trouble?"

"Mmhmm." I release a breath.

"Do you want ice?" His voice is almost tender. He draws me up and helps me shift until I'm straddling him. He's still fully clothed and I'm completely naked.

"No, sir."

He cradles my cheek and smiles softly. "You don't always have to call me *sir*, trouble."

I nod. The energy seeps out of me. "Fuck, I'm tired."

Wyatt glances over my shoulder and I lean my head against him. Dante comes over and lifts me off Wyatt's lap. I curl into Dante. Drew has the covers down on the bed and Dante puts me down.

"Sleep for a few, pip."

I can't even open my eyes to protest.

Dante

Her breathing evens out and the line eases on her forehead. I smooth her hair back and pull the covers up over her. Drew kisses her temple before nodding toward the bar.

We head over there while Wyatt slips into the attached bathroom.

When he joins us, Drew pours Finn and I drinks.

"How are we doing this?" Drew hands a glass to Wyatt before lifting his own to his lips.

"Blindfold her." Finn sits on the bar stool and his gaze goes to the bed. "Tie her hands. We each take a turn."

She's out right now. It sounds so clinical when Finn describes it, but that's exactly what we're doing. We're taking her virginity and she doesn't want it to be just one of us.

"We need to work up to it." I blow out a breath. "Anyone have issues with being naked in front of each other?"

My gaze goes to Wyatt. Drew's already mentioned wanting to watch. Finn and I have been naked together with Sara.

"I'm willing to do what it takes." Wyatt takes a sip of his drink.

"Good. Because when it comes down to it, she's been saving herself for you."

He sighs. "I don't know that I'm the right guy for someone's first time."

"We're all going to fuck her." I glance over at her still-sleeping form. "Just one of us fucks her first. We should also work her up to anal today."

Drew chuckles. "Maybe we should compare sizes to see who goes first."

Finn rolls his eyes. "Who's actually done anal with a woman before?"

He raises his hand and so do we all.

"Dammit." Finn shakes his head. Pretty sure he was hoping he was the only one. "Kinky bastards."

"It doesn't matter who goes first or last, just as long as she's taken care of." Wyatt glances toward her again.

We all nod. She's the most important part of this equation.

Sara

I stretch and am suddenly aware of a few things: I'm naked on a bed with a sheet over me. Not surprising. My eyes are covered but little glints of light bleed in from the edges of the blindfold. And something is wrapped around my wrists, holding them secure near my head.

I tug, but the restraints don't move.

The sheet slips from me and I turn my face in the direction it's pulled away from my body. My pulse quickens.

The bed dips next to me and a hand brushes my cheek.

"It's okay, pip. We just figured it would be easier this way." Dante strokes his hand down my neck and cups my breast. Heat floods me.

"Uh, what way is that?"

The bed dips on my other side. A hand brushes my stomach.

"You don't want to know who's taking you, flower." Finn's voice comes from the end of the bed. "You have nothing to compare it to, so we figured we'd give you the fantasy. Hands touching. Mouths kissing. Fucking without seeing who's fucking you."

He grabs my ankles and pulls me down. I squeak as my ass reaches the edge of the bed. Finn chuckles. He lifts my legs over his shoulders and his mouth closes over my pussy.

My lips part on a gasp and Dante's mouth captures mine. I try to keep up with his kiss as Finn sucks and licks my clit. The bed dips again beside Dante and someone kisses my stomach up to my breast. A mouth captures one breast while another mouth captures my nipple. Oh, fuck.

I fall apart, moaning into Dante's mouth as they work me over. Hands begin to move over me, smoothing over my skin. Some soft, some rougher. Finn thrusts his tongue into my pussy over and over, while each mouth on my nipples worships me a little differently.

Dante's tongue sliding against mine distracts me.

When I shatter and cry out again, they move as I'm coming down.

Their hands trail over my breasts and between my legs as they shift. Someone else's mouth sucks on my clit as their fingers thrust inside me.

My pussy tightens on an aftershock around them and I suck in a breath.

Mouths taste my skin, my neck, before finding my nipples and sucking and pulling on them. Fire rages through me and someone kisses me. Someone's hand works beneath my hips and rubs lube on my puckered hole.

It's overwhelming. I can't track who's where. I shatter, coming around the fingers in my pussy. The fingers rubbing my asshole slide inside and I gasp into the mouth taking mine.

No one says anything.

I'm surrounded by their heat and can't move my hands. Sparks tingle through me.

I can't see them, but I feel them everywhere. Lighting me up, scorching me.

Hands grab my knees and pull them up, holding me spread open as someone sucks on my clit while fucking me with their fingers. They stretch my pussy open almost unbearably. Someone else fucks my ass with their fingers, slowly sliding in and out, massaging the muscles.

The mouth on mine moves down to my jaw, to my neck, nipping, sucking, licking, kissing.

I'm lost in a haze of release, falling and rising back up. I've never felt like this before. Never had so much stimulation at once.

They move away from me again. My legs are held up and hands still touch me everywhere.

"Are you ready, Sara?" Dante's voice, but I can't pinpoint where he is.

"Yes, boss."

A hand slides into mine and squeezes it. "I'm right here with you, pip. We all are."

Something thicker than a finger presses against my entrance.

Hands cup my breasts and then mouths suck on my nipples. The guy between my legs rubs my clit in slow, steady circles as he presses into me.

I arch as he keeps up the steady pressure, easing inside me for the first time. When he sinks in all the way, I feel his body against mine. Realizing I'm holding my breath, I gasp.

Dante squeezes my hand and brushes my hair from my face. His ocean scent fills my nose as he presses his forehead to mine. "Are you okay?"

Dante isn't my first. That's all I know. He's larger than Finn, so maybe they just wanted to take it easy on me. I don't know about the others. I haven't seen them naked.

"Pip?"

I gasp in another breath. "Yes, boss. I'm good."

"Pain?"

I shake my head. It's different and fills me so much more than their fingers, but there isn't really pain. The guy between my legs pulls out and thrusts back in. A breath shudders through me.

Then he pulls out. The guys shift again and someone else thrusts into me.

"Fuck," I whisper and whimper at the feel of someone new.

"Bad?" Dante didn't shift. He's still right here with me. Still my protector. Still watching out for me.

"Good," I pant.

The guy thrusts again and pulls out. My insides are pulsing with the need for release.

Another cock fills my pussy, pushing in slowly. As he eases inside me, his fingers tease my clit until I explode. I cry out as he sinks all the way in with my pussy clutching at his cock and then pulls almost all the way out and thrusts in.

He pulls away.

"Dante?" I whisper. There's only one left.

His lips brush over mine. "You ready?"

"Please." I want to feel him inside me, just like the others.

He kisses me softly before his hand trails down my body as everyone shifts.

His cock presses against my entrance and I wet my lips, remembering his taste and the feel of him inside my mouth. He slides in a little ways, and even with the others before him, his cock stretches my pussy.

His hands take my legs from whoever was holding them and pushes them up against me. He thrusts in deep. I catch my breath. His cock is so thick and long, touching me so deep it aches.

"Breathe, pip."

I suck in a breath. Fuck, he's big. His fingers stroke my clit as I adjust to his size.

A hand touches my face and draws me toward them. Lips meet mine and I recognize Finn. My body relaxes as he kisses me while Dante holds still inside me. Fuck, Dante is inside me.

He draws back and pushes back in.

I moan into Finn's mouth. He chuckles before kissing along my jaw.

"Can I be untied now?" I jerk on my wrists.

"One more first, flower." Finn steps away.

Dante draws his cock out of me and I whimper, wanting the fullness, needing it. I want to be fucked, not just penetrated.

Someone rolls me over. Hands smooth over my back and pull my ass cheeks apart. Wet fingers slide into my puckered hole. I'm not sure whose or how many but they thrust in and out together until I fall over the edge.

"Good girl." Wyatt's voice.

They pull out and something thick and blunt rests against my puckered hole.

"Ready, pip?"

My breath catches, but I nod.

"Relax, princess." Drew's voice is easy as the cock presses into me.

I try to relax but it burns just a little as whoever it is pushes in and keeps pressing. Fingers tease my clit, stirring the fire inside me to raging again.

"Fuck, flower. You're doing so well."

They're all watching someone fuck my asshole. I breathe out as I adjust to this new feeling of someone buried in my ass. He pulls out and presses back in and I moan at the sensation.

"Good, pip?"

I nod. The cock works in and out until he's fucking me, thrusting in over and over, rubbing along my sensitive nerves. My release barrels down on me and I scream into the bed as I shatter.

He pulls out before he finishes. Someone rubs a warm washcloth between my legs and ass, cleaning me up. I relax against the bed, waiting for whatever's next.

Chapter 35

Leverage

"Is anal good, flower?" Finn releases one of the restraints. Then his hands massage my wrist.

"I came." I blow out a breath.

"You can come from something you don't like, pip." Dante works on my other wrist, undoing the restraint and massaging me. "Did you like it?"

"Yes, boss. I'd like to actually have sex now though."

Wyatt chuckles as he pulls off my blindfold. I sit up. They're all naked. Fuck, I don't know where to look first. All of them stay in shape. It's hard to believe they were all inside me and someone fucked my ass for the first time.

"I feel like I should say something, but I really don't know what." My eyes collide with Dante's. "What next?"

"We'd like to keep fucking you, pip." He brushes my hair behind my shoulder and trails the backs of his fingers down my arm. "We'd love to come, but we want you to participate. Did you enjoy the restraints and the blindfold?"

I nod and turn toward where he sits against the headboard. It was intense and perfect.

"I liked being overwhelmed." Crawling toward him, I straddle his lap. "But I miss the visual stimulation and the talking."

My gaze falls to his hard cock before me.

"I like touching too." When I meet his light blue eyes, my hand steadies his cock. Rising up, I slide his cock back to my entrance. They won't stop me now. No more waiting.

His hands rest on my hips, letting me lead. I glance to the others as they sit around the bed, watching me. Their cocks hard for me. A shiver of anticipation races down my spine. These men are mine.

I focus on Dante. Our eyes lock as I lower my pussy down over his cock, feeling him stretch me open again. He groans as I take him all the way inside. A low moan escapes me. The feel of him sliding against my walls is ecstasy.

"You feel amazing, pip." He brushes my hair out of my face and leans in to capture my lips. My breasts press against his hard chest. He's all around me and inside me. Finally.

I stay there just breathing him in and feeling this. I don't want to think beyond this day.

His cock twitches inside me, urging me to give him more, to move. I rise up a little and fall back down on him. The head of his cock presses against my womb, sending shivers down my spine. I don't want to move, but also need to. His blue eyes search mine as we remain connected, like maybe he's shocked at how good this feels too.

Breaking the standstill, Dante rolls me onto my back and I wrap my legs around him as he claims my mouth. He pulls out and thrusts back in. I gasp into his kiss. Fuck, his kiss is almost as distracting as the fire blazing inside me. He kisses me as if we've never tasted each other before. He thrusts into me over and over and over again until I lose myself in the feel of him. It's so much more than what I've experienced with their fingers.

I can feel the others watching us, but I don't let it filter through my thoughts. This moment is mine and Dante's. It's been brewing since that morning he caught me masturbating, maybe even before that.

He's been with me as long as the others, but while Wyatt wouldn't acknowledge me, Dante always watched me, always pulled me away. Now he's fucking me like I'm his and it feels more than right.

"Come for me, pip." His voice is strained as he rests his forehead against mine.

I open my eyes and meet his. The intimacy of this moment is too much. The desire reflected in his eyes. The feel of him inside of me, surrounding me. Finally. My orgasm crashes through me like a tidal wave, forceful and overwhelming. I arch up into him with a cry of release. He continues to thrust, pushing me higher, as I ride the wave.

Groaning, he comes. As my pussy milks him, his cock pulses, filling me with his hot cum. It's an odd feeling, but it makes me feel more complete than I've ever felt before. He braces his arms on either side of my head, still buried deep inside me.

I can barely breathe as we come down. My heart races at what I've done. It was one thing to let them claim me. To lie back and let it happen. Now it's my turn. I get to claim them back.

His light blue eyes are almost black as he searches mine. He dips his head and our lips collide. I want more. I can't get enough of him and just want to do this again and again.

Wyatt

I wasn't sure how I'd feel sharing Sara, but she makes it as natural as breathing. Drew sits a few feet from me as we watch Sara and Dante. None of us came in her, that was part of it. She didn't want to know who was the first and she wanted all of us.

Now, she needs to be in control. This is her decision. She leads when we fuck her for real.

At least this time. We all have things we want to do with her.

We'll all get our time, just the two of us, but right now, this is all about Sara.

She's fascinating to watch, but Dante baffles me. For years, he's acted as referee in this game of ours. Sara lusting after me and me keeping her at arm's length. But right now, I can feel how deep their connection is.

And I'm grateful for it.

Dante is one of my best friends. He had a rough life growing up. His father skipped out on his mother. His uncle took them in and reminded Dante every day of how grateful he should be. Dante never felt like he fit in. But with us he always has.

Seeing him and Sara form a bond would have made me jealous before. Now I can't see it any other way. She's never truly been mine. Even when we were kids. She's always been ours.

Ours to protect. Ours to guide. Ours to hold.

Dante releases her and grabs a fresh washcloth from the towel warmer nearby. This suite has everything. He spreads her legs and cleans her gently as she watches him. She's not shy. That's good. He leans over her and kisses her again and she sighs into his mouth.

After he lifts her to sitting and heads into the bathroom to finish cleaning up, she turns with a smile. Her eyes meet Drew's briefly and he gives her a nod toward us. Finn and me.

Her gaze swings to me and our eyes lock. For years, I've held myself back from her, knowing I could never claim her as mine. But she's always been mine.

Her cheeks flush and she crawls across the bed to me. She stops and kneels with her butt on her heels and her hands on her thighs as she looks at me.

"I don't know how you want me." She's not being coy, but honest.

I slide my hand up her thigh and hold her pale green eyes captive with mine.

"You're perfect the way you are." My hand captures hers. My pulse quickens at the heat in her eyes. The desire. The need.

"Want more, trouble?" I draw her forward and she straddles my lap. Normally, I prefer a more dominant position, but right now, I need her to feel safe and wanted and comfortable.

She bites her lip. "Yes, sir."

"Hands on my shoulders."

She does as I ask.

When I smile, her eyes light up like she's won a prize. It won't always be this easy between us or even this tender, but I'm in this to give the girl of my dreams a day to remember.

"I want to be with all of you again." She wets her lips and her gaze drops to mine.

I tuck her hair behind her ear and she shivers at my touch. My fingers linger in her hair, following it down to her perfect breasts. As my finger brushes her nipple, she sucks in a breath.

"Did you enjoy having all our mouths and hands on you?" I toy with her nipple, watching her eyes closely. Her pupils dilate and her lips part.

"Yes, sir."

"Could you tell who was touching you?" I'm curious. In the future she might be able to tell, but she never saw Drew's or my cocks before the blindfold came off.

She shakes her head and I pinch her nipple, making her inhale sharply.

"Use your words, trouble."

She shivers beneath my softened touch. "No, sir. I couldn't tell who was who."

"Did you want to?"

"No, sir. It was perfect."

I cup her breast and slide my hand between her thighs, teasing my finger along her pussy. "Do you want more than one of us to fuck you at a time?"

My finger grows wetter, giving me her body's answer. I slide my finger up to her clit and circle it lazily.

"Yes, sir. I liked it when Finn went down on me while I went down on Dante, and the other way." Her eyes lose focus as I work her clit. Her hips rock with my touch.

She tightens her hands on my shoulders as her lips part on her soft breaths.

"What if I fuck this pussy while you swallow Finn's cock?"

Her gaze focuses on mine. "I want to take you one at a time first, but then I'm open to play."

Her hand trails down my chest as her eyes remain on mine, waiting for me to tell her to stop, but not this time. This time, she can be the one in control. Her fingers sweep down my abs and brush my hard cock.

"You're a beautiful woman, Sara."

Her eyes widen. I've never had the chance to tell her that. But I've always thought it.

She wraps her hand around my erection and strokes it. Her gaze drops to my cock as she runs her fingers over the head and veins.

"Will I be able to tell which one of you is fucking me?" She lifts her eyes to mine and I pinch her nipple as I thrust my fingers into her wet cunt. She moans as her pussy flutters around my intrusion.

"Do you want to? Do you want to know us so intimately that you could pick us just by the shape of our cocks?" I grind the palm of my hand against her clit.

Her mouth softens and her eyes unfocus as I fuck my fingers in and out while stimulating her clit. She squeezes my cock. When she cries out her release, her pussy drenches my hand.

I move quickly, taking her hands and pressing her back onto the bed. With her hands beside her head, I thrust my cock deep into her weeping cunt and she moans.

"Sore?" I pause, letting her adjust to my size, worried because this time I don't want to hurt her.

She shakes her head, then remembers. "No, sir."

I draw her hands over her head and grip her wrists together with one of mine, stretching her body out beneath me. I hook my other hand beneath her knee and pull it up next to her chest.

"Wyatt." Her eyes capture mine as I draw out and punch back into her. "Oh, fuck, that feels good."

"Eyes on me, trouble. I want to see your eyes when you come for me." I'm not as gentle as I was before, but everything in me knows she can take it. She was built for me. Her hips lift to each of my thrusts, taking me deep inside her.

"Keep this here." I release her leg and she pushes it against my shoulder to hold it there. I reach between us and rub her clit while I piston in and out of her tight little cunt.

"Oh, fuck," she shouts and comes on my cock. Her eyes stay on mine even as they lose focus. Her cunt milks my cock until I can't take any more.

Groaning, I thrust in deep and kiss her. My release takes my breath away as my cock coats her insides with my warm cum. This is what I always wanted. What I dreamed of. She moans into my mouth as an aftershock clutches around me.

If it was just her and me, I'd stay here, deep inside her, until I could fuck her again, but my girl is on a mission. When I get her alone, we'll see exactly how much she can take.

Sara

Fuck, I want to do that again. And again. And again.

Wyatt kisses me, thrusting his still hard cock inside me and making an aftershock shoot through my system. He pulls out and I want to draw him back inside. Instead, I reluctantly let him go.

Wyatt just fucked me. My brain spins dizzily. From what he said before, this isn't exactly how he wants me. But if this is any indication of what he can give me, I'm all in. He returns with a washcloth and leans over to capture my nipple in his mouth as he wipes me clean.

My fingers clench in his hair as I arch my body into his touch. Sparks scatter through me and I almost pull him back down over me and make him start over.

Do I want to get fucked by him while blowing someone else? Hell, yes. But I want to get to know the guys as individuals before more group stuff. I'm definitely interested in the group stuff though.

As I sit up, my gaze meets Drew's. He smirks and nods toward Finn.

I'm beginning to wonder if the guy wants to fuck me at all, but he did say he got off by watching others. Maybe watching me fuck someone else gets him there.

"Flower." Finn's green eyes meet mine and he gives me a cocky smile. Before I can move his way, he comes to sit next to me and catches the back of my neck. "Had enough yet?"

My eyes flick from his to Drew's and I shake my head.

Dante and Wyatt sit in their boxers on the couch, watching us. Finn rises up on his knees and draws my back against him. His cock slots between my ass cheeks, and I flush remembering someone took me there and it felt better than I imagined.

Is that what Finn wants to do?

Finn grabs my neck and holds my head against his shoulder. His hand slides down my stomach. Sparks follow in the wake of his touch. "I love an audience, flower. This arrangement will work nicely for that."

Drew smirks as he strokes his cock lazily. My pussy pulses in anticipation. His gaze follows Finn's hand as he slides his fingers over my clit back to my entrance.

"We could spend days fucking you and not get tired." His lips move against my ear as he presses two fingers inside me. "Would you like that, flower?"

When I gasp, he tightens his hand around my throat, not to cut off my breathing though, just to hold me there. He slides his fingers back to my clit, working me into a frenzy as I focus on Drew's hand on his cock.

None of them would be considered small. I'm not even sure they're regular sized. Dante's is the biggest in both length and girth. But not by much.

Precum beads on the tip of Drew's cock and he spreads it down himself. I wet my lips. How will he taste?

Finn draws his wet fingers up over my stomach to my nipple, coating it in my wetness, teasing the tip to a hardened peak. "Do you know how beautiful you look spread open, taking cock into your pussy?"

"I don't," I whisper.

"Want me to show you?" he whispers in my ear like it's something wicked.

"Show me."

He draws back and I look over my shoulder at him. "Lie down."

I move onto my back and he grabs my knees to drag me closer.

"Wedge."

I furrow my brow. Drew passes him a pillow wedge over me. Drew smiles down at me and brushes my hair from my face.

"Lift your hips, flower."

I do and he slides the wedge beneath them so my pussy is lifted up to him.

"Look up."

My gaze shifts above us. "Fuck, I forgot about the mirror."

Finn laughs and spreads my legs. "You can watch my cock slide in and out of your perfect pussy as I fuck you."

The way he talks makes me so wet.

His cock lines up with my entrance and he eases in. I suck in a breath at the feel of him inside me and watching it happen at the same time. Drew lies on the bed and rests his head beside mine so his hair touches my shoulder. I meet his dark gaze in the mirror.

"We can play with the mirrors in this room all you want, princess."

I shiver as Finn's cock fills me full. The sight of his hips pressed against mine floods me with heat. He pushes my legs wider and slides his fingers over my clit. When he draws out of my pussy, his cock glistens with my wetness before he slides it back in.

His finger draws circles around my clit, winding me tighter and tighter.

"You'll be able to watch as we fuck you together." Drew's voice is soft in my ear. "Watch our cocks slide in and out of your tight pussy and warm, wet mouth. We'll work up to you taking someone in your ass at the same time, until you're so full you can't stop coming."

I cry out, arching, tightening all through my body as my release takes me. For a moment, I hang in that feeling, watching Finn pump into me. His gaze on his cock and my pussy.

I fall back into myself and gasp in a breath.

Finn winks at me in the mirror. "We can do better."

Chapter 36

Preferred Stock

Sara

Wait, what? Finn pulls out and flips me over. Before I can get my hands under me, he draws my hips up and sinks back into my pussy, filling me completely. His cock pushes in deep and I press my forehead against the bed.

"Ah, fuck." It should be illegal for anything to feel this good. I should also be mad at these men for making me wait for it. But I can't do anything but feel as Finn pulls out and sinks back in. Every inch is ecstasy.

Drew tips my face his way. Our eyes lock. His pupils are blown with lust. I bite my lip as Finn fucks me hard and fast, pushing me closer and closer to the edge.

Leaning in, Drew kisses me upside down. This kiss is filthy with tongue and teeth. It's more of a claiming than a kiss.

Finn grabs my sore ass cheek and squeezes, sending a bolt of pain and pleasure to my core. "I can't wait to fuck your ass while someone fucks your pussy. Your pussy is already so tight, but it will make you feel even tighter around our cocks."

I whimper as his words and his cock build the fire hotter and hotter inside me. I'm riding the edge, just waiting to fall over. His wet thumb presses against my asshole, slipping inside.

Crying out into Drew's mouth, I shatter. Every inch of me shivers as sparks course through me. Drew pulls away and brushes my hair from my face. My breath comes out in pants.

When Finn continues to drive into me, my fingers claw at the bedspread at the overstimulation. My pussy still throbs around him.

"I'm going to love playing with you, flower." He reaches between my legs and pinches my clit as he thrusts in deep.

I can't breathe as I spiral into another release. Stars burst behind my eyelids. Warmth floods me as Finn groans and releases his cum into me. Panting, I open my eyes and realize Drew isn't right next to me anymore.

Finn draws his cock out. I suck in a breath as hands grab my hips, keeping me from falling to the side. Drew slams his cock into me. I cry out as an aftershock rips through me, pulsating around his cock.

"So warm and tight, princess. Didn't want anything to drip out." Drew thrusts in and out. My insides sizzle as he works me back up to the edge. His hands caress my ass. "How did it feel to take four hard cocks in this pussy?"

I press up onto my hands with my head hanging between my arms and push back to meet his thrusts. "So fucking good."

He draws me upright until his chest touches my back. His cock rocks within me, driving me higher. "You thought about what our night together would be like, didn't you? The first time we'd fuck?"

I bite my lip as a moan works out of me. "Yes."

"Did you imagine it like this? Your cunt full of three other men's cum? Still warm and wet from the last guy? How many times have you come, princess?" Drew's lips caress the back of my ear with every word.

I can't think. I can't even process his words. His hand slides up to toy with my breast. Need, want, desire all slam through me, making me weak and supple to his demands.

"I want your cum." I reach behind me to grab his hips as I match his thrusts. My whole body buzzes with the need for release.

He chuckles darkly. "Greedy little whore, aren't you?"

"Drew." My pussy clenches around him at his words. "Fuck."

"You want to be my naughty girl, princess?" His fingers slide between my legs to work my clit. "You want to be a whore for me?"

"Yes, please. Make me your whore."

He fucks me roughly, every stroke taking me higher.

"That's why you wanted me, isn't it, princess? You don't want another man to worship you. You want one who will defile you. Make you do things you never thought you'd want to do. Make you filthy."

My orgasm overwhelms me, drawing him into his release as he thrusts in deep. Every pulse of his cock makes my breath catch. When he kisses the side of my neck, I take in a shaky breath.

"Better than I imagined, princess." Drew eases out of me and Finn catches me against him. He uses a warm towel to clean between my legs.

"How are you, flower?" His green eyes search mine.

"I'm good." I'm sure my smile is sloppy, but damn, I just got fucked by four guys and I feel euphoric. Because I'm hoping to do it all over again.

"Come on. Let's get some food and a drink before round three."

My pulse increases at the heat in his eyes. I'm definitely ready for round three.

Drew

Sara slips off the bed and I wrap a silky robe around her shoulders, searching her eyes for any censure.

"Was that okay, princess? Or did that make you uncomfortable?"

She shrugs on the robe and I draw the fronts together, pulling her against me. Her pale green eyes dance with amusement.

"You can call me a whore all you like as long as I'm your whore."

She pushes up on her toes, grabs the back of my neck, and presses her lips against mine. The tightness in my chest unravels as I take over the kiss.

Wyatt liked it when I called her my whore. His eyes lit up. I checked out all their consent sheets, and the fact that Wyatt likes domination and primal play doesn't really surprise me. The man is stiff and poised in his social life, determined to be exactly what everyone expects.

Letting loose during sex, taking control of another person. Fuck, I can get on board with that. Pretty sure all of us could when it comes to Sara. And that control will be hard won.

I lift my mouth from hers. "Drink?"

"Mmm." Her eyes darken and drop to my lips. "Did watching the others fuck me make you want me more?"

Her gaze lifts to mine. She's being bold, but there's hesitation in her eyes. This is all new to all of us and it's going to take some time to get comfortable.

"I enjoy watching, but that includes watching me fuck you." I squeeze her sore ass cheek and she whimpers. "Did you enjoy your spanking?"

Her eyes light up and she smirks. "Maybe."

Wyatt comes up to us and hands us each a drink. Sara smells hers and smiles.

"Manhattan. My favorite."

He grabs the back of her neck and kisses her fiercely. "I know. I want you relaxed for this next part."

Her smile is for both of us as she slips over to where Dante sits. She's intoxicating enough that I don't need the whiskey, but Wyatt taps my glass with his.

"Still not one hundred percent on board with this, but she's amazing to watch with anyone." Wyatt's words aren't lost on me.

I'm the odd man out in this equation. The one she brought into their group. It probably would've been easier for them if I just backed out, but I'm not willing to give up Sara.

She chose me. She wants me.

I'm going to keep her no matter what.

"You'll find we blend very nicely when it comes to things we want to do to our princess." I sip my whiskey. She straddles Dante's lap on the couch and kisses him.

I'm not a possessive man. Not usually. I'm usually the one unwilling to commit to one woman. Whether the woman knows about the other women or not is up to them. Some don't want to know, but I've never promised faithfulness.

Not until now.

"I should put in an order for food." My phone is over on the bar. It's only a little weird to be in only my boxers with these guys. After all, we were all on the bed naked together.

"Already done. Dante took care of it." Wyatt's gaze turns thoughtful as he watches Sara with Dante. "If you decide to take on anyone else, we need to know." He turns and faces me. "We know your past with multiple women, but if we're all sharing Sara, that means she's the only one."

I shake my head and smile. "She's the only one. I already promised her, but I'm all in on this until she ends things. If she ends things."

I don't see an end to this, but maybe these guys do. It doesn't matter if the future is with them or not, but I can see my future with Sara. This is what she needs right now, but if they end up being dicks and dropping her again, I'll still be here.

I'll be the one to sweep up her broken pieces and put her back together again. Wyatt doesn't believe that, but I don't need to make him believe. I only need Sara to believe in me.

Wyatt makes a noncommittal noise. His gaze once more focused on Sara. Her forehead is pressed against Dante's and they speak in a low tone. Finn brings over a drink and sits next to them.

There's a comfort already forming between the three of them. Makes sense since they've done things with her together.

"You going to have the same talk with him?" I nod toward Finn. "His reputation is almost as bad as mine."

Wyatt blows out a breath. "This is different. She's different. All those other women didn't mean anything to us."

"I understand and feel the same way," I say.

His gaze meets mine. "Thank you for the other morning."

I grin and slap him on the shoulder. "You would have got there on your own eventually."

He shakes his head. "I still don't know how Tom will react when he gets back."

"Ah, yes, the brother." I rub my jaw. "Those men haven't been in lately. I have a guy tracking Crystal to see if they can find anything else."

"I have Sebastian Cross looking into Tom." Wyatt sighs. "But when Tom wants to disappear, he's good at it. But Cross is also trying to figure out what else Tom might be running from."

"I've worked with Cross before. If there's something to find, he'll find it." Cross works security for Heath Duncan, but is a good man to know if you want information.

My phone buzzes on the bar and I walk over to it. Wyatt goes to join the others.

"Food's here," I say.

"I'll get it." Dante moves Sara to Wyatt's lap and goes over to pull on his jeans.

After checking to make sure I don't have any messages, I set my phone down. "I'll go with."

Dante nods as I pull on my pants. We go to the door bare chested and shoeless, but fuck it, I own this place. There's a discreet knock on the door. I open it and step into the hallway with Dante.

Amethyst's brown eyes widen as she takes in the tall, blond, built man beside me. I know I look good or I would never have a chance with Sara next to this man. Amethyst wets her lips.

"The bouncers are bringing it back." She gives Dante a smile. "If you ever want to play..."

"I'm taken." Dante's eyes are cold as he looks at Amethyst.

"The good ones usually are." She sighs. The bouncers show up and Amethyst gives me a look that says Dante's hot. I just smile. I honestly don't care what anyone thinks is happening in that room. As long as they keep the rumors to a minimum.

Sara still has a reputation to protect and I'm bound and determined to protect it.

Finn

When Dante put Sara on Wyatt's lap, I shifted into Dante's empty spot.

"Everything good so far, trouble?" Wyatt tips her chin up.

Her eyes are darker and her lips part. I want to cup her pussy and see if she's still dripping wet for us. Fuck, I'm a little obsessed with her. I haven't even fucked anyone else since that first night I tasted her.

Now, I can't imagine going to someone else for release.

"Yes." Her eyebrow cocks up like she expects a reprimand for not calling him *sir*.

The corner of his lips twitch like he's holding back a smile. "Do you want a matching set of pink cheeks, trouble?"

She grins. I bet she does.

"No, sir."

"Soreness?"

"No, sir."

"Anything you don't want to do again?" He reaches up and sweeps his thumb over her lips.

"No, sir."

Dante went through a similar line of questioning with her already. She's more than ready for more. We just need to get her fed.

The others come in with bags of food. Wyatt smiles at me as he shifts Sara onto my lap.

"Hello, flower."

She straddles me. She has to be leaking our cum. What does that feel like? I've never gone raw in a woman before.

"Finn." Her fingers tangle in my hair. "Was it okay?"

What she's really asking is, was *she* okay. Sara usually hides those nerves so well, but never from us. We see through her. I slide my hand between her legs under the robe and find her pussy wet. I thrust my fingers inside.

Her lips part on a gasp. Her eyes soften.

"I don't know how I'm going to get through a day at work without fucking this sweet pussy, flower."

Her hands tighten in my hair. She blinks at me. "At work?"

"We've left you alone this week, but you might have to put in a few extra hours to keep up."

Her pussy clenches around my fingers and I give her a lazy smile.

"We should eat." Dante's voice almost turns Sara's head, but I snag her chin before she can look away.

"One more." I search her lust-filled eyes.

She shifts her hips over me, rocking on my fingers.

"You're amazing, flower." I lean forward and press my lips against hers as I fuck my fingers in and out of her. "I can't wait to have a night to tie you to the bed and count how many times I make you come."

She cries out as she gushes around my fingers.

"And I'll punish you for each of those orgasms, trouble." Wyatt caresses her cheek.

Sara's eyes widen as she meets mine.

"Don't worry. I'll make each one worth it."

Chapter 37

Appreciation

Sara

Finn draws his fingers out of me and holds them to my lips. Meeting his steady gaze, I open for him and he slides them inside, letting me taste myself and all of them. I suck on them as our eyes lock. When he pulls his fingers out, he leans in to kiss me.

His tongue caresses mine, sharing the taste of us. I could get used to this so easily. A ripple of pleasure chases through me.

"She needs energy and hydration to play, Finn." Dante's voice penetrates the haze of lust forming around us.

Finn smirks. My pussy throbs for more. Will I ever get enough of these guys?

"So many orgasms," he promises, rubbing his thumb over my lower lip.

I shiver as he helps me stand and guides me over to where the food is laid out. My stomach growls and Drew chuckles.

"Worked up an appetite?" He draws me down onto his lap. His jeans are rough beneath my bare legs, but his chest is warm through the thin robe separating us. He grabs a container of pasta and hands me a fork. "Don't worry about the carbs, princess. We'll work them off."

My cheeks heat as my gaze lifts to Dante, Wyatt, and Finn. Working it off won't be a problem with these guys. I push the pasta around with my fork, trying to figure out how to ask them how the rest of today will go. But in the back of my mind, I can't help but wonder how long this can last.

We haven't set an end date. Sure, it's just beginning. But no one's talked long-term, except Drew.

Drew isn't even friends with the others. Tom will eventually come back. Will that mean everything ends? Will I know what it feels like to have these guys just to lose them again?

Watch them fall in love with other women. Be invited to their weddings. Smile at their beautiful brides. Play with their children. Grow old and resentful that I had them once upon a time.

"What's on your mind, pip?"

My gaze lifts to Dante's soft blue eyes. I want to curl up in his arms and let him take care of me. Make everything okay. Lie to me that everything will work out for the best.

Instead, I smile and shake off the blues. The future is a long way off. Today, I'm taking charge of my sexuality and doing all the things I should've done for years. If all I get with these guys is a few stolen moments, then I'm making the most of the time I have.

I can cry when they're finished with me.

"I'm just wondering how the rest of today will go." I stab a few penne noodles and bring them to my mouth. The rich cream sauce almost makes me moan.

"Do you want to know exactly how we'll fuck you, flower?" Finn's voice sends shivers down my spine. I definitely can't wait until my night alone with him. If I get a night alone with him, we haven't set up guidelines.

Just today.

"Can we do more things together?" I ask tentatively. I want to feel overwhelmed by them again. Like with the blindfold and when Dante and Finn played with me in the dining room.

Wyatt's nostrils flare and a muscle ticks in his jaw. Dante's eyes soften. Finn smirks and leans back in his chair. Drew slides his hand between my thighs and rests it right below my pussy, clutching the inside of my thigh.

"Anything you want, princess," Drew offers.

My breath catches and I lean back against him. "Anything?"

Dante chuckles. "Careful. She's got that needy look that only means one thing."

"Trouble," Wyatt says softly. His dark eyes capture mine as I take another bite of pasta. Awareness scatters across my skin. I can still feel him deep inside me. My heart flips over.

I have history with these three that Drew and I don't. But Drew has something none of them do. Newness. There's no preconceived notions of how I'll react to something. He didn't wipe away tears when I fell. Or threaten to kick my boyfriend's ass if they screwed me over.

He's not best friends with Tom.

He wants to date me. Something none of the others have mentioned. Yes, we all want to fuck each other, but there's more to it, if I'm being honest with myself. This is fun, but my heart is already bruised from Wyatt's lack of attention for years. These guys have hurt me before. Who's to say they won't hurt me again?

"What do you want to experiment with first, princess?" Drew's fingers lightly caress my pussy beneath the table.

My pulse quickens. I bite my lip, trying to think of what I want to do first with these four guys. I take a few bites of pasta, aware that nothing will happen until I finish my lunch, unless Drew stops teasing me with light caresses and really touches me.

"I'm willing to direct if you need me to, pip."

Dante's smile makes my toes curl, remembering how he controlled me while I fucked myself. His dark words in my ears as he took me over the edge. I could get behind that again.

I wet my lips and take a drink. They watch me expectantly, letting me lead if I want. I could be the one in charge, commanding these men to pleasure me. Right now, I don't want to be in control. I don't want to think at all.

"I'd like that." Heat fills my belly at Dante's smirk.

"Good girl." Oof, that makes me want to do more than curl up on his lap. He was hard when I sat on him earlier. His smile relaxed as we talked quietly.

I love how he checked in with me. Asking the questions that I'm not sure the others would. How I'm feeling about this? If I want to stop? If I need a break or some time to myself to examine what's happening?

He takes care of me, knowing when I need him close and acknowledging when I need space. My heart squeezes a little as his eyes collide with mine.

"Any word on Tom?" Drew's hand settles back on my thigh.

"Nothing." Wyatt leans back in his chair. "Whatever he's hiding from, he's doing a damned good job of it."

"What about the client he was working with?" I rest my head on Drew's shoulder. "Someone else in the office has to have done some work on it. Tom doesn't usually do everything himself."

"Beth's been on a cruise this whole week and impossible to reach. She's Tom's senior accountant." Dante taps his fork on his container. "She should be back Monday."

I make a mental note to seek out this Beth in the office. "There just aren't a lot of clues."

"No, there aren't." Finn shakes his head. "I've gone through all his digital files, but nothing. Whatever he has on these clients he must have taken with him."

I set my fork down and lean forward with my elbows on the table. Tom left of his own free will, but something drove him to it. My stomach churns and my hands feel clammy. "Do you think he's really in trouble this time?"

"It's possible." Wyatt leans in. "But Tom's smart. If he's off the grid, there's a reason for it and he won't come home until it's safe."

"If he truly thought you were in danger, pip, he would have taken you with him." Dante stands to clean up our lunch.

Maybe. Maybe what Tom's hiding from isn't major. Maybe the person who broke into our townhouse just wanted to frighten me into contacting Tom. Maybe the guy I thought was watching me was just a figment of my overactive imagination.

"He'll be okay, flower." Finn's hand touches mine. His green eyes are soothing. "He wouldn't want you to worry."

I nod, feeling bad about enjoying today when I have no idea what is going on with my brother.

Drew helps me to my feet. "If you want, there are toothbrushes in the bathroom, princess."

I force a smile to my lips and leave behind the men who are changing my life to hide in the bathroom and worry about my brother for a few minutes.

Tom will be fine. He always is. Does he get tangled up in strange stuff occasionally? Yes.

But he always finds his way out. Usually with the help of his friends. I breathe out a sigh. He's not leaning on them this time and I'm not sure why. Why would he push me into their space when he's done everything he could to keep me away from them?

I straighten the tie around my waist and try to fix my hair a little. We won't find anything new out about Tom's situation this weekend, so I'm going to enjoy what I have here.

When I walk out, the conversation stops. Four sets of eyes turn to me and my insides sizzle to life. Today is mine.

Dante

"How do we want to play this?" Drew looks at the bathroom door where Sara is. After cleaning up, we moved to the couch and chairs next to the bed to wait for her.

"It depends on her." I rub my hands together. "But we should start slow and ramp things up. Start with her taking two of us."

Finn smirks. "Are we going to try DP or hold off until she's a little more experienced with anal?"

It's a valid question. She doesn't seem to be sore from anything, but if we take it too far, she might need some recovery time. Or decide she doesn't like something.

"How is this going to work after today?" Wyatt rubs the back of his neck. "We're going to be working and living with her and you're —" He gestures to Drew. "Going to date her?"

Drew spreads his arms along the back of his chair and grins. "More than happy to take my princess out to wine and dine her. Afterward, we can see where the night takes us."

Wyatt's jaw ticks. He could never have her to himself in his mind. In any of ours really. After all, how could I sit back and watch Wyatt take her without my insides being torn to pieces? Yes, I want her happy, but that doesn't mean I'd enjoy her being happy without me.

"It's not like we can all date her." I clasp my hands between my knees. "It'd get back to her mother fairly quick. Sara may not care about her reputation, but I do."

They all nod their understanding. Sara's always been a wildcard, but she plays well in society and doesn't make waves. If this arrangement were to get out, her reputation would be in shambles.

If Tom doesn't kill us all for fucking her, he would for that. His family's reputation has always come first with Tom, which is why he didn't want Wyatt with Sara. Besides the kink, Wyatt could make waves that would drown her.

"Then we'll figure out a way to keep this all under wraps."

The bathroom door opens and Sara stands there. She seems so small and vulnerable right now. I want to draw her into my arms and hold her, but I know she needs me to help her through this.

I do like to tell others what to do. I hold out my hand to her and she steps forward with a little more confidence. When she takes my hand, I draw her between my thighs. Drew and I are still wearing our jeans with no shirts, while Finn and Wyatt are in their boxers. Beneath that silky robe, Sara is gloriously naked.

Her gaze goes to each of them before it settles on me.

"How do you want to do this, pip?" I tug at the knot of her robe, loosening it.

Color flares up her neck and into her cheeks. Her breath catches.

"I want you to choose for me." Her pale green eyes are nearly black. "I want you to take control."

"Anything you don't want?" I sweep the robe over her shoulders and it falls around her feet. I could spend all day looking at her perfect petite body. A solitary freckle on her left hip draws my attention and I rub my thumb over it.

She bites her lip, but doesn't shift her gaze away from me. "I want to try everything, boss."

Fuck, my cock twitches at that name on her lips. I've been hard since before lunch. Watching her take the others was hot as fuck.

"Two cocks or three okay?"

Her breath shudders out of her. "Yes, boss."

"How does your ass feel, pip?" I glide my hands up the outside of her thighs.

"Good."

"Do you want someone to fuck your ass again?" My hands slide around to cup her ass cheeks.

"Yes. It felt good." She steps closer to me. Her breasts heavy next to my face. Her nipples hard little peaks, waiting to be devoured.

"How about we start easy?" I slide my hand between her legs. Her pussy is hot and wet. I could pull her down on my lap and be inside her again so easily. If it were just me and her, we'd fuck our way through today and tomorrow since it's a holiday.

"Okay, boss." She whimpers slightly as I graze her clit. So fucking responsive.

I force my attention away from the flush of arousal rising over her breasts and turn to the guys watching her with hungry eyes.

"Are you cool if I run the show?" My gaze stops on Wyatt.

He's not the type to take orders, but for her, he will. He nods sharply.

Finn smirks as I glance at him. He's already standing to take his boxers off. I'm not sure if this is a game or more to him. Finn keeps his cards close to his chest, even from us. But there's something in his eyes that I've never seen before when he looks at Sara.

My attention lands on Drew as I slide my finger inside Sara and she moans softly, almost folding over my hand.

"What about you? Can you handle a few orders?" I arch an eyebrow. It's a challenge to accept him as part of this, but I've seen the way he looks at Sara like she's something precious to be treasured. And the way Sara looks at him. She wants him, and maybe part of her needs him to be part of this. Needs someone outside us.

"I'm good to follow your lead every now and then." He smiles and his darkened eyes shift to Sara as her lips fall open. "I might ask the same in the future."

I give him an acknowledging nod and turn all my attention back to Sara. Her pussy flutters around my finger. Her fingers dance on her thighs.

"Do you want to touch yourself, pip?"

Her pale green eyes meet mine. "Make me come, boss."

Holding her gaze, I lean forward until my breath coats her pussy. I shift up and kiss her stomach. It trembles beneath my lips.

"Slide your hands into my hair and guide my mouth where you want it, pip."

Her eyes widen, but she doesn't hesitate to put her hands in my hair and guide me lower. I smile as my mouth brushes her folds.

"Use your tongue." Her words are unsteady.

I slide my tongue over her hot clit and she sucks in a breath. Her legs tremble as her fingers tighten in my hair and she pulls me closer. I love the way she tastes and the hitches in her breath when I find just the right spot. I thrust my finger in and out of her tight pussy. The beginnings of her orgasm clutch around my finger.

"Dante," she whimpers. Her hips rock against my face, but I grab them to hold them steady. My tongue thrusts inside her and she shatters. It's beautiful and mesmerizing. I sit back and drag my arm across my mouth.

Her satisfied gaze meets mine, and she straddles my lap before taking my lips. I open for her and she explores my mouth with her tongue. Her nipples brush against my chest, but it's not just me she wants to play with.

I pull back and brush the hair from her face. "Hands and knees on the floor."

She eases off me and lowers to the floor. Her body dips in the center and her breasts hang down. She waits for whatever is next, pretending to be the perfect little submissive. But she isn't.

Her gaze remains on me. Not because she likes to give up control or wants me to have all the power. She'll do this because she wants what I can give her. We understand each other.

"Finn, fuck her mouth. Drew, fuck her pussy." I can just imagine how wet my words make her. Her breath comes out in little pants as Finn lowers in front of her.

He tips her chin up. "If you need something to stop, tap on my thigh three times or hum a song. Do you understand?"

When he rubs his thumb over her lips, her tongue darts out to flick his finger. "Yes."

His eyes turn mischievous. "Open up, flower."

She opens her mouth and he slides in, not too deep, but enough that she moans.

Drew finishes taking off his jeans and boxers and kneels behind Sara. His hands part her ass cheeks and he drags his finger over her clit to her entrance, circling it, making her squirm and rock her hips back to him.

"Easy, princess. You want to take two dicks, you need to make sure no one goes too deep at first." His gaze lifts from her pussy to Finn.

Finn nods and draws his cock out of her mouth. "Soon you'll be an expert at giving head while taking a cock in your pussy or ass, flower."

She drops her head and waits patiently as Drew touches her pussy. Wyatt drops into the chair next to me, since it has the best view.

"Fuck, why did we wait so fucking long?" Wyatt's words are soft, for my ears only.

"She wasn't ready for us before, but she is now."

Chapter 38

Accountability

Sara

I'm soaking wet as Drew brushes his fingers over my entrance again. I want to growl and demand he fuck me. Maybe next time I will, but right now, I'm caught in this feeling of being under Dante's command.

He makes me want to obey him.

"She's ready for your cock, Drew." Dante's loud voice carries. It sends shivers through me.

Drew notches his tip against my entrance and slowly eases in. He pulls my hips back to meet him. A moan slips from my lips as his hips meet mine. I don't think I'll ever get used to the feeling of them buried deep inside me.

Finn lifts my chin and brushes his thumb over my lower lip. "You good, flower?"

"Yes." I flick my tongue out to lick his thumb and lift my gaze to his. I'm ready for more. Fuck, I've been ready for a long time.

He smirks and brings his cock back to my lips. I lick his slit clean of his precum as Drew draws back. When Drew eases back in, I part my lips and slide my mouth onto Finn's cock. I gag a little around him, but I don't pull away, wanting him as deep as Drew is.

Finn rubs my jaw as Drew's fingers spread my ass cheeks. Both touches are almost tender, speaking to a part of me that desperately wants this to be more.

Tingles rush through my veins. I have two guys inside me, not unlike the time Finn and Dante took me. Except it's so much fuller with Drew's cock instead of fingers. My whole being trembles with the need for release, the need for them to actually fuck me.

"She needs it faster. Don't you, pip?"

I moan around Finn's cock. Drew and Finn draw back almost as one before thrusting back inside me. Fuck, my eyes close at the building pressure. Finn's abs touch my nose and I swallow around his tip.

"Good, pip? Tap once on Finn's leg for yes and three for no."

I tap once.

"Good girl." Dante's voice wraps around me, caressing me. "Show her what it's like to get fucked."

I whimper, but then they're moving together. In and out. Thrusting in deep, pulling almost all the way out. The pressure builds higher and higher until I can't take any more. I moan around Finn's cock in my mouth as I come, pulsing around Drew's cock.

"Fuck, princess." Drew thrusts in deep and his cock throbs within me as he coats my insides with his cum.

I suck on Finn as the sensation floods my body.

Finn groans and his cock spurts into my throat. I swallow him down greedily, taking every last drop. When he draws away, I pull in a gasping breath.

"Such a good little whore." Drew smacks my ass, making me tighten around him.

"Fuck, trouble, you're gorgeous getting fucked by two men." Wyatt stands and lowers his boxers, revealing his hard, thick erection. An aftershock ripples through me as Drew draws out of my pussy. I wet my lips in anticipation.

"Take her ass, Wyatt. Get her ready to take more." Dante's gaze collides with mine and he smiles. "You want more, don't you, pip?"

"Yes, boss." There's a part of me that wants to be defiant. But right now enough of me wants this, what he gives me, that I ignore that defiant impulse.

Wyatt walks to a drawer and pulls out a bottle of lube. Sure, someone fucked my ass before, but Wyatt is almost as big as Dante. I know I can take it, but I'm worried it will hurt. But for all I know, Wyatt's the one that fucked my ass and I'm worried over nothing.

Wyatt opens the bottle and squirts the lube onto his fingers.

His dark eyes find mine and he smirks. Anticipation wells hot and needy in my center as he strokes his thick cock.

"Down on your elbows, pip. Push that fine ass up in the air for your man."

My man, fuck. Moaning at the rush of wetness to my pussy at those words, I lower myself down, spreading my legs, wanting all of this, all of them. Wyatt is mine right now. Just like I always wanted.

My heart clenches because I can't help but worry it won't last. That Wyatt will decide this is too much work.

My gaze locks on Dante, sitting on the couch with his jeans still on. His cock is hard and presses against his zipper. Wyatt's slippery fingers slide over my puckered hole.

I huff out a breath. The nerves are sensitive and the fire in me rages even though I just came.

Wyatt slips a finger inside and I whimper at how good it feels.

"More," Dante commands.

Wyatt draws his finger out and pushes two back in, scissoring them inside me, pressing on the walls, making space for him. Oh, fuck, the thought of him easing inside my ass throws me right to the edge.

For seconds or minutes, he thrusts his fingers in and out, stretching me. I lose track of time as he fucks them a little faster and a little deeper.

"More." Dante's voice has me dripping wet and needing more.

Wyatt draws out his fingers and three slide back in. I cry out at the fullness and ecstasy of his fingers in my ass.

His thick cockhead brushes against my entrance before pushing deep into my pussy with his fingers still buried in my ass. I shatter into a million pieces before he can even pump once. My pussy convulses around his cock, drawing him in deeper, as my ass clenches around his fingers almost painfully.

"That's it, trouble. Come all over my cock. Relax into it. Let me fuck this sweet ass."

"Yes, please, sir." I want this so fucking much.

He draws his cock out of my pussy before taking his fingers out of my ass. I've never felt so empty in my life. Need has me panting and practically begging for more.

"Shh, trouble." Wyatt's hands pull my ass cheeks apart and then his cock is pushing on my asshole. He's bigger than his fingers, and as he slips the tip in, I pant and struggle to relax. I want this so badly. It's making me tense up.

"You're being such a good girl, pip." Dante's words make me smile. "Soon his cock will be buried in your ass. You liked the feel of a cock in your ass last time. You came so hard."

"Yes." I'm breathless as Wyatt continues to ease in, stretching my walls.

"You're so fucking tight, trouble." Wyatt massages my ass cheeks. "When I'm done with your ass, we're going to shower and clean up. Then I'm going to fuck your mouth while Dante and Finn fuck your pussy and ass."

I whimper as a little aftershock tightens my muscles around Wyatt's invading cock.

"Relax, pip, he's almost in. Just a little more." Dante's words are gentle and soothing.

Impatient, I push back against Wyatt and take the last length of his cock inside. I lift my gaze to Dante and he smiles.

"Good girl." His pale blue eyes sparkle with pleasure. I take that pleasure and feel it down to my toes.

Wyatt draws almost all the way out, sending sparks skittering through my bloodstream, before he thrusts all the way in.

"Can you take me harder, trouble?" Wyatt pulls out a little before slamming in harder.

A charged moan leaves me. "Yes, sir."

"Good." His smile is obvious in his voice. His thrusts quicken and his cock pushes in deep with every hard thrust.

My pussy drips down my leg as Wyatt fucks me. My breath comes out in pants and my hips rock with his, chasing the release I know is barreling down on me.

Awareness floods me. Wyatt inside me. Drew, Dante, and Finn watching him fuck me. My skin buzzes with sensation. I clench my fists as I scream my release.

I'm pitched into the stars as euphoria fills my blood.

"That's it, trouble." Wyatt fucks in and out of me a few more times before he pushes in deep and warmth floods me. His cock twitches inside me as it empties.

His hands rub my ass cheeks as his cock remains buried deep.

Fingers touch my pussy and clit, rubbing lightly.

"Come for me one more time, trouble." Wyatt's fingers thrust in and out of my pussy while his thumb circles my clit. Everything is so sensitive already. I'm thrust into oblivion. My moan fills the air.

"Good girl," Wyatt whispers as he eases out of me.

I can't move an inch. My whole body feels twitchy, but I want more.

Wyatt lifts me against him so we're both kneeling, but his front is pressed to my back. His hot skin slides against mine. I'm still trying to catch my breath as Dante closes in. He stands in front of me. His cock a little above me.

He undoes the button and zipper on his jeans. My mouth waters in anticipation. Wyatt slides one hand over my breast and the other between my legs. He pushes his finger inside my pussy and holds it there.

His voice is quiet and dark in my ear when he says, "The video doesn't do justice to the way you give head, trouble. Show me up close and personal how you take a cock as huge as Dante's."

Whimpering with need, I lift up on my knees and stare up into Dante's eyes.

"May I, boss?" I lift my hands to his pants.

Dante smirks. "Since you asked so nicely."

I reach into his jeans and pull his cock out. When I bring it to my lips and run my tongue over his head, Wyatt pinches my nipple. A jolt of lust fires down to my pussy.

"How does that taste, trouble?"

My eyes remain on Dante's. "So fucking good, sir."

"Show me more, trouble."

I'm sure Wyatt can tell how wet his words are making me. My insides are on fire, needing friction, but he just holds his finger inside me. I part my lips and take Dante's cockhead into my mouth, sucking on it, figuring out what I like and what he likes.

Wyatt pulses his fingers against my clit, making me moan. When I take Dante deeper, Wyatt begins to fuck his finger in and out of my pussy. I do my best to work Dante's cock while Wyatt alternates between fucking his finger in my pussy, pressing on my clit, and pinching my nipple.

As I get closer to the edge, I get sloppier. Dante wraps his hand in my hair.

"Let me take over, pip."

I almost sigh in relief. Instead, I give him full control, relaxing my mouth and my throat. I can feel Wyatt's hard cock between my ass cheeks as he works my body like a maestro. Dante fucks my mouth, making me take him deep like that first time in the shower.

The act and Wyatt's touch is enough to shove me over the edge again. I moan and swallow around Dante's cock.

"Fuck, pip." His face contorts as he groans and his release pulses down my throat.

Wyatt kisses behind my ear as he takes me over the edge one

more time, shattering me and leaving me breathless. "Thank you, trouble."

Dante lifts me into his arms and carries me into the bathroom where the shower is already running. Drew waits for me, naked in the shower. Dante sets me down and pushes me into the shower with Drew.

I glance over my shoulder, but Dante smiles and steps out of the bathroom.

Drew captures my hips and pulls me against him. The warm water cascades all around us, but the heat of his body is more tempting.

"How are you doing, princess?" Drew brushes my hair out of my face.

"Not your little whore?" Smiling, I arch an eyebrow at him.

He grins. "Not always. That's just for play time. This is aftercare."

I've heard about aftercare. Read about it. "So this is where you check in with me to make sure everything is good?"

"Yeah, princess. And I take care of you." He wets a pouf and pours some soap on it. "Even if we like to cover you in our cum, we also like you clean."

I glance up into his brown eyes. "Is that why you took me right after Finn?"

He smirks and trails soap down over my breasts and stomach. "Honestly? The heat of your body and the heat of his cum is an experience that few get to have. It's decadent, princess, and I'm all about decadence."

I grab a pouf and put soap on it. "Is that why you like to watch?"

"I like to watch because it's sexy as hell." He turns me to face the wall and scrubs down my back.

I'm not immune to his touch. It's sparking every fire back to life under my skin. I'm just also curious. I've never been able to be this open about sex with anyone.

"I liked watching, but participating too," I say.

His hand trails down over my ass cheeks. I suck in a breath and press my face against the tile of the shower. He sets the pouf to the side and fills his hand with soap.

"I definitely want to participate." He rubs his hands together and then works the soap over my ass cheeks and between them. As he rubs my asshole, lighting sparks throughout my body. "I love being inside you, princess."

When he washes his hands in the water, I turn to face him, leaning back against the wall. "You don't mind sharing me?"

It's the question that's been buzzing around my mind. I know he's said it before, but the reality might be different than what he was expecting. I might not be what he was expecting. After all, this is the extent of my experience and he's used to a certain caliber of woman.

He rubs his hands together with fresh soap and closes in on me. Towering over me, he runs his hands between my thighs. "I get to have you. To take you out and show you off as mine. To fuck you and watch you get fucked by three other guys, but everyone will think you are all mine."

My lips part as he keeps rubbing my pussy.

"So no, princess, I don't mind sharing you. Do I think it will last? Maybe. I think at least two of those three are already devoted to you and the other one doesn't seem to show his emotions very well."

I glance toward the open door. If I asked, would he tell me which ones? Do I want to know who? If when Tom arrives, we all go back to the way we were before?

I lift my gaze to Drew's darkened eyes. "If this all goes to shit, what will you do?"

Smiling, he rubs circles around my clit, winding me tighter and tighter. His gaze falls to my hardened nipples. His brown eyes search mine. "If for some reason those bulldogs can't pull their heads out of their asses, then I'll be happy to keep you for myself."

He pinches my clit and my orgasm steamrolls over me. I moan as his fingers keep the release going before he draws me against him and pulls me under the water, taking my mouth in a decadent kiss.

My hands lift to his hair and I realize I'm still holding a soapy pouf. When I rub the soap on his shoulders, he chuckles against my lips.

He kisses the tip of my nose. "We're going to have a lot of fun. You and me, princess."

Chapter 39

Consolidation

Wyatt

"You good, man?" Finn claps me on the shoulder as I stare at the bathroom door.

This sharing shit is fucked. I want to rush in there and tear her out of Drew's arms. I was okay when I knew what he was doing to her, but now... With them alone?

Is it always going to feel this way? It burned when I saw her with other men, before I knew she was still a virgin.

Instead, I draw in a breath and turn to Finn's knowing green eyes. "Yeah, I'm good."

"Lie better next time." Finn pats my shoulder and heads to the bar to pour some more drinks. None of us have been drinking too much as we want to be present for this. Present for her.

There's a second bathroom in this suite, so I've showered and put my boxers back on. Now we're just waiting for Sara and Drew to finish. Could I barge into the bathroom and join them? Maybe?

This whole thing is kind of put together with rubber bands and Elmer's glue. I'm not sure it will hold until we put something down that we all understand and agree to. Make sure we're all on the same page when it comes to Sara.

"Stop worrying." Dante hands me a drink. "Sara can hold her own with him."

I grunt and take a sip of the scotch. Sara can hold her own with the four of us. It's impressive. But I've always known she was special. She just can't be mine.

"She's made of tougher stuff than most women." Dante sits in the chair, holding his glass between his knees. He's also in his boxers and has taken a shower so his blond hair hangs wet around his shoulders.

"She's stubborn. That doesn't equal tough." I sit in the chair next to him because I can see the door to the bathroom from here.

Sara is soft and warm. Someone could easily use her. Which is the reason I helped Tom scare her boyfriends in high school.

Shouldn't someone go check on her and Drew?

"You've ignored her for the past six years. The fact that she's willing to accept you now after everything proves she's strong." Dante leans back and blows out a breath. "Besides, you agreed to include him."

Drew Young. Who would have ever thought Sara would want a guy like him? He's rich, sure. New money. Dresses nicely. Keeps himself fit. Is attractive, if all the matchmaking mothers and notches on his bedpost are anything to go by.

But that's just it. He's a man whore. He doesn't hide it. Like a point of pride, he flaunts it. And I've let him touch Sara. Let him fuck her. Knowing who he is.

He's said he's committed, but for how long? What happens to her when he strays?

"What do we actually know about him?" I tip my glass toward the door and lean toward Dante. "We haven't really had anyone dig into his background. Just the surface stuff that tells us his credit score and that he hasn't been convicted of any crime. *Convicted.*"

"Wyatt." Dante's voice is calm, but that's who Dante is. He's the rock of our group.

"What?" I down more of my drink and feel it burn its way to my gut.

"He's a good guy. I asked around." Dante takes a sip. "Yeah, he sleeps around, but he hasn't so much as stepped out with another woman since he started dating Sara, which is some sort of record for the man."

"It's not like they've been dating long," I scoff.

"You can hate him all you want, but Sara likes him." Dante runs his finger along the rim of his glass.

"You don't think it's a little convenient that Tom used to go to his club and that's the only lead we've had so far?" My mind spins with possibilities. "What if Drew *is* the new client Tom is running from? And we're all just letting Drew fuck his sister? What if that's the reason Drew's interested in her?"

Finn settles in the seat next to mine. "We can go through all the conspiracy theories later, but right now, we have a woman to fuck."

I run my hand through my hair. Yeah, we do. My cock twitches. I'm good with vanilla sex for the most part. I hide the part of me that most women don't find acceptable until I truly know someone. Because in the kind of sexual relationship I want, there has to be trust.

She needs to trust me to stop if she says her safe word. And I have to trust her to use it. Especially when things get rough.

Just thinking about holding Sara down and making sure she's completely overwhelmed with cock makes me hard. Fuck.

The door to the bathroom opens and Sara comes out in a towel with her damp hair hanging over her breasts. Her makeup is all gone. She looks fresh and innocent.

I hold my hand out to her and she bites her lip, but she comes forward. Satisfaction burns in my chest as she sits on my lap. I hold my drink to her and she arches an eyebrow, but takes it and swallows a mouthful.

When she hands me back the glass, I set it to the side and draw her mouth down to mine. Our tongues touch and the smoky taste of the liquor lingers in our mouths. The kiss goes on as we explore each other. When she sucks on my tongue, a bolt of need courses through me.

We draw away from each other. Her green eyes are almost black with her desire. Fuck, this woman has always been mine, but now I can own her and claim her. For how long?

I can't think about my friend's inevitable return with what I'm about to do, because right now, Sara's the most important person in the room. And she wants to feel everything.

She loosens the towel and drops it on the floor beside the chair, leaving her beautifully naked on my lap. I run my fingertips down her side and a shiver ripples through her.

"Are you ready for us?" I've already told her what we want to do to her.

Her eyes flick to Dante and Finn before returning to mine. "Yes, sir."

Drew chuckles darkly. "I'm willing to watch this time, but I'm on board for participating in our girl's pleasure."

When she stands, I trail my hand over her ass as she walks past me back to Drew in his chair. With her hands on his shoulders, she bends over and kisses him. Fuck, her body is everything I ever dreamed about.

Finn grins my way before moving behind her and sliding his hand over her pussy. She moans into Drew's mouth and spreads her legs for Finn. So fucking willing to do what we want.

After pushing his boxers down and stepping out of them, Finn lines his cock up with her pussy and thrusts in deep. She gasps and Drew reaches up to cradle her swaying breasts as Finn thrusts steadily into her. My cock twitches, remembering the feel of her surrounding me.

When she moans her release, Finn pulls out before he comes. His hands caress her smooth ass. "Come on, flower. Let's show Drew how much dick you can take."

Rising, she smiles at Drew before following Finn to the bed. Her heated gaze lands on me and Dante as we approach, taking our boxers off. We've never shared a woman before, but Sara makes this all feel natural. Like this is the only way we could've ever had her.

"You ready to be manhandled, flower?" Finn wets his lips as he sits on the edge of the bed and draws her down to straddle him.

"Always." She rises above him before lowering her pussy down onto his cock. She releases this little sigh of pleasure that makes my balls ache. Dante moves to the end table where the lube sits and applies it liberally to his cock.

With wide eyes, Sara watches him.

"You worried, pip?" He glances at her from the corner of his eye.

She shakes her head and swallows. "No, boss."

Dante pours even more lube on his fingers before walking over to her and Finn. Dante and Finn lock eyes. Finn nods and draws Sara down with him on the bed.

I stroke my cock as Dante's fingers slide over Sara's ass. Her asshole is tight and hot. I loved every minute of fucking it. Honestly, if I didn't want to fuck her mouth, I'd take her ass again with Finn buried in her sweet pussy, making it even tighter.

Sara cries out, bringing my focus to where Dante has three of his fingers sliding in and out of her ass while she squirms on Finn.

"Good girl, flower." Finn holds her ass cheeks open as his cock remains buried inside her.

Dante slides his fingers out of her ass and wipes them on a wet towel while studying her asshole. It's open for him, ready and waiting. Sara pants softly as her eyes open and land on me.

Dante lines his cock up with her asshole and she bites her lip at the brush of his cockhead. Then he eases in a little way.

"Fuck, pip, you're so fucking tight." Dante's focus is solely on her ass taking his cock.

"It feels so fucking good, though, boss." Sara curls up on Finn and he strokes his hands up and down her sides. She makes this little mewling noise as Dante slides in deeper.

"Almost there, flower."

"Wyatt?" She holds her hand out to me and I step forward to take it. She lets out a shuddering breath as Dante pushes in a little farther.

"You remember your safe word, right, trouble?"

"Yes, sir." Her green eyes lock on mine as she breathes through taking two cocks inside her.

"You shouldn't feel pain, Sara." I step closer. "Pressure, yes, but if it's painful, we can stop."

She smiles like she thinks I'm being cute. "It doesn't hurt. It's just a really tight fit."

I want to use her safe word for her. She can take it. I've been inside her pussy and her ass today, but double penetration is a lot for the first time. We're a lot for the first time. Maybe we should have only had one person fuck her.

But not Sara. She's always been an overachiever. Smart as a whip and determined to do what she wants.

Her hand clutches mine and she cries out.

"Fuck, pip." Dante grits his teeth.

"Are you all the way in, boss?" Her words are practically a moan.

"Yes, and if you don't stop coming, I'm going to join you."

Sara lets out a shaky laugh. Her face is flushed and her breathing is still heavy but it's a little more even. "Better, boss?"

Dante smacks her ass cheek.

"Ow, what was that for?" She releases my hand and pushes up on Finn's chest.

"For being trouble." Dante shakes his head and draws her upright against his chest. He grabs her hair and turns her head so she's looking at me. "Would you help her learn when to keep her words to herself?"

Dante's eyes hold mine for a moment. His hand slides down to play with her breast.

"Don't mind me. I'm fine where I am." Smirking, Finn puts his hands behind his head. My gaze drops to where he and Dante are buried deep inside her. Fuck. I want a turn at that.

"I think he wants you to fuck my mouth, sir." Sara arches an eyebrow as her lips curve into an impish smile.

It sets something off in me like a bomb detonating. I jerk forward and take her hair, tipping her head back. She gasps and her eyes widen, but not in fear. In anticipation.

"How do you make this stop, trouble?" I take her nipple between my fingers and pinch hard. "Use your words."

She pants as her green eyes focus on mine. "I tap on a body three times or hum a show tune like *Phantom of the Opera*. If my mouth is free, I say *mercy*, which I most definitely am not saying now. Is that what you want to know, sir?"

She blinks up at me like an innocent lamb, but she's not. Nope, she's always been trouble.

"Tomorrow, I'll teach you how to be respectful to your owners. Open your mouth."

She gives me a little pout before she parts her lips. Her gaze drops to my swollen cock, desperate for release.

I bring her mouth down over me until I feel her gag. When she controls it, I push into her throat and she swallows around me. No one has ever felt better than Sara.

"How does it feel to be stuffed full of cock, princess?" Drew sounds breathless. When I look over at him, he's stroking his cock.

"She can't exactly answer you right now." I pull her off my cock a little and look down into her watery eyes as she gasps. "She's busy."

"No worries, I'll remember my question for later. Please proceed." Drew can see everything from where he sits. For a moment, I consider going and sitting with him while the other two fuck in and out of her needy holes.

But then Sara's tongue begins to explore my cock. Fuck.

My eyes practically roll back in my head, but instead, I open my eyes to her sparkling ones. Oh, my sweet little Sara. She's asking for more than she can take, but I'll give her every inch of the rope she needs.

I wink at her before I raise my gaze to Dante and Finn. With a slight nod, we all move at once. Fucking in and out of her as she makes these needy little noises in the back of her throat. Her fingers curl around Finn's biceps as Dante holds her ass cheeks apart, watching his cock and Finn's shuttle in and out of her.

Meanwhile, my little vixen keeps licking and sucking my cock like it's her favorite piece of candy. Milk chocolate truffles. Watching her eat them when she was eighteen almost made me bust a nut in public.

Now, I tug on her hair to make her open her eyes and see who's fucking her mouth. Her eyes collide with mine. She freezes as her body tightens. Pleasure ripples over her naked body in a beautiful pink flush and her throat opens on a scream.

I push in deep, feeling her throat constrict around me. The groans Dante and Finn release fill the air as they come deep inside her. Watching her tremble at the feeling of them, I unload my cum down her swallowing throat. For a moment, we're all frozen in the pleasure, until time catches up.

Yanking my cock out of her mouth, I bend down and cover her mouth with my own as she gasps in my air. She moans and I can tell a little aftershock works through her body as both of the others groan, almost in agony.

I press my forehead to hers as both of us pant like we've been running a marathon. "You're mine."

Her green eyes meet mine. "I'm yours."

Chapter 40

Pooling of Interest

Sara

I don't know who Drew really is, but I'm pretty sure he's a god. Because after I take my three guys, Drew opens up another door to a warm bathing room. It's like a scene from a movie set in ancient Rome.

The floor is sunken into almost a pool, but only three feet deep, with plenty of seating like a hot tub. And it smells amazing, like flowers and herbs. Large enough for a fucking orgy, which is pretty much my new standard for my sex life.

I'm thrilled to finally have a sex life. Even if things are a little achy.

"Come on, princess." Drew's hand falls on the small of my back. He leads me toward a shower off to the side. After he turns it on, he slides his boxers off. He has a beautiful body, strong, not overly muscular, but defined. And his thick, hard cock... My mouth waters and my thighs clench against the aching need.

I'm insatiable. It's odd to go from never being fucked to having four guys worship my body over and over again. And still wanting more.

Drew's knowing brown eyes lock on mine. He draws me into the shower and against his warm body. My hands go to his chest. His smile makes my insides melt.

"How are you feeling now?" He soaps his hand and slides it between my legs.

I gasp as he works my clit softly while he washes me.

"Good." The word is barely a breath as my eyelids lower. Pleasure fills my blood. I can hear the others talking low and the water shifting behind me, and I know they're waiting for us to join them in the bath.

Well, mostly me. I'm not sure how they feel about Drew yet.

From here I can see them and they can see me. With Drew, if they look. Drew touching me feels clandestine, but if they look over here, they can see exactly what he's doing to me.

A shiver works through my body.

His eyes darken as he backs me into the warm spray. "I liked watching you get fucked. Taking three cocks at once."

When his fingers slide into my pussy, I clutch his arms and my lips part. I could get used to this.

"Filling every greedy hole in your body." He dips his head next to mine, brushing my cheek with his. "Watching you take them and come so fucking hard."

He twists his fingers and rubs my clit. A tremor works through me as the stimulation becomes almost too much. I pant into his ear. My nipples are pebbled against his chest.

"Did you feel overwhelmed, princess?" His breath caresses my ear as his soft words heat my blood. "Did you like the feeling of three hard bodies pressed into yours?"

"Drew." His name is a soft plea on my lips.

"Tell me what you want, princess. Whisper it in my ear so only I know what you need." His words are tipping me closer to the edge with every thrust of his fingers, but I want more.

I wet my lips. His hard cock presses against my hip.

"Fuck me," I whisper and reach between us to stroke his cock.

His low groan in my ear makes me even wetter. Can he feel it? How much I want him?

"How?" His voice is deeper.

"Thrust your cock into my pussy and fuck me until we both come." I release a shuddering breath as he pulls his fingers out of me, leaving me empty.

He lifts me against the wall and my arms and legs wrap around him. Our eyes lock as he thrusts deep inside me. My moan reverberates off the walls around us. The low murmur of voices pauses.

It's like I can feel their eyes on us. The tile I'm pressed against puts us in profile, leaving very little to the imagination.

Before I can look at them, Drew takes my chin and shakes his head. "No, princess. This one is all mine. They can watch how I fuck you, but I want your focus on me."

I tangle my fingers in his thick hair. "Make me come."

He grins as his hips rock against mine, more grinding into my clit than fucking me. A rush of heat floods my body as we stay connected, our eyes searching each other's.

"Do you know why I like to watch, princess?" He pulls out farther and thrusts in hard.

I bite my lip. "Decadence?"

His dark chuckle lights up every inch of my skin. "It's not the act that gets me. It's intruding on someone else's intimate moment."

He takes my knees, unwrapping me from his waist and pulling my legs wide, opening me up more to him and making it easier for the others to watch.

"When people fuck, they lose a little of themselves to each other. They shed that face they show the rest of the world. The mask slips and reveals who they really are." Drew's words are soft, for my ears only.

"Who are you?" I search his eyes, wondering if I can see who he really is.

"To you?" He smirks and rests his forehead against mine as he drives his cock into me. "I'm whatever you need me to be, princess.

But in this moment, I want to be the one taking you over the edge into ecstasy one more time."

Lifting my legs more, he thrusts in, hitting that spot inside me that stokes the fire hotter and more intense. The flames are almost painful.

"Keep your eyes on me, princess." His voice is tight, like he's struggling to hold back.

My eyes open to his almost black ones searching mine. It's intimate and consuming. My release swells over me and drags me under. His lips curve into a satisfied grin as he thrusts in deep and fills me with his cum.

We breathe each other in, still connected, still searching as we come down. Our breathing slowly evens out.

"We should really get you soaking in that water. You've been fucked more than most women will allow in a day. I'm sore for you right now." His smile turns cocky and some of that intimacy vanishes.

I rest my head against the wall, in no hurry to get down or to have him pull out. "I see what you mean."

He arches an eyebrow and runs his thumbs along the inside of my knee. Sparks light beneath my skin.

"There's this moment when everything falls away and we're our most primal selves." I tug on his hair.

He chuckles as he pulls out and lowers my legs. He backs me into the wall, crowding over me, dominating me.

I shiver, but stand my ground.

"Trust me, princess, when we get primal, you'll know it." He holds my gaze for a hot moment before his attention shifts to the guys.

I follow his line of sight and Wyatt's dark eyes collide with mine. A shudder flows through me. I can't wait to find out what happens when Wyatt drops his mask.

Drew draws me into the shower and helps me clean up so we can join the others in the bath. The oils fill the air with a thick scent and steam. My muscles begin to relax as Drew shuts off the shower and takes my hand to lead me to the steps down into the warm water.

"We drain these between clients and scrub them." Drew explains as I step down into his so-called decadence. "I requested Epsom salts to help with any aches you have."

When I'm waist deep, he brings my hand to his lips and kisses my knuckles before releasing me to go sit down. The guys are spread out around me, almost in the four corners. I could sit somewhere between them, but everywhere feels like a choice I don't want to make.

This is why I didn't want to know who took my virginity. It's too big of a step. Yes, I would have gladly given it to any of them. But knowing I could have all of them...

"While I love seeing you naked in a billow of steam, flower, you won't hurt our feelings when you choose someone to sit with." Finn's green eyes shine with sincerity. "We could use a break in the festivities too. Rehydrate."

He holds up a glass of water. Condensation runs down the sides.

My gaze settles on my Viking, my protector. I could sit with any of them, but I feel most comfortable with him. Dante's smile grows as I move through the water his way.

It's a little confusing how the one guy I used to dread seeing is now where I seek comfort. But his days of dragging me away from Wyatt are done, and there's something between us that I'm not willing to overlook anymore.

When he holds his hand out to me, I take it and let him draw me down between his legs with my back against his front. I can't see him, but it lets me be part of the conversation.

He wraps his arm around my waist and I sigh as I lean back against him.

"You didn't have to choose me again, pip." His voice is soft but the room is very quiet.

My cheeks flush as I realize time and time again I've been drawn to Dante today.

Wyatt clears his throat. "We need better guidelines for how this —" He gestures to all of us and says, "Works."

I slide my hand over Dante's on my stomach and tangle our

fingers together. Is this where Wyatt walks away? We barely got started. Wyatt Hawkins has rejected me all of my adult life. I didn't realize I was preparing for it again until this moment.

Dante squeezes me and kisses the top of my head. "It's okay, pip. We're just trying to sort out how we make this work for all of us. *All* of us."

I draw a breath into my starving lungs. Fuck.

Wyatt sighs and drags a wet hand through his curling hair. "Fuck."

His gaze captures mine and holds me pinned in place. Longing like I've never seen is laid bare in his dark eyes. Dante's arm releases me before I even realize I'm rising and moving over to Wyatt.

His hands catch my hips as I draw closer and he pulls me down to straddle his lap. Our naked bodies collide as his arms wrap around me, holding me close. "If I could take back those years, I would, trouble."

I close my eyes and breathe in. His woodsy leather scent rises with the flowers and herbs of the water. My arms tighten around him, like I could hold him to me forever and stay locked in this moment where he's mine.

But I'm not the girl who believes things work out for everyone.

Madison and her guys aren't me and my guys. This is a flash in the pan. A moment in time I'll never forget or regret, but I know it will come to an end. There's too much history with us. Too much at stake when Tom comes back.

Fuck, too much at stake when my mom comes back. She wants me married off to someone of a higher social standing. All these guys have that in common, but she wants me married to one, not four.

Can I imagine a future with these men? I want to, but I shouldn't.

"Hey." Finn's voice and his hand on my back make me realize I'm shaking in Wyatt's arms.

I open my eyes to his green ones. He cups my cheek and his smile sends my heart into overdrive.

"We just want to make sure that everyone is taken care of in this situation. To make sure *you* are taken care of." Finn brushes his thumb along my jawline. "Today has been exceptional, flower, but we need to plan for the next few weeks at least."

"We need guidelines to help us respect your limits and ours."

I turn to Drew, not releasing my hold on Wyatt. If I can hold on to him, maybe I can hold on to them all.

"We need to figure out how this goes forward." Wyatt's chest rumbles next to mine with every word. "And what to do when it ends."

My heart plummets into my stomach. But I swallow down that feeling. This isn't forever. I knew that going into it. We're just having fun.

I release Wyatt, but he doesn't immediately release me. He kisses my temple. His arms tighten before he finally lets me go.

I climb off his lap and back into Dante's. His arms feel like safety, like home. I wish it were an illusion. Something I made up in my head, but it's not. These guys have always been my safe place when the world was cruel.

Dante draws me down with him so we're all closer.

Wyatt takes my hand. His is so much bigger than mine.

"We want everyone on the same page, Sara." Wyatt's dark eyes try to convince me, but I know in a way this is just another rejection.

"You mean you don't want Tom to know about this." The words fall off my tongue.

"Tom is complicated." Wyatt runs his other hand through his hair. "He'd never accept this. Do you think your mom would accept this?"

I blow out a breath, feeling the twist in my stomach tighten. "Can we not talk about ending this? Can we just figure that out when we get there? I don't want to be fucking you and thinking this is the last time. I want to enjoy our time together. However long it ends up being."

"I think that's fair." Drew draws a stool up to sit in front of the four of us. "But we do need to talk logistics. After all, you're living with the three of them and dating me."

"Not every night can be an orgy, flower." Finn winks at me, trying to lighten the somber mood. "Though I might be able to pencil in lunchtime orgies."

His smirk draws a smile out of me.

"Is this going to be some sort of contract deal?" I look at each of them, looking over my shoulder at Dante.

"We could put it down in writing, so everyone feels safe." Dante runs his hand over my hair. "I can put something together that will get us started. But each of us will have our own demands on you, pip."

His hand runs down my arm, his fingertips graze my breast, sending a shiver through me.

"So each of you will have a contract for me and I'll have a contract for all of you. That way we know what we want and expect." When my gaze collides with Wyatt's, I scoff. "I always figured sex contract negotiations would be a lot sexier."

Drew chuckles. "You're sitting in bathwater naked with your four lovers, princess. What's sexier than that?"

"Okay, how about some basics to tide us over?" I lean back against Dante. "I'll go first. No one fucks anyone outside of this group or they're out."

"That's a soft pitch, princess. None of us plan on straying while we can be buried in you." Drew winks. "I get at least one weekend night as date night to take you out, and I want Sunday brunch."

Part of me melts, knowing that we're supposed to be talking sex. I smile.

"Sara always sleeps at our apartment." Wyatt's words have a little bite to them.

"Then I'll be staying some at your apartment too." Drew gives me a cocky grin. "I'm not just fucking Sara. I want to spend nights with her."

My cheeks flush with heat until I realize...

"Uh, that means I'll be having sex in Tom's bed?" Some part of me is seriously icked by the idea.

"Not his bed, pip." Dante shifts me against him.

"What?" I turn my head.

"I had the mattress replaced before you moved in. His mattress is in storage." Dante tucks my hair behind my ear. "I want you to be comfortable in our apartment."

Fuck, these guys are going to dig into my heart if I'm not careful.

"What's your one thing?" My eyes search Dante's. "Blow job every morning?"

"Can I amend mine?" Drew smiles and I laugh.

"No. You should have thought of it yourself." My cheeks hurt from my smile.

Dante tips my chin his way. "If this gets to be too much for you at any point, you tell us. Promise me."

I cup his jaw, feeling the slight stubble beginning. "I promise, boss."

"Well, fuck, if he's not going to take it." Finn smirks when my gaze snaps to him. He chuckles. "I don't know about the others, but I'm used to getting some on a fairly regular basis. I'd prefer us not to schedule sex though."

"So no sex schedule is your one thing?" I clarify.

"If I want to fuck you, and you're amenable, we should just fuck, flower." His green eyes glow with mischief and the now familiar craving rolls through me.

I do have a hard cock pressed against my ass. Fuck it.

"Okay, so no other sexual partners. Weekend date and brunch for Drew. Sleeping only at the apartment. Tell you if it gets too much. And no sex schedule. And we'll put together our specific requests in writing." I glance around until they all nod at me. "Are we done with the legal shit now?"

"Did you have something else in mind, pip?" Dante's lips caress the back of my ear, sending sparks through me.

"I mean." Tracing my hand up his thigh next to mine, I follow my progress with my gaze. "I know a lot about sex, but haven't gotten to experience it until today." I look over my shoulder to find Dante's cool blue eyes. "There might be some positions I want to try."

Dante's smile heats my blood. "You get to lead today, pip. What do you want?"

I grin and let the heaviness fall off me. These guys are mine to do with what I please. I'm not giving the future another thought. "I'd like to play with the restraints more."

Chapter 41
Contingency

"This isn't what I had in mind, pip." Dante gives me a put-out look as I cuff his other wrist. But he did ask me what I wanted. And a Viking that's mine to do with as I please, stretched out naked on a bed, sounded enticing.

Wearing the silky robe again, I shrug and latch the cuff into place. "I can't tie all of you down."

Dante is a big guy, like all around. Arms, chest, thighs, cock. I really want to drive him out of his mind with pleasure the way they've done to me. A knock sounds at the door and Drew backs away from what I'm doing. They've all been watching with amusement.

"Yeah." Finn sits on the side of the bed, running a large feather through his fingers. "Don't worry. She'll be gentle."

He barely hides his grin. Dante rolls his eyes.

I set the feather out with a few other things earlier, after digging through the drawers. The selection of kinky sex items is amazing. I want to try everything in there, but I couldn't possibly get through them all today.

Speaking of kinky things, I'm tempted to ask Wyatt, who's

watching me like a hawk from a chair, about the dildo collection I found in his drawer. But now probably isn't the time to remind him I invaded his privacy.

When I finish with Dante's ankle, I sit between his knees and study him, trying to figure out what to do first. His hard cock strains against his abs. I wet my lips. I want to take my time to explore every inch of him. To see how he reacts to every touch.

I know I said I didn't want an end date looming over me, but not having one creates this sense of urgency. A burning need to try everything with these guys before this all ends.

Finn holds out the feather. "Go crazy, flower."

When I take it, Dante chuckles darkly, sending bolts of pleasure through me.

"Just remember, pipsqueak, turnabout is fair play." His pale blue eyes are delightfully wicked. My thighs clench against my aching center.

I smirk. "Fuck, I hope so."

Drew clears his throat. "I'm afraid we have a situation."

Wyatt straightens, instantly alert at the seriousness in Drew's voice. "What's happening?"

"Release me, pip." The command in Dante's voice makes me want to jump to attention too.

I pout a little. I haven't gotten to do anything to him yet.

"I'll let you play another time." His expression is indulgent. I love that he's willing to let me try this again.

Finn stands and works on Dante's ankles while I straddle his waist and untie his wrists.

"What's the situation?" Wyatt walks over to his neatly folded pants and tugs them on while glaring at Drew.

"Some men who Tom has met with here have a table. My bouncer recognized them from before. I don't know if they're the same men from the video."

Wyatt brings our clothes over and helps me off the bed. His hand squeezes mine gently. Everyone focuses on getting dressed while Drew continues.

"They're asking about Sara." His serious brown eyes capture mine. "My bouncers and the dancers that know you're here won't tell them anything. But I don't like that they know you could be here. My stake in this business isn't public knowledge. We need to get you out of here now."

My fingers shake as I try to latch my bra. Finn brushes them away and takes over the task. He's quick and efficient as he helps me get the rest of the clothes I packed on. There's worry in his green eyes as he straightens my shirt.

Those men are asking about me. Here. Do they know about me and Drew? We haven't been sneaking around, but we also haven't been super public about our relationship. Not really. But asking for me here? At Veiled Vixen? Means they know more about me than we thought.

And we know absolutely nothing about them.

Yet.

"Wait." I turn. Everyone is dressed. Dante is tying his shoe. "What if I talk to them? We can figure out what they want. It's not like they can do anything to me here."

"Absolutely not." Wyatt steps closer to me.

"Why not?" I cross my arms over my chest. "Again, you guys are here. Drew has trained bouncers. I'm safe. They're asking for me, so why not figure out what they want?"

"These may be dangerous men, pip." Dante straightens to his full height. His shirt stretches tight over his hard muscles. My body hasn't received the memo that fun times are over quite yet.

"Exactly. Do you want to wait until they track me down alone?" I arch an eyebrow as I look at each of them. "If it's the same guys, they had plenty of opportunity to harm me when I was alone in the townhouse."

I point to Dante. "You said they were sending a message. Well, fuck it, let's hear what that message is."

"She's right." Finn steps up behind me. His warmth surrounds me, and I lean back against him. "We don't have any clue what Tom has gotten into this time. Maybe it's time we meet with these guys, find out why Tom is running."

"You want to risk Sara's safety?" Wyatt's eyes burn. "We can find out another way—"

"We've been searching for a week." Finn shakes his head. "We still don't know anything."

"You'll be with me," I assure Wyatt. "It's not like I'm alone at my townhouse, facing them with only Peabody at my side."

Thankfully, my dog walker was able to take Peabody on short notice this morning and keep him for the day and night. It's nice to not have to worry about the furball.

"She's not wrong." Drew leans against the bar. For all intents and purposes, he appears casual, but there's this energy buzzing beneath the surface. We're still getting to know each other, but I'm beginning to notice more about him. Plus, it doesn't hurt that he's on my side.

Dante moves to stand beside Wyatt and puts his hand on Wyatt's shoulder. "We don't know the lengths they're willing to go to get to her. This may be an opportunity to actually figure out the potential danger she's in."

My insides shimmer with Dante's words. Only one more to convince.

I step forward and put my hand over Wyatt's heart. It pounds fiercely. My heart flutters in response. His dark eyes meet mine and a muscle in his jaw ticks. I've always had to hold my urges back when it came to Wyatt, but I don't right now.

Wrapping my arms around his waist, I rest my head against his heart.

"We're stronger together," I say softly.

His arms pull me in tighter against him and I release a little sigh. This is where I belong.

"If we do this—"

I pull back to grin up at him.

"*If*, Sara, if." The harsh planes of his face soften. His dark eyes search mine. "You don't take any chances. You stay with at least one of us at all times. You don't offer anything or give them any information. If they ask a question, think before you answer. Ask yourself, Will the information reveal something about me or Tom that they don't already know? Got it?"

I nod and bite my lip. We have no idea what these men do. At least the bouncers patted them down before they came in. I need to do this.

"I can offer my office if you'd like a more private setting." Drew steps in and brushes my hair behind my ear. I step back from Wyatt.

"Let's start in the club." Dante wraps an arm around my waist and tucks me into his side.

I pull away. I have no makeup on. My hair is probably a mess. "Before we do anything, I need to freshen up."

Stepping out of that suite feels like leaving this little secure pocket in the world where I could be with my four guys without any judgment. Outside of that room, I have a relationship with Drew, but not with the others. They're just my brother's friends.

Madison had to keep her relationship secret for a while. The guys even dated other women. I was one of those dates, which is how I got to know Madison and her guys. But this is different.

We haven't really defined what this is beyond today. Besides exploring this attraction.

Dante's hand rests on the small of my back, and I resist the urge to lean against him as we follow Drew and Wyatt through the club with Finn behind us.

My stomach twists with nerves as we walk, knowing I might be meeting the men my brother is running from. Fuck, maybe this whole false bravado is a bad move. Maybe I should turn around and take the back door out of the club. Disappear with my guys back to their apartment. Back to safety.

When Drew and Wyatt stop, I glance up at Dante. His fingers rub my back lightly to try to steady me. We need information. Whoever this is must have some, or why would they be looking for me? And how could they have found this connection?

"Good evening, gentlemen." Drew's voice is loud and boisterous. "You've been asking about my girlfriend?"

"We need to talk to Sara Morris." A man in a black suit stands up from the table.

I swallow, but I'm not going to back down now. Drawing strength from Dante's touch, I step beside Drew, but next to Wyatt.

"I'm Sara."

The man has brown hair and brown eyes. He's maybe six feet tall. He holds out his hand. "Jacob Price. This is my associate, Ethan Martinez."

When I lift my arm to shake his hand, Wyatt blocks me. His hand wraps around my forearm like a brand.

"What do you want with Sara?" Wyatt asks.

"We were hoping you could help us find Tom Morris." Ethan leans back in his chair and studies all of us. He has dark hair, dark eyes and tan skin. Those eyes don't miss anything as he focuses on Wyatt's possessive grip.

I step closer to Drew and Wyatt drops his hold on me. "What do you want with Tom?"

Jacob glances at Ethan and then looks at Drew. "Is there somewhere private we can talk?"

Drew glances at Wyatt who nods slightly. "My office. Follow me."

Wrapping his arm around my waist, Drew leads the way to his office. My guys follow the two men. A lump settles in my stomach. What the hell is Tom involved in?

When we enter the office, Drew guides me to the sofa. I sink onto it. Finn sits on my other side while Dante and Wyatt stand behind us.

I want to take someone's hand, but know I shouldn't give anything away. I clasp my hands in my lap.

"Please have a seat." Drew gestures to the chairs across from us before sitting beside me. He slides his hand into mine and takes it onto his lap, rubbing the back of my hand with his.

The two men sit and look at each other.

"May we have your names, gentlemen?" Jacob looks at Dante, Wyatt, and Finn.

"Who exactly are you and what do you want from Sara?" Wyatt's voice is emotionless.

Jacob clasps his hands between his knees and looks at each guy in turn. "We know you're Tom Morris's business partners."

Finn's fingers twitch like he wants to reach out and grab my hand. These men know a lot about us and we know absolutely nothing about them.

Ethan looks at Jacob before he turns to Drew. "Are there any recording devices in this room?"

"No." Drew squeezes my hand.

"Did you know what Tom was working on before he went missing?" Jacob asks.

"Missing?" The word pops out. I swallow down the sudden lump in my throat. Tom isn't missing. He left.

Jacob and Ethan exchange a look. One that doesn't spark confidence in me.

Fuck. Tom does this. He gets worked up over something and has to think about it, so he takes off. He always comes back. Always.

"Has he been in contact with you? Or did you know the clients he was working for prior to his..." Jacob pauses and looks at me before continuing, "his leaving."

"We don't usually give out client information." Wyatt's tone is professional, but I can feel the undercurrent coming from my guys. They're wary of these men. "While we're asking questions, why did you break into Sara's house?"

Jacob and Ethan look at each other again like they're trying to figure something out. Ethan nods. Jacob clasps his hands together.

"It's important we find Tom before other interested parties do." Jacob reaches into his back pocket and pulls out a black wallet. He opens it and sets it on the table between us.

My gaze falls to it. An FBI badge. My eyes widen and my heart skips.

"Tom may be in serious danger."

Find out what happens next in INDECENT OBSESSION.

Meet C.S. Berry

C.S. Berry is a combination of my love for writing and my love for reading. She began as an experiment and took off into something I absolutely adore. It's not often you can do what you love and it works as a career. As for me, I love reading and romance and heroines seriously getting railed. I assume since you've read my books, you do too.

If you want to discuss books or anything with me, come join my Facebook group, C.S. Berry's Spicy Executive Suite. And you can always catch me on Instagram @csberry.

Oh and me, I have a lovely family who aren't allowed to read my books. But are so proud, they keep leaking my pen name. My dog and cats don't care about my writing as long as I sit still long enough for them to snuggle.

XOXOXO,

C.S. Berry

Keep up with C.S. Berry
View the shop: csberrybooks.com
View the Patreon: patreon.com/csberry
Join her Newsletter on her website
Join the Facebook Group:
https://www.facebook.com/groups/csberryreaders
Checkout her Website: csberry.com

9 781957 657431